Seductions

ALSO BY LONNIE BARBACH

Turn Ons: Pleasing Yourself While You Please Your Lover
For Yourself: The Fulfillment of Female Sexuality
For Each Other: Sharing Sexual Intimacy
The Pause: Positive Approaches to Menopause

EDITED BY LONNIE BARBACH

Pleasures: Women Write Erotica
Erotic Interludes: Tales Told by Women
The Erotic Edge: Erotica for Couples

BY LONNIE BARBACH AND DAVID GEISINGER

Going the Distance: Finding and Keeping Lifelong Love

AUDIOTAPES BY LONNIE BARBACH

Smart Sex
The Erotic Edge

AUDIOTAPES BY LONNIE BARBACH AND DAVID GEISINGER

Secrets of Great Sex

VIDEOTAPES BY LONNIE BARBACH

Falling in Love Again
Sex After 50: A Guide to Lifelong Sexual Pleasure
What Women Want
More of What Women Want
Lover's Massage

Seductions

Tales of Erotic Persuasion

EDITED BY

Lonnie Barbach, Ph.D.

A DUTTON BOOK

DUTTON
Published by the Penguin Group
Penguin Putnam Inc., 375 Hudson Street, New York, New York 10014, U.S.A.
Penguin Books Ltd, 27 Wrights Lane, London W8 5TZ, England
Penguin Books Australia Ltd, Ringwood, Victoria, Australia
Penguin Books Canada Ltd, 10 Alcorn Avenue, Toronto, Ontario, Canada M4V 3B2
Penguin Books (N.Z.) Ltd, 182–190 Wairau Road, Auckland 10, New Zealand

Penguin Books Ltd, Registered Offices:
Harmondsworth, Middlesex, England

First published by Dutton,
a member of Penguin Putnam Inc.

First Printing, January, 1999
10 9 8 7 6 5 4 3 2 1

 REGISTERED TRADEMARK—MARCA REGISTRADA

LIBRARY OF CONGRESS CATALOGING-IN-PUBLICATION DATA:

Seductions / edited by Lonnie Barbach.
      p.   cm.
      ISBN 0-525-94462-1 (alk. paper)
      1. Short stories, American.   2. Seduction—Fiction.   3. Erotic
stories.   I. Barbach, Lonnie Garfield, 1946–
PS648.S5S43   1999
813'.01083538—dc21   98-26993
                                                                CIP

Printed in the United States of America
Set in Sabon
Designed by Julian Hamer

PUBLISHER'S NOTE

For David Geisinger
whom I love and cherish
and only wish had
seduced me years earlier.

ACKNOWLEDGMENTS

First and foremost, I would like to thank the love of my life, David L. Geisinger, Ph.D., for his enormous help both in the conceptualization and writing of the Introduction. My assistant, Marilyn Anderson, did a remarkable job of maintaining the correspondence and organization of what turned out to be an incredibly complex project. Deborah Shames and Caroline Fromm Lurie offered invaluable second opinions on some of the submissions. I continue to appreciate the ongoing support of my agent, Rhoda Weyr, my editor, Carole DeSanti, and Carole's assistant, Alexandra Babanskyj. Finally, I would like to thank Tess Elyse Geisinger-Barbach for bringing joy into my life every day.

Contents

PART IV: THE ENVIRONMENT

PART V: THE DARK SIDE

Introduction

When I think about the most erotic moments of a sexual experience, I am drawn to the delicious and unpredictable buildup, the dance of seduction. A sexual experience often lodges in memory most vividly because of the events that lead up to the actual physical lovemaking: the invitation to sensually provocative play, the anticipation of an experience charged with pleasure and delight. Consequently, I have gathered a collection of stories that emphasize these openings, stories that set the stage for the sexual encounters that follow.

Seduction is the kindling of romance. It ignites the spark of sexual desire and intensity. Unfortunately, the art of seduction becomes a lost art in many long-term monogamous relationships, although it is usually an important part of nearly every courtship. This is a tragic loss because in its absence, relationships can become deprived of sexual liveliness and passion. The connection becomes humdrum. The mundane creeps in and the relationship is diminished.

The word *seduction* comes from the Latin term meaning "to lead away." In every seduction, some psychological or emotional resistance is implied and must be overcome. The resistance may be something as simple as the preoccupations and routines of everyday life, or it may be as complex as a romantic involvement with another. In either case, one person begins to entice the other, drawing his or her attention away from its current focus and onto a new agenda.

Yet, every seduction is a cooperative venture; ultimately, both partners must be willing to play the escalating erotic game. At any point one person could abdicate or drop out—

the seduced could rebuff the seducer's advances, and the inter-action would end.

Force and coercion are the opposite of seduction; rather than entice or allure, they control and violate a person's freedom. In the most extreme form, this can mean rape. This is not seduction. Seduction allows people to open up when they are closed. It is an invitation to be more vulnerable and hence more inti-mate.

Acts of seduction occur throughout nature and within virtu-ally every animal species. Without these alluring acts, most mating would not occur and species would die out. Seduction is a process that stimulates sexual readiness in a potential part-ner, thus increasing the likelihood of that individual's ability to contribute genes to the gene pool. Natural selection favors those who excel in the art of seduction.

Each animal species has its own distinct seduction rituals, and any or all of the senses, when stimulated properly, can be-come the gateway to the sexual overture. For some animals, the act of seduction uses visual allure as an attractant: The peacock struts and displays his elegant plumes to capture the attention of his prospective mate; for the jewelfish, the more brilliant the colors of the male, the more likely a female will choose him to father her young.

Sound is a major aphrodisiac in other animal species. The male porcupine produces a distinctive piercing whine to attract his mate. The bull elephant emits a unique trumpeting sound, bull alligators bellow, certain fish purr when they court, and male frogs and toads have a special croaking call during mating season.

Scent, of course, is among the most common pathways used throughout the animal kingdom to attract a mate. Animals with estrous cycles such as dogs and cats only attempt to mate when the scent of the female's urine or vulva signals to the male that she is fertile.

We humans, however, are always potentially available for sex. For human beings, sex serves purposes far greater than the biological and evolutionary functions of procreation. In fact, only a very small percentage of sexual experiences occur for the intended purpose of creating babies. Human beings use sex to express love, caring, intimacy: It contributes to a more soulful connection with a partner. In addition, sex provides intense physical and emotional pleasure and can result in deep, satisfying relaxation.

Because the rewards are great, human beings intent on dating and mating invest considerably in the seduction process. Energy is devoted to heightening all of the senses. The Dayaks of Borneo and the Maoris of New Zealand decorate their bodies with intricate tattoos. The Papuan people of New Guinea use brilliantly colorful paints to turn their faces and bodies into dazzling canvases of enticement. Those of us from more industrialized cultures may dress with the intent to allure; women may wear fashions or makeup designed to accentuate their most becoming features.

Sound has been used as an aphrodisiac throughout the ages. Poets have romanced loved ones with rhyme, troubadours with music. The Apache males blow flutes and the Trukese men who formerly used nose flutes now use the guitar or harmonica to woo young girls. And we all use conversation—words of love, of desire, the intimate communication and innuendo that occur between two lovers as they talk over dinner or under the bedcovers late at night.

The senses of smell and taste can also become ways to attract another, to waken desire. The use of perfumes and colognes calls attention to ourselves; in some cultures women even wipe their vaginal fluids behind their ears to attract a potential partner. For some of us, the most seductive scents are the pheromones, the natural smells of a partner's body. We may be captivated by the taste of someone's skin and the sweetness of their kisses.

And let's not forget touch: We may respond to the warmth and sensation of a prospective lover's skin, to being touched in particular ways or in certain places. From the holding of hands to the caress of the face, touch can add dimension and richness to a seduction.

In humans, romantic pathways are more extensive and complex than in any other species. We alone use fantasy and imagination as an important role in a seductive encounter. We have the capacity to raise seduction to a form of art, though we are still animals and our brains have been programmed to respond to someone we are attracted to through a physiological chain of events that heightens feelings of pleasure in both the seducer and the one being seduced. When someone excites us, our bodies respond with a gush of phenylethylamine, a natural chemical that stimulates the nervous system, causing us to feel euphoric, energetic, and optimistic. Our hearts beat wildly, we're turned on and may be falling in love—or at least in lust. We may experience a racy sense of exuberance and power at these times. With some creative thought and attention, an artful seduction can create a surge of phenylethylamine even in a relationship of long duration. We never lose our capacity to resurrect those pleasurable experiences. It remains with us for our entire lives.

The art of seduction can serve many purposes. It enhances the possibilities of procreation and perpetuation of the species. It can contribute to psychological well-being by increasing one's sense of self-esteem—the successful seducer feels powerful and valued, the one being seduced feels desirable and worthy. It is a gateway to passion, enlivening a person's romantic interest and creativity, so it whets the appetite for lovemaking and increases the likelihood that the sex will be exciting, fulfilling, and pleasurable. Finally, since true intimacy with a partner can only occur when we are vulnerable yet safe, seductions, because they are noncoercive invitations for lovemaking, add dimensions of safety and connection to long-term relationships.

To succeed in the romantic and sexual arena, to fully enjoy the pleasures our bodies hold, we must become skilled in the intimate art of seduction. Like most complex arts, what goes on in a seduction is partially learned through observation and experience and partially the by-product of our biological heritage. We glean ideas from movies, from books, from the confidences of friends, and from the techniques used on us by past lovers. We try them out, perfect them, then make them our own. But our own personalities, our tastes, strengths, proclivities of every sort, put their unique imprimatur on how we seduce, or, for that matter, how we respond to a seduction.

Some aspects of what may be called seduction—such as saying "I love you" or "You're looking great today"—are so common or subtle that they are almost invisibly woven into the fabric of a couple's daily life; other seductions can be so unique or elaborate that they remain unforgettable. There are seductions that develop from the context of the relationship while others are launched by the setting or circumstances that surround it. Sometimes a seduction is a fluid exchange between the partners that gathers momentum as it proceeds, while at other times it centers around one person's attempt to overcome the obstacles that appear to be keeping the two apart. And unfortunately, there is a range of destructive seductions in which the underlying motive is not based on caring or mutuality, but on the intent to undermine, hurt, overpower, or seek revenge.

The stories in this collection illustrate the various forms of seduction, from the spontaneous, subtle dance to the meticulously planned encounter. Some are humorous, others sad or serious, some warm and loving, others dark and menacing. But all of them are erotic at their core, and each encounter in these stories has something revealing or important to say about the art of seduction and how it can lead to uncharted places where new possibilities for adventure and delight await your discovery. I hope that they will stimulate your imagination and add color to your romantic relationships.

Read on. . . . And prepare to be seduced.

PART I

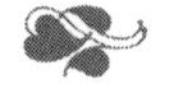

The Dance
of Seduction

A well-executed seduction is an artful dance. As with many dances, the success of the pair lies largely in the hands of the leader. The better he or she is able to artfully guide the dance, the more exquisite the performance. Like dance, seduction is a form of intimate communication. At its core lies a kind of reciprocity, a game that requires two people to play, two players who, in essence, choose to dance together. In the "power" seduction, one person leads and the other follows. When it comes to sex and love, the power of the seducer lies in his or her ability to influence, sway, control, charm, allure, and hence overcome a partner's resistance. A question constantly dangles over the dance: "Will he or won't he?" or "will she or won't she?" Uncertainty reigns until that moment when the follower makes the choice to be seduced. The question as to whether the resistance will, in fact, be surmounted fuels the erotic intensity. "Will they or won't they?" becomes the key question that maintains the sexual tension.

Personal power, charisma, a sense of sexual self-confidence are enormously attractive personality attributes in a potential partner. There is nothing as seductive as a partner's self-assurance, his or her unabashed interest in and desire for the object of his or her affections. This sense of self-confidence, coupled with a questionable outcome, forms an unbeatable combination in the creation of charged erotic intensity.

In Edward Buskirk's "The Other Woman," James, a long-married, monogamous man, is captivated by sexual fantasies of being seduced by his wife's best friend. Buskirk weaves a delightfully humorous tale, an unpredictable and teasing erotic who-done-it, with the wife, Brenda, actually orchestrating behind the scenes like an expert puppeteer. "A self-confident woman is the sexiest woman of all," says Buskirk. "Brenda is not intimidated by her husband's erotic daydreams about being seduced by another woman. She is sufficiently confident about her sexuality and marriage to have some fun with his fantasies." James holds his desires in check as the theme of "will they or won't they," and even "did they or didn't they," captures the three characters in their web of seduction.

Eroticism can be increased in the power seduction by slowing down the process. Looking into one another's eyes and jumping into bed can be one kind of sexual experience, with an intensity that is unique to the uncontrolled lust that underlies the act. But when the process is prolonged, when a sense of slowness and luxury dominates, erotic tension can be increased dramatically. With a slower pace, we submerge ourselves in the experience of the moment. The anticipation builds, and with it, the sexual vibrancy.

In "Lines of Fire," Tee A. Corinne entertains us with a unique lesbian story in which an electric first meeting sets the tone for a creative seduction that becomes an art form in and of itself. "Seduction is actually a dance," explains Corinne. "One person says, 'I want to,' and the other says, 'Show me.' My main character is not unwilling, but she's not jumping in either. Instead there's a pause that increases the excitement. Once the erotic tension has been created, she can open to it."

Another way erotic tension appears to be stimulated is through creating or encountering obstacles and then overcoming them. Every hurdle intensifies the question of "will they or won't they." Every deterrent calls into question the potential prowess of the seducer. The goal becomes more precious. As each successive obstacle is overcome, desire mounts.

In Doraine Poretz's story, "Only in the Movies," obstacles abound. Initially, union is impossible because the protagonist's college love, Beauregard Thomas Darcy III, is not Jewish. However, despite their separate marriages, Beau's passion never abates. "What is important in seduction is passionate engagement," offers Poretz. "But it must be subtle. Nothing is seductive if it is overt or blatant. Beau persists over the years despite the obstacles; he never gives up. And when he and Clare finally get the opportunity to make love, the years of abstinence and the accumulation of sexual tension and fantasy result in great joy."

Sometimes the dance of seduction is so fluid that it is difficult to determine who is the seducer and who is the one being seduced. In the early studies on rat mating, male researchers analyzed the ways in which the male rat enticed the female rat. But when a female researcher, with her female point of view, joined the team, her observations overturned their basic premise—the male rat was not the initiator of the seduction. She pointed out that the female rat's behavior actually incited the male rat's dance. His mating dance was a reaction to her initiation. She was the one who was leading and he was following. In these intricate dances of seduction, the roles of leader and follower can become obscured, as each partner reacts to the responses of the other. Hannah Katz sets up such a seduction in "Double Clicked," where lines of fantasy and reality blur. In this surreal story, seduction literally slips in the back door. "She was turned on to him," Katz explains. "In fact, the feelings were mutual, but he wasn't lunging at her by any means. Instead, he plays his cards carefully and waits for her to begin things. So really, who is in control when she brings his lips to hers—she in the doing or he in the waiting?"

In the dance of seduction, surrender plays a powerful role. In fact, it is the yielding that finally permits the seduction to take place. Yielding enables one to experience the intensity of a full surrender. By being overtaken, the one seduced feels the exhilaration of total abandon. One is not responsible for his or her sexual actions. In this way, the feelings of guilt instilled by society's antisexual attitudes are overcome. Surrender allows for guilt-free indulgence in the hedonism of the sexual encounter.

For Phoenix McFarland, the surrender comes in the form of pure physical enjoyment. In "The Last Seduction," McFarland shows us that you don't have to be young or sexually appealing to enjoy great sexual pleasure. Emma, strapped to life-support equipment, awakens to the ultimate sexual experience. "Someone is making love to Emma," says McFarland. "And she is without responsibility or expectations. She doesn't have to perform. She doesn't have to turn him on, or be young and beautiful or be anything other than herself. She can relax and let go. Everything is keyed to her pleasure and nothing else matters."

Whether the dance of seduction has a clear leader and follower or whether it is an intricate arrangement with subtly changing roles, the dynamics of power and surrender are central in all the stories in this section as well as many of the others in this collection.

The Other Woman
EDWARD BUSKIRK

"Have you ever thought about being with another woman, Brenda?" the thirtyish man behind the wheel of the dark green minivan matter-of-factly asks his wife, turning just far enough toward her to gauge her reaction and still keep one eye on the northbound freeway traffic. It is a hazy and sweltering mid-July afternoon, and it seems as if half of Chicago is escaping the city along with them. "Sexually, I mean."

It seems to take the attractive dark-haired woman a few moments to comprehend her husband's words. When she does, she looks up from the packing list she has been studying ever since they pulled out of their suburban driveway. (Surely they must have forgotten *something*, she had remarked a few minutes earlier. It wouldn't be a real vacation unless they left at least one absolute essential behind.) She blinks. "*What* did you just say, James?"

He laughs, obviously a little embarrassed. "I thought you were listening," he says, motioning toward the radio. "Someone just called in and asked Dr. Laura if she thought it was normal for a married woman to have sexual fantasies about another woman."

Brenda rolls her eyes skyward. "And you were just wondering if I'd ever had those kinds of fantasies about another woman?"

He grins sheepishly. "Just curious."

She cocks her head. "Did you have any particular woman in mind, James?"

"No, not really."

"Are you sure?" she says. "Maybe someone like, say, oh, I don't know—Linda?"

Linda is Brenda's onetime college roommate and longtime best friend. She has invited Brenda to spend a couple of days at her lakeside cottage in northern Wisconsin. And why doesn't she bring that darling husband of hers along?

James and Brenda don't get away very often, but there is a summertime lull at both of their offices, and the kids are off camping with her sister. Brenda hasn't seen Linda in God only knows how long. Who knows when she will have another chance like this? James decides maybe he will go along, just for the ride.

"Okay," James says with a shrug, "just for the hell of it, let's use Linda as an example. Have you ever had those kinds of feelings about her?"

Brenda sighs. "No, darling, I haven't. I'll admit that Linda is very attractive, but I'm afraid she's not my type. She lacks a certain piece of equipment that I've grown rather fond of over the years." She turns back to her list. "Nice try anyway, James."

"What is that supposed to mean?"

"I know how your mind works," she says with a little smile. "It may not have looked to you like I was paying even the slightest bit of attention to the radio, but I was listening just closely enough to know that no one called in with that question you just asked me. You made it up, didn't you?"

"And why would I do that?" James says, putting on his best hurt-annoyed face.

"You really are pathetic," Brenda says. "Don't you think I know by now what a huge crush you've always had on Linda? I couldn't drag you three blocks to see any of my other friends, but Linda calls from two hundred miles away and you start panting like a puppy waiting for his leash. You've been daydreaming about her all week. I've seen that faraway look in your eyes ever since she called. I half-expected you to start calling me by her name when we were making love last night."

"That's ridiculous," James says, hoping his face doesn't look nearly as red as it suddenly feels. "I don't have the slightest interest in Linda except as a friend. Anyway, the question was if *you'd* ever had any sexual fantasies about her, not if I had. Which, by the way, I haven't."

"Liar," Brenda says. "I heard the question. And I know you well enough to know why you asked it. Somewhere in the back of that dirty little mind of yours, you decided that since Linda and I were roommates back in college, maybe we were lovers, too. After all, isn't that what half of the make-believe letters in the *Forum* magazines you hide under the professional journals in your den are about? Horny coed roommates who just can't keep their hot little hands off each other?"

"*Forum*? Never heard of it," James says, trying to keep a straight face. "You must have me mixed up with some other husband." How the hell did she find the *Forum*s?

"Oh, I think I've got the right husband, okay," Brenda says. "The same one who got the bright idea that if Linda and I *were* lovers back in school, like the girls in your magazines, maybe you could talk us into bed together one more time. And best of all, you just might be able to talk your way between the sheets with us. Mainly with Linda, which has been one of your main goals in life ever since you first laid eyes on her. And what better way to find out if I might be interested in going along with your little fantasy arrangement than to pose a phony Dr. Laura question to me?" She smiles. "Am I close so far, darling?"

"You couldn't be more wrong if you tried," James says, well aware that he probably doesn't sound any more convincing to her than he does to himself. How does she *do* it? It's downright scary the way she can read his mind.

Brenda leans close to him, patting his thigh. "I hate to burst your bubble, honey, but your magazines lied—not all college roommates are lesbian lovers. If you want to seduce my friend, you'll have to do it on your own, without my help."

She turns back to her list, smiling coyly. "That is if she doesn't seduce you first. I've seen the way she flirts with you. Listen, you two have at it. Don't worry about little old me. I'll find something to occupy my time."

"Don't fill out your schedule just yet," James says. "In case you haven't noticed in all these years, I'm strictly a one-woman man. This is your fantasy, not mine."

She laughs. "Whatever you say, sweetheart."

"I can't believe this conversation," he says. "I ask you a simple little question that I *did* hear on the radio, thank you, and before I know it you've spun it into this bizarre fairy tale about me cheating on you with your best friend, right under your nose. With an imagination like that, you should be writing for the soaps."

"Pajamas," Brenda says.

"*What?*"

She turns to face him, tucking her list into the glove box. "Pajamas. I just remembered what I forgot to pack—your pajamas." She smiles mischievously. "But then that will just make it all the more convenient for you and Linda, won't it? No cumbersome old pj's to get in the way."

James grins and shakes his head in exaggerated disbelief. Things are getting pretty bad when a guy can't even enjoy a decent fantasy without his wife figuring it all out and making him feel like a damn fool.

"Don't strain your eyes, darling," Brenda whispers.

James nearly jumps out of his skin. He did not hear his wife sneak up behind the chaise longue he occupies on the deck of Linda's pine-shadowed lakeside A-frame. He thought she was still inside, changing into her bathing suit.

Actually, he has not been thinking about Brenda at all. Nor about the John Grisham novel he holds on his lap. He has barely even noticed the splendid view of the gently rippling, sun-splashed lake the hillside cottage perches above.

His eyes are trained on their slim, deeply tanned hostess, who, wearing the tiny bikini top and abbreviated cut-offs she greeted them in (Is it all in James's head, or did the hello kiss she gave him linger just a little longer than your average friendly hello kiss?), is lying on a large white beach towel at the end of her plank dock, waiting for Brenda to join her.

"You haven't taken your eyes off her since we got here. It must be her new haircut," Brenda says with only the slightest hint of sarcasm, dangling her arms over her husband's shoulders and nuzzling his neck. "If I cut my hair really, really short like that, would you look at me the way you're looking at her?"

"Of course not," James says. He tries, too late, to correct himself. "What I mean is, I like your hair just fine the way it is. Anyway, I'm not looking at her. I'm reading. Really."

"Oh?" Brenda says, covering his paperback with her hand. "Quick, repeat the last sentence you read."

James grins. "Uh . . ."

"I thought so," she says, sliding her hand down over his stomach and onto the crotch of his khaki shorts. "My, my, what have we here? Maybe you'd like me to go into town and get a motel so you two can be alone. I'm sure Linda wouldn't mind. I saw that kiss she planted on you."

Lowering his zipper, Brenda snakes her hand inside, touching his erection. She loosens his belt with her other hand, freeing his rigid penis.

"What's got into you today, Bren?" James says, frantically trying to cover himself with his paperback.

Brenda smiles, curling her fingers over him. "You should have bought the hardcover."

James jerks as she tightens her grip on him. "Have you gone nuts? What if Linda looks up here?"

"You don't really think she'd mind seeing you like this, do you?" Brenda whispers, nibbling his earlobe, slowly massaging him, teasing a fingernail along the throbbing vein traversing the bottom of his penis. "I'm sure she's very well aware of the effect she has on you. Somehow I don't think she wore that skimpy little outfit for my benefit."

Just then Linda sits up, glancing their way. Shielding her eyes from the sun, she waves. Brenda waves back with her free hand, continuing her rhythmic massage with the other one. James lifts his knees in an attempt to cover himself, desperately pleading, "Brenda, please!"

Brenda ignores him. "I can see why you're so attracted to her," she says, squeezing harder, slowly increasing the tempo. "Those legs, that tan, those disgustingly pert boobs. Very sexy. You know, I'm even beginning to think that you two might look pretty hot together in bed."

"*Sure* you are," James says, his breathing becoming labored as his wife works him closer and closer to climax. He still tries to shield himself from Linda, but he is no longer urging Brenda to stop.

"Don't be so sure of yourself," she says, darting her tongue into his ear, slowly teasing her thumbnail over and around his circumcision, making him gasp aloud. "Maybe I used to be jealous, but I've mellowed, maybe even gotten a little kinky. I know that you've fantasized for years about seeing me with another man, so why can't I fantasize about seeing you with another woman?"

"Just because I know you never would," James says, peeking nervously around his knees at Linda. "Look, maybe Linda and I do flirt with each other a little, but it's all in fun. Nothing is ever going to happen between us. I am very happily taken. And if there was even the slightest chance that something would happen, I don't think you would find all of this nearly as amusing as you seem to now."

"Whatever you say, darling," Brenda says, kissing his neck, reaching down to caress his tight and swollen testicles. "But I'll bet you're just dying to know what she looks like under those cut-offs, aren't you?"

James, of course, is dying to know exactly that, but even in his vulnerable state, he knows better than to come right out and admit it. He grins. "I could care less."

"For starters," Brenda says, gently rolling a testicle between her fingers, squeezing just hard enough to make James wince, "unless Linda's become a lot more conservative in her old age than I think she has, she's probably not wearing panties. And I would guess that she's as tan under her cut-offs as she is everywhere else. She always hated tan lines as much as she hated wearing underwear."

She switches her attention to his other testicle and James grunts, so aroused that he momentarily forgets his modesty and lets one knee fall flat. Linda looks their way again, tilting her sunglasses up onto her forehead. Her mouth drops open. She clasps her hand to her lips in mock horror, laughing aloud.

Brenda slides her hand onto her embarrassed husband's erection again, milking up and down. "Oh my, I do believe you've been caught with your pants down," she says. "Maybe this is your chance to make your move. Time is wasting, you know. We'll be gone tomorrow. Would you like me to call down to her and see if she wants to trade places with me?"

"Don't you dare!" James pleads in a hoarse whisper. "You've embarrassed me enough already. This is beginning to remind me of a bad dream I used to have back in junior . . ." Brenda squeezes his root and his words trail off. He tenses, knowing he is only another squeeze or two away from climaxing all over John Grisham's latest.

But it is not to be. Brenda abruptly pulls her hand away from him and stands up. "I guess I'll go down and work on my tan for a while," she says. "Enjoy your book. And whatever you do, don't let that thing get sunburned."

"Why, you . . ." Red-faced, James struggles to tuck everything back into place.

She smiles. "What did you start to say, James?"

"Nothing," he says with a grin, struggling to adjust himself. "Just a two-syllable word we had back in high school for girls who did what you just did."

Brenda laughs. "Sweetheart? That's two syllables." Smiling impishly over her shoulder at her husband, she pads down to the dock and stretches out beside her friend, looking sleek and confident in her white bathing suit. She leans over and whispers something to Linda.

James can hear their girlish laughter. He has had the feeling of being the outside man on an inside joke ever since they arrived and he overheard Brenda telling her friend, much to Linda's glee, about their Dr. Laura conversation. His cheeks burning, he buries his face in his book, not realizing for several long seconds that he is holding it upside down.

"Zip me, James?"

James looks up from where he sits on the bed, tying his shoes, to see Linda standing in the doorway, clasping a short white dress to her neck. Behind him he hears the sounds of Brenda showering. The three of them are going out for the evening. Linda knows this great little club on the other side of the lake where they play nothing but sixties rock and roll.

"Sure," he says, standing.

Linda turns her back to him. Her dress lies open around her tanned back and shoulders to several inches below her waist. James clears his throat and reaches for her zipper.

"I hope those are dancing shoes you just finished putting on," Linda says. "The place we're going has a dirty dancing contest at midnight. I'm counting on you being my partner."

James clears his throat again. He has taken hold of her zipper and his eyes have fallen to the shadowed flesh beneath her dress. He sees nothing but tanned peach-shaped bottom. No panties, just like Brenda said. His fingers tremble and he feels an immediate stirring below his belt.

Linda smiles. "Having trouble, James?"

"No, no trouble at all." Damn her, she had to have known he would get an eyeful. What man wouldn't? He reluctantly tugs her zipper upward.

She turns to face him, planting a discreet 'thank you' kiss on his cheek, draping her arms over his shoulders. "You will be my partner, won't you?" She is so close that he can feel the warmth of her breath and smell the gentle lilac scent of her perfume.

"I'm really not much of a dancer," he says, trying not to stare at the thick points her nipples are forming against the front of her dress. He does not quite know what to do with his hands. He fights the urge to slide them down over her ass. "Just ask Brenda."

"All you have to do is follow me," Linda says, moving closer still.

"Hell, I'd follow you anywhere," he says with a grin, unable to get that momentary peek at her backside out of his mind. "Okay, let's do it."

Linda smiles. "You don't know how long I've waited to hear you say that," she says, stretching up on her tiptoes, her lips brushing against his. James's lips brush back. Just as he puts his hands on her waist, he realizes he doesn't hear the shower anymore. Brenda has just stepped into the room. He quickly pulls away from Linda but he knows it is too late.

"Are you two having fun?" Brenda says, tilting her head to insert an earring.

James is at a loss for words. Now he's done it.

Linda is unfazed. "I was just thanking James for zipping me," she says matter-of-factly. "And for being my partner in the dirty dancing contest tonight."

As she turns away, her eyes meet Brenda's. If James did not know better, he would swear it was all they could do to keep from bursting into laughter.

"Listen," he stammers as soon as Linda leaves the room, "it wasn't what it—"

Brenda silences him with a finger to his lips. "Sure it wasn't, honey," she says. She steps past him, shrugging out of her robe and into a flowered sundress.

"That's it?" James asks incredulously. "That's all you have to say?"

She smiles, her eyes meeting his in the mirror as she applies her lipstick. "It *must* be her hair," she says. "I really do think I'll get mine cut, too."

James knows he should feel relieved that she is not angry with him, but all he feels is frustrated. What the hell is going on here?

James has not been inside a place like this in years—noisy, smoky, dimly lit, and smelling of stale beer, sweat, and perfume. It is twelve-twenty and the dance floor is full of other people of their own era, dancing to a nostalgia none of them is old enough to really remember.

Linda has kicked off her shoes and is barefoot, her short dress swirling around her sun-bronzed legs, inching dangerously high on her thighs. There is a sheen of perspiration on her face and a faraway look in her eyes as she moves her hips to the early sixties music, a song that James should recognize from the Golden Oldies station but doesn't. James Brown? Little Richard? James's pre–Eagles/Fleetwood Mac pop music knowledge is practically nonexistent.

All James can do is to try to keep up with Linda and not look too foolish doing it. The half-dozen beers he has drunk have taken the edge off his fear of looking foolish, but they have done nothing to help him keep up. Besides, he finds himself repeatedly glancing toward a darkened corner booth behind a jukebox and pool table where Brenda sits watching, smiling, fending off an endless stream of would-be dance partners.

James is not sure why she seems to be enjoying this so much, why she practically insisted that he enter the contest with Linda, but he is beyond trying to understand anything that has happened today. Go with the flow, isn't that what they used to say?

And right now the flow is with Linda. Her hands on his shoulders, she moves closer and closer, her body churning and twisting to the primitive beat. James slides his hands to her trim waist. He instinctively starts to move them to her hips but catches himself at the last moment. Sooner or later, Brenda will have seen enough.

Sensing his hesitation, never missing a beat, Linda whispers, "Don't stop now. She gets you all the time. I only have tonight."

No guts, no glory, buddy boy, a voice somewhere deep inside James growls. Fighting an urge to glance back at his wife one more time, he slides his hands lower, over Linda's hips and onto her ass. She gasps, her eyes sparkling with excitement. Grinding her hips, she pushes close to him, her fingers burrowing into his back pockets.

She pulls him to her, breaking into a smile when she meets his erection. He can feel the heat of her arousal through her thin dress. Knowing she is bare beneath it excites him all the more.

The music slows and they move together as one. "I am so hot I'm dripping," Linda whispers, her lips touching his. James is pretty sure she is not talking about the room temperature.

"Shall we really give them something to talk about?" she whispers, her eyes on fire.

He glances once again at Brenda. She smiles. He turns back to Linda and grins, kneading her ass cheeks, bunching her skirt in his hands, slowly pulling it higher and higher. "What did you have in mind?"

"This," she says, her fingers clutching at him from inside his pockets. Stretching up onto her tiptoes, grinding her pelvis against him, she kisses him long and hard and wet, teasing her tongue between his teeth.

James hesitates, but for only a split second, before pulling her closer. He teases his fingertips beneath her hem, exploring the satiny curves of her naked bottom as they kiss, their tongues tangling and twisting together. He does not look in Brenda's direction now. He is certain that he has gone too far, that Brenda, in spite of her smile, will be furious with him. It is one thing to look, but something else entirely to touch and to kiss.

But instead of filling him with guilt and apprehension, that fear of impending doom seems only to heighten his arousal. It is a feeling of danger and frenzy that he never wants to end, no matter how terrible the consequences.

Seeming to sense his excitement, Linda stretches higher, pressing yet closer, her hips moving back and forth almost as if she is in the throes of orgasm. As the music fades, she seductively sucks his tongue between her lips, curling her tongue over and around it as if it were a wet pink cock.

The bar lights go up. James looks around to see that they are the only couple left on the dance floor. Their audience hoots wildly. A bearded bartender rushes out with a hundred-dollar bill. Linda tucks it into her bodice with a brazen flourish. The bartender makes a loud crude remark about needing a fire hose to cool them down. Everyone laughs. James is afraid to look to see if Brenda is laughing, too.

As they walk off the floor, Linda takes James's hand and whispers into his ear, "If I know Brenda, she'll want the two of us to stay up all night reminiscing after you go to bed, just like we always do. And sooner or later, just like always, she'll fall asleep on the couch. Don't be surprised if you have a visitor." Her eyes fall discreetly to the juncture of his legs and she smiles. "It hardly seems fair that I do all the work and she gets all the benefits."

Before James can say anything, they are back at their table. Brenda rolls her eyes toward the smoky ceiling in mock disgust and says, "Listen, if you two want to go on back to the cottage and finish what you just started out there, don't mind me. I'm sure I can find a ride home." There is a glint of amusement in her eyes and a smile on her lips.

James breathes a deep sigh of relief. Thank God. But as relieved as he is that his wife is not angry, his heart is in his throat. *What the hell is it with Brenda? She should be irate. And what about Linda? Can she really mean what she said? What will he do if she does come into the bedroom? Will he be able to do anything? Will he even want to? For years he has been dreaming about just such a moment and now he is scared to death that it might really happen.*

James finally drifts off to sleep to the happy chatter of his wife and her best friend as it floats up the stairs. Everyone has had a good laugh and the flirtation game is over. Never in a million years would Linda really sneak into bed with him. Tomorrow night he and Brenda will be home, and while it will take him a few days to live down his foolish antics, no damage has been done—except, of course, to his dignity.

At first it is just a pleasant dream, the kisses on his upper thighs, the warm breath on his testicles. But now he is awake, or thinks he is awake, and the sensations have not gone away. They are even stronger. A wet tongue teases over the head of his cock, around the crown of his circumcision, making him gasp and start. Warm lips push over him and he feels himself swell and harden.

"Brenda?" he whispers sleepily.

Nothing.

He reaches for the light and remembers that he is not in his own house. The lamp is on the other side of the bed. He squints but Brenda pulled the heavy drapes before going downstairs and everything is pitch-black.

Well, it has to be Brenda anyway. It is one thing for Linda to goof around about paying him a surreptitious visit, but she wouldn't just come in here and do *this*.

Becoming more and more aroused as his visitor bobs up and down between his legs, sucking harder, taking him deeper and deeper into her mouth, he reaches down to caress his wife's head. His breath catches in his throat. His heart seems to stop. He is suddenly wide awake. The hair he is touching is short. *Very* short. *Linda* short. *Oh, Christ!*

James quickly pulls his hand away. He starts to say something, but he has no idea what it would be even if he could somehow force his lips to form words. He knows he should tell her to leave, but a part of him does not want her to leave at all. Her lips are engulfing his erection, her tongue performing magic on his excited flesh, and it feels so damn good.

He leans back, his heart pounding, his excitement growing ever more intense. He wants to touch her, to kiss and caress her, but he does not dare. He suddenly feels very shy. *What is the protocol here, anyway?* he wonders with a bemused grin. He just leans back and lets it happen, reeling with the rush of it all.

Just when he feels his climax nearing, his visitor pulls off of him with a wet sucking sound. Sitting up, she straddles him. He gasps aloud and she leans forward, touching a fingertip to his lips to silence him.

Pushing up onto her knees, she takes him into her hand and guides his throbbing head to her slippery crease. His hands go to her waist as she slowly pushes down over him, not stopping until his balls caress her ass. She pulls up, ever so slowly, halting her upward movement only when it seems he will slip out of her velvety grasp. Down. Up. Down. Increasing the tempo until James stiffens and explodes into her, grabbing her ass and holding on for dear life, shooting torrent after torrent of warm sperm into her deepest reaches.

Spent, James falls back against the pillow, gasping for breath. Still she does not stop, riding his shrinking member until at last she, too, tenses. Leaning back, holding her wrist to her mouth to muffle her cries of release, she squeezes her vaginal muscles over him, trapping him inside her, not releasing him until the clutching spasms of her orgasm have subsided.

Leaning forward, she touches her lips to his for a lingering moment. Then she is gone, padding barefoot to the door and slipping silently through it before James can even catch a fleeting glimpse of her. All that lingers is the faint aroma of her lilac perfume.

James lies in bed as long as he dares the next morning, last night's exhilaration dulled by nagging guilt and an intensifying apprehension. He hears his wife and Linda talking in the kitchen. He cannot make out their words but they are laughing. Well, that's a good sign, at least. Linda has obviously not told Brenda about their nighttime adventure. James suddenly realizes that for the rest of his life, every time Linda and Brenda are together, he will have to worry about the previous night's events slipping out in conversation. The thought makes him shudder.

Finally, unable to put it off any longer, he goes downstairs. Linda leans against the counter, sipping a cup of coffee. She smiles at James. James blushes, averting his eyes.

"Hi, hon," Brenda says from around the corner. "Have a nice night's sleep?"

"Like a log." He does not look her way. He fills his coffee cup, not looking at either of them. It is not until he has turned away from the coffeemaker that his eyes catch Brenda's. He nearly drops his cup.

"What do you think?" Brenda asks with a smile, her eyes dancing, cocking her head. Her shoulder-length tresses are gone, reduced to the same boyishly stylish length as Linda's hair. "We did it last night, while you were sleeping. You know how I've been threatening ever since we got here to get mine cut just like Linda's? Well, she got out the scissors and voilà. Do you like it, honey?"

James grins and nods, speechless.

"What's the matter, James?" Brenda says with a girlish gig-
gle. "You look like you've seen a ghost."

James feels relieved and disappointed all at once. Of course it
was Brenda. He should have known so all along. He should
have seen it coming, what with the way the two of them had
been whispering and laughing behind his back. They had obviously planned it together right from the start. Let's really put
one over on old James.

But then again, maybe it wasn't Brenda after all. Maybe the
haircut is just a weird coincidence. Hasn't Linda been flirting
with him for years, hinting that she might be interested in something just like what happened last night? And the way she was
rubbing up against him and kissing him out there on the dance
floor—well, that sure as hell didn't seem like any prank. And
then there was the perfume. James could have sworn it was
Linda's perfume he smelled last night, not Brenda's.

He takes his coffee and retreats to the deck. He can hear the
women laughing softly.

They are nearly home before Brenda wakes up. She has been
curled in her seat, fast asleep, almost since they left Linda's cottage. And all that time, James has been trying to decide if that
is just the barest hint of lilac perfume he smells on his wife, or
if it is all in his head.

Brenda yawns and stretches and pats James on the thigh,
snuggling close. "Did you enjoy yourself?" she asks.

"Oh, yeah," James says. "It was good to get away."

"Linda was certainly in prime form, wasn't she?"

James nods. "Linda was really Linda."

Brenda tucks her legs beneath herself. "Aren't you glad I'm
not the jealous type?"

James grins. "Uh-huh."

"Listen, I know it was all in fun between you two," Brenda
says. "But if she really would have . . . Well, you know. Would
you have?"

James shakes his head. "Never. You should know by now
that you're the only one for me."

Brenda kisses him on the cheek. But as she settles back into
her seat, he cannot help but notice the sly little smile that curls
over her lips.

James has a feeling he will never know for sure. Brenda will never tell him. She will enjoy watching him wonder way too much. And he will be damned if he's ever going to ask her. If he asks and it wasn't her . . . Well, that little thought sends an icy chill racing down his spine.

But a guy can dream about being seduced by his wife's best friend, can't he? It's just that when the guy's wife is someone like Brenda, he should never ever dream out loud.

Lines of Fire

TEE A. CORINNE

One of my lovers, it doesn't matter who, took me to see Gina Lomand's films one night. They were thirty minutes each and filled with poetry. I sat in the dark in the small, ornate old theater and felt as if my dreams were being played out on the screen. One showed a smoky close-up of a woman's face exploring someone else's body. In another, breasts undulated and changed colors, reversed into other tones, merged with the background and came forward once again. Flesh became ruby, then emerald, iridescent. It looked the way I felt when I made love. My own breasts throbbed against the so-fine silk of my shirt and I wanted to touch them, to comfort and quell the longing in my thighs, between my legs. The sweetly scented air pressed in upon me, caught in my throat. I reminded myself to inhale deeply and relax.

Although the event was open to the public, I can't remember seeing any men there, just wall-to-wall women. I thought we must be breathing and shuddering in unison, but maybe not. My companion stroked my arm. Her soothing rhythm lacked the urgency of my own blood.

At the end, Gina sat on the side of the stage and talked about her work, answered questions with a charm and a hint of the South in her voice. Her hair, an electric red that didn't come from any bottle, seemed to punctuate her comments. Her hands flashed with controlled gestures that bridged the gap between words and images.

My companion wanted to leave long before I was ready. I could have let her go alone, but I was hungry for food and something else as well. We had planned a late dinner at a new

Japanese restaurant. I wrote on my business card, "Your work is wonderful!" and moved forward just as the formal discussion was breaking up.

Gina was surrounded by a barrier wave of women, two and three deep. I held up the card and caught her eye. Reaching out, she took the card, glanced at it, then back at me. Her eyes took in my face in an almost physical act. It was as if she were measuring the moment, pressing in, devouring me. The sexual muscles in my pelvis spasmed with a flow of reaction so intense I feared it would show. She smiled, lips and teeth and eyes, and we were alone in some place outside of time, furtively held in those cataclysmic seconds. I registered her freckles, soft green jacket, russet turtleneck, gold earrings. But mostly I saw her eyes, turquoise blue and radiant.

I circled my fingers and called out the word "exquisite." She nodded, then her attention was called away. She glanced back at me and seemed to start to say something. Someone's hand touched her shoulder and she turned her head, leaving me with an image of softly open lips like a Renaissance angel.

My retreat was hot. Every nerve in my body seemed awake, alert, commenting and clamoring for attention. Food, later, was a balm—raw fish, vinegared rice, the music like water falling on stones. I cooled myself in it, although I know I also must have carried on a conversation. The real world had become muffled. Other images played across my inner screen, mixing Gina's beauty with her art.

The next day in my studio I passed over a block of pale yellow alabaster, choosing instead pieces of automobile bodies, yellow and red. I wanted to work fast, while the memory of the evening was still vivid. I pulled on the heavy leather apron, goggles, and gloves, adjusted the oxygen valve, and struck the first spark. The shapes seemed almost to free themselves from the larger pieces of metal, parting at my will, at the tip of the flame.

I stopped for lunch, but hardly noticed the food, so intent was I on returning to the forms laid out, ready to be assembled. Back at the workbench I braced two pieces for the first weld, changed the head on the torch, and picked up a brazing rod. The roar of the oxyacetylene torch filled my ears. The heat intensified over the course of the afternoon as seams were matched and filled, forming a vaguely heart-shaped form with curved, inviting crevices. *Cunt on Fire* I called it in my mind, but knew I'd have to find a more judicious name before my next scheduled show. My dealer, solid and devoted, would not approve.

As I worked, my body hummed with memories of Gina and her movies. I channeled these spinning, fragmentary neurological events through my hands into the evolving piece.

Late in the afternoon as I sat studying the piece, the phone rang. "Dinner?" she asked without saying "Hi," without identifying herself, but I knew who it was and she knew I knew. She added, "I need to take a break."

I paused between the exciting but safe world of my work and the enticement of her slight drawl, the promise of intelligent company.

She registered my hesitation, but did not hurry to fill the silence.

"I'm filthy. Give me time to shower and change," I said, stepping over an invisible line.

"There's a bistro called Sammy's, I think it's near where you live. Want to meet me there?"

"Half an hour," I said.

"Forty-five minutes," she answered.

She was waiting when I arrived, a cool drink in front of her, loose pages filled with drawings spread across the table. She bundled them and reached out to shake my hand.

"I seem to carry my work with me. It's what I'm like," she said with a smile. Her hand was intensely present in my own. Reluctantly I let go, but she seemed in no hurry to pull away, so our hands almost drifted apart, carrying imprinted sensations. My thoughts jumbled for a moment, then cleared. I held up a folder. "Me too. I brought these in case you were delayed, but thought you might want to see them as well."

"What? Show me."

"They're photographs of my newer work. Forms in transition, just like me." I wondered why I had said that, even though it was true. Was I going to blurt my entire life story to this woman I hardly knew?

Her eyes, which seemed to see too much, studied my face slowly. "I saw your last two shows," she said, not hurrying her words. "You make forms dance."

Immensely pleased by her comment, I felt an old caution threaten to hold me back. "What happens when two creative individuals get together?" I asked, trying to keep my tone light.

Her eyes seemed to sparkle and her beautiful hands opened like flowers. "Perhaps they work together."

The waitress arrived. I ordered cannelloni, noticed the background music for the first time, progressive jazz; had it been playing all along?

Gina's eyes flashed to my face. "I'll take the cannelloni, too," she said, turning to the waitress, "and perhaps a red wine, the house wine will do." Her eyes returned to me with that quality of absorbing whatever she was looking at. Will she take me, too, I wondered, casually, like the cannelloni?

The moment broke. The waitress hurried away. I handed Gina the folder. She studied the photos one by one. There was an excitement rising in me, an anticipation that she would see into the core of what I was doing. The sculptures were small, most under a foot in height, sensuous and inviting to the touch. She paused at one of my favorites, turned it upside down and sideways, then right side up again.

Raising one hand in front of her, she made a gesture as if pressing the hollow in the sculpture with the palm of her hand. A corresponding jolt of energy shot through my body. My face must have betrayed me. A brief look of pleasure crossed hers before she lowered her eyes.

The music grew louder, the lights dimmer, food was served. She returned the folder with a smile. We ate. There was a satisfaction in being near her, studying her hands, the disorderly curls of fine hair around her face. Still, I felt a distance. She caught me looking at her, put down her fork, folded her hands, and just looked back. I felt the daring, the enthrallment of her gaze. We laughed at the same time, at nothing at all, but there was a nervousness in me.

Dessert was Spanish flan, the custard smooth and satisfying, edged with the enticing sweetness of caramelized sugar. The odor and taste of spiced coffee sent a ringing through my body. Perhaps I would work all night.

A woman came toward us, tailored, striking. "Gina," she called out, her voice filled with pleasure, but carrying also a command.

"Maria Louisa!" Gina's delight was immediate. "Come. Sit down. Meet my new friend."

"I can only stay a minute," she said, pulling out a chair and sitting carefully. "I have some good news for you about money. My friend with festival connections says your film will be featured, if only . . . but I am interrupting and this is a social gathering. I have no manners." She gingerly raked me with her eyes and held out her hand. "Maria Louisa Piscadore, at your service."

I told her my name and decided to leave. Whatever their relationship, I felt left out, superfluous. "I must be off," I said, as casually as I could manage. "Work calls." I put money on the table to cover my tab and a generous tip.

Gina stood and hugged me, almost my height and warm, so warm. I hurried away.

Walking home I replayed our conversations, the disorienting effect of her proximity. I wasn't sure that I wanted a wild passion. I wasn't sure what it was that I wanted at all.

In the studio I studied the sculpture a long time. With the right base it would seem to twist in space.

Much later, sleep came slowly, interrupted by flashing images of her face and hands, the sculpture, the intense beating of my heart.

Throughout the following day my mind touched on that final hug that had happened so fast, yet lingered. The sensations would return to me in a flash of kinesthetic memory, her body against my own once again as I constructed an openwork base to hold the sculpture high, supporting it, but not demanding attention.

That evening, just as I was going to call her up, she dropped by my studio unannounced.

"Want to go for a walk?" she asked, her head tilted back, an enigmatic yet inviting smile on her lovely lips.

"Your timing is perfect," I told her, pleased to see her, but disturbed by the rush of pleasure her nearness brought. I was caught by the color and depth of light in her eyes. If she said more, I didn't hear it. I closed my eyes in order to turn away, pulled on a light jacket. We bumped into one another in the doorway. It was not accidental.

We wandered along the tree-lined streets. Overhead leaves

threw dancing patterns of light and dark on the sidewalk. Within this light show, we moved together so smoothly it was as if we were dancing.

"Do you always pick up strange women in theaters?" she asked.

"No," I answered, deciding not to tell her I had rarely been so bold with someone I didn't know. Instead I started talking about the only film I'd ever made, a graduate school assignment in which I had explored the plants in my lover's garden, a very satisfying experience. She kept glancing at me as I talked, a smile playing across her mouth. What was she thinking? She seemed both so present and so illusive.

She took my arm as we walked. I could feel her breast pressing through the layers of fabric. We walked a ways in silence. I lost track of time. My awareness of each point of contact, the slight friction of our movements, was all-consuming. She asked, "Do you have many lovers?" Her voice was quiet, steady.

"One who's leaving me for a job back East. A few hopefuls on the horizon."

"You could go East, too," she said.

"No," I said, shaking my head with an emphasis that surprised me. "No, I think it's over, has been over for some time. Habit, perhaps, or convenience, kept us together. She moved here with me, but never settled in."

"Places have personalities," Gina said, gesturing with her free hand. Perhaps it was a trick of the light, but she looked like some figure in a thirties movie, perhaps in *Morocco*. "I studied film in New York City," she continued. "Loved New York then. But I make better movies here."

As we came to a more populated area, she let go of my arm, but lingeringly, reluctantly. I knew I would cherish that gesture, the feel of her body against my own. I etched it in my mind.

We had been walking toward the riverfront, paused on a terrace with an excellent view of water, lights, traffic. "I love it here," she said. "I never want to leave." She leaned against me briefly, then pulled away. I felt my body cleave to her, but held myself in check.

"And you, do you have many lovers?" I asked.

"I have in the past. Maria Louisa was one. She dumped me for a singer, now she's trying to win me back."

"Will it work?"

"I don't know." She looked at me intently. "No, I don't think so."

We walked on in a pregnant quiet, making a large transit before reaching my building once again. I knew what I needed to know, at least for the time being.

I held out my hand and she took it, brought it to her lips in a gesture I had only seen in movies. The flickering lights gave her face a constantly changing expression. Her lips were sweetly soft. I released myself by an act of will.

"Yes," she said, as if answering some unasked question. She turned and walked away. I longed to call out to her, reach out to her, but held back. I noticed that I almost always hold back. From what? What did I have to lose? I went up to my studio, lay down on the couch. My response to her was lodged in my body, sensitized at every point of contact. I slipped my fingers inside my pants, found myself wet with longing, touched myself as if I were touching her, as if she were touching me.

Is there a way that desire can bind you to someone? I felt the danger of imagining her in this most private of my activities. Yet the connection between her image, her touch, and my body was so rich, so strong, I gave myself over to the experience. My hands explored my fantasy of her body as I was exploring my own. The smell of sex rose around me as the memory of her lips on my fingers moved to the palm of my hand, the inside of my arm, my breast, my stomach, my pubis. Despite my excitement, release was not immediate. Her imaginary fingers were inside me when I came.

Sleep must have followed pleasure. In the early hours of the morning I woke, languorous. The smell of loving remained. I carried her presence with me as I climbed into my loft to sleep again. In my dreams we were sitting with our legs wrapped around each other, kissing and rocking, nude. In that fluid way that some dreams have, our bodies seemed to float. Effortlessly we changed positions. I pulled her to me. She kissed my face, caressed my neck, my shoulders, my breasts.

When I awoke to daylight, I felt imprinted with her arms and legs, breasts, torso, fingers, hands.

Leafing through an art magazine at breakfast, I found an article about Gina. It praised her artistry, damned the critics who were put off by the content, frightened by the intensity, the passion in her films. Maria Louisa was mentioned as a producer with whom Gina had often worked. Done with breakfast, I washed and put away the dishes before turning to the sculpture whose surface rippled in the light.

After putting Strauss waltzes in the CD player, I returned to finish *Cunt on Fire*. Filled with hunger, yearning, it was unlike my other recent forms. I filed the welds, smoothing, refining. As the music wove a magic around me, my movements took on a special kind of grace. I forgot to eat lunch, continued working until the piece was done. By then the afternoon sun had warmed the studio. I sank into my favorite chair admiring the sculpture. I dozed.

She phoned. "I want to see you."

"Where? What time?" I was still half-asleep. She seemed to be part of some exceptionally pleasant dream I had been enjoying. Absentmindedly I rubbed my hands across my breasts, stroked the side of my face, slipped my fingers through my hair.

"My place. We are having a party, sort of, a working group to discuss my latest film. I would like very much for you to join in."

"Yes," I said, knowing that I hadn't begun to know what I was agreeing to, but ready to engage with her on her own ground. "Yes, give me the address. Shall I bring food?"

"Finger food or wine."

The address was close enough to walk. I showered with care, enjoyed the anticipation, ate before I left to stave off desperation, wore comfortable, loose-fitting clothes.

This city I had learned to love was jittering with color, reflected in the after-sheen of a light rain. Everything smelled cleansed and clear. I imagined her filming my walk, tried to see my transit through the camera of her eye. If I were in a movie now, my body would be transparent with blinking neon signs, arrows, fragmented words.

The entranceway to Gina's home was a long outdoor corridor that led between the buildings to a heavy wooden gate. Had she built the gate herself from boards washed against the shore? I asked when she responded to my ring.

"Yes, but that was long ago." She laughed and pulled me across a small, overgrown garden, flowers blooming everywhere. Her hair floated about her face and her eyes were bright. Once inside she gave me a brief hug. It was over so quickly I didn't have time to respond, but it echoed against me in waves.

Her living room was brown and cream and gray, not what I would have thought at all. No one else was there. "I wanted you to come early, to see my nest before it was full."

"I expected color," I said, taking in the textured covers, pots and baskets, weavings on the walls.

She closed her eyes, ran her hands through her hair, and sighed in a most engaging way. "I want neutrality at home, a nonintrusive world, no competition for my attention, which is often elsewhere."

I wondered how much time she had for lovers, how much of herself she was willing to extend. She took my arm and patted it, as if she knew. "Enough," she said.

She took my bottle of May Wine, saying that it was a favorite, then led me to the kitchen, where she settled it with other varieties, some fermented, some not. She beckoned and I followed her through a narrow hallway to a bedroom, where I lurched inside at the sight of the bed, soft with dark pillows and a magenta-colored comforter. I hurried to catch up as she disappeared through yet another door.

"This is my studio." She spun in a circle, making her clothing float out from her body. "It used to be a two-car garage." The walls were painted black. A central area was clear, lights around the edge. Order was everywhere.

"Some people think I am like my movies, but they are my imagination set free by the structure of my life. You comprehend. I know you do."

"Yes. When reaching for form, a vision, an almost hallucinatory dream, I want my tools right where I can find them. However, there is a great deal more dust where I work," I said.

"Dust is the enemy of film." She laughed. "I had to be successful enough to hire someone else to clean."

"And are you?"

"Yes, but only because I teach, as well."

Chimes from the gate rang through the house, but she touched my face, my lips, with the tips of her fingers. "You are very beautiful. Not ordinary beauty. Unique. Shapes that settle in my mind. I want to make a film of you."

I put my hand against the side of her face. If there had been time, I might have done more.

She hurried off and I followed slowly, replaying the touch, the words, the energy that briefly wrapped around me and then was gone. I remembered her movies and how strongly they had touched me. How much would she ask? How much was I willing to give?

There were women in the kitchen, moving quietly, as if they each knew their way around. They smiled and introduced themselves. Musicians, writers, artists. Some names I knew already. I felt their attention even when they weren't looking at me. Twice a shifting of bodies let me see Gina clearly. Each time she looked directly at me, held my gaze until her face was once more blocked from my view. What was the woman thinking? What did she want from me? Where might she lead? Did I want to follow? The tug of attraction was so strong. Did anyone else notice?

More chimes. More women came. Appealing-looking women with strong faces. We sat in the living room, fifteen? eighteen? The soft, intimate lighting dimmed to extinction as slides were projected on a screen: global maps, green and blue with bright red lines.

"There are lines of fire around the earth," Gina said, her disembodied voice warm, hypnotic, "places where the earth's core breaks through, where land masses shift, volcanoes overflow."

Images of eruptions followed, of lines of fire moving, caressing mountains, sliding into the edges of the sea. Aerial shots—were they from satellites?—with overlays of fault lines, points of precariousness, instability.

"I want to make a film about a woman's body as the earth, her sexuality breaking through like lines of fire. I don't know how to do it yet. I want your help."

The intimacy in her voice was compelling. I felt as if she were speaking directly to me.

The images changed and merged, women's bodies overlaid the maps, the landscapes. Torsos defined the territories, crimson arcs articulated subterranean activities. I was drawn in, turned on. My body. I wanted it to be my body cracking open, exploding with lava, delicious relief. I wanted to give my body to her project, to her art, the way I had transmuted my feelings for her into tangible form. It would be a giving, but also an exploration, a journey.

Suddenly I went numb. I couldn't do this, shouldn't do this. I needed control, my internal rock of self-security.

Someone started to play the drums, another the flute. Had they come prepared? Did they know what to expect? Did all her movies start like this? In this room?

She continued showing slides, lush with color, mesmerizing. "I want a woman to make love to herself," she said. "Yourself. I need you to be willing to be present in a sexual way, slow motion, letting me intrude, delay, define your intimacy." Her face, illuminated by projector light, had an ethereal, disembodied quality. She looked around the room. Did I deceive myself in thinking that her eyes lingered on me?

I was at war with myself. Was I the kind of person who could live with the consequences of this act? Could I be safe while being this vulnerable? Was her charisma pulling me into places I wouldn't go with someone else? The images changed quickly now, maps, details, the camera stopping actions that were sometimes slow, sometimes explosive. How much would I regret my failure to act now?

"Gina," I called out, and the room became quiet. "I want to do it, if my body is acceptable," I said, surprising myself.

"Oh, yes," Gina said, murmurs of approval all around.

The lights came up and someone took my arm. "Come," she said, leading me toward the bedroom. "Let me help you change your clothes. There are warm kimonos in the closet." She unfastened my garments, wrapped soft cloth around my body. "In a little while the marks from your clothes will be gone. Want some food?"

"Juice?"

"Sure. Come into the kitchen."

People were moving all around me, not fast, but clearly with a purpose. Tingling, I drank a mixture of cranberry and apple from a long-stemmed glass, the tart, bright flavor matching the crystalline liquid color.

My guide took the empty glass from my hand, then gently led me toward the back of the house. If I was going to change my mind, the time was now. What had I gotten myself into? Could I go through with this? Did I want to? The workroom had been transformed into a miniature set. Lights were on. The camera focused on a central area draped in shades of blue. There was a transparent shimmering of suspended panels as if some fabrics were laced with gold.

"Is there anything you want?" Gina whispered to me.

Did I want to back out? No. I kissed her lips and she said, "Later. Much more later." The taste of her lingered on my tongue. As in my dream, she touched my face, my shoulders, my breasts, but lightly, her hands quick, almost fluttering. Then she moved away. The scent of spices, cinnamon and cloves, remained.

The flute music began again, a delicate line of sound. I entered the world of blue veils and bright lights as if into an altered state of consciousness. The drum seemed to find and hold the rhythm of my heart. And then the guitar joined in, twelve-stringed, a sympathetic vibrancy.

My body ached with longing. I closed my eyes. In my mind, Gina danced before me, an ancient dance. She called me to her with her movements, dared me to explore a larger sense of self, to join with her in an exquisite act of creation. Sensuously I danced with my fantasy of her.

The robe fell off my shoulders, brushed my body on its way down. Music formed an exclamation point, dramatizing its fall. My loins were ignited. I smelled my heat rising, felt the flush as I touched, slowly, one hot spot and then another, traced the lines upon my body where the earth shifted.

The drumming altered with me, became more complicated, layered complexity. I felt it on my tongue, in my fingers, buttocks, a vibratory echo deep inside. I knelt, rocking, swaying, merging with the music, alive with intense sensations. I was aware of women watching, imagined them excited by my body, by my movements. Their attention energized the very air around me.

Desire engulfed me. I had never felt like this before. Who was I? Who might I become? I lay back on a pile of softness, spread my thighs, and offered myself to her.

Could she follow with the camera? One hand, both hands, how independently they each knew what to do. How long had this been going on? How long could I continue? I felt as if I were about to explode. I cradled my vulva. Squeezing. Touching. I arched, tense, drawing energy in. I was carried by intense sensations, but also saw myself from a distance, as if through the camera's lens, then envisioned the movie finished, projected on a screen. The fantasy amplified my overloaded senses. I wanted more, but more what? I felt as if my creative energy and my sexual energy were flowing together, lifting me, carrying me beyond the familiar, beyond the person I had always known.

My lower lips were swollen, slickly moist. Did the earth swell this way, engorge? Time slowed, extended, paused. I quivered on a hypothetical edge.

In a waking dream I imagined Gina kneeling before me, naked, hands open. "Come for me," she said, but only in my mind.

For her, I thought, but also for myself, for who I can become, shaping and reshaping myself.

Then, speeding in slow motion, I was the mountain cracking open, was the melted rock flowing forth. Mine was the voice crying out in each of many rocketing explosions.

Shudder and be still. I was the cooling, reshaping, solidifying surface once again.

Time must have passed. The lights were gone, but candles glowed. I was alone in the room with Gina, who knelt between my legs, touching, caressing, tears lacing her face. Not a dream anymore, she was so real I wanted to sculpt the curves she made in space.

"You were so beautiful," she said, stroking, soothing, exciting my body once again.

"I want you," I said.

"Here I am," she answered, stretching out beside me.

Only in the Movies

Doraine Poretz

Having assured my seventy-year-old Polish-born, Jewish father I had safely arrived in the heathen wilderness of Atlanta, Georgia, I hung up the phone in the university cafeteria and fell in love with Beauregard Thomas Darcy III.

Looking back, I think it was his walk; the way his feet barely touched the ground, his hips swiveling slightly, accentuating a straight spine and broad shoulders. Or it might have been his smile, more precisely his absolutely perfect, white teeth. In any case, in that moment, I dropped my eyes as well as my change purse, and nickels and dimes scattered all over the linoleum tiled floor.

He helped me pick up a few of the coins and stayed behind me as I edged toward the cashier and paid for my tuna fish sandwich and Coke. Nervously, I made my way toward one of the few vacant tables, feeling grateful I had not tripped on the way.

In 1965 I was eighteen years old. Up until that momentous takeoff from La Guardia airport, I had never left the environs of Manhattan, never flown in an airplane, and never been in love. Now everything had happened in one gorgeous rush. And all on an empty stomach.

The cafeteria was noisy, and I concentrated on eating, all the while feeling he was looking at me. It was then I casually slipped off my eyeglasses and rubbed the bridge of my nose. (Everyone always said my eyes were my best feature.) When I looked up, I noticed he was sitting catty-cornered from me, sipping an Orange Crush. His beauty made it hard for me to look too long; so *achingly* handsome he was, like some Hollywood movie star or West Point cadet. He even had a cleft in his chin. And then there were those teeth.

I was thinking about the braces I had to wear until I was sixteen, doubting if he ever needed help—of any kind—when I heard his voice, a slight drawl, smooth as tapioca: "Would you mind if I joined you?" And I responding as suavely as possible: "What, me? Oh. Yes. Thank you."

Long nights on the telephone followed. I in my flannel pajamas, stretched on my back on the floor of the dormitory hallway, the typewriters snapping in the adjacent room, the girls whispering or giggling on some landmass far away. His voice held me like music. He told me stories about growing up on a farm, about riding a horse to school. He knew how to fix cars and build houses. No boy I knew had ever done any of those things. And what did he like most about me? That I was a poet. I wasn't a poet, I'd tell him. I just happened to like literature, especially poetry, and especially Dylan Thomas. But he'd insist, "Oh no, you're a poet, I can tell from the way you talk. Deep, real deep. And that mind of yours, the way it goes all over the place. Now tell me again about this guy, Thomas. He was the one who drank and had all the women, right?" And laughing, I would place the mouthpiece of the phone closer to my lips and talk on and on, my eyes following the cracks in the plaster ceiling, marveling as they became one, then another, constellation of stars.

Our typical date on Friday nights was eating pizza and drinking Cokes or an occasional beer at Jerry's outdoor pizza parlor. Beau would chew the mozzarella off my mouth and kiss me, right there on the sidewalk. After a while I got used to it and wasn't so embarrassed. He should be the poet, I thought. He's the spontaneous, passionate one. And the way he *looks* at me.

I couldn't name then what I saw in Beau's eyes, but eventually I realized it was that ineffable quality of delight. Such delight was something I had never experienced from anyone, and never having experienced it, I could not accept it. I could only distance myself and wonder or worry about it because I was sure he would come to his senses soon enough and realize I was not anything that he imagined me to be.

If suddenly I'd get nervous and say how impossible it would

be, how my father would never let us marry, he would let loose with that warm bravado of his and totally mesmerize me: "Now listen, you, of course your father will let me marry you. Why, I'll take such good care of their Clare, just like any of those ol' Jewish husbands are supposed to. In fact, it will be better with me because I'll have to *work* at it, seein' it won't come naturally, right?" And laughing, he would kiss a dozen kisses all over my face. And I would laugh too, kissing him back, believing his magic. But in the midst of this sudden joy, something in me insisted that I didn't have a right to any of it. I remembered my mother confiding in me that her first real love was a Scandinavian boy who took her ice skating from time to time. But when her father found out, she was forbidden to see him, the *shegetz,* the non-Jew, again. It was impossible, my mother had said, impossible. And then she sighed: "That kind of love doesn't exist in real life. In the movies, maybe. But not in real life."

He called from a pay phone somewhere in Pennsylvania on his way to New York that summer. He had decided to introduce himself to my parents, to let them know his intentions. I pleaded for him not to, that it would be terrible, terrible, but he insisted. He told me he had spoken to his grandmother, who was wise and had "the sight." She saw us together for years and years, and anyway I was the kind of girl who had a strain of steel that would enable me to stand up to anyone or anything that didn't let me be myself. I was not to worry. He would take care of my parents. They would not refuse him, for they would see that he loved me more purely than a blessing.

I looked out the window of my second-story bedroom and saw the '58 Chevy pull up. Before I could force myself away from the window, so frozen with fear I was, he had rung the bell. My mother called me, and coming down the steps, seeing them together—my mother absentmindedly running her fingers through her hair, fussing with it a bit, smiling—made me feel less full of dread. She too had been instantly smitten by Beau.

Just then my father came in from the backyard. After folding his newspaper, he shook hands with Beau and invited him into the den for a drink. I sauntered in and sat down next to Beau and, surprising myself, took hold of his hand. We all had a pleasant chat about classes and future plans. My mother brought in a tray of little sandwiches. Beau told my father he planned to go to law school and would become a very successful attorney. He also made it clear how strongly he felt about me.

Later, I saw a kind of panic in Beau's eyes. He pulled me to him and asked me to take a walk around the block or at least to see him to his car. I could do neither; for I knew at that moment, standing on the worn carpet of my childhood, that if I stepped out of my family house to walk with him, I would not return. We embraced, and I promised to call him that evening. Then I watched through the screen door as he walked away.

When I entered the living room, my father was sitting by the piano in a green club chair. He looked up at me and shook his head, a mixture of sorrow and disappointment. He had never asked anything of me, had he? He had only given me his care, his tenderness. I was his *süss*, his sweet one. I had never done anything that shamed him; I was bright, beautiful, and respectful. All this, yes. So how could this boy, this boy as nice a kid as he was, how could I encourage him to think that he could marry me? I knew he wasn't Jewish, didn't I? Didn't I? And little by little I watched as my father, a small narrow man, grew large with fear and righteousness.

He burst from his chair, grabbed my arm, and I realized in that moment he had never held me so passionately before. All of his strength, all of the patriarchal dominance and insistence imbedded in his bones for four thousand years, exploded. He kept shaking and shaking me, repeating over and over: "I will not send you back to that school, do you hear? I will not send you back unless you swear you will not see him again. This I will not allow!" Trembling, I gathered enough strength to pull away from him and run upstairs to the bathroom, where nausea overtook me.

In minutes I was vomiting into the toilet bowl, crying and vomiting, alternating between the two until, exhausted, I sat down on the cold tile floor. Holding my gut, rocking like an abandoned boat, I realized with terrible confusion that I was tethered to a man, my father, whose perception of life was meaningless to me. And yet, I knew that because I loved him (Was it from love? Or from fear that if I were to assert my will,

I would commit a terrible sin?) I would obey him. I was under some ancient tribal law that insisted I uphold the holy alliance of Father/Daughter, which dictated absolute loyalty.

I heard my mother's voice: *Impossible, it was impossible.* I had no choice. And because I believed I had no choice, I did not even feel the outrage of my predicament; only the bewilderment that I had to sacrifice being passionately delighted in, for this other, this Law. And this belief—that I had no right to assert my will—would keep me unconscious for years: fainting out of the arms of my father into the arms of my husband, later out of my husband's arms into the arms of one lover after the other until finally I woke to the woman I had betrayed and asked her forgiveness. But my father's influence aside, the passion I had for this stranger, this Southerner with the absurd name of Beauregard Darcy III, a boy who refused to have sex with me before we were married, had to be illusion. Beau's love for me made no sense. How had I earned it? How could he ask nothing of me except that I . . . be? This young man, in all his clarity and tenderness, was a mystery. And this mystery was more than I, in all my self-effacement, could bear.

I returned to the university in September and spent the first part of the month avoiding Beau. I wrote him a long and painful letter instead.

One night he came around to the dorm and refused to leave until I appeared in the lobby. It was raining, and he was leaning against the tan-colored wall, wearing a soft lambs-wool V-neck, smoking a cigarette. He said the letter wasn't enough. He inhaled the cigarette and threw it on the floor, rubbed his foot back and forth over the butt, and insisted we talk outside. I couldn't move. He hissed that if I didn't go with him that instant he would make a scene and embarrass me in front of my friends; so I followed him out to his car; and once there, he jerked my hand and pushed me inside the open door. As soon as we were inside, his hands were all over me: squeezing my breasts, pulling my hair while he kissed my face, my neck. I was frightened and excited at the same time. He had never handled me like this. He kept calling me bitch and tease and said he would not lose me, would marry me and take care of me and kill me if I thought of leaving him. I started crying, and suddenly he realized how truly frightened I was, and this woke him, snapping open his terrible grief. He pulled me to him and let loose an awful, low cry, pleading with me to be strong, to understand that nothing worth having was easy. And anyway, what was this all about? This wasn't the Middle Ages, was it?

We sat in the car a long time, kissing passionately, stroking each other's bodies. He felt he had me, that it would be all right, all right after all. But I knew my heart had broken off a long time ago, long before I had met Beau. I told him it was hopeless. I couldn't see him anymore. I just couldn't do it to my father. He looked at me and knew I meant it. "Get out," he said. He spit out the next words: "Get the fuck out."

I pushed the heavy car door open and felt my body slowly move into the humid rain. His voice calling after me was harsh: "You're a stupid, pathetic coward; and you'll be sorry."

It was another 100-degree day in Baton Rouge. The fan was blowing the spelling papers I was trying to correct off the table. Since the dining table was covered with so many stacks that needed work, I couldn't place the fan anywhere without one or the other stack blowing away. My husband, Richard, was in the air-conditioned bedroom studying for his pre-med exams. After he passed his pre-med exams, I reasoned, I wouldn't have to grade sixth-grade spelling papers anymore. That was worth his having the air conditioner.

It was not that I didn't want to be a good teacher. I did. And generally speaking, the children liked me. But in the important things—important to my senior advisor, Rose Garland—I seemed to fail miserably. My lesson plans were never complete; my attendance record was a bruise of red pencil; and apparently I allowed the children to ask too many questions, thus "bogging down course content." Too, it seemed that my "Yankee ingenuity" exasperated Mrs. Garland. Desks were supposed to be in *rows,* not in clusters. Children needed, above anything else, a sense of order.

One afternoon Mrs. Garland, who had been sitting in the back row observing my class, handed me a wooden paddle in front of the twenty-four startled faces staring up at me and instructed me to reprimand a beautiful blue-eyed boy named Douglas for talking after the quiet sign had been raised for the second time. I was horrified. My stomach crumpled, and my hands whitened with sweat. I appeared to have no other choice but to go through with this double humiliation. I managed to pat the child lightly on his bottom. Most of the children laughed.

Mrs. Garland asked to see me after class. What I wanted most was to slap Mrs. Garland—hard—for violating both me and the children. But I did nothing. Instead I listened to her quiet harangue, feeling the tension in my neck build.

I was thinking of Rose Garland, the heat, and my lack of courage, when the telephone rang. I picked it up and went cold. It was Beau. It had been over three years since I had seen him. I pulled the phone to the corner of the living room and sat down slowly.

He was telephoning from a bar, having finally mustered the courage to call me. Yes, he was married, and he and his wife were in Chicago while he was in law school. And no, he hadn't stopped thinking about me, even though he knew he and I were married to other people. And anyway, I couldn't be all that happy with my husband. Well, was I? Finally, he told me that his grandmother had died, but that he refused to forget her words that eventually we would be together. And if I didn't want to hear from him he would try not to call again, but he couldn't promise. I asked him how he got my number. My mother gave it to him, he said.

The calls continued sporadically for the next several years, mostly waking me in the middle of the night. I told Richard about some of the calls. He didn't seem to mind very much. Maybe Beau's calls made me more desirable to Richard; I never knew, for my husband wasn't one to express his feelings.

After each one of Beau's calls, I would feel painfully out of sync and would turn to Richard to ask again and again if he loved me, if he found me beautiful. Richard would never answer me directly, but instead would give me another question to ponder: "If I didn't love you, sweetheart, would I have married you?" Or: "Why would I marry you, if I didn't think you were beautiful?"

By the time we moved out of the South and into a spacious home in upstate New York, my daughter, Karin, was two years old. I awoke one night to what I thought was my child crying but realized it was the ringing phone. Richard, being a heavy sleeper, hadn't moved. I picked up the receiver, and Beau's voice floated up. It was 3:00 A.M., and I was exhausted; my daughter had been sick all week.

"Beau, what is it?"

"I need you."

"Listen, Beau, this really has to stop. I have a child now. It's late, and—"

"She's dying, Clare."

"What? Who's dying?"

"My wife. She's in the hospital."

"My God, Beau, I'm sorry, I . . . ."

"And you, you're the only one I want to talk to. I need you to come over right now. Please."

"Where are you? What are you talking about?"

"We live in Riverside, not far from you."

"You mean you're in New York?"

"My wife's family lives here and we . . . listen, are you coming or not?"

"Beau, I . . . How can I? I mean, my husband . . . and I don't even know how to drive our car; it's a stick shift; mine is—"

"Take a cab, okay? I'll pay for it. Clare, I am asking you for this favor."

I stammered and told him to hold on. I woke Richard and explained the call. He mumbled and said yes, to go if I had to, and then fell back to sleep. I got the address and called a cab.

Waiting for it to arrive, I thought I was crazy. Maybe Beau had made all of this up. Maybe he was doing this to get me alone, and in some way retaliate for my rejecting him. He could still be furious with me. After all, I had abandoned him, abandoned us. Suddenly scared, I nearly canceled the cab.

The driver dropped me off at a low, rambling house, half-hidden by shrubbery. I stumbled on one of the stone slabs that led to the doorway. Beau was waiting for me outside, leaning against the sliding screen door, drinking a glass of whiskey. It was summer; the morning air was brisk, not cold. The emerging sun had painted the mountains black against the pink and turquoise sky. Everything seemed innocent, peaceful. When I got close enough to really see Beau, I saw how painfully exhausted he looked. But besides that, in eight years, he had not changed at all.

He pulled me toward him and held me, thanked me for coming. Then taking my hand, he directed me into the living room and asked if I wanted anything to drink or eat. I shook my head.

"I think I need another." He walked to the bar, pointing on the way to a photograph in a silver frame. "That's Nick. Four in October."

I looked at the grinning child and Beau next to him, wearing a rabbit mask that was pushed back onto his head.

So, this was his home. The living room was done in shades of greens and peach. I assumed his wife had decorated it. I pictured her blond, pretty, and all-American and wanted to see if there were a picture of her around but didn't find one. I felt like a trespasser. Just looking at the objects about the room, sitting on the couch next to Beau, made me feel I was betraying his wife.

Beau, sipping his Scotch, explained how he had wanted to stop his obsessiveness about me. He told me that even though he knew I was living close by, he had promised himself that he would never call.

"But tonight, tonight, I . . . it is crazy but true . . . you were the only one I felt could help by being here. Maybe I wanted someone here who I'd known for a long time. Does that make sense?" He rested his head against the sofa's pillows, and I watched his face collapse. "She's dying, Clare . . ." My impulse was to put my arms around him. But I stopped, not knowing if I had that right.

"What is it?" I asked. "What exactly is wrong with her?"

"Leukemia. It was sudden, no warning. Hey," he said laughing, "I'm too young for this."

I watched his eyes fill up, and I immediately touched his face. I couldn't help, then, but to pull him toward me. My arms encircled and held him fast, grateful to be near him, to be of some comfort. I smelled his hair, his skin. Everything was so familiar.

We sat silently for some time, then pulled away from each other and began talking. We talked about his wife's illness, about our children, about my struggle with writing a novel that I had started a few years before. When he asked me about my marriage, I didn't know what to say.

The chasm between Richard and me was widening. I lived

with it, rationalizing that the lack of intimacy was the way for most marriages. In other words, that passion and delight were "only in the movies." The fear of rupture paralyzed me.

"Richard is a good man. I'm lucky to have him."

Beau scrutinized me. "You don't love him."

I protested. "I didn't say that." I brushed his cheek with my hand and smiled. "You still wear the same aftershave you wore in college."

I leaned back on the cushions and closed my eyes. If only he had made love to me at school. Maybe that would have changed everything; maybe then I would have belonged to him as much as I believed I belonged to my father. If only I'd been jolted, forced through the shock wave of our electric selves, maybe that would have startled me back into a remembrance of myself.

Sitting on the couch, there in that strange house, I suddenly cried. I cried because we were both so poignant, so bright in our loving. I cried for myself and I cried for Beau and his wife. And too, because the morning was washing the room in such exquisite pink and amber, I cried at how fortunate we were to be part of it. I looked at Beau; his beautiful face was finally relaxed, asleep.

I had just shoved a box of books into the corner of the living room when the doorbell rang. Expecting to find one or two men from the Small Town Moving Company, instead I found Beau standing in the doorway. I hadn't seen him since the night he had called, six months before. He phoned only once after that, to tell me his wife had died.

"Beau, God, how are you?"

He smiled and hugged me and looked around. "Okay, I'm okay. Hey, what's this?"

I felt almost embarrassed to admit it. "Well," I hesitated, "Richard and I . . ."

"You're moving?"

"*I'm* moving."

He was smiling. "I don't believe it. What happened?"

I shrugged my shoulders and moved a box closer to the door.

"We're separating for a while." I indicated a bottle of mineral water. "You want any?" He shook his head.

"You're splitting. I can't believe it." He laughed. "Did it happen suddenly?"

"No, it's been happening for a while."

"For a long while?"

"I really don't want to talk about it, okay?"

"Is there someone else?"

"No."

"With him?"

"No. Hey, listen. I said I didn't want to talk about it. So please, shut up."

He took a long look at me and shook his head. He walked around the large, empty room. The ceiling was high and vaulted. There was a stained glass window on the opposite wall.

"This place looks like a church, you know? What were you two doin' livin' in a church, anyway?" He stopped a moment. "Damn," he said. "I just don't believe it. I mean that for all this time you weren't even in love with him."

"I did love him," I insisted. "Of course I—"

"No, I mean *love* him, like deep, crazy, meaning something more than a good catch or—"

"Beau, stop—"

"No," he continued, "I don't wanna stop. You see, I'm sitting here looking at you, and you know in eight years you don't look any different from when you were sitting in the front seat of my beat-up ol' car, you telling me it was over because some man in some European suit had decided we were still living in the sixteenth century; and now you tell me the guy you did choose, the one you finally wanted enough, was someone you weren't totally crazy, totally out of your mind over? Boy, you are an ass, you know that, girl?"

"Thank you," I said. "Thank you very much."

He came over and sat down on the floor next to me and brushed the hair off my forehead. "Really," he said. "How are you doin'?"

I told him I was scared. Suddenly, I was a culprit. I was breaking up the perfect marriage. My family insisted I couldn't do this to my daughter. I couldn't be so selfish. But, I told Beau, so much of the waking hours were lies; I felt practically schizoid. One part of me going through the motions with Richard; the other part living an imaginary, passionate life. I confessed I was leaving Richard because my will had broken through, making itself felt for the first time in my life. Some force was pulling me up from the roots, flinging me out toward something other, that other woman, perhaps, that larger one I was destined to meet. It was as if some stranger (an angel?) had made herself manifest in order to guide me. I didn't recognize who I was anymore.

Looking at Beau I said, "And I still don't recognize myself."

"Oh, but I do." His gaze was steady. "I recognize you perfectly." Trembling, I let him embrace me. For a long time, we were very quiet.

"And you, how are you doing?" I ventured.

"It's hard. I won't say it isn't hard." He looked around. "It's sure a beautiful house. You'll probably be sorry about losing it. What are you planning to do?"

"Karin and I are moving into an apartment, not far from here. I hope to get a job. Something not too demanding, something that will give me the time to . . . to write."

"Yeah." He laughed. "You're the poet. You see, I knew it all along."

"No," I insisted, "I'm just beginning. And a poet, well, that, that's a whole other thing, a whole other—"

And that's when he kissed me. Cutting off the next word. And the kiss led to a longer kiss and a deeper kiss after that, and I remember thinking that I could probably make a whole career of kissing Beau Darcy, an art, in fact. I'd forget the writing; there had been thousands who succeeded in the art of writing; but in the art of kissing Beauregard Darcy III, well, that was another matter. This was an art that could take years to perfect and that few had the particular gift for—one that I felt, at that very moment, I had.

Biting, teasing his lips, I used my tongue to travel around the inside of his mouth, then over those perfect white teeth. Meanwhile, his tongue traveled deeper into my mouth, toward the well of my throat. We explored our mouths' darkness; and swirling in the wetness, swallowing a sticky glissando of tongues, we sucked each other up through a gloss of sweetness and need.

Soon his kisses spread from my mouth to my neck, small, delicate grace notes, making a trail from my ear down my neck to my shoulder and then back again; and each time he kissed me, he would lick the kiss off. Then his mouth on my ear nibbling and sucking the delicate ridge of my earlobe, until finally his tongue whirled inside my ear. The shivers through me were so intense, so uncontrollable, that I had to pull his head away. Seeing me so flushed and excited, he smiled and pulled me up off the sofa.

"I want to be on a proper bed," he said.

I nodded and he followed me upstairs, his hand grazing my buttocks as I climbed the steps in front of him. It's a dream, I thought. This can't be real. But while thinking that, I knew everything *was* real because it felt perfectly natural, even inevitable. Here we were. About to make love. The way we were meant to do all along.

The bed was unmade, the sheets disheveled from a night of restless sleep. He gently pushed me down on them and got on top of me. His aftershave, pungent and full of memory, enveloped me.

Then ever so slowly he opened each small pearl button of my blouse. He did this very intently, not rushing at all; and I imagined that he knew he was finally making Time his own. My breasts underneath the silky brassiere were his breasts to do with whatever he'd want, for however long he desired.

After he unhooked my bra and I wriggled free, he cupped one breast then the other and, looking at them, murmured how beautiful and vulnerable they were. Then his mouth fell upon them, and soon I was arching my back up to his lips and his tongue, which flicked back and forth, teasing one nipple then the other, and Oh how I loved being tasted like this! His lips sucked, his teeth bit, he sucked and bit and I shuddered from the pain and the pleasure of it.

Licking as much of my flesh as it could, his tongue traveled down toward my navel. His hands unbuttoned my jeans, pulled them down along with my panties, and opening my legs, he pulled my body to the edge of the bed so that my legs were dangling, my feet barely touching the floor.

When he looked up at me, I saw the swoon of desire that shadowed his face. Soon his face disappeared, and all I felt were the electric waves of his mouth on my cunt, kissing and pulling and sucking me up. My hands were on his head, into his thick hair, and I held on, bucking up and down from the intense pleasure of it. I felt I could climax any moment, but didn't want to. Not yet. I wanted to give him his pleasure first.

When his face emerged, I bent down to kiss his wet mouth then slipped off the bed, pulling him up to stand before me. And now, belly to belly, my lips pressed to his neck, kissing it, I undid the buckle of his belt, then the button of his pants, and unzipping the fly, I reached in to feel his cock through the soft cotton of his underpants. Slowly I dipped my fingers underneath to feel his cock growing hard. The silkiness of it delighted me. I rubbed and stroked it, teasing the head with my fingertips.

In moments we were both naked, I on top of him. I could finally see his cock, how pink, how shining it was. I loved it. I found it beautiful. I put my mouth on it.

"Harder," he moaned. "Suck harder."

I did. Even though my mouth ached, I kept sucking and licking, my one hand stroking his balls, caressing them. I was wild with giving him pleasure. He stopped me, telling me he wanted to be inside of me.

I got on top of him and rubbed my breasts all over his chest while I studded his face with kisses. His hands were on my butt, stroking it, patting it, teasing the crack with his fingers; and soon he was in me and I was riding him, looking down into his gorgeous face, my long hair falling over him, sweeping his chin and shoulders. I kept pumping up and down and quickly he rolled me over, and now lying under him, I felt his strong thrusts in me, each one sending new shivers into my soul. His eyes were closed; and he was gone, having disappeared into himself. He kept fucking and fucking me, reaching what I thought would be a climax; but no; instead he stopped thrusting. Instead he began to gyrate his hips, soft and easy, soft and easy, allowing his cock to explore its new home. I relished watching him, the pleasure on his flushed face apparently endless. After a few moments, he became conscious of me again, and looking into my face he smiled, murmuring, "Nice and easy now. You like that? Nice . . . and . . . easy . . ." Then suddenly he began thrusting hard, and after a few more strokes, pulled out of me, turned me over and entered me from behind.

Richard had never made love to me with such abandon; and

I found myself swept onto the beach of another country; and now his fucking me from behind was more thrilling than anything I had known. It felt as if not just his cock but his whole body was entering me. While he continued to thrust into me, he used one hand to rub my moist cunt; his fingers pulling the lips apart, delving deep. All the while, he talked to me, his voice hoarse with desire: "We're going to make it together, baby. Ready to fly, to fly, girl?" He kept pumping and fingering me, rubbing my clit, stopping for a moment, then rubbing it again, and soon I felt the rush of a cum cry gathering in my chest, pushing up toward my throat, and soon the sky broke open for both of us and Oh, and Oh again!

Afterward, we lay together on the cool sheets, our heads angled up on the pillows, our bodies pressed together, his fingers stroking my pubic hair.

"Well," he said, "it's finally come round. Just like my grandmother said."

"Married, in fact. Too bad not to each other." I laughed.

"Well, that can be taken care of."

At that moment I shivered. Beau smiled, thinking it was my expression of delight. But I knew it meant something else.

"It was good, wasn't it?" said Beau.

"Good? You call that *good*?" I began tickling him. "Definitely not good." I kept tickling him and he started slapping my hands away, laughing. "How about *very* good? Or maybe *fantastic,* or maybe simply the best thing since . . . since . . ."

By now he was tickling me back and together we roiled around silly and giddy until finally, out of breath, we called a truce, and fell back onto the pillows.

"After all this time . . . all those fantasies . . ." He sighed and slithered his hand under my butt. "You have a great ass, you know that?"

"No, I don't. It's too flabby."

"What are you sayin', girl. It's perfect. Turn over."

"No."

"Come on. I want to kiss it."

"No." I squirmed. "It'll embarrass me."

"Really? Well, now, that's crazy. Come on, nothin' to be embarrassed about."

He flipped me over and began kissing my ass, and it tickled

and felt good and I started laughing and he kept kissing it more and more until I felt his tongue angling into the crack and then I went out of myself and began pushing my butt up toward his face, on my knees now, and soon his fingers were kneading my buttocks and as one finger began edging toward the hole, I drew my torso up; his finger had entered me by now and his other arm was across my chest, his fingers playing with my breast.

In the soup of this desire, I heard the rush of a sports car motor in the driveway. It was Richard's car.

"Beau, stop. We have to stop! It's Richard!"

"What?"

"Richard. He'll be at the door any minute. He has a key."

Beau kept stroking me and took his time to pull his finger out and in that last reverberation of pleasure, the doorbell rang.

Beau was actually tickled; he thought it was high time that he and Richard meet. He pulled me onto the bed, full of glee over my predicament. I broke away, threw on a robe, and ran down the steps. Looking over my shoulder, I glowered a warning at him that he stay there and stay quiet. He looked back at me with a stubborn, impish grin.

Richard and I exchanged a few words downstairs. He had come by for a particular wedding gift he was fond of. I found it and gave it to him. We walked out into the front yard because it felt uncomfortable talking between the boxes, in the midst of our empty house. Richard took both of my hands and held them tightly before he turned toward his car.

I walked slowly back into the house, then ran up the stairs to see Beau step into the shower. He had to go pick up his son at school. He wanted to see me later. I told him I wasn't sure. Too much was happening too fast. I needed time. He thought that was a very funny thing for me to say.

A week later, I got a letter from Beau asking me to marry him. He was planning to move back to the South, was offered a partnership in a law firm there, and this, well, this was the time we had been waiting for, wasn't it? His grandmother had been right, after all.

How truly strange this all had become. At the moment that I was free to choose Beau, I couldn't. This other, this angel of mine, was preventing me. I was no more ready to be another man's wife again, to live out the obligations of that commitment and raise another child, in addition to my own, as I was able to stay in a passionless marriage. It had nothing to do with Beau. It had to do with this stranger, the one who was goading me, daring me to retrieve the lost parts of myself. If I had known how very difficult that journey would be, maybe I would have hesitated writing back to Beau that although I loved him, I couldn't marry and live with him.

Now and again, a big wave will come up, mostly when there's a humid rain, Southern weather, I call it. I'll get this feeling that I want to talk only to him, hear that sweet tapioca voice of his, a voice like no other. I want to say to him that it was good we never married, good we've had no time to hate each other, grow numb. Instead, there is this still time, time for us both to rock in each other's heads, seduced by our mysterious connection.

I smile now, thinking of my ancient father, how poignant he was a few months before his death, asking if I ever "think of that boy, that one from school." And when I said yes, that we had been in contact, he looked at me with his soft, gray eyes and said quietly, "Well, maybe it wouldn't have been such a terrible thing . . ." Moved by the guilt in his voice, I assured him that everything had worked out exactly as it was supposed to and that I was genuinely satisfied living alone. He sighed then, filled with the confusion of his descending age, not able to take comfort in my words.

And I? Well, I expect at any moment for my daughter, who is now a few years older than I was when I met Beau (but certainly more astute), to come bounding in during a semester break and excitedly tell me that while getting lunch at the UC she met a young man from Georgia, a law student. His name would be Nick, Nick Darcy. And after the first shock wave had settled, I'd casually mention that life was much more interesting than the movies, much more mysterious and unpredictable. And she would look at me, wide-eyed and wise for her years, and respond: "Of course, it is, Mom. Why wouldn't it be?"

Double Clicked

HANNAH KATZ

In spite of the warm night air, Salana could not stop shivering.

"It's okay," Wolff said, drawing her into his arms. "It's okay."

Salana relaxed against his chest. Listening to the slow drumbeat of his heart, the sounds of the African night eased into a symphony full of stories and mystery. She pulled slightly away, no longer frightened but feeling self-conscious and awkward. His nearness, which moments earlier had been comforting, now evoked thoughts that fled scrutiny, like zebras silently appearing from, then disappearing within, the shadows of the trees. "I am really sorry I woke you and you had to come in here. I must have heard those hippopotamuses in my sleep and just . . . oh, what's that sound?"

"Probably a lonely baboon."

Salana turned away, embarrassed again by her fearful outbursts in front of a man she barely knew. "I guess you must think the publisher was foolish to send someone so inexperienced."

He brushed her hair off her face and she blushed at the gesture. They had touched throughout the day, in the casual way colleagues might, crowded alone inside a small jeep loaded with photography equipment. Yet with each random sweep of an arm against a shoulder, or unintentioned whisper of a hand across a chest, or accidental rub of a knee against another, Salana could not deny her attraction to this stranger. Nor could she deny her wish and fear that he would be as drawn to her as she was to him.

"You'll get used to it here," he reassured. "The animals never bother you at night if you stay inside your tent."

"They've promised?" Being funny always helped her feel more in control when something or someone was making her feel very out of control.

Wolff gently returned her head to his chest. "I've promised," he said, struggling to keep his passion in check. Throughout the day he had longed to hold her, to run his hands over her sunbronzed skin, but his hunting instincts cautioned him. Although he had put down his guns for cameras and his bullets for film, the instincts still remained. So tonight the skilled hunter waited, limiting himself to nuzzling his chin against the side of her temple, quietly inhaling the scent of her hair.

"Oh!" Salana again pulled away, but this time faced him more fully. How well he reflected this country, she thought; his hair and the sun-parched grasses, his eyes and the cloudless September sky, his movements and the grace of the cheetah. "Your chin is scratchy," she teased, placing the palm of her hand delicately on his cheek.

Slowly Wolff drew his fingers up the sensitive underside of her arm and took her hand in his. Salana watched transfixed, as Wolff brought her hand to his mouth, first kissing, then moving his tongue in small circles around the center of her palm.

"You taste good," he murmured.

Salana shivered.

"Still cold?"

"Yes," she lied. His body was warm, providing a heat that both soothed and frightened her.

"Here." He shifted her body so that she was lying down on the cot. "Maybe I can warm you." He smiled that grin, a grin that, like him, spoke of continuing contrasts; passion with distance, safety with danger, intensity with mischief. He lowered himself next to her, wrapping his right leg over her.

His closeness was new and electrifying. For what seemed like an eternity, she stared up at him, waiting. Even though her nightgown covered her, she felt naked as he returned her gaze. And then, as if controlled by an outside force, she put her hand behind his head and brought his lips to hers.

"Mom."

Her lips

"Mom?"

Her lips parted.

"Mom, where are you?"

Sally turned and faced the interruption.

"Oh god," Megan groaned as she entered her mother's bed-room/office and peered with distaste at the light blue computer screen. "Not again. What is the matter with you?"

"Now, Megan," Sally reassured as she quickly clicked off the computer file. She never saved the Salana and Wolff stories. "It's not a big deal. There's plenty of time for me . . ."

"No, there isn't." The teenager paused to see if there was to be a reprimand for her interrupting. "Your agent has already renegotiated your due date. If you don't get this book done . . ."

"It'll get done. I'm just having a little trouble"—Sally hesi-tated, eyeing her daughter apprehensively—"a little trouble staying focused. That's all."

"Mom, let's be real. This is supposed to be a book about the animals of Botswana for sixth and seventh graders. Instead, you keep writing this, this, oh, I don't know what to call it." She plopped herself on the bed across from the desk.

"Meg . . ."

"Mom, I love you. You've always been there for me, and if you want to change direction and write something other than educational stuff, I don't care." Megan could feel herself start-ing to cry. "But if you don't get this book done, we won't have the money to go to Mexico like you promised. We've *never* had a real vacation."

Recently, Sally had been having her own concerns about her writing sessions. Her disciplined devotion to supporting herself and her daughter had always prevented men, love, and sex, es-pecially sex, from entering Sally's mind. That her writing should now be taken over by these romance novel/erotic images both perplexed and disturbed her.

"Mom? Talk to me."

"Sorry, sweetie, just thinking." Sally pulled her focus back to her daughter. "I know you're worried, honey, but it'll be okay. It's not like I have a writer's block. It's just that lately, every-thing I write ends up kind of, um, well . . ."

"Sexy?"

"Uh, yeah. Sexy." Sally always admired her daughter's candor, which was in sharp contrast to her own inhibition.

Megan tugged at her earlobe, a sign Sally had learned over the many years of being a single mother meant that her daughter had more to say.

"Is something else bothering you?"

"Noooo." Megan turned away, ostensibly to pet Fred and Ginger. The tabbies had nestled themselves on top of the pillows and, at Megan's touch, immediately rolled onto their backs, paws listlessly raised in the air. "Well, maybe there is one thing."

"Like what?"

"Well, I'm not trying to be rude or anything. It's just that for a while now, you've been acting different." Megan picked up Ginger and placed her on her lap. Fred, unwilling to be left out, rolled back onto his belly, stretched, then jumped across the narrow gap, landing clumsily on the desk. He rubbed the side of his whiskered face against the computer monitor.

Sally lifted him off the desk and settled him on her lap. "Like how?"

"Well," Megan started, putting Ginger back on the bed and brushing the cat hair off her shorts, "in the past two months you've been playing that weird music and wearing makeup, even around the house. You've lost ten pounds, and even though those are good things, combine that with the stuff you *are* writing instead of what you're *supposed* to be writing—it's just kinda weird."

"Are you worried about me?"

Megan took Fred from her mother's lap. "Noooo. I mean you are thirty-eight years old and I think it would be really great if you had a date once in a while. Dad's already been married twice."

Sally's stomach churned at the mention of her ex. Just the thought of her college sweetheart turned compulsive philanderer still hurt, a hurt that her new friend, Teala, said kept Sally wedded to a convent-type life.

"Is that all?"

"Oh yeah," Megan continued, petting Fred more vigorously. "And you bought this weird-o computer from that weird-o woman who opened that weird-o head shop who's become like your friend."

"Anything else?"

"No. You asked and I told you."

Sally nodded solemnly. "Well, let's see. I can't tell you why I've been paying more attention to my appearance these past couple of months, but I just have. People go through stages you know, even mothers."

Megan rolled her eyes.

"And that weird-o woman has been very helpful. Her name, by the way, is Teala."

"Like that's her real name."

"And it's not a head shop. It's a New Age shop called Inspirations. And I needed a new computer."

"Mr. London, my computer teacher at school? He said he never heard of a computer company called Machine Mystery."

"Machine Magic," Sally corrected. "And that's because it is a very special, individually handmade piece of equipment. Teala says these computers are so ergonomically and uniquely designed to the specific needs of the buyer that the company is very particular about whom they'll sell one to. So they don't advertise or really make their computers public."

"Oh, please. What a bunch of bull."

"Megan, watch your language." Sally had had some of these misgivings herself. But there was something so comforting and wise about Teala that Sally had trusted her.

"Sorry, Mom. It's just that you can't call them, because they don't give you a phone number, and you can't write them, because they don't have an address."

This had also made Sally uneasy, but again, her worries were quelled by Teala's assurances. "Teala says that's because their computers are so unique, they didn't want to take out a patent and disclose how they're made. So they have to stay very, very secretive."

"Owww. Stop it, Fred," Megan yelled. Fred had developed a habit of chewing on the fingers of owners who held him but became so involved in conversation they forgot to keep petting him.

Sally took Fred back onto her own lap. "Anyway, Teala assures me that their customers are always very satisfied and never have any complaints. I was really very lucky Teala knew the company well enough so that when they had a customer back out on an order, I could pick one up cheap."

"Well, I just think it's weird. You didn't even get a modem." Megan shook her head in disbelief.

"Well, you can shake your head, young lady, but in the past five months since Teala got me this computer, I've completed two projects and gotten this rush job proposal landed. I have never before been so focused and inspired."

Megan freed a sheet of paper sandwiched in between Ginger's fluffy orange body and a pillow and began reading. "Wolff's lips brushed teasingly against . . ."

Sally grabbed the paper out of her daughter's hand.

"Is this what you're calling inspired, Mom?"

The insistent honk of a car's horn saved Sally from answering. Fred, the watch cat, jumped out of her lap to check out the sound.

"That must be your dad. You all packed?" Sally stood up, wiping her hands clean of any remaining cat hair onto her jeans.

Megan copied her mother's behavior and nodded.

"I love you, Meggers," Sally said, giving Megan a big hug. "Don't worry. When you come home at the end of this weekend, *Beasts of Botswana* will be all done, and we'll be off to Mexico."

Megan smiled broadly and gave her mother a peck on the cheek. "I love you too, Mom. I really do."

"Okay. Go on. You know how your dad gets if he has to wait. And don't forget to bring back your tennis shoes."

Sally sat in her living room listening to the silence. Megan's bi-monthly weekend visits with her father had been occurring for the past seven years, yet Sally still felt at a loss.

She walked over to the front door, squinting through the old patched screen at the even older front porch. Megan was right, Sally thought. Other than these visits to her father's or the vacations at Sally's mother's, the adolescent had never been away. And though Sally wrote about exotic places, she hadn't traveled in years. What extra money she had been able to earn had always gone for something seemingly more pressing, like a new roof or refrigerator. But as much as this aged farmhouse had been a financial drain, it had also been a sanctuary. Three hours away from the city, the old home had provided Sally a retreat from the betrayal of her marriage, friends, and men, and the opportunity to explore her career as a writer.

A writer. Megan was right about that too. Things had been going so well on the last couple of projects, as if Sally's fingers and the new keyboard had a mind of their own. Once she finished the research, the words just seemed to flow from her, almost without her conscious awareness. And then, like magic, the books would be completed and the money would be on its way.

At least that's how it had been with *Great Animals of the Galápagos,* and *Wondrous Whales.* But lately, everything she wrote turned into some kind of erotic drama, and while she feared she would indeed miss her deadline, she had to admit that she had been mesmerized by her own stories. Entranced actually—almost as if it was she who was being kissed, she who was being loved. And this morning, when she sat down to write the section on the hippopotamus, she realized with horror that she was eager for Salana and Wolff to appear.

"Salana and Wolff," she mocked to herself, shaking her head. "Could there be a more classic pair of romance names?" Before her divorce, Sally had never read much romance or erotica. After her divorce, the genre seemed frivolous, boring, and made her uncomfortable. And yet, here she was, for some unknown reason, writing and enjoying the very thing she had so successfully avoided in the past.

"What is going on?" she wondered. "Could I possibly be thinking about meeting someone?"

"No," she quickly answered herself. "Impossible. I'm perfectly happy with my life."

Whatever was going on, however, Sally was determined to fight it and complete her project on time. So with full resolve, she poured a cup of tea, marched into her office/bedroom, and once again sat in front of her Machine Magic computer to teach the world about the African Lion.

From the far reaches of the delta, the great African Lion calls to his pride. The low rumble beckons with the promise of food for his lionesses and his cubs. He has eaten what he wants from

the prey and is now willing to stand guard while his family con-
sumes the remainder.

Salana stood outside her tent, listening to the great beast's
roar, wondering if this deep resonance came from the magnificent cat they had seen earlier in the day. She had been fascinated
by the animal's dignity, his unnerving command. He carried his
golden mane with respect, and all around him, animal and
human alike, silently heeded his wishes.

Throughout the day, Wolff had watched Salana being mesmerized by these exceptional animals. It was not the curiosity
of the idle tourist Wolff had seen, but some kind of reverberation between Salana and the regal cat. And now, watching her
silhouetted by the bright African moon, listening to the distant
call, he knew that he too was being called.

Salana became aware of Wolff's hands on her sides before she
heard him whisper her name. She felt him place kisses on the back
of her neck, then softly nibble the side. She heard the crinkling of
her crisp cotton blouse as his hands reached further, cupping a
breast with each hand, his thumbs idly brushing her nipples.

Still standing behind her, he pressed her closer to him, while
he deftly undid the buttons of her shorts. She could hear him
breathing, steady and strong, as his teeth and tongue played
sensuously with her ear. He held every bit of her attention, first
maneuvering between her khakis and her panties, and then between her panties and her belly. Exhaling her name, he slowly
kneaded then caressed the tops of her thighs, while his thumbs
stroked her soft curly hair. She could feel his arousal as he held
her even more tightly against his abdomen. She wanted to turn
and face him, but dared not disrupt the path his fingers were
taking. His left hand returned to her right breast while the fingers of his right hand pushed further down between her legs.

Salana shifted slightly, broadening her stance to allow him
greater access to her, her normal need for control overruled by
her growing desire. Wolff's breathing became heavier, drowning
the night sounds, as his fingers now fully explored her sex.
Under his commanding hands, Salana's body rocked hesitat-
ingly at first, then rhythmically, and then with no other purpose
than to meet and match his touch. A powerful longing was developing deep within her, compelling her hips upward in an intense need for contact.

Suddenly,
BBRINGG, BBRINGG.
Suddenly, Wolff

Sally looked at the ringing phone, then back at her screen, her fingers resting motionless on the keyboard.

BBRINGG, BBRINGG.

"Keep going," a voice within her commanded.

BBRINGG, BBRINGG.

"Keep going," the voice repeated. "You need to finish this . . ."

BBRINGG, BBRINGG.

". . . to move on."

Sally returned her focus to the screen and the ringing stopped.

Suddenly, Wolff withdrew his fingers, and for the briefest of moments, Salana panicked. But then he was facing her, and kissing her. In one smooth movement, he gathered her up into his arms, carried her to the back of her tent, and laid her down at the foot of her cot. Silently, he unbuttoned her blouse and removed her shorts and panties. She felt his fingers enter and reenter her, sliding easily from one hidden pleasure place to another, while his lips pulled and tugged on her nipples.

The night sounds of the African delta no longer existed. Salana was lost somewhere between heat and touch and desire. From a distant place Salana knew Wolff's tongue had left her breasts. Positioning himself on the canvas floor at the end of the narrow bed, he parted her legs. Salana gradually realized he was looking at her sex, watching his hands stroke her thighs, his fingers disappear and emerge, back and forth, spreading her dampness over her glistening mound. His fingers were making larger and larger circles within her, while his thumb gently rubbed and ignited her passion. With each brush of his thumb, or circle of his fingers, Salana's heart beat faster and her breath quickened. He was looking at her secret place, and though completely exposed, Salana's hips again moved without constraint, her inhibitions surrendering to the rising fever.

"You are so beautiful," he murmured.

An erotic electricity shot through Salana's entire body as his tongue now curled against her most sensitive spot, while his fingers continued massaging her wet and aching inner tissues. She jerked reflexively, small movements from muscles stimulated and tissues engorged.

Wolff read her movements, her moisture, and knew it was time. He slid his fingers out of her, not to leave, but to hold her private lips open, so his tongue could enter and caress and taste. Then he stopped and pulled slightly away, leaving Salana with only her longing and the heat of his exhalation. With increasing pressure his tongue and fingers began again, opening, savoring, probing, only to stop and let his breath carry her. Salana's body desperately pursued the pleasure, pressing her inner thighs against Wolff's head, directing. But Wolff remained in control, drinking her excitement, then pulling away, leaving the few inches between his mouth and her pleasure filled only with his hot breath. In those brief moments, Salana felt a yearning so intense, nothing existed but Wolff's fingers and mouth and tongue. Her wanting was overpowering, but Wolff now owned her body and seemed intent on keeping Salana on this teetering precipice.

Waves of heat were gripping her now, luscious spasms from muscles seeking an answer to the emptiness. He pulled away. "No!" her body begged, or was it her voice? And then he was kissing her neck, her ears, and her mouth. She tasted herself and her excitement as his kisses grew more fierce. Wolff was now over her, and around her, and finally within her. He was hard and firm, splitting her tightness with a delicious warmth.

"Salana," he moaned softly, as he rotated his pelvis from side to side, keeping the contact intense.

Now, deep inside, Wolff moved her every muscle, lit her every nerve. She had no thoughts other than having him buried and full within her. Her legs gripped his thighs. Her hands clutched his buttocks, forcing him further, to own him, as they rocked in frenzied unison. She was everywhere and nowhere. Her back arched, and the urgency—to find, to press, to hurt, and soothe. It came as a torrent, with Wolff large and

CRASH, MEEOOOWWWRRRR.

Sally's head jerked around toward the sound. Fred sat in the far corner of the room cleaning his paw, completely ignoring Sally and the spilled tea that was currently making a large irregular circle on the pastel Indian rug.

"Fred!" Sally yelled, as a flash of orange scampered away.

Her heart was beating rapidly, but not from Fred's accident. Grabbing some tissues from the bedside table she quickly blotted the rug and then her damp forehead.

It was not just her forehead that had become damp. This is absurd, she thought. Not only have I wasted an entire afternoon, but now I'm feeling . . . She glanced at the softly glowing computer screen. Had it gone from a tranquil blue to a rosy shimmer? Maybe if I just allow the rest of this story to unfold, she rationalized, I could get the rest of my work done. She studied the screen carefully. The cursor no longer seemed to quietly blink at her, but to pulsate, to . . . throb.

"No!" she yelled, and quickly shut off the computer. She sat on the bed, in the same space her daughter had sat earlier, and for the first time in years, thought of her life and her loneliness, of the humiliations of her marriage, and of her body, which hadn't been touched in years. Then came the tears.

Eventually, Ginger curled up next to her, the pet's loud purring bringing Sally out of her painful reverie. She glanced at her watch. Five-thirty. Still an hour or two of daylight left. Perhaps tending to her little garden at the back of the property would make her feel better.

Few things are as powerful as the memory of a fantasy. Though time had always flown whenever Sally had gardened, this afternoon, as day gave way to dusk, she could not shake the longing that had been stirred at the computer. She could smell Wolff's scent in the blooms she clipped. Her body ached to be embraced as she extracted the weeds from the beds. Her roses became paintings by Georgia O'Keeffe, the roots of weeds taking on an earthy male quality. Sally's own Pandora's treasure chest had been seduced open, and she could find no escape from its contents. With a sigh, she gathered up her tools and headed back to the house.

She heard his greeting before she saw him.

"Hi," he said warmly. He was standing on her front porch. Ginger was rubbing against his leg. "You must be Sally."

She studied this intruder carefully. Six foot three, maybe 180 pounds, fortyish, or younger.

"I'm from M&M." He pointed to a cobalt blue BMW with *Machine Magic* written on the side.

A BMW?

"Yeah," he smiled as if reading her thoughts. "We're kind of a unique company."

Sally nodded, still keeping her distance from this attractive stranger. White cotton shirt, khakis.

He looked at her quizzically. "So Teala didn't call you?"

The phone had rung, Sally recalled to herself, while Salana and Wolff were . . . She shivered.

He stared at her in a manner that seemed eerily familiar. "Teala didn't tell you I was coming?"

Sally shook her head.

He chuckled. "She gave me the directions here, otherwise I'd never have found it."

That had always been the idea. A swimmer, maybe basketball.

He shook his head and grinned, a funny, mischievous grin.

I've met you somewhere, Sally thought, but only said, "Excuse me. Why are you here?"

"Well, as you know, you purchased a very special computer, from us, a very special company, and since our clients can't come to us, we come to you."

His hair was the color of straw, a bit curly and unruly, thickly framing his face. He smiled broadly, as if aware and amused by her staring.

Sally nodded and averted her gaze, aware that he was aware she had been staring into his crystal-clear blue eyes.

He looked at his clipboard before continuing. "Right. We know our machines so well that we can pretty much guess when you're, that is, the machines, are going to be in need of periodic maintenance. So"—he stared intently—"here I am."

Sally swallowed. He made her uneasy, and yet she found herself unwilling to just tell him to leave. "Well, um, there's nothing wrong with my machine, so I . . ."

"Really?" he interrupted. "Because I would have bet my life that by now you're . . ."

"Do you have any documentation?" That felt better. Take charge.

He handed her the clipboard, which had all her original application and purchase contracts. Ginger, still rubbing against his leg, meowed at his side.

Sally gave him back the clipboard and watched, transfixed, as he tucked the clipboard under his arm, picked up Ginger, and stroked the persistent feline. Where had Sally met this man?

"If you're uncomfortable," he gently offered, "I'm happy to come back at another time."

"No," she said quickly, realizing that for some reason she did not want him to leave. "I guess since you drove all the way out here you may as well take a quick peek. My office is in the back of the house."

"Great." He put Ginger down, climbed the rickety porch steps, and held open the screen door, waiting.

Never before had Sally allowed a strange man into her house, yet something made this situation feel different. "By the way," she said over her shoulder, self-consciously leading the way, "what's your name?"

"Wolf," he answered with a twinkle. "With one f."

The Last Seduction

Phoenix McFarland

Silence is the perfectest herald of joy.
—William Shakespeare,
Much Ado About Nothing

Emma lay motionless in the bed. The hated tubes that perforated her body crisscrossing her like lines on a road map. But all of that disappeared from her awareness. For the first time in she couldn't tell how long, she had felt something. She never had sensations anymore. Not when the nurses turned her or stuck her with needles or when the therapist moved her arms and legs around to exercise her muscles. Yes, she had known what they were doing and why. She just couldn't feel it.

It began as a presence. A feeling that someone was in the room. People had become mere shadows to her. Shadows that drifted in and out of her room like pleasant or unwanted breezes. Once identified, she dismissed them from her attention. But this one was different. His aura seemed to fill the room. She felt a hint of compassion in it, so he must be one of the doctors. Perhaps an important visiting physician.

He was out of her field of view, but she could sense him near. She didn't know how she knew it was a male except to say that she knew the way any woman knows that an attractive man is in the room. She strained to listen to his breathing pattern, a cough, a distinctive shuffle in his walk that would make him known to her. He was silent. There was no sound but her own labored breathing and the ever-present hum of the machines that powered her bodily functions.

She grew uneasy waiting for him to step around to the foot

of her bed so she could see the person responsible for these new feelings. It had been many years since she had felt this kind of energy working in her body, but she had never forgotten those sensations. Now waves of those feelings washed over her old and motionless body, flooding her quiet nerve centers with input. A tingling, a longing, a need was born in her and it was in reaction to him.

Emma lay still on the bed, her eyes closed, savoring the mystery. She had so few distractions she was making the most of this one. She never had a visitor. Everyone who might visit her was dead. She had outlived them all. She'd been there almost twenty years, lying motionless on that bed. Her husband died twenty-five years earlier and no man had touched her since, not that she'd missed it except in a general sense. It was the closeness with Harry, the whispers, the rasp of his whiskers, the smile of satisfaction that he got when they'd managed it. Emma would always smile lovingly. It wasn't about sex anymore, anyway. It wasn't the fucking. It was about Emma and Harry sheltering each other from the ravages of time with the comfort of shared memories. The mediocrity of Harry, after all those years together, had developed a kind of momentum of its own. It swept her along. It was a comfort. But it had not been a joy. Then Harry died and after that, her stroke and the stillness fell like night upon her twilight years. Until today.

She waited to catch a glimpse of this man, but the effort was so great that she collapsed into sleep without even realizing it. When she awoke, he was gone. The ward was silent. The room was in darkness except for the dim lights of her machines. She held the memory of the man softly in her mind. Stroking it like a dream, afraid it would vanish upon remembering. She rolled the sensations over and over in her mind. Hesitant lest they fall away to dust, yet eager to have something new to think about.

Things did not often change in the limited world of Emma's perceptions. It had been years since anyone new had entered her field of view. It had been perhaps forty years since any man had aroused her like that. "Fancy a reaction like that in such an old woman," she mentally chuckled. She was as proud of her physical reaction to that stranger as Harry had been of his lackluster erections.

She waited through an uneventful morning with only her favorite nurse coming in to check on her. She did not bother to open her eyes, but mentally extended her spirit to the caring young woman. The nurse hurried through her duties and stopped to brush her hand over Emma's white head. Emma could feel only her sad, tender smile.

Alone again. The afternoon lumbered monotonously forward. Suddenly she felt his presence again. She had not heard him approach. The halls of the ward were silent. Her door had not swung open altering the light patterns against her eyelids. He was near. Very near. She held her breath to try to hear him. Suddenly, she felt a warm and nuzzling kiss on the side of her neck, moving wetly up to breathe hot moist air into her ear. He had kissed her like a lover. "Who would kiss an old woman like that?" she wondered, then quickly thought, "Who cares!" She could feel it! She felt kisses again. Kisses! Sweet, silky, sexy, slow, wet kisses. She grew tipsy on kisses. Her head swam with the sensations circulating through her body.

She still couldn't tell who he was. But she no longer cared. Her skin tingled, actually *tingled* from the contact. She waited for her heart to stop pounding, waited for the next sensation, but none came. She listened for clues as to who the man might be, for she could not see him, but she knew for sure it had been a man this time, because she had felt his rough chin scrape deliciously against her skin. She didn't know who he could be. Even from outside her limited field of vision she could recognize most of the staff. Every doctor, nurse, intern, and most of the other patients who shuffled by her door had distinctive sounds they made and subtle smells she had learned to discern that marked one from another. He was outside her field of vision and this person was as silent as she and she detected no smells associated with him. Emma longed for his touch, but he had vanished once more like a vapor, a wraith. Her world was once more the torturously slow routine of the last twenty years.

Another day passed before he returned. Emma had been napping. A pressure on her nipple awoke her. A large masculine hand enfolded her breast, kneading it and sliding his thumb and finger together to squeeze the erect nipple. The sensation was wonderful, so wonderful! Emma felt a mouth encircle the nipple and alternately suck and bite at it until she was flooded with the flowing fire she had known so well so many years ago. The mouth moved over to her other breast, where it lazily suckled. She simply surrendered to the feelings, abandoning all resistance. Letting her inhibitions slide away from her mind was profoundly erotic to her. She wasn't even self-conscious about her advanced age and withered body. She was radiant with joy. She felt sixteen again. She was twenty-eight and forty-two and sixty again. She was all those ages at the same time. She was ageless and timeless. With a great effort, she opened her eyes, the only motion she retained in her still and silent existence. She opened her eyes, but she saw nothing. No one.

She stared straight ahead at the tubes and the smooth white sheets and the shapes that indicated her shriveled little legs. "You're dreaming, old woman!" she scolded herself with a mental sigh. But the questing tongue defied her reality and continued to move down her body. Hands spread her legs although the legs beneath the sheets did not move as Emma stared at them in growing excitement and confusion. Fingers caressed her clitoris as the tongue probed her labia and flicked inside. She let her eyes slide closed, no longer caring why she could not see him. Emma's body was flaccidly unmoving but her mind was exploding with pleasure. The sensations grew more powerful. "Yes," she thought. "There!" The tongue captured her clitoris. "Oh God!" Each stroke of the tongue, each dart into her was perfection.

Never in all her adventurous long life had a man with such skill pleasured her like this. It was as if he knew exactly what she wanted. Knew it even better than she did. She felt his love wash over her. His desire to please her. She felt his love for her just the way she was. She felt beautiful again. He reveled in her. She had never felt so wanted. Whatever she longed for was lavished upon her. When her body yearned for a man, for the fullness of a man inside her, suddenly she felt a pressure against her labia. Pressing and releasing, milking sweet wetness from her dried-up body. Patient, tender, young. She felt that he was young but at the same time experienced and wise with age. She settled on ageless. He anointed the shaft of his penis in her essence like a priest with holy water performing a sacred rite.

Then as she moaned inside her silence, he slid in. He was not huge, but seemed snug and perfect for her, suiting her small body to perfection. He seemed to fill her more than the seven-foot-tall piano player she had done it with in the blues bars she used to sing at when she was a young woman in the jazz age. Lord, she had forgotten about that. Dark corner trysts behind the dusty, red velvet curtains of the Paradise Ballroom. Knowing the curtains could suddenly part and expose the slender redhead and her giant lover only added to the excitement. She was suddenly awash with memories of the past. The way her body once looked and felt. The evenings she wore glitter sprayed all over her nubile body and how it shone in the moonlight and dazzled her partners. The war and the torrid lachrymose nights spent with soldiers snatching at life while the world was at war. As he slid into her, all her lovers flooded her memory, their scents, tastes, smiles, and how it felt to lie beneath them. They all became him. It was as if they were all making love to her at once. His cock seemed to go on forever, filling her up but never hurting her, even after all these years of abstinence. It was a lovely cock. Thick too, and hard as wood. It slid in slowly, deliciously, just the way she liked it. *Exactly* the way she liked it.

Then with short strokes against her cervix it pulled out, leaving her poised on the edge of expectation. She felt the tip bumping against her labia again. Circling and circling, painting pictures with her honey. Teasing her. His penis went in a little then back out to slide up to her wildly jumping clitoris. Alternating until she floated on waves of pleasure. Icy hotness flooded into her limbs. Just as she approached orgasm his penis drew back and pounded into her once again.

Unseen fingers circled her still buttocks and, bathed in her wetness, slid slowly into her ass. Into the silence, Emma screamed with pleasure, but the silence hid the sound. The pounding cock pushed her higher and higher. The questing fingers drove her beyond pleasure. Her ears were ringing from the sounds of her silent bliss, a cacophony of ecstasy. She felt a mouth on her clitoris sucking the hard little button. "This can't all be happening at once!" she raved. But it was. Memories of young women drifted back to her. Soft hands, women's hands stroked her arms and legs, their soft fingers in her hair. Soft, round, red lipsticked mouths were sucking on her toes. Kisses. Sweet kisses. Soft women's kisses. Hard, prickly whiskered men's kisses. Both mouths bent to kiss her at once. Three tongues met and mingled.

Emma hadn't lived a sheltered life. She'd loved many able-bodied men and once or twice explored between the sweet legs of mysterious women and she'd found satisfaction with them all. But it never felt like this! Nothing could have prepared her for whatever was happening to her now. Her mind turned toward the women she had loved. Instantly, she tasted a wet pussy dancing beneath her tongue. As she sucked on the clitoris, she could hear a woman moan and feel her writhe. As always, another woman's excitement fired her own. As Emma tongued and probed the woman so she herself was tongued. She sucked and bit and made the unseen woman scream with delight. Emma gasped as the cock pulled out and glided up to bump into her own engorged clitoris. Flashes of heat flared over her like lava down a mountainside. She could hear the blood flowing in her veins, her heart pounding.

The magnificent cock, "The penis of a God!" Emma thought rapturously, poised throbbing at the shining dark lips gleaming like moonshine. He waited for her command. The lips suckled at her clitoris, tonguing it past pleasure, past lust, past human understanding. The cock slid slickly between her legs, waiting. She bucked against it, asking for it. It pulled away as she advanced. She wanted the cock. The lips sucked her nipples hard as rock candy. The fingers plunged into her ass but she wanted the cock. She whimpered for it. But it lingered outside her, bathed in her mellifluous perfume. Finally, she screamed for it, howling like an animal. Only then did he plunge into her, tearing into her with the rhythm of a wild beast.

The sensations were completely out of the realm of what Emma had ever experienced. The pleasures so much more intense, the desire so much greater. He pounded into her, reaching for her cervix and capturing it with his hardness. Fucking it. Reaching deeper than any man had ever gone. She wanted to open up, to feel him fuck her uterus; she wanted him in her tubes, spurting into her ovaries, anointing her withered eggs like a spawning salmon. Her pleasure was undeniable, unutterably grand. "Oh God!" she gasped silently. She opened her eyes in the final throes of bliss and looked into the eyes of her favorite nurse gazing down at her.

Emma experienced a release that transcended mere human experience and sent her soaring back through all her human lives and past her ancestral animal lineage. From the trees back to the water and out into the galaxy seeking the origin of stardust. Emma was thrown higher and higher in her pleasure, far above her body, far above the universe. Finally she came. In great writhing echoing pleasure she screamed out into the dark between the stars in cacophonous rapture that to her ears sounded like the singing of a million beautiful voices. It was the sound of the stars. The music of life itself. It was the sound of her own conception.

"Nurse Miller?"

The woman turned toward the door. "It's Miss Emma. She's gone. Poor thing."

"Miss Emma?" exclaimed the supervisor who crossed to the bedside and felt the old woman's pulse. "Oh, dear, the poor old soul," she said as she switched off the machines and filled the room with empty silence. "Well, she's in a better place now."

"Must be. You know, I've been taking care of her for years now and never saw anything but blankness in her eyes. But just now, she opened them and looked straight at me right before she died. There was such happiness there."

"Yes, I've seen it many times before. They all have that look. It's like . . ."

". . . Rapture."

"Yes. It must be joining with God for all eternity that makes them look so blissful as they die."

"That's what they say, anyhow."

Drawing the smooth white sheets up over Emma's head, the supervisor bent and whispered, "Go with God."

PART II

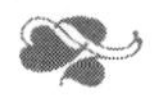

The Unknown

Seduction is enhanced by mystery, the unknown, the unfamiliar, or the unpredictable. Each unexpected turn of events increases the sexual passion. The unknown is an integral part of any new relationship. During a first seduction, virtually everything is unknown—the potential partner's sexual likes and dislikes, their sexual style, as well as their body's unique sexual responses. The wonder and surprise that accompany each revelation increase the erotic urgency and heighten the sexuality.

In Dave Clarke's "Nothing to Wear," the unknown, the fascinating, and the mysterious are combined as an Arabian prince with a private plane, palace, and unimaginable wealth transports a woman into an extraordinary and extravagant seduction. "The story is about a voyage into the unknown," says Clarke. "This mysterious, beguiling man meets a woman in a department store. He finds her so incredibly desirable that he is unwilling to hold anything back. The gala ball he transports her to becomes the event of a lifetime."

The sexual experience can be heightened when mystery is coupled with the taboo—when a potential partner is from another race, culture, socioeconomic background, or sexual orientation. Since this culture has treated the whole notion of sex as taboo, anything that couples sexuality with the forbidden builds on that fundamental prohibition and increases the erotic charge.

In "Knowing," Kate Fox chronicles her protagonist's first sexual experience with another woman. "The shock is an important part of the seduction," says Fox. "The whole experience is a surprise, the young woman is surprised that she has these feelings in the first place, then she is surprised that she is actually acting on them, and finally she is surprised at the lovemaking that follows. The forbidden aspect of the lesbian experience does play an important role, although I find that almost anything erotic has some element of the forbidden in it."

But you don't have to be in a new or taboo relationship to experience surprise and novelty. Actually, with a little imagination, some planning, and a sense of adventure, you can create this kind of newness and mystery in a long-term relationship. This is what Saskia Walker shows us in her eye-opening story, "The Welcome Home." According to Walker, "Seduction is delicious and it does not have to end once a relationship has become established. Sex can continue to be exciting, fun, and mysterious if you continue to explore each other and life together. People do not stop developing and changing when they settle into a relationship. You can continue to flirt, play games, and exploit your knowledge of each other to heighten your sexuality." Her main characters, a couple married for five years, help to maintain a lasting passionate sexual connection through the device of acting out fantasy games and assuming a variety of roles and identities.

Renate Stendhal develops the elements of mystery and surprise quite differently in her comedy of manners, "Guest of Honor," set in nineteenth-century France. Stendhal uses humor to couple the danger of discovery with the forbidden. "The important elements of the seduction in my story are the surprise, the ruse, the game, the unexpected," says Stendhal. "Breaking taboos is at the heart of the story. Seduction is a challenge, a serious affair, yet it can be extremely comical at the same time. My task was to combine all of these elements and to set up resistance, suspense, and, of course, surrender."

Risk is always involved when a person enters into a new or unique sexual encounter. He or she risks being rejected, exposed, or in some other way hurt emotionally. Anticipation grows keener as the anxiety of failure contends with the possibility of success. Since seduction is a risky game, those who succeed must be sufficiently self-confident to overcome their fears. And this self-confidence, itself, becomes an integral part of the seduction.

In "She Went Shopping This Morning," Joseph S. Teller

presents us with a woman who is willing to take enormous risks as she engineers a totally unique shopping excursion, one with an erotic twist. According to Teller, "The woman in my story has tremendous self-confidence; she knows she is beautiful and sexy as well as excited and mentally turned on. Not only does she have the creativity to envision the scene, she also has the courage to carry out her fantasy. Even though she is self-confident and determined, danger is in the air. The sexual tension builds as she plans the seduction and then carries through with it."

In Ethan Monk's story, "The 5:20 Encounter," the main male character, a gay man, has quite a different approach from Teller's female character when it comes to facing the risks involved in seduction. As he watches Kim, an attractive Asian male, across the aisle of the commuter train, his erotic fantasies build. "Seduction is largely an exercise of the mind, of the imagination, but a great seduction requires action, confidence, courage—and perhaps, a little luck," Monk explains. "My main character tends to be bolder in his thoughts than his actions. He knows that holding back, instead of following his intuition, produces nothing but regrets. Still, he finds himself fighting his patterns, the wounds derived from his past." The question of whether he will be able to take the risks necessary to overcome those patterns and wounds heightens the erotic tension that draws us into Monk's psychological drama.

Whether it is a new relationship, an old one, or somewhere in between, when the seduction is infused with risk, novelty, surprise, and particularly when coupled with a touch of the forbidden, we have a recipe for a potent sexual cocktail.

Nothing to Wear

DAVE CLARKE

Despite a walk-in closet bursting at the seams; despite six extra-wide dresser drawers filled with neatly folded tops and accessories in virtually every style and color she would look good in; despite three floor-to-ceiling racks of shoes and who knows how many more pairs under the bed, Rebecca once again found herself in the middle of Bloomington's designer boutiques, strolling from Calvin's to Ralph's to Anne's, I and II.

She floated between the Chinese silk dresses and the Egyptian cotton chemises, picking up an outfit and appraising its every aspect with one eye, all the while scouting the racks with the other, for the one she had to have.

"Nothing to wear?" a richly Mediterranean-accented voice startled her from behind.

Rebecca turned and saw before her the most beautiful, most perfect man she had ever seen. Tall, but not too much so, hair so black it looked almost blue. His skin, the color of cocoa butter, glowed as if it had just been buffed. His suit draped on his lean frame as if it hovered around him, never quite touching him. His eyes, two polished panther-black marbles, seemed to reach inside her the second they met.

"I have something for you to wear. And . . . somewhere to wear it," he said, his penetrating dark eyes reaching so deep inside her, Rebecca swore she could feel them tickling her soul. "Tonight is my people's annual celebration."

"Oh?" she played into him. "What are they celebrating?"

"Me," he said in all modesty. "It is our annual Prince's Ball and, I confess, I have no one to be at my side."

"Prince?" she queried, moving closer to him, and she was

startled again as the bodyguards she hadn't noticed earlier came in closer, in sync with her every movement.

"At your service," he said, taking her hand and bringing it to his full, dark lips.

"This celebration, wouldn't that be in your country?"

"Of course," he said with a smile, melting her heart with his honey-smooth voice.

"I don't have—"

"Anything to wear. I know. Don't worry, we have everything you could possibly need or desire. I will personally guarantee it."

"Well, I at least need my passport and I—"

"Please," he said, feigning insult. "You are with me. That's all anyone needs to know."

He held out his arm and Rebecca took it. Without a second thought, without knowing his name, without even knowing where his country was, she took his arm, and it seemed when she opened her eyes again her champagne glass was half-empty and the Royal Jet was touching down on the thin, black ribbon of runway that had suddenly appeared over the bright white desert horizon.

A gleaming black Mercedes the length of three cars was waiting at the end of the air stairs they had rolled next to the plane. In a matter of seconds, they were inside behind the cool, darkened glass, the sand dunes speeding past like lilies on a pond. After a time, the prince rolled down Rebecca's window and the warm desert air rushed in, her hair swirling behind her.

"It is just there," he told her as the palace rose on the horizon. In the middle of this vast sea of sand, a building, its roof glittering with gold, its walls so white it hurt just to look at them, took shape before Rebecca's eyes. As if commanded by the heavens, the wrought-iron gates parted before the limo. They parked at the massive red-tiled entry, a stream of servants studding the driveway and continuing under the palatial, columned alcove, right up to the bronze-covered doors that stood fifty feet tall at their pointy, Moorish peak.

The entry hall, with its high, domed ceiling, rivaled anything Europe could offer. A statue, depicting a sultan, sword drawn, mounted on a rearing horse that stood twenty hands or better, filled the rotunda. And if size alone wasn't enough, a shower of sparkling fountains drew the ears as well as the eye to the piece. "My father," the prince explained.

A servant, dressed in flowing white robes, approached them and bowed protractedly before the prince. "Your Highness."

"Raja."

The servant rose straight up. "It is so good to see you again, Your Highness. Everything is as you requested."

"I can always count on Raja," he told Rebecca with a broad smile. Then, remembering something else, "Oh." Before he could speak again, the servant produced a small box and handed it to the prince.

He handed Rebecca the case, its inlaid olive wood polished and glistening in the shafts of sunlight streaming into the grand chamber. "Something to wear."

She took the box and lifted off the fitted lid. Inside, she peeled away the swatches lining the case until she came to the object it protected—a crimson, heart-shaped piece of silk, no bigger than her palm, the slender, silken strands sewn to it little more than a thimbleful of thread. She held it out and watched as the prince's grin broadened. "It's beautiful," she barely managed.

"I only hope it will do you justice." He looked at her and sensed her anxiety as her eyes darted around the room. "Is something wrong?"

"What will I wear with it?"

"With it?" he asked.

"To the ball. It's magnificent, I love it. But what else is there? What other garments?"

The prince looked surprised and, if it were possible for anything to pierce his perfection, even a little wounded. "This is it. Everything. So it has been since the very beginning here. So it shall always be."

"I'll be . . . as good . . . as naked," she told him.

Now the prince looked truly touched. "How can you say that, my angel? You will be manicured, pedicured. Your every pore from head to toe will be cleansed and oiled and powdered smooth as satin. You will be coiffed and made up by the finest artisans money can buy. Your eyes will sparkle like stars, your cheeks will glow like the sunset on a summer's eve. Your ears will drip with diamonds as big as the plumpest grapes on the vine. You will be perfumed in the most intoxicating fragrances my gardens can offer. Oh no, my love. You will be completely dressed up, your every perfect feature brilliantly displayed. I have no doubt you will be the envy of every woman and man in the room. No matter how hard they try, they will not be able to take their eyes from the magnificent creature before them. They will speak of your extraordinary beauty to their children and their children's children," he assured her, taking her in his arms. "You will see, surrender is good. Even sweet. It is simplicity itself."

Rebecca looked into those eyes and knew she could do nothing but surrender. Immediately, he saw it inside her, as if she had signed it on a parchment with her own hand.

The prince smiled broadly at her. "This is Haseem. She will prepare you."

The woman who had gracefully slid to Rebecca's side was tall and slender, with skin the color of honey. From the vacant stare in her eyes Rebecca knew immediately she was blind. Nonetheless, the servant took her hand without hesitation and led Rebecca away, her sightless steps far more steady and assured than Rebecca's.

Haseem, little more than a girl of perhaps eighteen or twenty years, took her along the vaulted corridors, deep into the palace. She led Rebecca along the plush ribbons of carpeting, past the paintings and the vast, oversized portraits of the royal family. She led her past the colorful tapestries, past the bronze casts, past the polished marble tables lined with tall, hand-painted vases filled with fresh-cut flowers of every kind. When they had walked what seemed to Rebecca a half-mile or so through the maze of hallways and doors, Haseem stopped at a large set of double doors. A pair of peacocks, their broadly fanned plumes painted with thick oils and gilded with the strokes of a brush no more than a single hair wide in places, made the doors unique in all the palace. "The Chamber of Fair Maidens," Haseem whispered, opening the portals.

"The harem?" Rebecca asked.

"The prince has no harem at this palace," she explained, leading her inside.

The room was enormous—as long and wide and high as a grand hotel lobby only more sumptuous in every richly crafted detail. When they realized the door had been opened, the dozen or so handmaidens, as Rebecca would soon learn they are called, stopped in their places. They held a curtsy until Haseem signaled them to return to their business with a gentle clap of her hands, which they did with warm, gracious smiles for their guest.

Rebecca felt a slight tug at her foot and looked down to find Haseem kneeling at her side, ready to replace her street shoes with a pair of embroidered pink satin slippers. She gave way to the young woman and they slipped on as though they were a pair of custom-fitted gloves. Haseem stood up. "We'll begin in the baths," she said, leading Rebecca toward the wisps of steam rising up at the far corner of the room.

The baths, a suite of boldly colored marble and gold fixtures, was misted in steam from the nearby pools. The lingering scent of jasmine made the rooms seem serenely surreal. A pair of maidens peeled the clothing from Rebecca and led her to a tub filled with clear, sparkling waters. Using golden jugs of the water, they soaked Rebecca from head to toe. With soft loofas they gently whisked her skin clean. When they were done, Haseem appeared with a robe as thick and soft as if it were the sheep's own cloak. She took Rebecca's hand and led her to a large marble table on the terrace. "Please," she said, motioning her to lie down.

Laid out there, Rebecca could see all of the palace grounds and the sienna-kissed mountains in the distance. Immediately behind the palace were the gardens—several acres of perfectly clipped lawns, alabaster statues, sparkling fountains, and the sculpted date palms, their leaves rustling in the soft breeze. The gardens yielded to the riding grounds. As the maidens began, Rebecca could see the prince below working one of his shiny black mares. The two, rider and ridden, became one under his smooth, powerful command. His manner was firm, yet loving, and the animal seemed to revel in performing exactly as instructed.

Four women now attended Rebecca. Removing the robe, they swathed her torso, her arms, and her legs in large, dark green leaves they pulled from a pair of steaming clay pots, one on either side of the table. Each time they lifted one of the moist leaves, they released the pungent, cleansing aroma of the soak into the air and the breeze curled around it and carried it away. Only her sex was left exposed.

When she was wrapped tightly, each woman took a hand or foot and began first trimming the nails then soaking them in a thick, creamy goo. As they worked, Haseem placed a hot towel over Rebecca's face. The towel smelled minty and made Rebecca giddy and light-headed as she breathed it in. "We will take the impurities, whatever and wherever they are," Haseem whispered, then began trimming the soft tufts of hair between Rebecca's legs, leaving only the barest hint of discretion around the pink mound.

Though it seemed an eternity, the handmaidens soon peeled away the dressing. When she looked out across the fields for the prince, he was gone, and the breezes crossing the terrace gave her a slight chill.

Haseem's hand brushed ever so lightly against Rebecca's erect nipples. "The breeze will close your pores and make the skin firm and tight." She took Rebecca's hand, leading her to a plush upholstered chair, then pressing her into it. The burgundy velvet was soft beneath her skin, seeming to Rebecca as though she were seated on a bed of rose petals.

Four new maidens approached, each taking a hand or foot and applying a polish in a shade of pink so pale, it was nearly clear. A fifth followed close behind and, using a brush with bristles so soft they could not be felt, began working Rebecca's hair. She worked it in smooth, swift strokes until the effect was one of glowing radiance and silkiness. In one move, the woman pinned the hair up, holding it in place with a diamond-studded pin so it spilled down and rested just above the shoulders.

The desert air, bereft of moisture, had already dried the polish on her nails. The women retreated silently into the chamber, bowing as they left. In their place, a tiny woman appeared. Her feet as small as a child's, she took halting little steps in the platform shoes that raised her barely chest high. In the slender fingers of her petite hands she carried a small, leather-handled box and set it down on the stand next to Rebecca's chair.

The woman had long, thick black hair that hung past her knees, and her features, though clearly Oriental, seemed betrayed by the delicate porcelain pallor of her skin. She opened the box and set her things out on the stand. She stared hard at

Rebecca, then traced her face with the tiny, doll-like fingers, like a young child exploring its mother for the first time.

She began to paint Rebecca with her thin brushes. She worked swiftly and assuredly, her fingers smoothing the blushes until they blended perfectly, coating each eyelash with a mascara so rich it held in a single stroke. When she was done, she stopped without a word, repacked her case, and retreated in the same halting half-steps that brought her.

Haseem reappeared and took Rebecca's hand. "The sun will be down soon," she said, leading her inside. The maidens from the baths arrived again and placed Rebecca on a pedestal near the center of the room. They buffed her with a sweetly fragrant cream that melted into her skin like butter on a warm bun. The application complete, they pulled small crystal bottles from their pockets, dabbing at Rebecca with the stoppers, laying a lilting, fruity perfume at each passion point along her smoothed skin.

When they were done, Haseem brought the olive wood box and removed the tiny heart. She stretched out the slender threads for Rebecca to step into, then, gliding it in place over her thinly shorn pubes, fitted the strands square between her cheeks.

From a nearby cart, Haseem began to accessorize Rebecca. First, a pair of earrings, the diamonds so big Rebecca nearly lost her breath when she first saw them. Next, the woman removed a necklace. Layers of gold clustered with so many precious stones they covered Rebecca's chest in a V down to her sternum and accentuated the naked breasts in a pair of crowning half-circles. A thin ribbon of gold was hung around Rebecca's waist, then another chain, more slender still, was clasped around one ankle. Rebecca was coaxed into lifting a foot, and another diamond, this one mounted into a slender platinum setting, was slipped onto the toe next to her biggest one. Haseem arose, removing the last two articles from the case on the cart—two tiny golden bells, each no larger than a pea. She clipped them to Rebecca's nipples, their gentle, tinkling sound echoing softly in the giant chamber as she breathed.

A pair of heels, little more than a few golden threads between the toes on a leather sculpted platform, were slipped on her feet and the straps tied crisscross up Rebecca's calves. Haseem stood and moved in close to Rebecca. "May I?" she asked holding her hands to Rebecca's face.

"Yes," she whispered.

The woman began at the top, sensing the position of the hair and the clasp holding it. With a touch as light as the desert breeze she slowly traced the rest of Rebecca's trembling form. The fingertips caressed the face, gleaning its every contour from the cheekbones to the lips brushed a deep wine red. She moved to the ears and down the neck to the broad, jewel-studded necklace, tracing the full breasts. She glided along the smooth, lean stomach and with the touch of a butterfly traced the moistened lips below. She ran her fingers to the back and rounded the plump, muscular buttocks, coming back to the inside of the thighs and down the calves until she rested at the perfectly polished toes. She stood and said, "A more magnificent woman we have never had. Come, it is nearly time to present you."

The grand ballroom of the palace was a cavernous open-air space with walls that melted into the clear, dark night sky. Columns, as big around as oak trees, rose up to meet the stars. At the far end of the hall was a broad, grand staircase leading to a sheer white curtain at the top of the room. Rebecca waited in the ante way with Haseem until, after a few moments, the prince arrived.

His flowing white robes gleamed around him, shaping his lean frame. He gave the blinded maiden a gentle touch, sending her back into the catacombs, and turned to the woman before him. "Flawless. A gift from the gods," he said, taking her hand, leading her to the precipice of the ballroom.

The crowd silenced, a blare of trumpets announced His Royal Highness as they stepped into the room. Rebecca looked at the hundreds of pairs of formally dressed eyes focused on her and felt her entire body turning crimson. As the heat radiated from every exposed inch, the crowd took great notice with their hushed oohs and ahhs.

"Your modesty pleases them," the prince whispered, squeezing her hand.

As she started to walk, Rebecca felt the dampness sticking between her legs.

Curling his nostrils and picking up her scent, the prince added, "Your excitement pleases me."

They descended into the crowds, which parted for them, then enveloped the couple completely. For the next few hours the prince entertained his guests with Rebecca at his side. Between caviar and champagne and delicacies of every sort imaginable, he kept her close at hand. He discussed matters from international politics to sports to fashion and art, seeking out her opinions on each one and making her feel at ease with each word she spoke, as though her thoughts and feelings were no less important than those offered by any minister or cabinet official or jet-setting tycoon.

When the shank of the evening arrived, he led her to the grand staircase and started up, keeping her at his side. When they reached the curtained balcony, a hundred feet above the crowds, he turned back to the people below. "I thank you, my friends. You are truly what makes our nation great." He waved, then parted the sheer curtain for Rebecca. There she found the largest four-poster bed she had ever seen. The bed, layered with pillowed shams and silvery, silken linens, stood at the center of the room, its farthest end against a picture window opened to the dark, cool air.

The prince smiled handsomely at her. "You see? You see how much you impressed them? They will speak of your beauty into eternity."

He slipped from his robes. His physique, each muscle, so lean, so perfectly proportioned, his golden, tanned complexion, made her grow weak in the knees and he but touched her shoulders and she fell to them, the silk pillows cushioning her.

His cock, the shaft stiff now and thick as a stallion's, shined before Rebecca as he brought her head gently toward the tip of the shaft. His fingers deftly parted her quivering lips as he slowly slid himself inside her. She took him in, as much as she could in comfort, and began to kiss and lick and pleasure his organ. He stood over her, running his hands through her hair as she slid back and forth on him. His bold, musky scent mesmerized her as she tasted the sheer power she held within her.

When he began to throb, he deftly slid himself out from her warm mouth. In one smooth motion he carried her to the bed, laying her on her back across the pile of pillows. He began at the nape of her neck, nibbling behind the ears, then down her shoulders. He pressed his lips to the spot between her breasts and continued down her smooth belly. When he reached the red heart, he raised her hips and slid the tiny garment from her. He parted her lips and sent his fiery tongue inside her. He stroked and pressed and lapped up her sweet juices as quickly as she released them. Three times he climaxed her, his deft, assured hands and his schooled, strong tongue pressing against her beady, throbbing clit to new heights of pleasure and then he turned her over, positioning her for the mount.

He set her head toward the pitch darkness of the open window and slipped his thick member inside her from behind. The tiny golden bells tinkled in the night air as she became aware of them tugging lightly at her flushed, erect nipples beneath them. The width of his cock filled her up, stretching her and reaming every wrinkle from her cunt so she throbbed as it lay just inside her. When he began to move, the pleasure intensified still more, causing her to cry out and reach for the bedposts to steady herself against the increasing thrusts.

He pushed against her flesh, coaxing the pleasure from deep inside her, and she began to understand what the mare had felt that afternoon. The thrusts grew faster as he guided her slender hips against him with his large hands. As he pressed the muscles in her buttocks and reached around to hold her waist, the pleasure became excruciating. She thrust back at him, giving as fiercely as she got, and when the euphoria became so intense she thought she might burst, she relented, relinquishing every ounce of her soul to him with a final joyous scream, his hot liquid bullets filling her, spilling out and down the inside of her still pulsing thighs.

As she collapsed beneath him, he stayed with her, inside her, until she came to. When her eyes opened she looked out the window expecting to see the stars that guided her to this magical place. Instead she saw the same faces that had hung on her every word throughout the first part of the evening. As the color again radiated within her, the faces began to smile, then to applaud, then finally, to shower her with roses until the balcony was a sea of fragrant petals.

"A legend," the prince said proudly. A fashion legend for the ages.

Knowing

Kate Fox

Telling my roommate to go home without me, I'd stayed in the city late that Friday night under the guise of doing errands I didn't want to have to do over the weekend. In actuality, I was avoiding him, and I was sure he knew it. I was never a very convincing liar.

We'd been living together for a few months, and although he quickly proved to be easy to live with, and a pretty nice guy in all respects, recently some subtle changes had taken place. He'd stopped averting his eyes when I emerged from the shower in just a towel, and had stopped courteously moving away from me when, in a crowded subway, our bodies were pressed together by the crush of commuters.

One week ago, we'd gone out drinking after work with some friends and had both ended up completely smashed. During the cab ride home, as we were laughing about something, the cabbie made a sharp turn and my head ended up in my roommate's lap, my face turned toward the ceiling. Our laughter quickly subsided, forgotten. I closed my eyes as he traced his fingertips down my forehead, over my nose and lips, and down the curve of my chin. After two or three passes, I unthinkingly parted my lips and allowed his fingers to slip into my mouth.

I was beginning to feel dizzy when he unexpectedly jammed his other hand in between my legs. I pushed his hands away and sat up. We had a long talk about it later, the experience having quickly sobered us, and I rambled on about how a sexual relationship would be too difficult and uncomfortable due to circumstances. I insisted that I didn't want to get involved with someone I lived with or worked with, let alone both.

All of that sounded good in theory, and had appeared to placate him at the time. Still, I'd been stupid to hope it would all dissipate just like that. Quite the contrary was true; things soured quickly between us. At least, from my point of view. He seemed to think that the true reason I had pushed him away was either out of propriety or, worse, that I was playing hard to get.

His casual glances at me in my towel or nightgown now became long, surveying looks. He spent more time hanging out in my room, sitting on my bed, than he ever had before, and it was getting more and more difficult to find polite ways to kick him out. This morning, though, on the subway on the way to work, he'd finally crossed the line. A wave of people entered, shoving me from behind, and I ended up pressed tightly against him.

"Well, hello," he smirked. "Fancy meeting you here."

"Very funny," I muttered, trying to extract myself.

"So, what are we going to do tonight?" he asked casually. "Going out drinking again?"

"I don't think so," I answered. "I have some stuff to do after work."

"Like what?" he pressed.

"Just stuff," I said defensively. "Errands."

"Why don't you come out with us? Have a few drinks. I promise I'll be gentle," he said, raising an eyebrow and giving me a grin that he probably intended to be enticing, but which came across as more of a leer. It was not becoming.

"No, thanks," I said, looking anywhere but at him. I was actually beginning to feel sick to my stomach.

"What's your problem?" he asked me, his voice low, trying to mask his wounded tone with something more like derision, but failing.

My eyes widened in surprise. "My problem?" I asked, incredulous. "You're the one with the problem."

"No," he said condescendingly, with just a hint of a whine. "Your problem is that you want me, and you know you want me, and I know you want me." Pausing for a moment, he puffed himself up a little. "You're just too uptight to do anything about it."

Seeing red, I refused to look at him for the rest of the trip, although I could feel his smug, knowing glare on me the entire way. I avoided him for the rest of the day and took off after work without saying a word to anyone. I seethed as I walked around Midtown, his pompous, knowing tone echoing in my ears.

How had things gone so badly so quickly? I'd been uneasy about having a male roommate, but he seemed to be a pleasant guy and a good housemate. Until . . . until sex came into the picture. That was it. Everything changes as soon as sex becomes an issue. I knew that, and I was stupid to let things go as far as they had in that cab. Now he was under the illusion that there was some unspoken truth I was suppressing. Well, maybe there was. Maybe that was why I was in the city tonight. Looking for truth in the only place I could find it: within myself.

I found my way eventually down to the Village and wandered around the streets for several hours, ducking constantly out of the way of couples or groups of friends chattering happily and obliviously, passing me on the sidewalks.

I paused outside a club that had a black wall behind glass so that I could check out my reflection. As usual, my eyes and hands went first to my hair. The perm I'd gotten the week before had turned out much wilder and frizzier than I'd hoped, and being that my hair was barely chin-length to begin with, the blond locks jumped out from my head at all angles, with no rhyme or reason. I gave up trying to smooth down the curls and instead just stood and stared at my reflection, my shoulders slumped and my eyelids heavy.

Without warning, the door to the club swung open, just feet from me, releasing with a cloud of smoke and burst of music a pair of women, laughing. The music faded away as the door closed behind them. Not seeming to take notice or care of my presence, one reached for the other's neck, encircling it with one hand. She pulled the shorter woman toward her and dipped her head smoothly, claiming the waiting, parted lips to her own.

I stood silently, unable and unwilling to move or to take my eyes away. As I watched, the taller woman's free hand reached unabashedly to cover a welcoming breast. The other woman moaned slightly, deliciously, from inside the kiss, and was promptly backed up against the wall, not three feet from where I stood. As tongue twisted with tongue, fingers massaged breast, pelvis ground into pelvis, I stared, mesmerized.

After several extraordinarily long moments, one pair of eyes opened, languidly, and acknowledged my presence. Without breaking from the kiss, she met my gaze levelly and drank me in. Her eyes dipped downward a little, heavy-lidded, and I allowed mine to follow. Through her thin T-shirt, between her lover's fingertips, the outline of her tiny, hard nipple became visible.

The door to the club suddenly opened again, and I quickly looked away from the two of them. An older woman stepped out. She held the door, obviously thinking I was heading in, and, completely disconcerted, not trusting myself to speak, I stepped inside.

The club was open, two levels, and more brightly lit than other clubs I had been in. A large, masculine woman in a black T-shirt and black jeans sat just inside. "Five dollars," she told me, giving me a once-over, and I fumbled inside my bag for the cash. As I handed it to her, I wondered, somewhere deep inside my dumbfounded mind, what I thought I was doing. She stamped my hand, a dark pink triangle, and I moved away.

Glancing around, I tried to appear as though I were looking for a friend. Spotting a tiny empty table in a corner, I made a beeline for it and sat down. It was darker and quieter in the corner, which I was thankful for. Immediately, I busied myself looking for some imaginary item in my bag. What a search it was, too; it must have lasted five or six minutes before I was interrupted by a voice.

"Ready for a drink?"

I glanced up, one arm in my bag almost up to the shoulder. A tall, athletic-looking young woman stood over me, casually swatting her arm with a dishrag. She had thin, straight brown hair that hit her shoulders and she wore no makeup. The look on her face was unsmiling but pleasant.

"Uh, yeah, sure," I mumbled, looking around, noting a majority of beer bottles in hands and on tables. "Beer."

"What kind?" she asked.

"Surprise me," I said before I realized the words were out of my mouth, shocked when I heard them hit the air.

A hint of a smile touched her lips, and she walked away. I sat back in my seat. The place wasn't packed, but it was definitely crowded. There were women everywhere, talking, laughing, hugging, and, yes, kissing. So this is what it's like in a lesbian bar, I found myself thinking.

She returned with a Corona and a glass with a slice of lime. "Three-fifty," she told me as she set it down on my table. I fumbled for the money and came up with a five. "Keep the change," I said.

A look of mild surprise washed over her features and she watched as I gulped down half the beer straight from the bottle. "She stand you up?" she asked, sympathetically.

"What?" I looked up at her. "Oh. Uh . . ."

She shrugged. "Sorry. It's kind of easy to tell, though. I mean," she quickly amended, "just for me. Because I work here. I'm sure no one else would know."

I stared at her for a moment. "Well, enjoy," she said, patting me on the shoulder before turning away.

Keeping my head low, I nursed the beer, not tasting it, as I took a longer look around. There, in the corner, were two women standing at the jukebox, one's hand resting casually on the other's buttock. There, at the bar, was one woman sitting, with another standing in front of her, in between her knees, their arms around each other. And there were two women dancing, laughing, playing with one another's hair. As I watched, they exchanged several light, affectionate kisses.

"Aren't they great?" a familiar voice asked from my shoulder, and I looked up to see that my waitress had returned. "They're regulars," she told me. We watched them dance for a minute or two. I was very aware of the tall woman's presence next to me, her hip almost touching my arm.

"I like the dark-haired one," she observed, referring to the plumper woman, whose curly chestnut hair swung casually almost to her waist.

"She is beautiful," I agreed, glancing up at the waitress, who returned my gaze, and suddenly the realization hit me that I found her beautiful, as well. Her eyes were oval, some light shade of hazel or brown, her nose was long and thin, and her small lips surrounded white teeth that were endearingly crooked.

She must have noticed a change in my face, for she smiled. "There, you're feeling better. Or maybe it's the beer hitting."

I smiled a little. "No, I am feeling better. Thank you."

"No problem." Her smile was wide.

"How long have you been working here?" I asked her.

"A couple months, off and on. I only work a couple of times a week. Usually not on weekends. My girlfriend has been working here a long time, but she's off tonight."

"Oh." I nodded, looking down, ashamed at the sudden disappointment I felt, and took another long swig of my beer. Out of the corner of my eye I saw her head turn toward the bar, and she nodded.

"Have to get back to work," she told me.

"Yeah, I have to get going," I said, rising and picking up my bag.

"Oh, well, it was nice talking to you," she added, casually resting her hand on my arm.

"Yeah," I said, allowing one quick glance at her warm eyes. So unfair. "You, too."

When I stepped outside, the two lovers were gone. I moved toward the street without looking back, not wanting to know what the name of the club was. I hailed an oncoming cab.

"Queens," I told the driver, giving him the address, and he took off for the 59th Street Bridge.

When he dropped me off around 11:30, I glanced up at our third-floor living room window, which was dark. My roommate must have gone out, which I was thankful for. I didn't want to have to face him in my present state.

I let myself in, went straight to my room, and shut the door without turning on the light. Dropping my bags on the floor, I peeled off all of my clothes and stood next to the bed for a moment, uncomfortably hot and out of breath. I climbed into bed, kicking off all the covers except for one thin sheet.

Wide awake, I tossed and turned. I was still dazed from the evening. And I couldn't get my waitress's face or her lilting voice out of my head. I reached over my shoulder to scratch an itch. The scratch soon turned into a caress, and I found myself rubbing my shoulder and neck. My fingers trailed down to my breasts, and I traced wide featherlike circles around each one. Closing my eyes tightly, I recalled the image of the women on the street. Imagining the one's fingers on the other's breast, I played with my nipples.

Ripples of pleasure immediately swooped from my breasts to

my thighs. Sighing, I slipped one hand between my legs and began to rub myself. I didn't bother starting out slow and building up, as usual. I was too keyed up for that. I massaged my clitoris with a vengeance, the image of my waitress's warm eyes burning into my closed lids.

I came suddenly, hard, the top half of my body rising momentarily off the bed. Almost before the first orgasm had finished, I surprised myself by pushing on for another one. Within a minute I was coming again, and for a moment, it was another woman's fingers I was rubbing against.

Spent but unsatisfied, I fell back on the bed and lay awake for a long while. At about 12:30, I heard a key in the front door. Under my bedroom door a sliver of light appeared, then disappeared just as quickly. Heavy footsteps moved from the door to his room, which struck me as odd. He normally had reasonably light footing and was usually conscientious about keeping quiet.

It was about ten minutes later that I heard the noise. I strained, listening, and in a moment I heard it again. Was that . . . a moan? It couldn't be. But it was.

"That—" I whispered, stopping, having no idea what my next word would have been. As quietly as possible, I rose from the bed, opened my dresser drawer, and pulled out a short nightgown, slipping it over my head. I moved silently to my door and opened it carefully, leaning ever so slowly out and craning my neck to look into his room.

His door was slightly ajar, and I could see, at the foot of the bed, two pairs of bare feet twisting languidly around each other. Almost immediately, I felt the heat in my body return, and I slowly turned myself around so that the front of my body and my cheek were pressed against the wall. As I did, the sound from inside the room became audible. I could hear the swish of sheets, heavy breathing, and the moans, which were not emanating from my roommate.

She was tall. That was the first thing I noticed as I moved my head slightly to get a better look. Her feet fell farther than his over the edge of the bed. Her legs were smooth, I could tell in the moonlight, which glinted off the thick blond hair on my roommate's calves.

They were already close to nude. He had only boxer shorts

on, and she wore just panties and a bra, which were some pastel color that I couldn't make out in the faint light. Perhaps lilac or peach. They lay on their sides, facing each other, her back to me. He had his arm draped over her waist, and as I watched, he slid his hand into the back of her panties and squeezed her buttock.

She moaned again and ground her hips into his, the muscles of her thighs contracting. I felt my own do the same, imagining what she was feeling. His hand reemerged and slipped up the curve of her back to unhook her bra. It took him perhaps fifteen seconds, which I had to admit was pretty good for one hand.

He shifted his weight so that he could pull her bra off and toss it carelessly on the floor, and ended up on top of her. Almost roughly, he kissed and sucked at her neck, then moved down to her full breasts. He took one of her nipples into his mouth, flicking it with his tongue. Her head tossed back and forth on the pillow, and my heart jumped into my throat, afraid that she would spot me.

He slid down on the bed so that his knees rested on the floor and his stomach against the foot of the bed. Hooking his thumbs under the sides of her underwear, he pulled them down her thighs. She raised her feet, allowing him to slip them off, then parted her legs, dropping her knees to either side.

Just before he leaned forward, I was granted a perfect view. Her pubic hair was thick and dark, opening to a glistening crevice, the sight of which sent a delicious shudder through my body. His head swooped down, obliterating my view, and I watched as it bobbed up and down. Her breath began to turn into gasps, and her hips rolled with his head.

Soon, he pulled away from her and, instead of climbing back onto the bed, stood up to remove his boxer shorts. The outline of his body was perfectly visible against the window, and his penis stood straight out in front of him, somewhat muted under his thick belly. I took the opportunity to look once again at her, feasting my eyes on the pink flesh between her smooth thighs. Incredibly, I found myself wondering how she would taste.

Turning away, he opened a dresser drawer and I heard the crinkle of plastic. Out of the corner of my eye, I saw his elbows moving, his head down. He returned to the bed and knelt in be-

tween her knees, dropping his elbows on either side of her
chest. Relaxing his weight on top of her, he pushed his hips
slightly, once, twice, then something gave and he slid fully in.

A gasp slipped through her lips, and became a way of breathing as he thrust in a steady rhythm. I finally succumbed to my
own desires and slid one hand down between my own legs, rubbing myself in time with his thrusts. I watched not his buttocks
or her thighs, but her face, eyes closed and mouth open, breathing hard, almost panting.

Then, unbelievably, it was over. He grunted loudly with two
or three deep thrusts, then collapsed on top of her. Her breathing quickly returned to normal as she lay there, eyes closed, de-
ceptively calm. I couldn't tell what she was thinking or feeling.

Suddenly realizing the compromising position I was in, I
began to move my head away from the wall so that I could get
my balance enough to step back into my room. I was planning
to move slowly and delicately so as not to make a sound, but,
as his bedsprings creaked, I saw that he was getting up to head
toward the bathroom.

I jerked my head back and darted clumsily, almost tripping,
into my room, closing my door as quickly and quietly as possible just seconds before he entered the hallway. I stood on the
other side of the door, out of breath, listening to his padded
footsteps on the carpet, then to the bathroom door closing. I
leaned my head against the wall and closed my eyes. I remained
in that position for a long time.

That bastard. He'd left his door open on purpose. He knew
I was home. He knew I'd hear them, at least. And he knew I'd
end up hot and bothered. At that, though, my eyes opened, and
I allowed myself a small, if ironic, smile. He'd misread one aspect of his little scenario. Obviously, he was expecting to be the
object of my desire.

Finally, peeling my cheek off the wall, I crept back into bed.
My legs splayed, my hand automatically found its way back to
tonight's spot of choice, my fingers spreading the labia to have
better access. However, after more than ten minutes, I hadn't
been able to bring myself to orgasm, and I gave up, still frustrated.

I hadn't heard anything in several minutes. I surmised that
she was staying the night and that one or both of them were

asleep by now. Slowly, I got out of bed and moved to my door. I opened it slightly and listened. Hearing nothing, I tiptoed out into the hall and walked softly to the kitchen to get myself a drink of water.

I took the bottle of filtered water out of the refrigerator and closed the door. As I turned, I saw a figure standing just a few feet from me in the darkness, and I nearly jumped out of my skin.

"Sorry," she said softly, her voice just above a whisper. She was wearing an oversize T-shirt, maybe one of his. I couldn't tell if she was wearing anything underneath it. "I actually was looking for the same thing. May I have some?" She indicated the water bottle.

I looked down at it as if it were something foreign in my hand. "Oh," I mumbled. "Yeah." I crossed to the cabinet and took two glasses out. I poured water into each of them and handed one to her.

"Thanks," she said, a little louder, and I glanced in the direction of the bedrooms.

"It's okay," she reassured me. "He's asleep."

I prayed she wasn't going to tell me how they'd met or where she knew him from, or whether they'd been together before, and, thankfully, she didn't say any of those things. She just watched me drink my water.

I finished mine off and went to the sink to put my glass in it. Unexpectedly, I felt her move smoothly up behind me. The fingers of one hand rested gently on my hip.

"I saw you," she whispered, her breath tickling my ear. "I saw you watching."

Her body was warm behind mine. I turned, slowly, but she didn't back away. We were face to face.

"Who are you?" she asked softly. I knew she was looking for something much deeper than my name.

"I don't know," I replied quietly.

She reached up and brushed a curl from my forehead. "How sad," she murmured.

Closing my eyes briefly, I knew that whatever I said or didn't say would set the tone for the rest of the night. I reached for her, stroking her short, fine hair. "You're beautiful," I whispered to her.

She responded by pressing her lips to the side of my neck. Her hand brushed my hip. "Mmm, you're warm," she whispered into my ear. "Have you ever made love to a woman?"

"No," I answered after a slight hesitation. "Have you?"

"Umm-hmmm," she replied, tracing her soft fingertips over my ear and neck. "You like women, don't you?" It was an observation rather than a question.

"Yes," I admitted, my voice barely audible.

She was silent for a long, excruciating moment. In the darkness, I sensed her watching me. Finally, she murmured, "What do you want?"

My first instinct was to say, I don't know, but it was a falsity. I knew exactly what I wanted. I was just terrified to voice it.

"Come on," she whispered, and leaned forward to run her tongue in a long, slow, wet line across the side of my neck before moving away, taking my hand to guide me.

I glanced once more with trepidation as we passed my roommate's room, but he appeared to be solidly out. She led me into my room, leaving the door ajar. She stopped next to the bed, releasing my hand and turning to face me. Slowly, she took her T-shirt by the hem and pulled it over her head in one motion. She was indeed naked underneath. Her skin glistened in the moonlight.

I stood, trembling, and my fingers played with the hem of my nightie. She saw this and met my eyes. Her gaze, almost apologetic, told me, "I can't do it for you."

Taking a deep breath, my heart pounding mightily, I lifted my nightgown off and dropped it on the floor. She took a half step closer to me. With one fingertip on each hand, she traced lines all over my body: my arms, my neck and face, my stomach, my shoulders, in between and around my breasts, my thighs. Finally, I caught and grasped her hands, pulling her onto the bed. She lay down on her side, facing me, and placed the flat of her hand on my waist. Gently but firmly, she gave me a tug.

I groaned and rolled into her, crushing her full breasts to my smaller ones, running my tongue along the side of her neck where it met her chin. Slipping my hand around her waist, my fingers tingling against her soft flesh, I pulled her close, dipping my head to kiss her fully on the mouth.

Her lips were soft and sweet, a startlingly pleasant contrast to male lips, and without the onslaught of hair growth to scrape my cheeks. I savored the taste of them, alternating between pressing them against mine and licking each one slowly. She parted her lips, offering her soft, moist tongue to meet my own. I took it in my mouth and sucked on it, gently, almost as if I were sucking on a man's penis. For the first time, she moaned softly into my mouth as I had heard her moan earlier, and all the blood in my body seemed to rush to one pounding, throbbing area.

"Oh, God," I murmured against her lips.

"Umm," she responded, her mouth covering mine hungrily, sending dizzying waves of pleasure down my spine. I tightened my arm under her neck and slipped my other hand down past her waist, exploring the soft skin on the small of her back with my fingertips. Recalling what I had seen my roommate do earlier, I slid my hand down onto her buttock, how smooth and cool, so unlike a man's, and attempted to pull her hips into mine.

She tightened her muscles, preventing me from doing so, and removed her lips. "What do you want?" Her voice was husky. "Tell me."

I was reeling with lust. I had to try my voice twice before it worked. "You didn't come. In there. Did you?"

I thought I felt her smile. "No."

"That's what I want," I whispered.

"What?" she teased me.

She wasn't going to let me off the hook. I wanted her so badly my whole body vibrated with liquid fire. I was terrified of the magnitude of my desire, but it paled in comparison to the terror I felt at the possibility of her slipping out of my bed as easily as she had slipped in. "I . . ."

She stroked my cheek with soft fingertips. "It's okay," she murmured. "Just close your eyes and let it out."

My eyes were squeezed shut so tightly I saw stars. "I want to make you come," I managed, with no small effort.

"Oh, yes," she breathed and slid her thigh over mine, wrapping her knee around my leg, using it to pull the lower half of my body over her own. I rose slightly so that she could move closer to the center of the bed, returning my tongue with great relief into her mouth, then shifted most of my weight onto her.

She sighed with pleasure and ran her hands down my back, gripping, then massaging, my buttocks. Resting on my elbows, I placed my hands on either side of her head and stroked her hair back away from her face.

As I licked and sucked on her lips, I spread my legs so that one was in between hers and the other one rested to her side. I felt her moist warmth on my thigh and, in turn, rubbed myself against hers. Her fingers tightened on my buttocks and she breathed hard into my mouth. I drank in her sweet breath and plunged my tongue deep into her mouth, exploring every recess.

She murmured unintelligible syllables around my tongue. I slipped my hands down around her neck and forced her head gently up. Showering kisses over her chin, I moved downward, kissing and licking her neck. I began to nibble gently in the curve between her neck and shoulders and she drew a sharp breath, her hips bucking just slightly under me. I took the hint and bit on her neck a little harder, not nearly hard enough to draw blood, but enough to elicit deep guttural moans that sent shivers down my spine.

I continued to bite and suck at her soft flesh as she rolled her hips underneath me. I tried to shift slightly with each roll, attempting to position myself so that our pelvises would be grinding together. I wanted nothing more than to be pressed against that heat, lips against lips, maybe even separated enough for those tiny knobs of flesh to slide against each other. But I didn't even know if that was possible, and I couldn't seem to get the right angle. I gave it up for the time being and drew my outside leg in between hers, sliding her thighs apart.

I moved downward on her body, trailing kisses from her shoulder to her upper chest, pausing when I reached the swell of a breast. My blood pounded as I let my hands slide from around her neck and down her chest. I traced circles around her breasts with one finger as I had done to myself earlier that night, which now seemed like an eternity ago, another time in another place. She trembled, and in the dim light I saw her nipples grow erect, the areolae tightening into tiny wrinkles around the hard little nubs.

Gently, I flicked my tongue and brushed her nipple with the tip. She arched her back slightly and gripped my upper arms. I licked her nipple again, more fully, with the flat of my tongue, and she moaned and pushed her pelvis up into my stomach. Her wet curls tickled the taut skin over my ribs. I began to suck, gently and eagerly, on her nipple and felt a rush of relief so great that I was afraid tears would spill over my cheeks onto her warm skin.

As she drew a sharp breath, I tugged harder on her breast with my lips, my tongue massaging the hard knot. I placed my hand flat on her other breast, squeezing the nipple between two fingers in a soft scissorlike motion. She breathed hard and fast through her nose, muffled moans audible through tightly closed lips. Oh, God, I was in heaven. I moved easily from one nipple to the other, pausing often to circle her entire breast either with tongue or fingers, not wanting to miss so much as a millimeter of her skin, relishing the goose bumps I encountered at every turn.

Somewhere in the back of my mind I was beginning to wonder if I was going to be able to follow through with what was inevitably going to come next, when she made that decision for me. Unabashedly, she slid her hands from my upper arms to my shoulders and gave me a firm push downward.

Trailing kisses down her ribcage and stomach, I veered to one side and licked the warm, slightly wet skin of her hip and thigh. Her thick, musky scent filled my nostrils as I rested my cheek on her thigh, so close that her hair tickled my nose. I ran my hand down and then up her opposite leg, sliding it onto her inner thigh on the return approach. She trembled as my fingers slowed to a crawl, tracing my fingernails over the last firm curve of her thigh and stopping.

Closing my eyes, I reached inward until my fingers brushed her damp hair. I pulled softly on the ends, wrapping it gently around my fingertips before letting it go. I curved my hand slightly, covered her so that her hair brushed my palm and the insides of my fingertips. I moved my hand upward and touched her skin under her belly where the hair began. Without lifting my fingers from her skin, I slipped downward, pressing the curls down in my path.

I kept my eyes closed, knowing her because she was me. I knew where the mound of flesh covering her pelvic bone began before I reached it because I knew myself. I kept my palm curved over the rest of her as I continued down, and reached the spot where the skin began to part. I pressed gently and split my fingers to follow both halves down. Finally, I slipped my fingers in between, teasing back toward the top.

I found her there, the center of her, moist and engorged, and I brushed it lightly with my fingertips. She moaned then, earnest and loud, and I almost paused, then gave my conscience a swift kick. I wanted her loud, ear-shattering, unheeding. I pressed her clitoris firmly, knowing exactly what to do, and felt her body jerk. Using two fingers, I moved in slow circles, the way I liked it done to myself. Her hips began to rock gently in response.

My own body was on fire. Blood pulsed into my clit, causing a delicious frustration. I moved my head closer, just slightly, so that my lips brushed the side of her labia. One of her hands snaked into my hair and established a firm grip near the base of my skull. Dizzy with lust, I licked the crevice between her thigh and her labia, and she gasped. I slipped my fingers down and found the slick wetness. I parted her lips with three fingers and rubbed them all around, soaking them, and slid all three of them up to moisten the rest of her.

I lifted my head from her thigh, just an inch or two, and rolled the lower half of my body over and down. My knees hit the floor and my thighs were flat against the side of the bed. I was able to press myself against the mattress, relieving some frustration yet creating even more. I spread her labia apart with my three fingers and, with my middle finger, began to probe. Rather than pushing my finger inside, I felt as though it were being pulled in. She was slick and tight, and I moved my finger in circles as wide as I could, exploring.

Her fingers tightened in my hair, almost pulling, as she tried to force my head down. I allowed her to push me into her. My lips found her first, and I showered her with open kisses. I pressed my mouth around her clitoris and licked her, slowly. I ran my tongue in wet circles, sometimes soft, sometimes firm. I kept my finger inside her, not thrusting, just holding it firm against the top wall.

The moans came again, and didn't stop, but punctuated every breath. I licked her steadily and rubbed myself against the mattress in rhythm. Her hips rolled against my face, and I pressed harder into her with my hand to hold her still. I gave up licking and began to suck on her clitoris. Her moans came from parted lips now, fuller and more vocal.

Without warning, she gripped my hair hard, pulling my head up, and sat up in one quick motion, forcing my hand away before I knew what had happened. I stared at her, my face wet, my blood pounding. Her hair was in spiky disarray and her chest heaved. Finally releasing my hair, she grasped my hands and pulled me up. I half-climbed, half-slipped onto the bed, and before I knew whether she wanted me to sit or lie down, she was kissing me hungrily, licking her own wetness off of my lips and chin. She forced her tongue into my mouth and I sucked on it.

In a blur of arms, legs, and mouths she had me lying on my back and she was on top of me, her knees bent, one of my legs in between hers, the other up over her hip. She slid herself up into me and I gasped into her mouth as her labia covered mine. She rocked steadily, pressing her pelvic bone into me. I felt her clitoris slide against mine and we moaned together, grinding harder into each other.

The bed rocked with us. Somewhere far away I heard the headboard knocking against the wall. I took her breasts in my hands and squeezed her nipples as she filled my mouth with her tongue. Her movement was erratic, desperate, and I raised my hips farther off the bed to help her continue the rhythm. Her heat was almost unbearable. All at once, her body started to tremble and her moans turned to cries. She bucked her hips against mine, coming hard into me. Almost immediately, I followed her lead, my orgasm a spectacular explosion, longer and harder than anything I could remember.

As our rhythm gradually subsided, she collapsed on top of me, breathing hard into my mouth, her legs slowly stretching out. My leg dropped from her hip and we lay sprawled, spent and stunned.

Rolling off of me, she rested against my side, one arm gently tossed over my waist. I looked at her, mouth open, chest heaving, skin glistening. Her eyes, heavy-lidded, met mine for a moment, and I kissed her damp forehead. I realized that I was exhausted, and she looked ready to doze off, so I pushed myself up, with great effort, to grab the one last corner of the sheet still clinging to the foot of the bed, and lay back, pulling it over us. Immediately, she curled into me, resting her head on my shoulder.

I lay on my back, one arm under her neck, one thrown over my head. A slight noise made me look at my doorway.

In a sliver of faint light emanating from his room, my room-mate stood, still naked, his penis engorged, one hand on the doorjamb and the other holding my door half open. Our eyes met for a moment. His were a confused mixture of stunned and aroused. Perhaps entertaining one last, egotistical notion of being invited into bed with both of us.

Possessively, I rolled toward her, turning my back to him, wrapping my other arm over her. Her eyes closed, she snuggled into me, sliding one thigh in between mine. After a long, tense moment, I heard his footsteps retreating into his room, as he closed his door behind him. Finally. Knowing.

The Welcome Home

Saskia Walker

When the phone rang she wandered over slowly, pacing herself, and let her hand rest over the receiver. The vibrations pulsed gently up her arm, humming over each nerve ending, drawing every fiber of her being toward its call. Before she lifted it from its nest, she pictured him snuggling inside the phone booth, waiting for her to answer. He wasn't going to hang up; he knew she was there, just waiting for him to call.

It was always like this when he was traveling. His work took him away at least once a month, and their reunions were something to look forward to. They were anticipated, deliberate, and passionate encounters. They never merely settled for the hurried coupling of reunited lovers. Instead, they pursued the drawing together of separation, reunion, and new discoveries; they elicited each step of that very special journey from one another with careful deliberation. Revealing their passions for each other, slowly, they built its joint fires to fever pitch, intentionally, until finally, within its heat, they melded their lives back together.

He was phoning her from the airport. With grace and charm he invited her out, on a date. She accepted. He suggested they meet at a cocktail bar and then head on to a little Cantonese restaurant he knew. He spoke to her as if it were the first time he had ever suggested a rendezvous.

He made his plans when he was away from their shared space. When he flew in he would send his bags to the office, unburdening himself of the material evidence of their time apart. The first time he had done it, she had been expecting him at home for a quiet long weekend. Instead, he had telephoned her and requested she put a few things in a bag. Then he collected her and took her to a rambling cottage in the countryside that he had rented for the weekend. They made love in every one of the rooms before they left the place. Another time they had simply met at a cinema and she had lost the plot of the film halfway through, as his hand on her thigh had gently stroked her whole body into a fever of longing.

They never ran out of ideas for each other. On his previous return home she had phoned his office to find out when he would be flying in. She deviated again, from their nonroutine, by waiting for him at the airport. When he walked through the gate she noted his purposeful stride with pleasure. He wanted to get to her; her body throbbed with desire and anticipation. As he drew close to the place where she stood, she turned and walked out in front of him, heading toward the exit. When the heat of his eyes had fallen over her, she slowed her steps and dropped her bag. As she bent to pick it up and rescue the bottle of scent that rolled across the floor, he bent alongside her and offered to help. As she glanced at his blue-gray eyes, sparkling at her from beneath the straight line of his brows, she returned his knowing smile.

They walked on, together, discussing the weather, anticipation crackling between them. He was eyeing the full cotton skirt that swung over her thighs as she walked. She offered him a lift to his destination. He accepted and followed where she led. She had parked the car in a darkened corner of the multistory car park. When he climbed inside, he leaned over her, pushed up her skirt, and sank his mouth into the naked warmth of her sex. His sudden movement drew her sudden relinquishment. Her legs fell apart, her sex throbbing. The desire she felt for him ran hot and sweet on his tongue. She had never come so quickly.

After his call beckoned to her this time, she bathed and dressed with care and attention. She ordered a taxi; it wasn't far, but it was about to rain. As usual, she added some new dimension to her look, displaying some new aspect of her personality that she had not revealed to him before, even after years together. Tonight she wore a new choker against her throat. Black suede, with a small silver chain hanging in the center, some two inches wide. It rocked against her throat when she walked into the bar; his eyes followed it as it touched her skin.

He stood up, lifted his travel coat from the stool beside his, and gestured to it. They didn't embrace. Their greeting was restricted to the gentle cheek kiss of new friends becoming lovers. He held the brief breath of her scent in his lungs as she settled onto the stool he had reserved for her. She smoothed her black satin dress over her thighs as she crossed one leg over the other. He watched her movements. He knew she was naked beneath the dress, she rarely wore underwear when they met like this. Once she had, but that was part of the surprise. As he glanced down at her breasts, he saw that her nipples pressed their full outline into the soft fabric. Her only other covering was the choker at her neck and the black suede shoes that let her polished toenails peep back at his enquiring eyes.

They talked as if they knew very little of one another, concentrating on the time they had been apart, the desire that gap had left weighting each word, each statement. Their conversation was meaningful, laced with hidden needs, the pain of being apart drawn, slowly, into the pleasure of their forthcoming reunion. As they walked to the nearby restaurant they maintained the distance of friendship, finally closing together as they crossed the road, his arm beneath hers; the physical arousal of contact grew more tangible. They each knew, and understood, the pleasure in anticipation. They savored it, each and every morsel.

She asked him to order for her. She couldn't think of food, she was hungry most of all for him. She watched as he spoke to the waitress, and the young girl laughed over his comments about chopsticks. He was so attractive and charming, and she was so in love with him; sometimes it made her feel totally incompetent. He swept his dark blond hair back in his hands. It wasn't long, but in need of a cut, teasing the edge of his collar. He liked it that way, and so did she. It fell forward again, as he turned back to her. It was difficult to stop themselves sliding into the familiar, but it was a challenge not to. It led to a sort of awkwardness between them, akin to that felt on a first date.

She watched his fingers rolling a spoon back and forth across the tablecloth between them, as she listened to his description of the cities he had visited when he had been away. He mentioned their lonely streets as he looked deep into her eyes.

They folded Peking duck pancakes for one another and he

noticed how well she looked, but didn't comment on it. Her skin glowed with a light tan, she must have been spending time in the patio garden tending her cacti collection, while he had been away. As she described the photo shoot she was working on, he focused on her elegantly dressed hair. It was swept up against her head, and reminded him of the time he had phoned her and simply given her a room number and the location of an out-of-town motel. She had arrived in a Grace Kelly dress and fifties-style sunglasses, a fuchsia scarf wound round her head and throat. She had looked so elegant he couldn't bring himself to touch her. He had lain on the bed, his arms folded behind his head, as she unwound the scarf from the dark chestnut tresses hidden beneath the vivid pink chiffon.

The light from the red lanterns of the restaurant sent a sheen across the silken surface of her hair as she moved her head. Her hands wove the shapes and patterns of her image-plans from her mind, into the space between them; sharing her ideas with him. He absorbed her again: her mind, her physical presence. How he had longed for the touch of those hands on his body when he had been away.

He obviously hadn't shaved since that morning; she noticed the dark shadow of stubble on his chin and reached for her glass, to distract herself from the desire to stroke it. She twisted the glass by its stem, then skimmed its edge with one finger while he watched and her words faded into the silent need between them. She ached to have him inside her. He picked up the sliver of duck that remained on the dish and tore at it with his teeth. She crossed her legs higher on the thigh.

The main dish arrived. He had ordered Green Jade and Red Coral; he knew the fusion of broccoli and crab would appeal to her artist's eye and her taste buds. When he asked for her dessert suggestion, she turned to the waitress and requested lichees in syrup, for his sweet tooth. He gave her an accusing glance, his eyes twinkling, and she hid her response by touching her napkin over her mouth. They barely maintained the self-inflicted distance, taunting each other with their knowledge, while feigning innocence. When they sat over coffee, he asked if he could escort her home. With a downcast of her eyes and a gentle smile, she accepted his gentlemanly offer.

She let her gaze linger on him across the backseat of the

taxi. He looked out at the passing streets, the rain blurring and distorting his view of the city. He was wearing a linen shirt, white. It glowed in the darkness against the charcoal gray of his long raincoat. How she adored his chameleon nature. Tonight he was like a puma dressed in a man's clothing. His animal sexuality was disguised in fine manners and entrancing words, but it was visible to her nonetheless. As this thought occurred to her they sped past the city zoo and she smiled into the night.

Once he had called for her at the house by taxi and they had gone to the zoo. It was spring and all the animals were in pursuit of one another. After they got home, they had made love all night. As they drove alongside the entrance gates he was smiling too, remembering how wild she had been. The animal in them both lurked, just beneath their groomed surfaces.

They got out of the taxi and he lifted his coat over their heads, to protect them both from the rain shower that fell over them. By the time they had run the path to the doorway, the coat was drenched. She was laughing, breathless; he beginning to quiet, his desires simmering, in check.

The door closed behind them and his coat fell back into place. They stood in the gloom of the hallway, their breathing fast, but out of sync. As it slowed, it synchronized. The tide of longing between them could not be held back much longer. They walked to the bedroom, in unison. In silence. They closed another door behind them, standing against it, locking themselves into one another's space. A quick glance around the room showed him she had arranged a new cover on the bed; dark red velvet, printed over with a raised rose pattern, her favorite. It was good to be home, but he tried not to be distracted from her by the comfort of it.

She stayed close to him, breathing in the sharp musk of his body. He smiled at her, his mouth in that familiar curl. She smiled in return, but dropped her eyes from the familiar, to the newness of the fresh white linen over the skin of his chest. His fingers closed into the chain that hung from the suede at her neck. He tugged gently on it, caressing its newness. She brushed her hand down the linen of his shirt, felt the familiar outline of his chest through the crisp material, smiling still, as her fingers wound their way around each new, tight button. They addressed the newness that they found in one another, in a meeting of eyes.

He brushed his lips over hers, a tentative kiss that ran electric over her skin. He drew back when he felt its charge. Her expression showed how hungry she was for more. After a moment, he reached into his coat pocket and drew out a CD. Without taking her eyes from his, and without a blink of surprise, she accepted the disc from his hand. She turned from him and walked over to the niche in the wall, to one side of the bed, that housed the stereo. As the new disc nestled into its well and slid discreetly inside the player, she breathed determinedly into the interlude, keeping herself in check, waiting for the sounds to begin.

She undid her hair and let it fall over her shoulders as the first notes chimed out from the speakers. The music began gently, caressing her. It was a remix of a familiar song; seductive, intimate. She absorbed its rhythms, immersing herself into them. He stayed fixed against the door, watching her. She walked over to the bedside lamp and reached through the trailing filigree of beads that hung from its shade. A warm orange glow spread out through the clinging strands that stirred against the back of her hand. Their lingering brush on her skin seemed to brush against his own skin. His hips flexed. His hand slid along the wall and he switched off the main light, immersing them in the soft orange light of the lamp.

As she walked back to him she reached up and began to undo the zipper on her dress. Seeing him standing in the shadows by the door, she paused in the middle of the room. His look was so intense, the fire he felt for her was glowing in his eyes. Their strange grayness reflected the combination of leashed physical desires and freed fantasies. His gaze fell to her red gloss toenails, as she slid them slowly out of their suede casing. Her naked feet pushed the abandoned shoes to one side and then the black satin dropped, like a glossy shield, vanishing away from her skin. She began to move sensuously, slowly following the undressing into the rhythms of the music, her hips swaying, her spine curving. As the black coating slid into a pool of oil on the floor, her hands flowed over her body and she writhed under them, her eyelids falling, her lips parting, her breath being drawn in, audibly.

Her body glowed luminescent in the darkness, a halo of light behind her, caressing its voluptuous curves. She was following the path of the sound, moving back and forth in small spirals. She let the sounds seduce her senses, unfolding herself into the music he had carried with him and offered to her. He leaned his back against the door, watching her still, an undeniable smile teasing the corners of his mouth. He had known the suggestive intimacy of the music, its sensuality, would draw on her like this.

He caught her eye, and nodded his approval. She came closer, her eyes heavy with arousal and suggestion. Her mouth opened and she breathed in time with the music, her expression taunting him to follow her. Her naked skin brushed gently against the surface of his coat; the wetness still lying on its surface leached itself to her, sheening over her skin. She moved against him, a gauzy touch through his coat, until he began to move his hand to touch her, then she stepped away. His hand fell through space as she stepped back through the sounds, toward the bed.

When she touched against its surface, the soft coverings gave against her legs and she felt the resistance of the surface beneath. It was like the hardness of his body, beneath the covering of his clothes. Unable to stop herself, she turned again and moved back to him. Turning her back against his body, she moved up and down; her back against his chest, her hair sliding up against the side of his face. Strands of it caught against the shadow of stubble on his chin.

A quiet moan escaped her at the feeling of his contained tension against her rippling body. He did not try to touch her this time, but closed his eyes and felt her movements, the swaying of her flesh against his, the promise of her rhythms building the energies within him.

She snaked up against the line of his body, slowly moving in against him, her head going back against his shoulder, then she stepped slightly away, leaving a painful distance of mere inches between them. The strands of her hair that clung to his beard seemed to transfer the electricity between them. He automatically descended, his mouth ready to close over the gap, to brush across her shoulders. His warm breath hovered over her skin and she cried out, instinct taking over; her body flicked itself back against his, in demand. He rested his mouth against her warm nape, the pungent smell of her desire rose through the exotic flowers that overlaid her skin. He drew his head back to rest against the hard surface of the door, his eyes shut, his mouth closed in a determined line. But his hands locked around her hipbones, drawing her hips in against his.

She uttered a low captured sound, then moved again, within his grip. He moved with her, his hips thrusting forward; their bodies slowly following the rhythms that stirred out from the stereo toward them. She pressed herself up against him, her head falling forward, her hair tumbling over her shoulder. Their locked bodies pivoted against the door. He looked at the line of her neck as the hollow of her sex moved against his clothes, against his hardness. He lifted one hand to trace the indentations of her spine, swaying with her as she rippled in his grasp. His touch was too heavenly. She drew away suddenly and crawled onto the bed.

She rolled onto her back, against its giving surface, her body sleek and lissome as a cat, rippling over the velvet bedcover. It closed in ruches around her body, like knots of desire seeking to capture her movement. He wanted to do the same. He was frozen to the door. He knew that if he allowed himself to move, he would be unleashed; then he would have to claim her, thoroughly. He tried to restrain himself a moment longer, as she unveiled her desires to him.

She drew her knees up, her feet on the bed, exposing her soft inner thighs and her sex to him; her hands roved over her hipbones and then rode over her breasts in deep caresses. She was showing him the desires she had felt in his absence, releasing them from her body, offering them for him to claim back as his own. Her moans of need were building, her sight of him fading as the desire inside her clouded her perceptions. It was so potent, it weighed heavily, an insistent need. Soon, it had to be soon. And yet, he waited. They were torturing each and every ounce of anticipation from one another.

Her fingers stole into her open mouth, running against her full lower lip, she traced a damp path over the skin of her throat, then they traveled between her breasts and down to nestle against the darkness of her pubic hair. Her hand clenched over the soft fullness of her flesh and she turned her face into the pillow, her eyes closing, mouth open. The veiled sensations that flew out from her own grip were too divine, they spread like liquid fire over her pelvis, moving fast, then sinking slowly, deep inside her body. She wanted him to do the same.

The tension emanating from the place where he stood was equal, yet opposite, to that flowing forth from her body on the bed. Her thighs fell wider apart and he watched as her fingers sank into the folds of her sex, her fingers slicking against the moisture inside her. As her fingers moved deeper, and her spine curled to allow them to explore her wetness, his body seethed its response. He wanted to drown in her wetness, he wanted wave after wave of her body to overcome his.

He stepped forward from the darkness, moving through the luxurious rhythms of the music, toward her. She was following the path of her desires in regular strokes when she felt his coat brush against her legs. He leaned over her body, his hands on either side of her hips on the bed. Their eyes met; the music spoke to some innate force within them, while their expressions told one another of urgency and passion. His fingers held her by the choker on her neck as he bent to kiss her mouth. Her hands flew into claws over his shoulders, her teeth tugging gently on his lips as he kissed her.

He whispered softly against her throat, soothing her, before he moved to take the coat off. But she leaned up, her eyes frantic, and held it on his shoulders, gripping it at the collar, drawing him down to her quickly. He smiled and whispered his pleasure as his body sank against hers; the hardness of his belt, and that which was withheld by it, pressing against her. She cried out when she felt the pressure of his erection through his trousers, and her hips flexed and pressed demandingly against it.

He stripped open his belt and she writhed beneath him as he revealed the key that would unlock her. Her breath passed shallow and erratic over her parted lips as she took it into her hand and stroked it. Its potent vitality was smooth, hot, and rigid and she caressed it in adoring strokes, before leading it to the heat that awaited it inside her. When the firm wet warmth of her sex gave beneath him, he followed where it led, and ploughed deep within her.

His body rode up against her, taking her to the core. The clothes that he had worn as he traveled back to her imprinted themselves against her body, while the hard shaft of his naked flesh bowed inside her. Their pubic hair merged, the dark shadow of their animal origins, entwining together. Her legs slid up around him, pushing the coat back from his hips as she wrestled him deeper.

When his penis touched against that place where she had longed for the pressure of his body, her eyelids lowered over the sensation, her mouth releasing the intense pleasure in sound. The muscle of her sex closed in a fierce embrace, her body moving urgently beneath him. His breath caught, his desire to escape inside her and reclaim her, unleashed, as he gasped for air again. Pinning her flexing body down to the bed with his hands, he probed inside her, fierce and frantic, his heavy damp coat brushing over her skin in time with his thrusts. She fought him for the escape, her body moving against his, the hands that held her down making her wilder still.

He was animal; enclosed into a space he wanted to overcome, desperate for freedom, he roared back and forth inside the captive space. Her hips forged up against his, meeting each thrust, her hands grappling themselves free to clutch at his body. The release of pent-up passion raced her through sensation after sensation, like wildfires crossing the plains. They each sought to outpace the fire, but it was close behind them, closing on them with each stride. It beat against his back as she clutched at his body, fistfuls of his coat pulled from his back in her grip. He roared as the flames leapt up, rode through his body, and fired into hers, taking his strength and resistance from him. He fell into its release. His mouth rested against hers, breathing in her strangled breaths, as she rode the back of her orgasm.

Her body bowed up beneath him, her limbs arched. Her hips pressed harder, manipulating her pelvis against him as the fire sent waves of molten heat into the flesh of her sex. She was in the grip of its heat, her body taking what it needed for its fulfillment. As the feeling of weight descended from her womb, and the final spasms of heat rippled through her sex, freeing her from its grip, she drew his body closer against her, holding him lovingly in her arms.

He clung to her, his body nestled against hers, their limbs softly entwined. After a while she drew back and slowly undressed him, removing the traces of their time apart. Like any other semidomesticated animal, once he was freed, he wanted to return to his sanctuary and he watched and waited until he could be close to her again. Naked, their bodies closed together, their skins molded as one again.

"Welcome home, my love," she whispered.

Guest of Honor

RENATE STENDHAL

I threw the rope over the cornerstone in my usual fashion and hoisted myself onto the balcony. Her door was half open, allowing me to slide through without moving it. I slipped between the curtains.

She was standing in front of her mirror, her back and waist almost delicate in contrast to her elaborate powdered wig and crinoline skirt. She was humming to herself, twisting and turning her shoulders, her brocade bodice. I knew she was going through her repertoire. Her skirt bounced and swished like a punctuation mark to every movement she made. Did she know she wasn't alone in her room? She folded her hands behind her back. The corners of her mouth betrayed her approval as she arched her body and watched her powdered breasts struggle against her bodice.

In a noiseless leap I appeared behind her in the mirror, immobilized her hands behind her back. Her pretty lips opened to a sound that anyone else might have mistaken for shock. I knew my Angèle. I promenaded my gaze from her eyes to her cleavage with the smile of an accomplice. She leaned against me as though to attest, yes, she had been caught, she was at my mercy. But I would be merciful, wouldn't I, her gray eyes tried to dictate.

"My faithless angel," I threatened into her ear, holding her gaze in the mirror. I let her watch my hands reach up under her bosom and slowly force her bodice down. The pale crescents of her nipples rose over the horizon of the brocade. Her eyes darkened.

"Who is this for, my angel? Tell me."

Even before I brushed a fingertip, light as a powder puff, across the horizon, she had closed her eyes. I stopped. I needed her eyes to know if she was lying to me. She peeked at me through her lashes. A frown announced that she was growing annoyed. All of a sudden she took me in. Wide-eyed, she managed to leap aside and leave me to myself in the mirror.

"You are dressed up? You are NOT invited!" She glared at me, trying at the same time to take in as much of me as she could.

"I'm still going to be there. And in a costume that won't go unnoticed, wouldn't you say, *chérie*?" I turned and twisted in front of the mirror the way she had. A powdered dandy, white from top to toes. I adjusted a curl on my wig, beat the lace ruffles of my sleeves into place before tucking my hand in my hip, my legs in kneepants crossed to perfection. "Doesn't your ardent lover cast a figure worth being the guest of honor at your *fiançailles*?"[1]

Her face was torn between desire and disgust. "If you make a scandal it's all over." She threw up her chin. "I warned you. If you spoil this you will never see me again."

"Spoil it? I? Hasn't it already been spoiled? By Monsieur the Count—or is it Monsieur the Accountant? Monsieur with only the literal *bourse bien pleine*[2] while his other one, between you and me, will hardly count. . . ." I rotated my hips in derision. She continued staring me up and down as though unable to decide whether she was beholding a dream or a devil.

"You are mad!" She stormed out of the room before I could stop her. I grabbed her mask from her dressing table and raced after her, down the flight of stairs. The servants wouldn't recognize me. A dandy chasing after a lady, holding up his trophy, the lady's pearl-and-feather mask. It would be seen as no more than a frivolous game.

She banged a door shut and turned a key, but I caught up with her from the opposite direction, through the library. I found her pressed against the door, panting, arms spread as though to protect her feast. We looked at each other across the banquet table, laid out with the finest china, silver, crystal,

[1]Engagement.
[2]Well-filled purse; allusion to a man's endowment.

flower arrangements. Set for a good thirty people, I gauged. For everyone but her inadmissible passion, the impossible lover, the pariah. Me.

"Leave," she commanded. "Or I'll call for George."

"Yes, let's call for George." I approached. "I'll take off my wig and present myself properly. As the one with the most legitimate claim to your incandescent body."

"Please." She suddenly threw herself into my arms. I was expecting tears. "*Mon amour.* I love you. Please control yourself. Nothing will change between us, I promise. You can't marry me. Even if you wanted to. Would you really ruin your life over a dinner party?"

I considered. "I just want to be there. You will surely agree that I need to see it with my own eyes. How else could I believe it?"

"You will be thrown out, you'd better believe that. It would be a shame for your—"

"Reputation? You are too concerned about me, my angel. Isn't it rather your reputation that we should worry about, in case of a scandal?"

She let go of me with a scornful laugh. There were steps in the hallway, shouts, the clapping of hands.

"George is lining up the servants. You have one minute." Her chin pointed to the exit, through the library. I did not move. "*Tant pis alors.*[3] Stay and let George take care of you."

She undulated down the table, trailing her hand across the backs of the chairs. "Nobody will believe you," she challenged. "You know it perfectly well. Because you *are* unbelievable."

I was impressed with her *maîtrise.*[4] She looked more desirable than ever pretending to be cold, her eyes flashing with anger.

"There is room, you realize, for an extra plate at your table. For a surprise guest, let's say, an old friend of yours. Say anything you like. Could you have forgotten that I am always anything you like, and how much you like it?"

I could tell my words made a mark but she straightened her dress with determination.

"All I'd like you to be is *air.*"

---

[3]Too bad for you then.
[4]Control, mastery.

In the hall, George could be heard giving final directions. In the courtyard, a first carriage approached. Twirling her mask around on its stick, I pretended to walk out through the library. When I passed her, I fell to my knees, grabbed her hand, kissed her palm, dug my teeth into its center.

"Air I'll be. I won't be seen, I promise. Just let me be there, somewhere. Hide me."

She withdrew her hand as the door flung open. I ducked, protected from view by the table. I heard the servants line up at the door to take her orders. In a moment's inspiration, I lifted the hem of her dress and slipped under it, fast as a thievish cat.

"*Très bien.*[5] We will need to . . . Make sure everything is as it is supposed to be," she decreed.

"*Oui, Madame.*"

I clung to her legs for dear life. As long as I was where I found myself, everything was indeed as it was supposed to be.

"First of all, make sure the doors and windows to the garden are all open and fixed. No banging, *s'il vous plaît.*"[6]

I heard the rush of steps. Was she going to walk me to the garden and shake her dress out? I would not let her shake me out. I was determined to exert whatever control I had over her legs. I was just starting to enjoy the prospects of this position, when her skirt went up. I felt the shock of air and exposure, but in the next moment, she lifted the tablecloth, opening a discreet tunnel from one hideaway to another. I obliged on my knees, blowing her a kiss for the compromise with which she had saved herself. Through clenched teeth, she abandoned me to my destiny:

"*Faites vos jeux.*"[7]

I regretted losing my first hiding place, its comparative safety. She was going to leave the room, leave me alone with her servants. I heard her call one of them, Jean, and demand that he personally serve her at the banquet. She adjusted the chair at the head of the table as though to mark her place for me. Was she worried, in case I needed to rush under cover again, that I would pick the wrong skirt?

I made myself as comfortable as I could under my square

[5] Very well.
[6] Please.
[7] Place your bets; announcement at the roulette table.

tent. I stretched out on the solid center support of the table. It was high enough above ground to be hidden from a casual glance. I watched the lacquered shoes of the servants shuffle and pirouette around me. The thought that Angèle was worrying about my position inspired me. Should misfortune lead to an early discovery by the servants, I plotted to pronounce myself a gift, a surprise performance arranged by *monsieur le fiancé* for his beloved. But if the discovery were to happen during the banquet? In case someone insisted on retrieving, say, a potato gone overboard? Nobody would be more surprised than Monsieur. Probably Angèle's ill-famed great-aunt Maude would make a better story. Great-aunt Maude had exiled herself to Britain with an actor at the scandalous age of fifty-one. It would be just like her to arrange for a pantomime, a mock homage to marital happiness, as an engagement present for her great-niece.

One of the servants kept watch at the window, announcing who was arriving with whom, in what kind of a carriage, in what state of dress. There were ohs and ahs, snides and sniggers. Their observations provided me a vivid picture of the party.

The chamber orchestra in the adjacent room began to play and the flock entered in procession. The lacquered shoes finally took position, pair by pair, behind the chairs. I was impressed, to say the least, with the noise, the screeching of chairs, the number of knees and feet pushing in on me at once. Fortunately the table was broad. I would not be a likely target for the shorter legs. For more protection I could cower between the vertical posts of two cross-sections that ran perpendicular to the center support of the table. One of these comparatively safe barricades was situated at the feet of my enemy, the fiancé, the other one close to my ultimate salvation, the skirt of Angèle.

While wine and water were served, I amused myself with the fantasy of not knowing where she was seated or how she was dressed, and having to closely examine all the ladies' extremities in order to find her. . . . I noticed how many satin slippers got dropped almost as soon as the intake of soup began. Food was clearly bringing some desire for expansion, even extravagance, to the party. I watched one of those liberated little feet come to the encounter of an elegant brocade shoe only one chair away. The small foot explored the shoe and its inhabitant until it found a gap between the brocade and the arch, and slid its toes into the gap. A gentle wrestling match ensued that held my attention with the question whether the adventurous little foot was trying to strip its object of desire or if it was determined to fit into the same shoe. I was burning to peek up from under my tent to find out who the two daredevils might be that were so conveniently placed side by side at the table. In other circumstances, would I have suspected Angèle?

The hostess's feet, I noted, were still properly dressed. They were advancing in slow, probing movements along the floor and circling in midair. Having left me behind, she could not be sure about my whereabouts. I gave her time to wonder. The second course was being served, *Feuilleté à la Reine*,[8] as I could tell by that smell I loathe. I cat-walked along the center support to get a close look at my rival. On my way, I passed a pair of widespread, massive legs in pants so tight that the hairy hand of their owner had to relieve the itching apparatus in between. I knew this must be Uncle Edouard, the old hunter of all kinds of beasts. By comparison, the future husband's treasure appeared rather lost in its cage, a bird without feathers, not to speak of wings. I returned with a mixture of pity and rage.

Climbing back over Uncle Edouard, I was careful to avoid a kick that might have catapulted me straight into some questionable lap across from him. The two naughty feet were still at it. The small foot had usurped the brocade shoe, forcing its owner into the role of the attacker in order to reclaim it. The eagerness of their wrestling made me wonder about their owners' composure at their plates.

Meanwhile, a number of shoes had been left alone by feet searching for comfort of all kinds. Those who had not found a partner were kneading each other or the wood of the table, caressing the buckles and buttons of the shoes they had escaped, or lying innocently folded up on the floor, toe against toe, as if in prayer. It was time to liberate Angèle's feet.

I barricaded myself between the posts of the cross-section near the hostess and drew her mask out of my pocket. I let its crowning feather play along the rim of her slippers. The speed

[8]Queen's Pie.

with which she kicked them off might have been called inde-
cent. She was wearing her thinnest silk stockings, and I sent my
feather on a promenade across her soles and toes. I noticed a
little silence at her end of the table, then her father's voice:

"Does the wine make you sleepy, dear?"

I grinned to myself. The dear must have forgotten herself for
a moment and closed her eyes.

"Oh, I was just remembering . . . a lovely day in the Bois de
Boulogne . . . the day I first set eyes on—" She didn't pronounce
his name. It wasn't necessary. Everyone raised their glasses:

"To Hugo!"

I knew she was referring to our first encounter. I encouraged
her memory of me by lifting her skirts out of the way and
slowly, deliberately untying the silk ribbons that gathered her
wide, ruffled underpants in above her ankles.

"What happened, Angie? Tell, tell!"

I recognized her nosy thirteen-year-old cousin Lucille.

"I was driving to the races. This elegant rider came up from
behind, rode alongside my carriage, and suddenly threw a rose
into my lap."

I wished I could repeat my debut performance right at this
moment, coming up from behind her with a rose in my teeth. I
came up with a few nostalgic bites on her heels.

"How charming. . . ."

"What an encounter. . . ."

"Right into your lap?" Lucille wanted to know.

"Well-aimed." Angèle laughed her throaty laugh. "A rose
white as snow. But that was only the first time. It happened
again. The next Sunday, it was a pink rose. Then, the third—"

"Haha! Now we know your secret, Hugo, old boy!" Uncle
Edouard burst out as if unloading his gun at a prize boar. "I always wondered. . . . Ha!"

I was the only one who had the pleasure of watching the res-
olute grip of his hairy hand below his belly, telling himself
where the true boar was housed.

The fiancé cleared his throat. "*Ma chérie,* I remember we
were introduced at the races. . . ."

Everyone broke out in admiration over a couple so romanti-
cally suited. I remembered how Angèle had peeled each rose to
the core while I was riding at her side, and how she had sent the

petals flying out of her carriage at me. Was she telling her guests our story to torture or entice me?

The high mood at the table was carried over into admiration of the artichokes with their exquisite vinaigrette. I decided to claim my share of the feast by peeling the hostess.

With the little stick of her mask I probed whether the moment was opportune. My poking up her skirts just enough to stroke along her thighs was met with welcome, especially when I erred a bit from the path and let the stick slip into the ravine that couldn't resist opening for easier access. I was in no hurry. In order to pursue with proper manners I crawled out of my stronghold, lifted her skirts back over me, and slipped onto my knees in front of her. She quickly closed her thighs. I gave her time while I enjoyed the faint lime and cinnamon scent that rose from her body through the layers of cotton, silk, and lace. Then I began rolling up her ruffled pants little by little, driving a slow path of kisses up from her ankles to her knees. Her knees gave in under my tender assault and allowed me just enough room to further roll up her pants. I reached the different silk of her skin above her stockings. Devoutly I tasted that skin with my lips and tongue, from the coolness on the outer sides to the beguiling warmth of the insides of her thighs.

"Ah! This is so *good*. . . ." she sighed. "Isn't it?"

There was resounding agreement around the table, and new bottles were uncorked while *mademoiselle la fiancée* unlocked her legs for me.

"Woman is a bun spread with white marble," I recited to myself. I turned into an artist, I drew the exact contours of her padded mound with my little stick, added curlicues for decoration and finished with a central, vertical exclamation mark. Then I pressed my mouth to the fine white cloth that covered the mound, sending hot air down her flesh. She pressed against me. Impatiently, she ordered Jean to remove the artichoke leaves. I obliged, gently pulling the cloth aside to enlarge the opening in her pants. And there, jutting out from its cotton frame, was *my* artichoke heart, pink and pouting.

The beast, I thought. Powdered. As though she had known and prepared for me, her connoisseur. Was it all her scenario, the scene in the mirror played out for me, her running down to the table, pretending to send me to hell as a foretaste of salvation? I circled around her like a cat around hot milk. Who was serving whose plot?

The next course was delayed. Her father said a few formal words, addressing the happy occasion. The husband-to-be rose to deliver a toast to the day, to the very special privilege he enjoyed in being there. . . . Being where, exactly? I showed Angèle, taking a sudden mouthful of her with a short bite as the finish. A shriek rewarded me. A glass was thrown over. I saw the splashes on the floor. I ducked halfway under her chair to hide from the servant who was rushing to clean up and who might want to look for drops under the table.

"*Pardonnez-moi,*[9] *cher Hugo,*" she giggled. "I am so excited by it all, you know? Please, *mon amour,* go on." The last words were uttered with an insistence that left me no doubt as to whom they were meant for. *Cher Hugo* went on rhapsodizing, while she couldn't stop giggling. I could tell he was troubled by her reaction. He went quite out of character telling stories, trying to be funny. Had he known it was my little feather that caused her such amusement, teasing her pout with strokes and tickles, his story might have taken an unsuspected turn.

Angèle must have had something similar in mind. With sudden irritation she commanded, "Let's get serious now! Let's get to the point!"

The fiancé scrambled to an end of his address and fell back on his chair. The company cheered and the seafood course was carried in.

I caught myself fantasizing about powdered lobster on a plate. Appetites, I had to admit, can be disarmingly obvious. I comforted myself by delicately separating her lips, delighted to see them close up again, no longer under the restraint of her pants. Her lips were forming an ever more pouchy pout, and between them, her glistening pearl was rising to my encounter. I had to hold back in order not to lose my head—and my game—in my hunger. She squeezed her thighs against my shoulders with urgency, almost panic, but I refused to be predictable. I kept spreading her and at the same time cooling her by blowing gentle breezes, waiting for the main dish to come on.

[9]Forgive me.

"*Bon Dieu*,[10] it is hot," she blurted out. "Where is my fan? Jean, my fan! Isn't it amazing, such heat in June? I can't remember anything like it."

This led to a lively discussion of the weather in June. The main course, deer by its smell, was served.

"More! I want more," my greedy Belle announced like an unruly child.

Some voices sounded hushed alarm.

The future husband took it upon him to send reassurance across the table, "But you'll have everything you need, *ma chérie. . . .*"

"I'm not so sure." She sulked and kicked her heels into my groin. Several servants rushed to fill her plate.

I was satisfied with our communication. I felt more and more present at the table. In order to tell her so, I took her into my mouth and slowly let my tongue slide all the way down the ravine.

"This is too much," she exclaimed ravenously. I heard her gulp down her glass of wine. Everyone politely laughed and speculated how such a healthy appetite would serve well for the purpose of founding a family. I didn't like these speculations. She is mine, I raged, nothing and nobody else will fill her, and I plunged my fingers into her as though sending a warning to everyone present. She must have thrown her body backward, coming toward me as though all dams were breaking.

"Ah, *la vie est belle*,"[11] she shouted. "Let's all sing together. Let's sing Hugo's favorite song!" And she began, "*Boire un petit coup c'est agréable. . . .*"[12]

The company showed goodwill falling in and seesawing along, while she rocked against my hand. I followed her rhythm with well-placed kisses. The embrace of her thighs tightened. When I felt her widening voluptuously around my fingers, I doubled the beat of the song with my tongue.

"*Boire un petit coup c'est doux. . . .*"[13]

In an instant, her cup ran over and spilled its shameless sweetness, for me.

---

[10]Good God.
[11]Life is beautiful.
[12]To drink a little cup is such a pleasure; popular French drinking song.
[13]To drink a little cup is sweet.

I rewarded her with a dessert in creamy spirals served on my fingertips and topped by tiny bites. She thanked me with repeated rounds of shudders. When I heard her sigh over her coffee and reveal to her guests, "*Rien ne va plus,*"[14] I was certain I had saved her. She had gambled away her marriage. I, the woman she could not wed, had won the game.

[14]No further bets; final announcement at the roulette table.

She Went Shopping This Morning

Joseph S. Teller

Diana Carrington stared thoughtfully down Nob Hill at the dark beige Prescott Building. Because Walter had not left yet, she kept the smile off her face with effort and tried with even less success to repress the growing warmth in the bottom of her stomach.

From the bedroom came the sounds of Walter packing for his trip. He was making a lot of noise, and she knew when he was gone she would have to go in there and make things neat again. It was her role. "My duty," she thought with a sigh. At least until Maria came tomorrow.

"Did you call the cab, Diana?" Walter shouted.

She glanced at the clock and saw it was already nine. "Yes. It will be here in fifteen minutes," she called over her shoulder. She heard him grunt and then swear as he crashed into a piece of furniture.

Diana drummed lacquered nails on the smoked glass of the kitchen table and noticed that her silk dressing gown had fallen open above the knees. Way above the knees. Her long legs were her pride and joy, and although she tended to view them artistically, or even clinically most of the time, occasionally she allowed herself to see them as wonderfully sexy. Today was one of those days, and letting the gown lie open all the way up, she stared at them through the darkened glass.

After a minute she reached down and pulled her gown shut, then went back to staring at the Prescott Building. Although it was only three stories tall, its gray color with black trim made it striking among the plainer buildings around it. Diana glanced at the clock. It was still too early for it to be open; that would not happen for another hour.

She raised the ornately painted Chinese cup to her lips and took a sip of the special Sumatra blend, and contemplated again what she had heard at the Hartmans' the night before. It had seemed impossible then; too dangerous to be true. And yet she was certain a practical joke was not being played on her. It couldn't be. No one had realized she was eavesdropping.

It was Lane Chatham and Suzanne Hartman whom she had heard discussing it. In a way it was sort of a coup, since although she was more or less cordial with Suzanne, Diana's relationship with Lane was never warmer than an arctic spring. Lane would not have told her this juicy bit in a hundred years, and Suzanne was too sophisticated to pass it on.

Such was the problem with being a society wife, Diana mused. The really fun stuff was reserved for the men, and the wives were actually expected to be interested in gardening, dinner parties, and the opera.

Walter called from the hallway. "I'll be in New York until Wednesday, then Chicago till Friday. Pick me up at the airport Friday at five, okay? We'll go straight to Napa. Book a place up there for the weekend. We've got to entertain . . ."

"And blah, blah, blah," Diana muttered. She had stopped listening. She knew what to do. Had done it all a hundred times before.

"Okay, I'm going," he said from the hallway.

Diana got up and walked down the tiled hallway to the front door. "Have a good trip, dear," she said, turning her head.

"Yeah. Bye." He kissed her cheek perfunctorily, picked up his suitcase, and was gone.

Diana returned to the kitchen, picked up her coffee cup, and walked into the dining room. From there the expanse of San Francisco spread out below her through the floor-to-ceiling windows, and directly in the center sat Prescott's. As Diana stared down at it her mind returned again to what she had overheard Lane say.

The Hartman house was a sprawling, curving labyrinth of rooms and hallways. Diana had been returning from a trip to one of the four bathrooms and had heard women's voices coming from a secluded area of the patio. Thinking it unusual, she stopped behind a huge fern and unabashedly listened.

"I'm telling you," Lane was saying in her high, little girl's voice that Diana despised, "it's true! I mean, that's what Belinda says. She told me her personal shopper, a girl named Renee, told her about it but swore her to secrecy. If it got out she would lose her job, and Mark could be sued, scandaled, and everything else."

"Maybe he should be," Suzanne had remarked. "It's disgraceful really, when you think about it."

In spite of the danger of being found out for spying on them, Diana had taken the opportunity to peer through the leaves. She saw Lane roll her eyes.

"Oh, really, Suzanne," Lane said. "It *would* be disgraceful if he weren't so incredibly gorgeous. I would take down my panties for him anytime, and so would every other woman in this town."

"Don't be coarse, Lane."

But Lane Chatham had only laughed. "I'd bet that you would be one of those women, too, Suzanne," she had said. Then, after a coy second, "Maybe you already have."

"I have not."

Diana had ducked back behind the fern, but continued to listen.

"Well, maybe not, but you have to admit he is movie star quality."

"You're right about that. He's the closest thing to Cary Grant since, well, Hugh Grant. But that's what makes it all the more strange, Lane. Don't you agree? Why, if he makes women that excited, has that much control over them, does he need to peek at them through one-way mirrors in changing rooms?"

When she heard that, Diana had nearly fallen into the plant. Mark Prescott? *The* Mark Prescott, peering at women trying on clothes? It was wild, crazy, and unbelievable. Diane had stepped backward and caught her breath. She herself had contemplated seducing Mark Prescott once, or maybe more than once. It had never happened, of course. In fact, Diana had never done anything like that in her life. Thought about it, yes, but never done it.

When she returned to the rest of the group someone had commented on how flushed she looked, and she had claimed she was not feeling well. Walter had taken her home early but complained all the way.

Diana finished the last of the coffee in her cup and took it into the kitchen. The clock said a half hour had passed. Prescott's would be open soon. Diana glanced through the kitchen window again at the store. She was filled with a sense of wonderful exciting guilt, just for thinking what she was thinking.

Guilt, she mused, was one of those things that makes sin worth it if you do it right. Her first sexual experience had so filled her with it that she could barely enjoy it, then later, she found that only when she had a good sense of guilt could she come. Maybe that was weird, but at least she had good orgasms.

When she had orgasms, that is.

You had to have sex to have orgasms, and although she offered her beautiful young body to Walter anytime he wanted it, it seemed he rarely wanted it. Old Walter seemed to care for her only as a cuff link—something attractive on his arm. Diana was not pleased with the arrangement, even if she had married into it with full knowledge of what it meant to be an older rich man's young wife.

But lately she noticed that sexual fantasies had become most of her sex life.

A collage of images raced through her mind, all of them including Mark Prescott and all of them very erotic. Her favorite one was a dream she had the night after the fund-raising call, when she had seen him from the next-door window.

In the dream, everything was painted brilliant colors. The sky was electric blue, the sea a turquoise richness, and the sand below a dazzling white. She was on a horse, riding along the waves.

Warm winds had blown, their delicate softness on her skin making her aware that she was nude. Her hair blew backward, and she realized she was riding. The horse beneath her was huge, powerful, and her legs had to be spread wide to wrap around its muscled body. She glanced down and saw that it was not a horse, but Mark Prescott, and his hands were on her breasts.

She had awoken at that point, heart pounding and breathing hard. Fortunately old Walter was snoring away, unmindful of her state. But the images had been magical and lasting in her imagination ever since.

"I'm going to do it," she said out loud, and was immediately aware of her heart pounding in her chest.

At ten-thirty Diana walked straight past the large, ornate door to J. B. Prescott's. It was the third time she had done it, and this time she paused just as she had the previous two times.

It's going to take courage, she told herself. *No, something more than courage.*

She remembered Lane's voice saying, "In the back of the lingerie department. That's where he goes. He sits there and looks through a one-way mirror."

Somebody on the crowded sidewalk bumped into Diana. "Excuse me," the woman said icily as she stepped past Diana and went inside.

This is ridiculous. I've got to do something.

What she ought to do was to go home, of course. She was well aware of the common sense in doing that. But the tingling excitement deep in her stomach assured her that she would not be going just yet.

What am I doing?

Diana looked nervously at the people walking past her. If she did not move soon she would begin to draw attention to herself. So, taking a deep breath, she looked straight ahead and walked through the wide-open doors.

She felt like a bank robber. As soon as she stepped inside she nearly panicked and ran back out. It took all her control to go to a display counter and pretend to look at jewelry. For several seconds she stood motionless in front of a row of diamond rings and did not see them.

"May I help you?"

Diana looked up, startled. "Oh, uh, that's okay. No, I'm just browsing," she managed to say.

This is insane. This is crazy! Everyone must know exactly what I'm doing here!

She walked over to a row of winter coats newly presented and pretended to examine them. And thought about the changing room upstairs with Mark Prescott behind the mirror, watching.

The warmth inside her grew stronger.

Again she glanced around the store, certain everyone there knew what she was up to. But she saw that no one even noticed her.

Diana took a deep breath, swallowed, and went to the escalator. Although she pictured herself as the essence of calm, she tripped on the first moving step and nearly knocked another woman over. She stepped back quickly, apologizing.

But even with all this, as she rode upward she forgot about her tension, reveling instead in the excitement that continued to build inside her. She wanted more than anything to be touched, held, and stroked. The stockings she had put on under her skirt made her exquisitely aware of her inner thighs.

The escalator deposited her on the second floor and she walked around automatically to the next set of moving steps. Gentle, seductive scents emanating from the perfume counter caressed her as she walked through that department, and stayed with her as she rode up to the third floor.

The Third Floor.

The lingerie floor.

Where women bought beautiful, soft, sexy things. She had never seen the erotic side of such a department before. The negligees and underwear, yes, for when she wanted to wear them to excite a man. But not the department itself.

Now she saw it through different eyes, and for the first time she saw that the entire half of the floor could be viewed as a tribute to women's sexuality, and therefore as something sexy in itself. Something erotic for men, but also for women. Especially if there was a tall, handsome man hiding and not knowing that the woman knew he was there. Diana almost giggled.

She walked over to a gondola stacked with bras and began to examine them. As she moved along the display rack her mind wandered back to that time she had seen him from the neighbor's window. Mark had been sunbathing nude. He had been unaware that she had seen him from his neighbor's window, just as now he would be unaware that she knew he was going to see her.

That time Diana had been visiting his next-door neighbor on a fund-raising call for the Modern Art Museum, of which she was a charter member. After securing a donation from the wealthy matron whose home it was, Diana had gone to an upstairs bathroom. As she washed her hands she happened to peek out of the small window over the sink and saw him sunbathing on his deck. It only lasted a moment, but it had been enough for her to see his tanned and well-muscled body, and it had sent a shiver of excitement through her that had amazed her.

Diana moved on, past rows of silk panties dangling from plastic hangers. Her mouth grew dry as she realized she was close to the dressing room. What's more, the department was practically empty. In a moment one of the saleswomen would undoubtedly see her and offer some help. Diana's heart banged in her chest like a tin can knocked around in the middle of the night by an alley cat.

She glanced sideways and saw that she had been right. A middle-aged woman walked toward her from the cashier's stand.

"May I help you?" the woman asked, smiling.

Diana stared at her guiltily. "Um, I just wanted . . . that is, I'm looking for a new negligee."

The woman looked at her questioningly for a moment, and Diana's mind raced. *Does she know?*

"Of course. Right this way," the woman said, and indicated the back wall.

Diana followed her. For several minutes the clerk showed her some things that had just come in, but Diana kept moving from one to the next without expressing interest in any. As she had hoped, the clerk began to grow bored. Finally another woman entered the department and the clerk left Diana alone. "Please try on anything you like," she said as she moved away.

Diana picked up a black lace teddy and white silk gown, and swallowed hard.

This is it!

The impulse to run out of the department nearly overcame her. She hesitated, and her limbs locked in place. For a full minute she could neither move out of the department nor toward the dressing room. Then she saw a woman she knew get off the escalator.

It was Catherine Summersby, a mutual friend of hers and Lane Chatham's. Catherine might not know or even suspect what Diana was doing, but if she even happened to mention it to Lane then Lane would put two and two together.

Or, at least, Diana feared she might.

With that thought, she turned and walked straight into the dressing room and quickly shut the door behind her. At first she could not even look at the mirror-covered walls. She took two deep breaths and forced herself to calm down.

After a moment Diana raised her head and examined the small room. There was a soft overhead light, a clothes hanger on the back of the door, a small chair, and three mirrors.

Three mirrors!

She looked in the one in front of her and saw herself blushing. He might be looking at her right now!

A small grin formed on her lips, though she reminded herself that she must not give any hint that she knew he was back there. She bit her lip and looked down at the floor. Then she licked her lips and hung up her coat.

Well, this is what I'm here for.

Her fingers trembled as she reached for the top button of her blouse. As her fingers worked downward, she glanced in the mirror and watched her blouse open up, button by button. She couldn't get over the fact that he was back there, seeing her undress. She imagined him on the other side of the mirror, sitting on a chair and staring at her with his incredibly beautiful dark blue eyes, and a tremor raced through her.

Which mirror are you behind?

As the third and then fourth button came undone, and her lacy white bra became visible, Diana felt herself succumbing to the incredible heat beginning to permeate her. Suddenly it hit her: This was fun! The face in the mirror smiled back at her with increasing confidence, and the smile became warm and sensuous. She was undressing for a man whom she found very sexy, and he did not know that she knew that he was there.

It's the best possible seduction! I'm completely guilty and completely innocent.

She almost laughed out loud.

When the last button came undone she slid her blouse off her shoulders and hung it up, then allowed herself a brief, critical appraisal. She decided he was enjoying what he saw, and that made her feel the eroticism of the moment even more intently.

She turned a complete circle as she unzipped her long skirt, trying to appear nonchalant, as if she were merely appraising her body. But as the tension slipped away from the waist of her skirt and she tugged it gently over her hips, Diana knew that her feigned nonchalance was in trouble. Her own sensations were getting the better of her. She hung up the skirt and almost gasped at her own flushed face looking back at her in the first mirror.

A now scantily clad, undeniably sexy woman stared back at her. She put a hand to her head and brushed back a lock of soft blond hair. The erotic sensations turned to fire.

This is incredible. It's more sexy than I ever thought it could be. Which mirror are you behind, Mark Prescott?

Her breasts ached. She glanced down at them and saw that her nipples were hard, standing up erect through her bra. She swallowed dryly, and was aware that her knees were weakening. Again she licked her lips.

"If you go any further you'll be in trouble," a little voice warned her inside her head.

She ignored the voice.

Her bra seemed to come undone by itself. The woman in the mirror shrugged her shoulders and the light material floated away naturally. Her rounded breasts, small but firm, bounced free.

Trying not to grin, she turned a slow complete circle again to show herself to him no matter which mirror he was behind. Then she bent down and removed her stockings.

This was the most naughty part, and her fingers hesitated one last time. But she pushed down on the elastic of her panties and they slid across her thighs until soft golden curls of hair became visible. She was breathing harder as she pushed her panties to her knees, where they fell to the floor on their own. When she stood up straight and looked at herself in the mirror, she was completely nude.

Never in her life had she felt so sexy or so turned on. She could tell without touching herself that she was wet. But oh, how she wanted to touch herself! She looked in the mirror and watched as her own hands moved up to her breasts, and she moaned.

In the back of her mind she knew he was watching her, and that made it all the more intoxicating. In fact, she felt sort of drunk. The room seemed to spin.

He was watching her! From behind one of the mirrors he was watching. Did he have his cock out of his pants? Was it hard, was he looking at her driving him wild, as wild as she felt?

Her right hand moved down across her stomach. Her fingertips moved to the top of her bikini line, then down across the untanned skin until they touched wetness. Unable and not wanting to stop, even though what she was doing was beyond anything she had ever imagined, she let her middle finger slip inward.

Diana moaned, and gasped for breath.

The steady beat of her heart grew louder as waves of pleasure filled her. She watched herself in the mirror through a wall of lust so thick that it made her vision blur. Her nude body trembled under the light as it danced with her finger.

She closed her eyes, surrendering. Dizzy with lust, she blinked her eyelids open and saw the nudity of her back reflected in the mirror. She stared at her soft, shoulder-length hair, her narrow waist, and gently flared hips in surprise. And realized that the position of the mirror should not allow her to see herself.

Something was different. It was the mirror behind her; it had moved.

She watched in the opposite mirror, unable to prevent her own finger from continuing to ravage her even as she saw a man stepping through the narrow threshold of the mirror behind her. He wore only a pair of tiny green briefs that accentuated the rigidity of his cock.

She swallowed desperately.

It was not Mark Prescott.

This was a younger man, well built, with long golden hair and a gold earring in his left ear. He came up behind her quickly and brushed aside her hair, then kissed the back of her neck. She felt the hot wetness of his lips and tongue on her bare skin, and the waves of passion that had been building took off, rising uncontrollably like lava.

Diana was aware that her finger had not stopped, even as he spun her around and kissed her hard on the mouth. It did not stop its attack of pleasure on her until he grabbed her wrist and lifted it over her head. Then, just as quickly, he grabbed the other hand and held it, too, over her head. It made her wild.

"Fuck me," she whispered hoarsely. "Do anything you want to me . . ."

With one movement he tore off his underwear and lifted her up. She seemed to float for a second, and then he put her down onto his demanding cock. She slid onto it like warm butter and in a shock realized that she was coming.

But she was not to be freed. He pushed her against the mirror and pumped into her. Diana wondered if she were being split in two. She bit her lip and watched in the mirror, knowing that she had barely finished her first orgasm and the second one was already upon her.

She cried out and fought to stifle the sound. Her entire body spasmed, and then he put her down onto the floor on her hands and knees. Diana turned her head to watch in the mirror, wide-eyed and open as he entered her over and over until at last she felt herself carried away into a soundless explosion of passion with him.

There was a knock at the door.

"Is everything all right?" It was the sales clerk.

Diana tried to answer, but her throat was too thick. She coughed once, found her voice, and answered affirmatively.

He stood up and put his finger to his lips. Then he picked her up and kissed her once. "I'll be here next Thursday," he whispered. "Come back."

Diana watched him grab his briefs and disappear through the mirror-door, pulling it closed behind him. Then she picked up her own things and got dressed.

She would never come back, of course. Once was wonderful, but she would never do it again.

Never.

She couldn't.

Ever.

Diana looked around the small room once, then opened the door and walked out. As she left the store she remembered Mark Prescott and wondered what had happened to him.

She checked her watch. It was noon. Maybe a light sandwich was in order, she decided.

The 5:20 Encounter

ETHAN MONK

Charlie bounded down the steps and through the turnstile, then sprinted the last ten yards to the Outbound platform. He squeezed through the doors to the commuter train just before they closed, and swung into the seat opposite. "All right," he thought. This was a game he played virtually every day after work in the city. Trying to make the 5:20 train to the East Bay; sometimes, like today, cutting it close.

He settled in, put his briefcase to his side, and leaned against the window as the train pulled out. He glanced around the car, not really looking at the people riding with him, but sort of absorbing their presence. Then he saw him. In the seat diagonally across, sitting alone. Charlie looked down for a moment, not wanting the boy to think he was staring. He looked back up again. The boy across from him was looking out the window. He wasn't really a boy, of course. But in gay parlance, almost everybody was a "boy." Charlie guessed he was in his late twenties, maybe even thirty. He wasn't sure. He wasn't very good at pinpointing the ages of strangers. He turned his head, pretending to look in a different direction, but couldn't help return his gaze to this beautiful vision.

He looked so sweet—smooth skin, tousled hair. Just Charlie's type, he thought. He couldn't tell how tall he was, but Charlie guessed he was probably about medium height. Not as tall as Charlie, at six feet. He wore jeans and a white shirt, tucked in, under a lightweight navy car coat, and white tennis shoes. Real cute, Charlie thought. The boy turned away from the window. As he reached into the pocket of his coat, he looked in Charlie's direction. Charlie froze for a moment. For the first time, he saw the boy's full face. Beautiful dark eyes, with full, long eyelashes that gave him a sort of innocence. He had a small nose, and a sweet mouth. His skin had a light, golden hue, and Charlie guessed he was Vietnamese. Or maybe Chinese. Charlie was no better at determining race than he was at guessing age.

As Charlie stared, and pretended not to stare at the same time, the boy's eyes moved to meet his. Charlie turned quickly to look out his own window, worried that the boy had caught him. His heart picked up a beat. Charlie gazed out the window at nothing, then closed his eyes. The image of the boy's face was etched in his mind like a photograph. What was his name? Charlie wondered. Was it a Vietnamese or Chinese name? Something Charlie probably couldn't pronounce if he saw it in writing. Something exotic-sounding. Something beautiful. Though again it could be something extraordinarily common. Maybe it was a simple American name, like Bill or Tom. As the image of the boy, fixed so sharply in Charlie's mind a moment ago, began to fade, Charlie tried to call it up again. That face. That incredibly striking, sweet face. Those eyes—round and wide. At that thought, it dawned on Charlie that this boy might be Amerasian.

Charlie couldn't quite give enough detail to the fading image in his mind, so he turned his head away from the window. He looked straight ahead, rather than directly at the boy. Slowly his gaze moved toward the boy's direction. Charlie could see him out of the corner of his eye. He was reading a book. Holding it in his lap, his head bent forward. Charlie thought it safe to drink him in again, although he was careful to avert his look every so often so as not to appear to be leering. Charlie knew that you could tell if someone was "cruising" you. You didn't have to see the person doing it, you could just "feel" it.

He looked at the boy's hands. Long fingers, not delicate, but with a certain elegance. No rings. If he was straight, he wasn't married. If he was straight, Charlie concluded, that would be an incredible injustice. When Charlie was young, and coming to grips with being gay, he heard that gay people could tell if other people were gay, and he wondered how. After years of working in San Francisco, of being "out," of going to bars and places where "his people" were, he knew. With some guys it was easy, of course. Anybody could tell.

With others, it was hard for straights to tell, but most gays knew. Then with some, it was almost impossible. Charlie might not have been gifted at determining age or race, but he was very good at knowing who was gay and who wasn't. Charlie had grown up in a small town on the Oregon coast where you didn't want to make the mistake of assuming someone was gay who wasn't. Not that the question ever came up that much back there, back then.

Charlie decided at that moment that he would give the boy the name Kim. No good reason. He just wanted to give him a name. Then Kim looked up, and straight at Charlie. Uh-oh, Charlie thought, but before he could turn away again, the boy smiled. A small smile. Just as quickly he returned to his book. Charlie again looked toward the window. His heart was really beating now.

He smiled at me, Charlie thought. Or did he? Maybe it was just a reflex. Maybe he wasn't even looking at me but someone behind me. Charlie turned to look over his shoulder. There was no one in the seat right behind him. Two seats back was an old woman, packages on her lap, a blank look on her face.

He thought again of the boy's face. His quick smile made him even more beautiful. The hint of white teeth. The slight upturn at the corners of the boy's mouth. The arch of an eyebrow. Or did Charlie imagine that. It was so quick. Charlie wondered what it would be like to kiss him. Gently brush his lips against Kim's. To part his lips with his tongue and to slip it into his mouth. Would he be passive or return the passion? Would he be eager, or patient? Charlie imagined putting his hand on Kim's neck as their tongues explored each other. He imagined opening his eyes to look at him, while Kim kept his eyes closed. He imagined his cheek against Kim's cheek—soft, warm, smooth. He imagined gently licking Kim's neck.

The train was pulling into the Montgomery Street stop, and Charlie was jolted out of his fantasy. He looked quickly toward the boy. What if he gets off here? "Oh, don't let this be his stop," Charlie thought. The doors opened, but Kim made no attempt to move. Charlie muffled a little sigh of relief. Four people did get off, and another three got on. "Don't sit next to him," Charlie thought as he mentally moved the new passengers to other parts of the train. They seemed to oblige. The boy kept reading. Charlie feigned interest in the new commuters, but kept coming back to the boy.

The doors closed and the train picked up speed. Charlie wondered what Kim did. Charlie couldn't see the cover of the book he was reading. Maybe he was a student. No bookbag though, so probably not. Charlie hadn't seen him on the 5:20 before, of that he was positive. He wouldn't likely fail to notice someone who looked like this boy. He works in the city, Charlie surmised. Or maybe he was just visiting somebody. Or maybe his car is in the shop. Maybe he just moved here. Charlie thought of all the small details you learn about someone on the first date. Dating. For a moment, Charlie entertained the thought about going on a date with Kim. A movie. No, not a movie. A movie was a lousy date. Particularly a first date. No opportunity to talk, to find out about him, to look at him. Out to dinner. Somewhere nice, but not too fancy. Somewhere hip. Maybe dancing, although Charlie didn't really like the dance scene anymore. He used to go out dancing—at the after-hours clubs. Not so much to dance, he admitted, but more to see and be seen, to perhaps meet someone. Although he almost never did. Of course Michael used to love to go dancing. Michael. How long had it been since they broke up? Eight years. Michael had been Charlie's first and only true love, his only real relationship. Charlie thought about sex with Michael. They were young when they met. Young and horny. Sex had been great. They discovered intimacy with each other. They discovered experimentation with each other, and boy did they experiment. Charlie had been somewhat shy in bed. Not Michael. Michael had no inhibitions. But they set up house too soon. Probably, they were too young, and didn't understand how to work at making a relationship last.

Charlie thought about how many times he had had sex in the past year. Once with his friend Taylor, and *that* had been a mistake. Friends just shouldn't sleep together. It just complicated things. Who else had he slept with? A boy he had met in Golden Gate Park on a Sunday in May, roller-skating. A one-night stand, as it turned out, though Charlie had not meant it to be. Was that it? Charlie wondered incredulously. Work had been demanding, but had he really only had sex twice?

He looked back toward Kim, a little perturbed for allowing himself to become distracted. He wondered what it would be like to take Kim's clothes off, to fuck him. How did his friend Taylor put it, "take him for a test drive." That was so crass, he thought. But that was Taylor. There was always a thin line between the romantic and the raunchy. Charlie knew that while raw sex was exciting, it still felt somehow like it wasn't enough. Fucking someone you wanted there in the morning, when you woke up, was infinitely better. Cuddling was important. Being close was important. But he also knew he had a wild side. Sometimes the best sex was about the dark or embarrassing fantasies he carried inside himself. It was easier to be uninhibited when there were no emotional ties.

The train pulled into the Embarcadero Station, last stop before the tunnel under the bay. Half the people got off, and were immediately replaced by commuters. They crowded into the car, moving toward empty seats. Kim stayed absorbed in his book.

As the train reached full speed, the rhythm of its gentle movement was soothing. It made a sort of dull, purring hum, and Charlie closed his eyes. He thought about Kim again. He imagined them at Charlie's house, sitting on the couch in the living room. He fantasized about his arm around Kim, kissing him, feeling the warm glow brought on by a good wine. Kissing him. Slowly. Longingly. Tongues intertwined. Feeling the warmth of Kim's breath. He imagined Kim leaning with his back against Charlie, and Charlie lovingly kissing his neck. Nibbling. Licking. He imagined pulling Kim's shirt gently out from his pants, putting his hand underneath, and letting his fingers dance over his stomach. He could almost feel the warmth of the boy's skin. He fantasized about moving his hands up to his chest, to his nipples, then gently playing with each one between his thumb and forefinger, getting each nipple, in turn, erect. He imagined Kim's head leaning back on his shoulder. He thought about tracing the outline of Kim's lips with the fingers of his other hand. Then slowly putting a finger in his mouth, Kim moaning slightly as he ran his tongue around the finger, sucking it; letting Charlie explore his mouth. Charlie thought about pulling Kim back toward him even more, then moving his hand, under his shirt, down to his pants, and slowly sliding his hand inside, beneath the boy's underpants, feeling the edge of the soft pubic hairs, lingering a moment, then moving further down, and feeling Kim's hard dick, the boy holding in his stomach to make Charlie's quest easier. He imagined squeezing his dick, while turning the boy's face toward his, replacing the finger in the boy's mouth with his tongue. He could feel Kim move toward him, his hand now gripping Charlie's leg. He imagined undoing the boy's pants and feeling his hard cock as it strained against his briefs, then pulling them back, freeing the boy's pole. He imagined it standing straight up. The boy would probably be uncut, and completely erect, the head glistening slightly. Charlie wanted to see it.

Charlie stopped, remembering where he was, realizing he had a raging hard-on. He pulled his briefcase onto his lap to hide the bulge, and caught the boy looking at him again. Kim once more quickly turned his head back to his book, and Charlie wondered if the boy could read his thoughts.

Charlie opened his briefcase and looked through the Micro-Dot Account sketches to take his mind off the boy. Charlie was the director of the high tech accounts for Wilson/Potter, arguably the biggest and best graphics image consultants in the country. He'd been there six years, and was a rising star, or at least he hoped that's how he was perceived. Things were going okay in the thirty-second year of his life. He made good money, had bought a house in Orinda two years ago, and drove a classic old Mercedes. Style was essential to him. He took the train to work almost every day so he didn't have to hassle the traffic. He hated sitting in stop and go traffic. Made him nuts. And even though he would be the first to admit that he was a snob, for some reason he enjoyed riding the commuter train. Watching the people. It was, of course, politically correct, and he often let people believe that was the reason he did it, but it wasn't.

After staring at the drawings for a new corporate image for MicroDot, a new Silicon Valley Internet company, he put the papers back in the briefcase and closed it. His hard-on had subsided, but he couldn't focus on business, not when the boy was five feet away. He glanced over at Kim, and wondered why he was so attracted to him. It was something more than lust for the boy's beauty, want of his body. Hell, he had lust fantasies all the time. San Francisco was full of beautiful boys. Maybe he was just horny, maybe a little lonely. Maybe he wanted to find somebody and settle down again. Although he had affairs and brief encounters, it had been a long time since he had had a real relationship. A lover, a partner. Not since Michael, and that seemed a lifetime ago.

He had met Michael at the gym. Neither of them were body-builders, but both liked the way regular exercise made them feel, as well as the results. Michael was a Nordic blond, with a deep tan and blue eyes, He was shorter than Charlie, naturally athletic-looking, and he carried himself with a certain confidence. He had an easy way with people. Like Michael, Charlie was slim, his body taut and fairly defined without having to work at it. Charlie's complexion was olive, and when he had the time to lie in the sun for a while, it took on a rich brown patina that made him look Mediterranean. He had high cheek-bones, a warm smile, and green eyes that seemed to twinkle. With his long legs, clothes hung on his body well. He never considered himself really good-looking, although certainly a lot of other people seemed to. His dark hair tumbled over his eyes, and he had, or so Michael had told him the first time they talked, a "butt to die for." That had made Charlie blush. No one before Michael had ever been so direct. Being young, gay, and out, in San Francisco in the mid eighties, had been a hell of a ride. Before AIDS, and age, had changed gay life.

Michael had just walked up to him and casually remarked that he liked Charlie's butt. Maybe that was part of his attrac-tion to Michael, Charlie thought. He was so fearless. Never a doubt. Always totally comfortable, in charge. Michael was good at flirting. It was a gift. Charlie wasn't like that. He was more reserved, less sure of himself, at least where meeting other guys was concerned. He knew he blew opportunities being the way he was, but he couldn't seem to make himself like Michael. Confident. Cocksure and confident.

They had gone for a beer after their workout. Made a date for that weekend, and moved in with each other a month later. They stayed together almost two years, which was some kind of record given their age and the times. Charlie hadn't seen Michael in almost three years, but knew that he had had at least three lovers since Charlie. Michael was one of those guys who would always have a partner. He needed to be in a relationship, no matter how tenuous, how difficult. Michael had started cheating on Charlie within a few months after they became a "couple." Charlie was hurt at first, then angry. By the time he realized Michael had wandering eyes and would never change, Charlie had already stopped sleeping with him. Still, they remained friends. Not close, but friends. And Charlie thought for a moment that he should call Michael.

He smiled to himself. If Michael were here he would have sat down right next to that boy. He would have smiled at him and struck up a conversation, and no doubt the two of them would be laughing within minutes. Michael would turn on his charm and end up in bed with the boy by the time it was dark. He could almost hear Michael's voice now—"Talk to him, Charlie. What are you waiting for? Smile at him again, and don't look away when he looks back." Easier said than done.

The train was almost through the tunnel and would make its first East Bay stop in a minute or two. Charlie panicked. What if the boy got off right at the Berkeley stop? He should have said something to him. He should have smiled back. The train pulled into the station, but the boy remained in his seat. People got off, others got on, and the train sped off. Charlie looked directly at the boy, who was leaning back, holding his book a little higher while he read. It was still too low for Charlie to see the cover, and he craned his neck to try to make out the title. Kim looked up at him, and into Charlie's eyes. Charlie smiled. A little smile. The boy held the book up for him to see. *Degree of Guilt,* a courtroom thriller by a San Francisco author Charlie liked. "Ah," Charlie said to him. "Good book." Brilliant, he thought to himself. The boy smiled back. "Yeah, I like mysteries." "Figure out who did it yet?" Charlie surprised himself by asking the boy. "I think so. Don't tell me though." Charlie wanted to say something, but couldn't form any words. He knew he was thinking too much, and ought to just "be." But he didn't want to say something stupid, or insipid, even though he knew that anything would be better than nothing. He was paralyzed, and the moment was slipping away. The next stop was close. Kim closed his book and put it back in his jacket pocket, then zipped his coat up partway. As the train pulled into the next station, he got up and held on to the bar as he faced the exit door, waiting for it to open. Charlie watched him achingly. Just before the boy got off, he turned and looked at Charlie. "Have a nice evening," was all he said, and then he flashed a big, inviting smile—and melted Charlie's heart. Charlie smiled back. He thought he did anyway, but wasn't sure when he replayed the moment back in his head later. As the train pulled out, Charlie watched the boy move toward the exit. He looked so hot, and Charlie hoped he would turn toward the train one last time. But he didn't.

Charlie leaned back in his seat and closed his eyes. He thought of Kim's face, trying to fix it firmly in his mind while the memory was fresh. Those beautiful dark eyes, the small nose, the smooth skin, that infectious smile, and those white teeth, the straight, jet-black hair, slightly tousled. He imagined the boy naked, standing in front of him. Lean, but not skinny. His body naturally hard. A flat stomach with an "outie" navel. A perfectly proportioned chest, his tits slightly darker in color than his golden skin, nipples erect. Rounded shoulders and the curve of biceps. His arms at his side. A slightly embarrassed look on his face. Charlie imagined the small patch of black pubic hair on the boy's otherwise smooth body. He imagined the boy's cock hard, standing up straight, his soft balls tight against the base of his dick. He thought of the boy from the rear, arms down at his side, his torso narrowing to his waist. His ass cheeks smooth, rounded, with a narrow crack separating them.

He fantasized Kim as innocent and sweet, eager to please; if not submissive, then compliant. But he knew that could be completely wrong. Maybe Kim liked to be the aggressor, the one in control. He tried to remember his voice. It had been soft, without any edge to it; neither high-pitched, nor low, but sexy nonetheless.

The train pulled into the Orinda stop, and Charlie opened his eyes. He grabbed his briefcase and stood up to move through the doors as they opened. Instinctively he moved through the station, down the steps, and across the parking lot to his car, still thinking about Kim.

Once home, Charlie went straight to the refrigerator. He made himself a sandwich, grabbed a Diet Pepsi, and went into the den and switched on the TV. He lay back on the couch, and once again his mind drifted to the boy. He closed his eyes and savored the image. He thought of Kim lying naked on top of him, Charlie's hands squeezing his bubble butt, then running up the small of his back, feeling the weight and warmth of the boy's body against his. He fantasized about Kim licking his neck, then lifting his head up to look at Charlie, and smiling. He imagined the boy licking his tits and running his tongue down Charlie's hard stomach, licking Charlie's whole torso, his tongue moving up one side of Charlie's body to his armpit, across his chest, and down the other side, stopping every few moments and looking up at him as if to have Charlie confirm that he was doing it right. Then moving down to Charlie's hard cock. Cupping Charlie's balls in one hand, and wrapping the other around Charlie's dick. Stroking Charlie, then running his tongue gently up the shaft, then across the head of Charlie's cock, sending shivers up Charlie's spine. The boy repeated this movement, driving Charlie into ecstasy. He lifted Charlie's scrotum, moved his own body further down the couch and began to lick under Charlie's balls. Teasingly. He moved Charlie's legs further apart and took Charlie's nuts into his mouth, first one, then the other. Charlie moaned with pleasure. Kim's tongue darted under Charlie's sac, then back up to his erect cock. He loosened his grip on Charlie's dick, and took the head into his mouth, sucking gently and enveloping it with his tongue. His hand moved up Charlie's stomach to his tits and the boy expertly kneaded Charlie's right nipple. He took the whole of Charlie's seven inches down his throat as his nose grazed Charlie's pubic bush. He sucked Charlie's cock until Charlie thought he would explode in ecstasy.

In his fantasy, Charlie sat up, and put his hands on Kim's hips, moving him off so that the boy stood directly in front of him. Charlie buried his tongue in Kim's navel, licking his stomach while his hands squeezed his ass. Charlie could feel Kim's erect penis bobbing slightly against his neck. He stopped licking the boy's belly, and took his cock in his mouth, swallowing it in one gulp. He tickled the boy's soft, egg-shaped balls and sucked his dick. Kim let his hands rest gently on Charlie's shoulders, and let his head fall slightly backward. Charlie continued to feel the throbbing cock in his mouth, as the light musky smell filled his nostrils. The boy arched his back, and moaned ever so quietly. That turned Charlie on, and he quickened the pace of sucking Kim's beautiful dick. It felt warm in his throat, and Charlie could almost feel the boy's heartbeat as blood rushed to keep his young, eager cock engorged.

Kim continued to moan as Charlie brought him closer to climax. But Charlie didn't want it to end this way. He slowed down, then wrapped his hand around the boy's cock and took it from his mouth. He stroked it a few times, then looked up at the boy. "I want to be inside you. I want to fuck you." The boy smiled faintly, nodded imperceptibly, and just said: "Okay."

Charlie got up, went to the bathroom, and was back within seconds. He sat down on the couch, opened a jar of lubricant, and rubbed some on his dick. He imagined motioning the boy closer to him, and rubbing cream on the boy's cock as he rubbed it on himself. He put more of the gel onto his fingers and saw himself slipping them between the boy's legs. Charlie's finger slid up and down the crack of the boy's ass, while he felt for the opening. The boy moved his legs further apart and squatted slightly, all the while watching Charlie's ministrations. Charlie's finger probed the boy's crack, searching for his anus. Charlie found the hole, and rubbed the gel on the outside for a second or two before he let his finger slide inside. The boy quivered slightly and groaned, and Charlie let him get used to the feeling of having a finger inside him. He slipped the digit in and out, and began a rhythmic finger fucking of the boy's canal. Kim let Charlie in without resistance, and stroked his own cock while Charlie loosened him up.

Finally, Charlie returned to his own dick. He tore open the condom packet lying next to him on the couch and rolled it down the shaft of his dick. Leaning back against the pillows, he moved his butt forward slightly, and put his hands back on the boy's hips. He guided the boy to straddle him, with the boy's knees on the couch. Then he sat the boy down on his cock, and Kim obligingly let Charlie get up inside him. Kim draped his arms around Charlie's shoulders, and Charlie wrapped his hand around the boy's dick and begin to pull. The boy's eyes met Charlie's, and they looked at each other for a brief moment before Kim bent his head toward Charlie, closing his eyes, and slipping his tongue into Charlie's moist mouth. Leaning back, Charlie begin to slowly thrust into the boy, and Kim, in turn, moved up and down on the pole now deep inside him. Charlie was breathing heavily. "Oh yes. Oh, that feels sooo good," Charlie told him appreciatively. Kim just moaned. Charlie began pumping deeper, faster, and Kim moved with him. The boy's fingers slid down and absently played with Charlie's nipples. "Fuck me, Charlie."

Charlie didn't need any encouragement, though it heightened his desire to have the boy plead for it. "Fuck me, Charlie," Kim repeated, his voice full of passion. Charlie increased the thrusts, and Kim moved up and down with him. Kim had now surrendered to Charlie completely, and Charlie knew that, at this moment, the boy was his. They moved together with primitive abandon, Charlie fucking him faster and harder. Still he wanted it to last. He slowed the pace, let his hands play with Kim's cock, and then pulled Kim to him tight. Kim looked into Charlie's eyes, but neither said a word.

Charlie eased his dick out slowly, moved Kim off him and to his feet, stood up, and then got behind him. With one hand on Kim's hip, and the other on his back, he bent the boy over. Kim complied willingly, bending over the couch, resting one hand on a cushion, presenting his ass to Charlie. The boy could feel Charlie's hard cock brush against his ass as Charlie reached around and played with the boy's chest and stomach, squeezing him roughly. Charlie stood back, pulled the condom tight, and slid one hand under the boy's nuts. He toyed with his balls for a moment, spread Kim's legs further apart, then eased his cock back inside. His rock-hard dick entered deeply. Kim pulled his own dick as he moaned in unison with Charlie's thrusts. Moments later, Charlie knew he was getting close, and he stabbed the boy really deep. Kim moaned a little louder, but offered no resistance. Charlie quickly stabbed him again, even deeper. A second later, Kim pushed his ass tight onto Charlie's cock. "Ooh. I'm coming, Charlie. I'm coming." Charlie felt the well inside himself, and he began to ejaculate at the same time. Both bodies jerked and shuddered. Their breathing was hot. Charlie shot the last of his load inside Kim and collapsed on top of him. He said nothing for several moments, and the boy stayed motionless, supporting the weight of Charlie on his back without complaint. Finally Charlie reached around and stroked Kim's cock. Kim shuddered involuntarily as Charlie's hand slid past the head of his dick. Charlie stayed inside of Kim, who stood up and leaned his head back on Charlie's shoulder. Charlie kissed him tenderly on the neck, then the ear, his hand moving up the boy's stomach and chest. Kim's hands reached behind him to Charlie's ass as he tried to pull Charlie closer to him, to keep Charlie inside him.

As Charlie lay on the couch, his stomach and chest covered with the sticky, white, milky spunk of his masturbation, he remained still. Jacking off was often easier than actual sex, but never as fulfilling. This was pretty close though. Charlie couldn't remember ever having a more vivid, more erotic fantasy. "Thank you, Kim," he whispered as he drifted off to sleep.

PART III

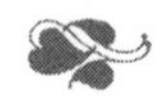

Escape

Rather than moving toward someone, the motivation behind some seductions is to escape from a certain set of circumstances. When life is depressing or distressing, when a relationship is having difficulties, we may find ourselves moving away from a drab or uncomfortable reality, seeking relief through an illicit sexual relationship or seductive daydream. We may seduce ourselves with a fantasy and create the "perfect" lover who will rescue us from the emptiness or the mundane problems of our lives. In some cases, the fantasy alone provides sufficient relief, as in Nancy Sasha Long's imaginative "A Life of Seductions." "For me," Long explains, "seduction usually comes in the form of a fantasy that is capable of overshadowing a rather bleak reality. It is the illusory promise of fulfillment, a temporary paradise. When reality comes up short, I retreat into myself, into a fantasy world where seduction creates the potential for fulfillment. Fantasies of wanting to be seduced or to seduce someone else help me to relieve the boredom, the frustration, and the feelings of powerlessness. It seems to me that the single most important element of seduction is its promise of fulfillment."

However, in other cases, life is breathed into the fantasy and escape is consummated in the form of an illicit affair. In "I Wanted To," Lisa Prosimo creates the quintessential boss/secretary love affair to lure her main character away from her sexually unfulfilling marriage. "It's about the unspoken," says Prosimo. "There is this chemistry of attraction that you can't quite put your finger on, but it charges the air between the potential sexual partners. There is the gloss of the 'new,' the 'untried,' the 'possible,' that is really the seducer in this case."

Sometimes, the escape is not from an unfulfilling relationship but from the stresses of modern life. The arms of a lover who provides true and lasting intimacy can represent the real freedom. In "Simply Seduced," Wickham Boyle creates an exceptional seduction out of an unexceptional evening at home for a couple married fifteen years. "It's easy to be sexy with a lover," says Boyle, "but I want to be able to have an affair with my husband. The elements of seduction for me are primarily anything that takes me out of what I call 'list land.' This is the place where I manage a complicated work life, remember birthday gifts, do the wash, and forget to mail the insurance forms—all the mundane details that remove me from a life between my legs." So Boyle creates a husband who charters the perfect escape route to enable his wife to eclipse harsh reality and melt into the netherworld of soft sensuality.

In these stories, when real life is stressed, or gray and sad, sexual passion, whether with an intimate partner, an illicit partner, or an imaginary partner, offers exciting color and promise and an escape from the ordinary into a far more enticing, exciting, Technicolor world.

A Life of Seductions

NANCY SASHA LONG

I chop the onions thinly, evenly . . . with a sharp-edged knife . . . bringing each stroke down onto the wooden counter . . . slow, clean strokes. He comes up from behind me. Circles my waist with his arms. Nudging his lips against my ear. I try to ignore him. Want to finish this. Guests are coming soon. I slice the broccoli, white cheese . . . "Hurry with that," he whispers, "I want you right here." Stroking the curve of my neck, his hands begin to travel down . . . tracing the curve of my back, the side of my hips, down to the insides my thighs. Firmly grasping my flesh, he rubs up against me. I must finish . . . Must hurry . . . Now what is next? Eggs? Two or is it three?

My lips swell with wetness . . . his desire rising . . . I feel hardness . . . his breathing, deeper now . . . my nipples grow hard, straining against the tight silk dress that binds me. "Hurry," he whispers. I put the soufflé in the oven. Turning around to him . . . we never make it beyond the kitchen floor. Heat rises . . . in me, around me . . . As I swell, my soufflé swells . . . rising . . . slowly . . .

The front door slams.

"Hi, hon, I'm home!" He throws his briefcase on the chair. . . . Loosens his tie . . . goes straight to the refrigerator, reaches for a bottle of beer, and heads for the couch. "Hey, it's great to be home . . . I'm tired . . ." I hear the familiar click and faraway blare of voices from the TV. I am still standing in the kitchen, wearing my new summer dress, now soaked with sweat from my thoughts, my desires, fantasies of someone else . . . far away from here . . . I look in the oven . . . soufflé should be ready . . . I open the door and stare, wondering what went wrong. . . . All I see is flatness, burnt edges . . . deflating . . . sinking further and further down . . .

I sit across from my husband at the breakfast table hoping for some reaction. He just sits there . . . tired-looking . . . quiet. I wonder what he's thinking . . . after hearing me tell about the dream I had last night.

"You live too much in a fantasy world, sweetheart. It's only a dream. You need to pay attention to reality," he says while finishing his coffee. He stands up. Straightens his tie. "Have to get to work. Will be working late again tonight. Would you pick up my shirts at the dry cleaners?" As he kisses the top of my head, I look down into my coffee cup. Swirls of dark float . . . still . . . on the liquid surface. I think, what has gone wrong? Married for seven years and . . . Did he hear anything I said?

I don't want to think about those things right now. My mind plays tricks on me. While clearing the table, my thoughts drift to the man I met at a party last Friday. He is a carpenter and has a table to sell. A table I may want to buy. He described the wood to me. I liked the sound of his voice . . . how he paused . . . made time for me to speak . . . how he listened. There was something alluring about him. I went away from the party feeling a warm glow. Something I haven't experienced in a long time. I walk to the bathroom . . . Get my shower ready. The water is warm . . . my skin softens . . . I close my eyes, my face in direct wet streams . . . continue my thinking about him . . . what it would be like . . .

I am boxed in. White tiles surround me. Little squares line the ceiling, on the floor cooling the bottoms of my feet. Water splashes everywhere from something jutting out one side. A glass door closes us in. He towers over me . . . Wetness everywhere . . . The hair on his chest curls along with the steam. We are contained. Nothing else goes in or goes out . . . Soap clings to his hands spreading a film all over my breasts, my nipples; hard from the twilight, the slight coolness, the white cubicle we are in . . .

In all that white haze he gives me gifts of lush fields, snowy soft cotton clouds, and fingers that make honey

flow from the deepest parts of my darkness. Laughter with
raging tears bubbles up to the surface; devouring me,
melting me suddenly too fast. He turns me around to enter
me, my lips touch the wall, hands propped up high, my
fleshy bottom enveloping his urgency . . . his desire . . . his
harsh whispers echo to the top of the ceiling then down to
the ground, where only our feet know where we stand.
Breaths sound louder, heartbeats seem longer. Torrents of
water beat down on skin like storm rain. My words are
washed away with no thought . . . "Take me away from
everything."

Storm stops. Silence . . . Only the sound of one water
tear hitting long shiny metal . . . Time takes on another
name . . . I turn around to see . . . Dewdrops resting on his
eyes, his fingers where he probed tight openings; lips full,
swollen from bites, my hunger. My tongue mouth lips run
moments along his back so strong, sturdy; he is built for
raging storms. He looks young to me; a glow in his face
after discovering something new, something right. His lips
taste of sweet blackberry wine and his eyes remind me of
the seas where I lived a long time ago . . . Eyes that follow
me home, eyes that are surprised wondering how they arrived to this place of bright white; eyes that remain in pictures in my mind . . . Blue, green sapphires, glistening,
staring down into me; beckoning me to come again . . . I
dry his damp skin with a cloth made of soft white cotton.
Slowly, smoothly I run it up and down his shoulders bare,
his thighs, his arms, the top of his head; but his lips I keep
wet . . . running dew water with my fingertips, keeping
them moist . . . keeping them all mine . . .

I awaken from what seems like a dream. Grab the towel and
slowly dry off my wet body. Catching a glimpse of my face in
the mirror, I think how I've got to snap out of this. My daydreams seem to be taking hold of me . . . too strong a pull . . .
What is real anymore? What is a fantasy? What do I want?

The carpenter calls me late that afternoon. Tells me about his
table again. It is long, dark . . . He tells me that his father would
cut meat on it and his mother kneaded dough. He tells me how

he carved it from the finest trees . . . with his hands . . . I remember his hands . . . Sensitive, rough in the palms . . . a carpenter who likes to build houses . . .

He asks me to come over . . . to show me the table, of course . . . I hesitate . . . What is going on here? What do I expect? I do not know him well . . . only that he smells of birch, pine, and oil that is used to polish wood. I am curious. We agree to meet tomorrow. That night I dream of tables . . .

I enter his room. It is empty . . . only one long table . . . dark brown . . . we both walk into the dim light . . . one small window in the corner . . . I watch leaves tremble on the tree outside flashing diamonds onto the walls . . . dancing on the ceiling . . . hypnotizing me . . . making me forget what is outside . . . He tells me to turn around and then he lifts my skirt . . . fingers travel up along the back of my thighs . . . forming straight lines of electricity . . . burning trails leading to tunnels wet, moist, waiting to spread wider . . . he asks me if I want him . . . I answer with a light stroke of one hand . . . he pulls on my hair demanding I say it in words . . . my silence provokes him . . . my touch beckons a hardness in him . . . fierce, rapid; he changes into another man . . . thrusting in deeply, his finger becomes fire . . . I lean on top of that table . . . my hands grabbing, holding steady, my nipples hard, rubbing the fine wood . . . My prayer is answered in more ways than I know . . .

Madness makes me turn around. I look at his face. My mouth reaches for his fingers . . . sucking the wood scent . . . easing the crazy yearning, endless craving . . . desire to be thrusted . . . till rawness overtakes my want for more . . . "Tell me you want it," he whispers. "Say it and I will do it." I drop his hand, unbutton my dress, and show him in words he'd rather hear . . .

The phone rings, waking me from my dream. It is morning. My husband has already left for work. I never saw him last night. He got in late . . . like so many nights lately . . . Didn't have a chance to talk to him . . .

I answer the phone. "No one will be home. A good time to see the table."

I hang up the phone. Something about his voice . . . I feel flushed. I go to my closet. Think about what he would like. I finger the black silk. This is crazy! Why am I so concerned about what to wear? I sit in front of my typewriter . . . got to get to work . . . my mind wanders . . . back to the party . . .

Hours pass. It is evening already. No word from my husband. I feel relief. A car horn beeps outside . . . My taxicab is here to take me to him. Maybe I should cancel . . . maybe I should stay home . . . this whole thing is a waste of time . . . Why am I doing this? He's married. I'm married. Just another fantasy . . . another escape, I hear that voice in my head. You're running away again . . . running away from reality . . . responsibility.

I enter the cab; sit down trying to catch my breath. "Are you okay, lady?" he asks. "I'm fine. I'm fine." I give him the address. Just want a few minutes to catch my breath. To think . . . I check my skirt; my blouse is disheveled, buttoned in the wrong places. I smooth my hair down. I feel my cheeks still flushed. "Hey lady, you want a cigarette?" The driver startles me back to the present. He is an older man, dark skin. He resembles my husband. I do not reply. I just sit there looking at his forehead, eyebrows, and eyes in his rearview mirror. His eyes . . . dark, probing . . . maybe he would know . . . an answer, a word, something to piece all of this together neatly in correct straight lines; not zigzags and curves all going in roundabout circles . . . At the stoplight, that's when I ask him, "Would you ever have an affair with someone who is married?"

I enter the apartment building . . . walk up the stairs. Knock on the door. He opens the door. A warm smile. "Please come in." He closes the door while lightly touching the small of my back. I feel a spark . . . light . . . a warmth I never experienced before. We talk for a while. He has a warm smile. His hair falls into his eyes . . . frequently he brushes it back. I find myself restraining the urge to run my fingers through it . . . He shows me the table. Tells me how long it took for him to build it . . . the hours of polishing, refining it . . . perfectly each and every angle, curve. "Like a woman," he says, "a man needs to give undivided attention to his woman . . . slowly, carefully, lovingly." There is a charge between us. I see an intensity in his eyes . . . I tell him that I need time to think it over . . . the table,

I mean . . . I linger, then decide to leave . . . "Need air," I say.
He smiles while opening the door. I say to myself how this
whole thing was a fantasy in my mind. Just another fantasy . . .
Probably better this way . . . I do not need any more confusion
in my life. He then embraces me. Pins me up against the wall.
We stand in the hallway . . . in the shadows . . . someone could
walk by. This is happening all too quickly. He slides his hands
under my blouse grasping my breasts. Stroking, caressing each
nipple with his fingers; twisting harder with each breath; making me moan, wanting more. I try to break away, but then I find
myself pressing my hips against him wanting to excite him;
tempt him. I feel his urgency. He then hikes up my tight skirt,
spreading my legs, both wrapped in black nylon, garter belt, no
panties. Just hair covering a place that is warm, moist, ready for
his touch. His fingers enter me, probing my darkness . . . a fever
inside of me mounting . . . making me lose sense of time . . . As
he kneels to the floor, I know what he is about to do. I want
him to. My lips are swollen, alive, pulsating for his mouth.
Sweat along with wet juice escapes me. I arch my back up
against the wall to gain time. He stands and whispers, "I want
you, here."

Just then I hear someone close by. I see a shadow from above
me. He looks like a man holding a bag in his hands. His footsteps stop near us. I see a shadow duck under a doorway. I
sense he is watching us. I grow more excited. I want this man,
this stranger to see my nipples erect sticking with sweat to my
blouse. I want him to see my hips grinding up against my lover's
mouth; my sweet pussy lips grow more swollen with each moan
that escapes from my throat. I see him leave; walk up back the
stairs, slowly. I wanted him to come back and watch us. All of
a sudden, I panic.

My eyes start to focus. I am not in a fantasy, a daydream.
This is real! With very little light from the faraway dim bulb on
the porch I still see the walls in the hallway; how cracked they
are. I tell him I am going. He pulls me to his chest, caressing my
bottom, beckoning me, enticing me to stay. His body is like a
magnet; fast, fierce, drawing me into his torso. Making it hard
to break away . . . I run out.

The night air is cool. My body still hot. Stars bright. I walk
home thinking about him . . . how he placed his hand on the

small of my back. That touch created a wonder . . . baffling me . . . catching me off guard . . . taking my breath away . . . creating a curiosity in my mind about how certain people come into my life . . . unexpectedly, bad timing perhaps, but maybe not at all. Maybe that is what I'm learning . . . how people, situations, come not in neat little preplanned perfectly timed packages; but, in waves, uneven, surprising, puzzling me yet delighting me; drawing me into another world . . . path . . . dimension I've never imagined before . . .

I walk into my house. It is late. My husband startles me for a moment. He is sitting in a chair in the dark. A glass filled with whiskey in one hand. His face looks worn, tired, lines run across his forehead. I have an urge to reach out and trace those lines with my fingers. Fingers that caressed another man's body hours before. Instead I take off my coat.

"Where have you been?" he asks. I go to sit across from him. Do not know what to say. Instead a lie flows out of my mouth. Telling him about the hallway episode would do no good. It happened so quickly. Too real. Too frightening. Shouldn't have gone over there . . . too dangerous . . . must forget about him . . . There is a marriage for me to work on.

I ask my husband if he would like to hear another dream . . . a dream I had last night. He leans forward. My whispers draw him in closer . . . he used to enjoy my little stories. Always, from the moment we met . . . how, attentive he looks . . . just like the carpenter at the party . . . Softly, I begin . . .

The light casts a shadow across his face. We sit opposite each other . . . at a table . . . I thought I knew him . . . Did I create this monster? This whole thing with my words, gestures; the way I move? "You walk for them, not for me; who do you think you are?" It wasn't the first time he said this . . . egging me on in public . . . where other eyes fill the room . . . Wearing a tight low-cut black gown, I thought my performance would please him. Earlier that evening, before going out, he tells me to wear it with the four-inch spikes, sleek nylon mesh panties, stockings that run lines up along my thighs, smooth glossy; fine to the touch. Standing behind me while hanging white pearls, he tightens the clasp close to my throat as he whispers what every man would want to do to me . . . what he would do with his hands, mouth, tongue, and leather belt. According to cue, I respond with cold indifference . . . he likes me that way, only that way . . . it makes him sweat, squirm . . . It is all a game . . . I play it well and he rewards me . . . a role I play, I slip into . . . like the fine silk gowns he gives me . . .

Now in the restaurant, I come back to the present . . . I rise slowly . . . Standing there hovering over him . . . his cold sunken dark eyes boring right through me . . . daring me to blow this whole thing apart . . . the pearl necklace nearly choking the words right out of me . . . cutting too close to my vein . . . Throwing my napkin to the floor, every head turns in that room . . . that fancy white linen, gold napkin ring, diamond chandelier type of place . . . where bottles of sparkle start never below a hundred . . . I throw it down with such force and stare into those eyes . . . those eyes that control people, things, everything around him . . . eyes that match Italian-cut tailored suits; eyes that buy fancy little-boy toys, yachts, cars, long white lines on shiny mirrors, and so-called promised trips around the world . . . eyes that could melt me if I slip for one second from my made-for-him mask . . . Into those eyes, I whisper only once but with such fury redness blurs my vision, "You will never possess me!" And, with that, I walk out . . .

I open my eyes. He sits across from me, dozing. Almost falling asleep. My throat tenses up. We do not move. I wait patiently. Anger, frustration, boil inside of me. I do not say a word. Slowly rising, I stand hovering over him wanting to spit in his face. That man face. That face that resembles hundreds in my dreams.

He wakes up and smiles. "I'm sorry, honey. What did you say? Need to go upstairs to bed. So tired . . ." While watching him climb the stairs my body shakes with rage. I cannot even express what I really want to say. Finally, I take my purse and coat and walk out the door.

*   *   *

I find myself wandering downtown. "You're running again," I hear the voice in my head say. "Trying to escape . . . You'd better start being responsible." Maybe I should have told him what happened in the hallway. Piece all of this together with him. I don't know. I can't even think about all of this right now. I have my marriage . . . my marriage . . . Do I still want it? I check into a motel room. Need to sleep. Need to think clearly . . . I'll do it later . . . tired.

I wake in the morning. Still in a daze. Ashamed of my feelings. I usually am in complete control. Not right to feel like that . . . Try calling my husband. No answer. Probably already at work. The morning is dark, overcast . . . clouds threatening rain. I decide to check out . . . walk downtown, do some window shopping . . . get my mind off of things . . .

Wind gets colder. I wrap my coat tighter around me. Breakfast does not appeal to me. I wander. Storefront pane glass reflects back to me a face that looks different. The face of a woman that craves something more in her life . . . a life filled with passion . . . desire. A woman who preferred safety . . . security . . . many years ago, but feels differently now. She smells something changing in the air. Something that reminds her of when she was young. As I glance away, my eyes meet those of a tall, dark, handsome man. We pass each other on the street. His briefcase in hand. Raincoat perfectly tailored. He smiles and says good morning. His eyes linger longer than usual. Electricity passes between us. I notice how he stops, turns around, and watches me cross the street. I am that woman in the window . . . A very different woman now . . .

A furniture store catches my eyes. The tables in the window lure me to walk in. Wood glistens in the sunlight. I turn my head toward the far corner of the showroom. I hear voices. A man lovingly describes a table. A voice that sounds soothing, familiar . . . I walk closer to the back of the store . . . following the voices . . . My eyes first notices hands . . . hands stroking the fine wood . . . slowly . . . I look up. I see that it is him! I should leave. This is getting too involved . . . complicated . . . but I find myself lingering . . . unable to leave . . . fascinated by the way he caresses the wood . . . running his hands slowly along the edges. "See the grain . . . so fine . . . so beautiful."

"Well, we'll think about it and probably come back." As the customers walk away, he looks up and sees me. Eyes meet. I hesitate. He doesn't. He comes right over . . . a place where we may go . . . a room far away from intrusion . . . I like the sound of his voice . . . low, deep, soothing . . . I take his arm and walk with him . . .

We lie on sheets, white with sweat. A raven cries outside our window. I see the flutter of black wings, frantic, beating the air beyond the pane glass while he speaks of a hawk circling his mind earlier that day. I turn my head to gaze at his lips so full from kisses. His eyes open, light against skin so cool, calm; away from the world outside. My fingertips reach out touching his chest, now bare covered with hair exposed for me to see. He asks for a story . . . a story of how we could be together . . . if things were different . . .

I tell him of a cottage . . . a place we can go . . . a place where my windows would be lit with dozens of pink candles surrounded with roses all long-stemmed, scattered with petals falling, blowing away in the breeze. I shall cook for you, build a fire for you, wash your hair in the morning sun. I will kiss you and spread thighs wide open for you . . . all with long blue ribbons covering tall bedposts and vines of jasmine close by. Wetness and rain, hard nipples and flushed cheeks . . . that is what will await you, I tell him, in a whisper, close to his ear.

I look at him and shudder . . .

He plays with fire while with me . . . Striking matches, hoping not to get burned. I do not say this, some things are better left unsaid . . .

So instead, I go on with my story . . . I tell him let's pretend we are in France. Away from the noise, the swirling colors of a much-too-fast life. I have a cottage inn where I grow my very own flowers and write in the evenings after my guests are asleep. He tells me that he will visit me . . . in summer for warmth, in winter, for fire . . . His car will be long with dark-shaded windows. No one would know who this mysterious man would be. This mystery man of mine who hides away. This man who holds danger so close to his heart.

*   *   *

He plays with fire while with me . . . striking matches . . . striking matches . . .

My story ends . . . I lie facing him . . . watching him . . . all with a wonder . . . my soul deepening, merging with his . . . There, I think, time has no ending or beginning in a dream. All in that room I find we have no past, no future to name, to interfere. Moments swirl as we press against flesh . . . we are different . . . brand-new . . . like shiny gold pennies that glow hot in the sunlight in palms eager to hold on to . . . jangle, jangle, we go, all around and around. Tumbling down into something . . . a spark, perhaps fire, down, all the way down . . . I am free when I am with him. My flesh turns pink from warm moisture, slow caresses, and hushed laughter in white-tiled cubicles that shower down rain . . .

A whole day has passed . . . I get up, brush hair, see in the reflection . . . I am different, soft, open, not ready to go back . . . to another time, another place . . . I glance at his eyes to remember the bright hue . . . perhaps to carry something back with me, to help carry me through . . . I hesitate; feeling a pull, hearing a whisper telling me stay, don't go . . .

He plays with fire while with me . . . striking blue, red, yellow matches . . . All smelling of glowing red flame.

I walk out of the motel room. Quietly I close the door so he may sleep. Stepping out into the night air, I look up at the moon. So full, bright . . . I want to keep him close to me . . . next to my heart . . . for just a while longer . . . I wonder what this man is bringing me to learn . . . find out about my life . . . The night air clears my head . . . What am I doing? Confusion begins to swirl in my head again . . . This affair, or perhaps my marriage, may not be right . . . What is the answer? Where do I go? My heart and thighs say one thing . . . my sense of responsibility says another.

I go home. My husband is not here. What has happened to him . . . to me? I sleep for a while . . . tossing and turning thinking about the night . . . my lover and his lips, tongue, thighs rubbing on top of me. The next morning I wake with a rock on my heart. A rock so heavy that it pins my chest to the bed.

Turning my head to look out the window, I try to make a bargain; strike a deal with the gods. It's a game I play when I don't know what to do. I used to play it all the time the year my Papa died. "I will do this if you do that for me. I swear I will give up that if this happens." Words flow in circles in my mind. I like to play tricks with myself. It used to take the pain away, but now it doesn't seem to be doing any good. All I feel is the coldness of wind that rushes in from gray skies . . . threatening me with storm . . . Things are different now. I'm not that little girl anymore.

As hard as it is I try lifting that rock off of my chest. Maybe there is an answer underneath. A word that would help me understand . . . I don't want to be pinned on that bed. All I want is to lie next to my husband on moist earth like we used to do; thighs, arms, feet touching; next to blue water, a carved tree, watching spaces between leaves on green branches that shimmer diamonded sunlight. I want to dance with him on rocks, hold hands reaching toward white ceilings and sit in caves that could be so dark that even the spirits prefer roaming around outside . . . The whispering of stories in ears; the tips of my fingers tingling with his light . . . But his heart has already gone . . . far away . . . he is not here for me.

The truth comes back to me as heavy as that rock; once again, weighing me down. With him I am dead. I stand up. Throw that rock out the open pane that shines brightly, clearly. My eyes catch colored leaves falling outside . . . passionate loving reds, yellows, browns . . . Whispering to me softly as they give way . . .

I Wanted To

Lisa Prosimo

I wanted to against the wall inside our Brooklyn project's apartment. I wanted to on the kitchen table where my mother's blueberry pie cooled. I wanted to in the tall scratchy grasses in the field before they built the A&P. I wanted to underneath the boardwalk at Coney Island while sand rained down on my bare breasts. I wanted to in the car under the street lamp on Myrtle Avenue. I wanted to under the blanket while I strained to hear the Beatles sing on *The Ed Sullivan Show*. I desperately wanted to, but I didn't. I waited until my wedding night and did it in a bed at the Plaza Hotel with my new husband, a boy who wanted to, but never did, either.

I remember how I cried atop our expensive rented bed, a present from our parents, who blushed when they handed us the reservation. "From us," they said. "Happy wedding night."

My husband was cross. "Why are you crying?" he demanded. I didn't know then how to tell him that he'd hurt and disappointed me.

"Mrs. Kennedy has three dead sons," I sobbed.

Bobby Kennedy had been killed a few days before our wedding while he was campaigning in Los Angeles for the presidential nomination.

"What? What!"

I looked at the fresh flowers, the antique furniture, and ran my hand along the plush bathrobe at the foot of the bed. "Bobby might have been president," I said, "if some jerk hadn't shot him dead."

"This is our wedding night, goddammit!"

"Yes," I said, looking down at the pink goo streaked along the insides of my thighs. "I know."

My husband looked like a giant bird flapping its arms in confusion. I closed my eyes. Fly away. Please. How ironic that all those nights of groping and twisted clothing, all the sweat and denial, should come to this.

At gatherings with friends, Ted sat with his arm around me, reached over to peck me on the cheek every now and then, squeezed my shoulder, and gave me a wink. His public display of affection annoyed me, but I hid my displeasure and smiled; pretended that yes, this was Camelot.

"Gosh, you two look so great together," said one of my girlfriends. "And he can't keep his hands off you."

But it wasn't like that in bed. No peck on the cheek, no squeeze on the shoulder. Each time we had sex I'd shut my eyes and see my uncle's barnyard the summer I spent on his small farm in Pennsylvania. When I got bored, I walked out to the chicken coop and watched the rooster jump on the hens, make a violent noise, and jump off. I felt like one of those hens. But the rooster, I remember, didn't fall asleep right afterward, and he didn't snore.

Sometimes I'd catch Ted staring at me, eyes hard, mouth grim, looking as if he wanted to kill me. Why should he look at me like that? Did I extract haste from his body? Did the fault for his going alone into some deep space during our lovemaking belong at my feet? No, I didn't think so.

Okay. So I was ripe. A dumb kid with a broken libido. What a combination.

The first time I saw Greg, that day he walked into our department as the new manager of sales at Cook's Plumbing Supplies, I didn't think much of him. He was older, tall, stocky, with a face that looked like it was forged by the elements of an unforgiving land. But Greg was an urban creature, raised on the streets of Hell's Kitchen, as I came to learn, whose manner and speech were absolutely direct. I guess that's what I liked most about him: the way his eyes swallowed everyone he looked at, the way he conveyed an order or a request. Inside the confines of his impeccable suits, I sensed a wildness about him that thoroughly intrigued me. I typed his letters and made his appointments and even brought him coffee in the morning, and all he did was smile and say thanks.

Until one Friday night, when everyone else had gone home. I had one letter to complete before beginning my weekend. All of a sudden I couldn't see the words I was typing. My eyes overflowed with tears. I didn't want to spend the weekend with Ted, go to his parents' for dinner, watch television until he fell asleep. I felt so idiotic, especially when I realized Greg was standing behind me. I don't know when I noticed his hand on my shoulder, caressing me lightly. He didn't say a word, but bent and kissed me on the ear. I turned my face toward his; he stuck out his tongue to lick a tear from my cheek, straightened up, smiled down at me, and walked into his office. All at once my body tightened as if I were wrapped in cords. The cords tugged at me, pulled me up, slithered over me like snakes, and produced a strange humming sound within my ears, like when you drink one scotch too many. I got up, shoved my chair back, and as if in a trance, walked to Greg's office. I pushed open the door and saw him leaning against his desk, his arms wrapped across his chest, a slight smile on his lips. I don't know how I got to where he stood, but suddenly I was there. It was like standing close to a fire and being blinded by the glow. All at once I was falling into him.

"I love that skirt you're wearing," he whispered. I had to look down to remember what I had on. It was the black wool, the one with buttons up the side, and a slit that exposed a good deal of my leg. Greg bent to stroke me through the slit, grasped my thigh, his fingers inflaming the skin beneath my stockings. The breath left my lungs; my panties, I realized, were soaked through. God! I had never felt like this. He lifted me onto the desk, told me to lean forward on my knees. I did. Greg began to undo the buttons, starting from the bottom and working his way up until the skirt fell away. He caressed my ass through my pantyhose, sending chills across my skin. He slowly pulled down the hose, along with my underpants, while he kissed and licked my cheeks and thighs, tiny wet kisses and tongue flicks that left small fires raging. I squirmed against him, could feel the heat of my sex radiate between my legs. His hot tongue entered me, searing the swelling flesh. I moaned. Greg moved his

tongue in and out of me in a lazy motion, rolling it over my clitoris, then pulling back. He did that for a long time, all the while
murmuring how sweet I tasted, how good I smelled. His strong
arms grasped me around the waist and turned me over until I
lay on my back, my legs dangling over the desk. He loomed
over me, reached up and unbuttoned my blouse, peeled the fabric away and undid the clasp on my bra. My breasts sprang
from the lace cups and Greg caught a nipple between his lips.
He sucked first one, then the other, drawing the nipple far into
his mouth, savoring it the way a child savors a tasty treat. "You
have magnificent breasts," he said, then brought his face up to
mine, kissed me long and tenderly. I could taste myself in his
mouth and became drunk on the flavor of my own sex.

During that first encounter with Greg, I thought of nothing.
At that moment, I was not Ted's wife, not the woman who visited Planned Parenthood and whose diaphragm was tucked into
the top drawer of her nightstand. There were only Greg's hands
kneading my flesh, his fingers finding their way inside me; his
lips teasing my breasts, my belly and that part of me I had never
named. Cunt. Greg teased my cunt. The word added passion to
the act. A word, inadequate at best, to describe that part of me
that usurped the rest of me. In my circle of innocence, women
didn't have cunts, they were cunts, especially women who gave
men a hard time. Lying on top of that desk, I had a cunt. A
huge, all-consuming cunt.

Greg stood up and pulled me against his chest. "Undress
me," he said.

My fingers trembled as I worked the buttons on his shirt. I
pulled off his undershirt and brushed my face against the hair
on his chest. My hands tugged at his zipper; it came down easily. I pushed his pants down over his hips, reached inside his
briefs, and touched him. "I want you to lick me," he said.
"Then I want you to take me in as far as I can go, as if you were
going to swallow me. And then I want you to suck me until my
cock can't get any harder, until the veins are bulging out and the
tip is dripping and purple and ready to explode."

His words, said in a hoarse whisper, excited me so that even
the hairs on the back of my neck responded. I wanted his
penis—his cock—in my mouth. In that moment, I could not
have wanted anything more. I did all the things he wanted me

to. I licked him, took him in as far as he would go; swallowed him. And when we were done, I wanted more.

I went home reeking of sex, but Ted had fallen asleep on the couch. I tore off my clothes, threw them in a bag destined for the dry cleaner, and took a shower. That night, as we sat across from Ted's parents eating his mother's pot roast, I could hardly contain my joy—what else could I have called it but joy?—and I sat there nodding as my mother-in-law told her tale of tearing lingerie out of the hands of fellow shoppers, my feigned interest cheering her on. Ah, the bliss of getting a Vanity Fair camisole at thirty percent off!

I look back, and I don't know how I got away with what I did. All those mornings leaving early, making love with Greg on his desk before anybody came to work; staying late, rolling all over the carpet, too lusted out to notice the patches of skin missing from my back until I undressed later, vaguely wondering why I felt as if I'd stayed out in the sun too long. We did it everywhere—in the executive washroom, in the Xerox room, in his car, me straddling him, my full skirt fanned over us, his body securely wedged inside mine. Those fucks, quick and furious, grinding down so hard, so fast, just to get it over with, just to feel and savor that eruption within me, that blast that never failed to surprise me, that made my juices rise like hot lava, spill over and sear my skin. At night, I'd look in the mirror and stare into eyes that sparkled with a secret, and under my breath ask, "Who are you?"

The same girl who stood before Ted the day he gathered all of us—his parents, my parents, my sister, his sister and brother—to tell us that he had joined the Marines. I thought his mother would faint.

Why?

"I've taken a stand. I believe in this war."

No. Impossible.

Yes.

Off to Vietnam. Just like that.

In my world, "free love" only happened on television between poorly groomed individuals. Now, here I was, suddenly free. Free to have my boss drive me home in the evenings. Free to make love with him in my own bed. Free to give in to daydreams of us together forever, sinful imaginings of Ted being blown to bits, or the victim of napalm, running in the streets naked, like that picture of the little girl running, on fire, the one all over the news.

Such things do not go on in a small Brooklyn neighborhood without notice. Mrs. Pongelli, my landlady, handed me a package the mailman couldn't fit in the box. Disapproval painted on her lips. "It's from your husband, poor thing. So brave to go fight over there in that jungle. Just to keep you safe. If I were you, I'd get down on my knees and thank the Virgin for sending me such a wonderful young man. You should go to church, pray—"

The key turned, I hurried into my apartment, slamming her voice in the door. Old bitch. My body shook, rage collected on my skin leaving me clammy. I stripped, flung my dress to the floor, hurried into the bathroom, and turned on the shower, anxious to feel the water on me, as if that would wash away the old woman's words. The water hit the tile, little needles that captured the remaining sunlight streaming through the window. I shut off the spray. I wouldn't shower.

We couldn't be together that night, Greg and I. He had obligations at home. That's all he would ever tell me. "I have obligations at home, Josie." I wasn't allowed to ask, although he never said as much. Just the way he said it, the way he looked at me as he said it, withdrew my permission. I gathered my purse, the novel I read during lunch breaks, and headed for the elevator with my coworkers, Harry and Belle. We were the last ones to leave.

"Josie," Greg called. "Before you go, would you show me where you put the Thompson contracts?"

The elevator left without me. Greg pulled me into his office; his hands traveled over my breasts, my ass, his cock pressed against my thigh. My mind began to form words, sarcastic words to remind him he didn't have time for me this evening. But his breath caressed my ear as he told me he couldn't let me go, how through the whole day he could only think about the touch of my hands on his skin, the taste of me inside his mouth. He kissed me until I was dizzy, pulled my dress up, my pantyhose down. His tongue slipped inside me, easy, painted the walls of my cunt, one coat, two coats, desire thick and luminous. I came in glorious shades of reds and oranges, lemon yellows and rich greens, riding the crest of a rainbow.

A whisper against my throat, "Josie . . . it doesn't matter that you go home to yours and I go home to mine. You belong to me. Do you understand?"

I nodded, yes, yes. I belonged to him.

Greg made me get up on all fours and crawl backward onto him. He plunged into me, his balls slapped against the base of my ass. He slipped his arm around my waist, pulled me up to him, clamped his mouth over my ear, whispered, "I want you to leave my come in you tonight. Don't wash me away . . . and later . . . I want you to think of us together, concentrate on the wet hot feeling between your legs and make yourself come again." His words thrilled me, my sex closed around him, gripped him snugly, milked him, and I came again, so overwhelmed by the intensity I couldn't make a sound. "You are full of me, Josie. You have everything. All of me." He pumped into me wildly, yelped like a wounded dog as he came, the force of his orgasm crashing against the walls of my vagina. I collapsed onto the rug, Greg's body over mine. His breathing came fast in my ear as he sighed my name over and over.

Inside my chest my heart thumped, under my clothes my skin glistened. Greg turned me over, kissed me, licked the salt from my lips. He smiled at me as if we shared old secrets and then murmured that he had to go. But he didn't move. He kept me there in the crook of his arm for a while longer. Finally, he got up, arranged his clothing, then helped me to my feet. He snapped off the light in his office and together we rode the elevator down.

That evening, I did exactly as he'd ordered.

As far as I was concerned, it could have gone on forever. I lost track of time, of the boundaries between my being Greg's lover and Ted's wife, whom I'd promised to love, honor, and obey. And write letters to. The pen pal who dutifully scribbled all the weeks' news, with one notable exception. Ted's letters spoke of rot and heat and putrid smoke, of snakes huge and slimy, of ruined earth where rice fields once stood. His words covered the pages in slow, languid sentences filled with introspection and retrospection, not like letters at all, but more like entries in a journal. Never any words of love, of longing, of missing me. I vaguely wondered if he might know, vaguely wondered if I cared.

Every day after leaving the apartment, I slipped over the edge of my world into Greg's world. For eight, ten, twelve hours, whatever time we had together, I was completely his. We worked well together grappling sales figures and juggling appointments, busy, always busy, and during those times, I'd get a sense of the familiar, a feeling of eternity. Contentment.

Smack in the middle of the euphoria, the bottom fell out. We stood, the whole office, drinking champagne and munching on canapés, a bit sloshed, high-spirited, as Mr. Meese from the home office congratulated our division for being first in sales. Here, here. He said we had a good man in Greg Morrison. The best. So good, he was being moved along to a vice-presidency, transferred to a city halfway across the country.

I watched a bird soar off the ledge of the building opposite ours. There was something terrifying about how it kept going higher and higher up to the sky until it turned into a silver dot and disappeared. Something squeezed my gut, my eyelids fluttered; then I disappeared.

I opened my eyes to the curious stares of my coworkers milling about outside the open door of Greg's office, where I lay on the leather couch, a washcloth on my forehead. What might have been suspicion for some was now certainty for all. But I was beyond caring, even as I heard Belle explain that I'd had too much to drink on an empty stomach. Her nervous laugh and hand gestures persuaded the others to go on with the party. She tiptoed back and shut the door, leaving me alone. Outside, Greg continued to be the man of the hour, accepting hugs and slaps of commendation.

Later, I cried as Greg explained, his voice patient, how he had worked all his life for this. I wasn't listening. He reminded me that he was nearly forty and I was just twenty. My throat closed, the pain inside like a gash across my windpipe. My chest filled with a grief so heavy I could hardly sit up. I heard him say, "I love you, Josie, but this is my life, my career. I never meant to hurt you. . . ."

*   *   *

Time heals nothing. For weeks I lay around the apartment dressed in an old ratty bathrobe, unshowered, unfed, unwell. I couldn't go back to the office, to a place where Greg had been. "Josie," Belle said, "at least call and tell them you quit. You've been a good worker. Don't you want a letter of recommendation?" I didn't care about a letter of recommendation. So I didn't call.

I had a friend in high school once who'd had a bad love affair. When she was hurting most, she liked to recall dead relatives. It made her appreciate being alive, she said. I'd never known my dead relatives well enough to recall them, so they stayed in their graves. Instead I recalled my dead relatives who were still walking around: my parents, whose lives seemed devoid of pleasure. My in-laws, who had the same lives as my parents. My friends, who had the same lives as their parents. Tears. Recalling dead relatives didn't work for me.

Time heals nothing, but if enough time passes, a kind of numbness settles in, a blurring of the nerves that allows you to go on. I got another job, even without a letter of recommendation, and stayed busy. At Christmastime, I dressed the tree, I went to parties, I bought presents for the dead, laughed at jokes, ate too much, drank too much, shit my brains out, puked my guts up. And faced a new year. And Ted.

Waiting for Ted's train to pull in at Grand Central, I wondered what I would say to him. Would I even know him? Would he know me? Thirteen months was a long time; it had been a lifetime for me. It was so easy to believe that Ted was gone. Not away at war, just gone. Now he'd be home for a couple of months, then he'd go back to being gone. In the meantime, what would I do? I wondered if Ted would see a change in me. Would my face reflect the experience I'd had?

The dufflebag came down first, then the feet, placed carefully onto each stair as if the shoes contained not flesh and bone, but heavy stones. Ted walked toward me, the expression on his face one I couldn't define. Even though Ted's mouth curved upward, the gesture did nothing to coax a smile from his eyes. When he reached me, he placed his arms around me and hugged me to him in a limp embrace. His lips brushed mine lightly. "You look good, Josie," he said.

"So do you," I lied. He seemed so much smaller than I remembered.

Ted had written that he didn't want anyone but me to meet his train; and in fact, didn't want our relatives to know he was coming home. "I can't stand the idea of a big party," he'd said in his last letter, "at least not the first night I'm back."

As soon as we settled into the cab for the ride home, Ted fell asleep. When the cab came to a stop, I touched his shoulder to wake him. He jumped, nearly hitting his head on the liner, startling not only me, but the driver as well.

"Sorry," he mumbled and got out of the cab, leaving me to pay the fare.

Ted walked around the apartment, pulled open closet doors, kitchen cabinets, as if he'd never been there before. "Has the toilet always been this close to the door?" he asked.

I didn't know him, this strange inspector of square footage.

All these months I had kept up the pretense of being married. What had I expected would change? Here was the boy whose arms I'd teased when we were dating, whose flesh I'd brushed up against with purposeful intent. But he was almost a stranger now, and unwelcome. What had I been waiting for all these months? Why had I avoided ending this farce that masqueraded as a marriage? No matter what our parents would say, no matter how much people would talk, I was suddenly anxious to end it.

"I need to tell you something," I said in a rush.

Ted looked at me steadily for a moment, then shook his head. "No, Josie, you don't need to tell me anything."

"I had an affair!"

"I know."

"It started before you left."

"I know!"

He knew. Why, then, were we standing here when it could have been over long ago? Resentment rose like bile and left a bitter taste in my mouth. I didn't feel my hand moving, but all at once there it was picking up the heavy crystal ashtray on the end table and hurling it toward Ted's head. He moved just a fraction and the ashtray sailed past his ear and smashed into the wall behind him.

I regretted missing his head with that ashtray. My rage

was in that ashtray. It was his fault we were in this mess, his fault for not turning out to be the husband and lover I had needed.

As if I had sprouted wings, I was suddenly across the room, flailing my fists at Ted, punching him in the chest and head. Each blow left only a weak imprint. His arms tightened around me, strangled my limbs in a grip that rendered me as helpless as if I'd been sealed into a straitjacket. From another place, a siren's wail cut through the neighborhood. The symphony of automobiles and shouting children on the street below faded into the background as the sound became louder and louder, packing my ears until it was finally silenced by the crush of Ted's hand over my mouth. Though his grip was savage, his words were tender. "Josie . . . Josie," he crooned against my ear, "I know you hate me. I know . . . and I'm sorry."

"You're not even real anymore! Why did you come back?" The words came out muddled by angry tears. His grasp was so tight, it was useless to struggle, and so we stood, his arms still around me, his breath at my ear.

"Where should I have gone?" Ted whispered. "This is my home. . . . If you promise to calm down, I'll let you go. . . . Promise?" I nodded and Ted loosened his hold.

"Will you please sit down?" he asked, gesturing toward the sofa. I hesitated. "Please. . . ." Reluctantly, I did as he asked, perching on the edge of a cushion. Ted hunched before me. "Every day I expected a letter from you telling me you wanted a divorce, Josie. But when that letter didn't come I figured it didn't work out for you and you just didn't know what to do, just like me."

Ted stood up and began to pace. He gestured with his hands as he spoke, as if he were fashioning his words carefully before presenting them to me.

"You have to know that it wasn't easy for me, either, Josie. I knew I wasn't making you happy in bed."

He stopped, perhaps waiting for a reaction from me, but I had nothing to say. So far, he was batting a thousand. "I didn't know what to do," he repeated. "I wanted so much to please you, but I didn't know how. And there was nobody to talk to. I couldn't ask my friends for advice, they all thought we were such great lovers. I tried to talk to my dad—that was a disaster." He laughed without joy. "And I couldn't kill you . . . so I went away."

The question, "Why didn't you talk to me?" never got past my mind. Though it was a seemingly logical question, I thought it absurd. If he had tried to broach the subject before he went away, while I had been spending every spare moment fucking Greg, I would probably have screamed, "How dare you, how goddamn dare you!"

"Listen, Josie. Every day, I came this close to getting my ass blown away." Ted spread his thumb and index finger apart about an inch to show me how close. "It taught me to leave nothing undone or unsaid." He shook his head. "In the beginning I was scared shitless. We all were. It took a while to realize that nothing you said or thought before you got there was valid. I wondered what the hell I was doing there. Had to remind myself I'd enlisted to get away from . . . this." He gestured toward me. "Yeah, I couldn't make it with my wife, so I ran smack into a fucking inferno. Jesus!

"You can live a lifetime in thirteen months. Ask questions and maybe find some answers. You want to know why I came back. Okay. . . . I came back because this is my home . . . and because I remembered that once we talked about movies and music, and we made jokes and ate pizza. I remembered that we had the same teachers, the same friends, and that you liked me. That's right, isn't it, Josie? You did like me?"

Ted's freedom of speech, the simple honesty in his voice, began to carve a path through the resentment I had stockpiled. My first instinct was to fight that empathic response, to hold on to my grudge. "No!" I could have said. "I never liked you. I have no idea what I ever saw in you in the first place." But I couldn't lie. I had liked him, once, a long time ago, before I noticed how easy it was for him to fall asleep, before he displayed what I thought was indifference.

"Yes, I liked you."

Outside, a sudden stillness settled over the city, obscuring the last of the sun's rays. In just moments, rain, thick and heavy, crashed against the sills and glass and pummeled the roof. The room grew dark, but neither of us made a move for the lamp. Ted stayed still, his silhouette almost black in the graying room. I listened to his breath enter and leave his lungs, setting a rhythm as soothing as one of those quiet melodies on an FM station. God, I was tired.

"There's so much I need to tell you, Josie. Will you listen?"

"Yes."

"When I got there, I couldn't sleep. Then, sometimes I slept so hard that waking up seemed like a dream. I'd open my eyes and see the tops of trees, so green against a sky so blue and I would think: paradise. But that lasted only a second and I quickly realized where I was, and why. I didn't give a shit about anything, started to take chances. Lit cigarettes during tower duty until the guy up there with me—Ben—screamed in my face that I was going to get us both killed. To keep me occupied, he arranged for a couple of girls from the village to join us. I nicknamed mine Josie. . . ."

I squirmed into the cushion. Picturing Ted with that girl he had given my name to made me bristle with an inexplicable jealousy, an emotion my intellect scoffed at, but one I couldn't stop my gut from reacting to. At the same time I had to laugh at the nerve of me for being jealous.

"Nothing unsaid," he reminded me. "She giggled the first time she hauled my dick out of my pants. I came all over her fingers even before she had a chance to get her mouth on me."

"Jesus."

"What's the matter? Do the details make you uncomfortable? Don't worry. I'm not going to ask you to give me details. I just want to tell you these things."

I peered out the window, stared at the smudged sky, massive with rain, angry with lightning. "Go on."

"There've been other Josies. Girls with sweet smiles and beautiful hair. And I learned something from each of them."

In contrast to the weather, and in spite of that small flash of jealousy, I realized that every bit of my anger was gone, replaced by an all-invasive sadness.

"Did you fall in love with any of your Josies?"

Ted laughed softly. "Sure . . . I loved them all."

"I feel so empty, Ted. So fucked-up . . ."

He reached over and squeezed my hand. "I know," he whispered. He stretched across me and snapped on the light; clicked twice until it gave off its softest glow. He smiled at me, leaned over, untied his shoes, and took them off. He did the same with his socks. Then Ted stood up, removed his tie, unfastened the buttons of his shirt down the front and at the wrists. I watched, like a spectator, as he pulled his belt free and unzipped his fly. He didn't take off his clothes, but squatted down in front of me and pulled off my shoes. With one hand, he grasped my ankle, and with the other, kneaded the instep of my foot, exerting a light but steady pressure. For months, my body had been numb. Now, even with Ted's hands soothing me, I felt like a bystander, a voyeur, as if he were touching someone else's body. When he was through massaging one foot, he started in on the other. "We're not so different, you and me. I found out something about us, about all of us. . . . Sex never lies, Josie."

Slowly, Ted leaned forward and covered my mouth with his, not forcefully as he used to, but almost as though he were sampling an appetizer, nibbling, tasting. I closed my eyes to the observer in me, gradually became a participant, a partner in the kiss. My hand slid between us, caressed the smooth skin inside his open shirt.

I'd been wrong about Ted's structure seeming smaller. I realized his body had simply lost the excess softness I remembered. As my hand traveled over his pectoral muscles, I couldn't help but appreciate the economy of his lean, hard frame. My senses awakened.

I kissed him back. Licked, sucked his mouth, his jaw, his neck, his chest. Ted reached up and lightly touched my breast, his fingertips barely brushing my nipple through the fabric of my dress. Immediately, my breasts felt weighted, ached for more. I pressed closer, aware of my ragged breath against his skin. He touched my chin, tipped my head back, and licked my neck slowly. Without stopping his tongue, he reached around and tugged on the zipper of the sheath; the zipper slid down easily, its sound like skis in fresh snow.

"Sit on my face," he whispered.

Ted slid the dress up past my hips. He quickly freed the tops of the nylons from my garter belt and rolled them down and off. He pulled me off the sofa, lay flat on his back, and tugged gently at my hips. I straddled him and shimmied along his chest, then eased down over his mouth. His tongue on my flesh was a revelation. Ted's strong hands grasped the cheeks of my ass and pulled downward, letting his tongue reach further inside me. I gasped. His strong arms lifted me off his mouth, let me hover over his lips and tongue while he blew warm steady breaths against my sex. I strained to reach his mouth, my hips dancing to a deep, internal rhythm, but he kept me at bay, teasing me, every so often licking the lips lightly while ignoring my clitoris. My God, I thought. Does he know what he's doing? Lick me there, for Christ's sake, lick me there!

Of course Ted knew what he was doing. Driving me crazy; proving he'd learned more than war in that steamy jungle. Suddenly, his mouth clamped over my warm, wet cunt and he began to suck. He burrowed his tongue, his lips, his teeth into me, as if he were devouring a ripe fig. The stimulation was so thorough, so unbearable, I arched my back, cried out as the fire in my spine shot into the pit of my belly, soared up into my brain and exploded there, sending down spasms of delirious pleasure clear to the soles of my feet.

I slumped over Ted, spent. After a few moments, he rolled me off his body, removed my ruined dress and garter belt, and tossed them aside. He pulled off his clothes as I lay on my back looking up into his face, trying to see the boy who'd gone away. He wasn't there. "All right," he whispered. "All right," and gently moved my hand to his tight, up-drawn balls. He kissed me as he hooked my legs over his hips and pushed into me, all the way, in one strong stroke. "Oh, Josie," he moaned, as I locked my ankles into the small of his back to feel him more deeply. "Oh, Josie," and for a moment I wondered which Josie he was feeling. "I'm going to fuck you so hard," he hissed sweetly. "So hard . . ." He moved against me and my cunt clenched around him, gripping him tightly. "Oh, God . . . that's it. Yes, that's it . . ."

The impact of his thrusts made me groan with pleasure. His strong, steady pounding brought me up to a level of sensation I'd never experienced before. Ted threw back his head, bared his teeth, gathered all his strength, and plunged into me again and again, harder than I thought possible. My fingers knotted in his hair, I drew up my hips to meet every sharp slap against my thighs. Ted lashed his tongue against mine; in the intensity of our pleasure we sucked and bit like ravenous hunters at a kill. Slippery mouths, sweaty bodies, building up speed like a great steam engine, sparks of passion flying as his iron-hard cock beat against my greedy cunt. Again he groaned, pulled his mouth free, and flung his head back. He let out a scream—pure animal pleasure—and mine followed, the power of my climax dissolving what was left of my mind.

Moments or hours might have gone by; I wasn't sure. When I opened my eyes Ted was smiling down at me. "You're beautiful, Josie," he whispered. "I've been in love with you since that day you stuck your foot out of the pew at St. Anthony's and tripped me. Remember?"

Yes, I did remember. That was the day I had fallen in love with him, too. We were ten. I nodded.

"I learned my dick will never bullshit me, Josie. It doesn't need to reason, it doesn't think about shame, and it's not a hypocrite. And it never forgets who it has loved, and why. Yeah . . . we both fucked other people . . . took what we needed. But we have a history, you and me, and I want us to go on. I want us to try to make this a real marriage."

I tried to suck back the tears, but they beat against my throat just as the rain battered our old building.

"It's okay to let go, Josie," Ted said.

I did. Cried out all those months of loneliness and confusion. Cried until I couldn't see anymore. I felt Ted brush my tears away, felt his breath, warm against my ear, felt his gentle kiss land on my cheek, a sweet and simple kiss, nothing sexual about it at all. A kiss of reconciliation. I reached out beyond the tears, encircled Ted's neck, and hugged him to me tightly. I needed to. I wanted to.

Simply Seduced

WICKHAM BOYLE

I love him. Don't let any of the tired jaded things I blabber about make you think anything else. There is a sway to his hips and a thoughtless toss to his head as he laughs that makes my inner sex boil. My husband, James, possesses what I call the starter. He can sidle up behind me, snuggle me, and send a frisson traveling the course of my body. It lodges between my legs. As much as I adore him, marriage and daily life take a toll on spontaneity and seduction. I long for the lists to melt into a background where the phone doesn't ring and the school projects are completed and marvelous.

The middle of the week is our busiest. Our son is scribbling an assignment about New Amsterdam. He intermittently munches on leftover chicken while he pastes pilgrim pictures on orange construction paper. His sister bustles with dishes while crooning to some boy, hugging the bashed-up kitchen phone under her ear. She giggles and loses her tenuous grasp on the phone. It bangs to the floor. It hasn't fallen into the sink yet, still its tone leaves something to be desired for adult conversations. If your voice is changing, phone clarity is not a top priority.

I find task after task to fuss over. James stands silently behind me and deposits a nibble to my neck and ear that charges my center. A momentary respite, then I hear the plop into the sink.

I charge into the kitchen, a mother herd animal rounding up strays and bedding them down. I wipe and straighten and bustle about. My cleaning motions augur tonight's final phone conversation. If this were a farm, I would be nesting the chicks and arranging clean straw for the donkeys. This is my domain. I love to restore order and usher my growing children safely to bed.

The world is sometimes not easy on a family of two blue-eyed females and two brown-eyed males whose colors range from "tree brown," as James describes himself, to me, the color of "vanilla puddin'." Our daughter resembles me, but with butterscotch skin and bright, sea blue eyes. Our son is a caramel-colored, almond-eyed beauty. The world is confused by us because we seem to represent a race continuum. We are not easy to categorize and I believe that makes some people nervous. People who are constantly worried about being judged seem to leap at the opportunity to judge others.

We, as a family, are often judged. Who are we? How do we all fit together, and why? We belong by dint of affection. We are bound together by love, humor, and a lust for life. We are a modern family and by that I mean we are often too scheduled in this urban life we call home. We rush with work, school, Little League, ballet, and lost socks. When I think of the ultimate seduction, it is founded on turning off my brain to the countless lists and shoulds that haunt my consciousness.

The boy goes pitter-patter to his bubblegum toothpaste. I sit down on his bed and wait for him. A dish towel is still wadded in my fist. James slides in next and wraps his arms around me. The little boy loves to see his Mommy as the child all held and cuddled. James gives me a big kiss, that always makes our son squeal with delight. James croons, "Go into our bathroom and relax, Baby. I have this under control." He turns to our son and enlists the little boy's help. "Tell Mommy to go take a float, Buddy. Tell her the bath is waiting." In an instant I am off on a novel experience. A mid-week relaxation adventure.

James has installed a state-of-the-art sound system throughout our TriBeCa loft. Even in chic downtown Manhattan our music and machines are the envy of all male visitors. The rooms are wired into distinct sound arenas. You can be in surround sound in the bathroom and not a drop of it escapes to the kids' room or the kitchen. There are moments when I resent his high-tech life. I imagine all wives find things that create wedges in a relationship. For me it is technology. I want to fall asleep by candlelight reading *Madame Bovary* while listening to Mozart, and James wants Jay Leno's monologue with a final click to

some cuts from Erykah Badu. Still, I can stay angry only for
short periods. My husband has the body of a Greek god dipped
in chocolate. At mid-forty he still glistens and vibrates with
youth and vigor. He has my heart wrapped and stored. He carries it with him everywhere. I melt when I see his lanky frame
sprawled across our boy's bed. His tight black curls are rolled
around a chubby child finger; our son toys with his hair while
James spins a story.

I kiss both kids good-night. My daughter is happily shocked
by the fact that I am actually doing "a girl thing." She has a
wonderful sense of self-indulgence that I am still trying to learn.
At thirteen she understands that doing something for yourself is
not a selfish act, but one that brings personal joy and enriches
the lives around you. At nearly fifty, I am struggling to acknowledge how important it is to take care of me, as well as
everyone else.

James encourages me to pamper myself. He says I need to in-
dulge, relax and let go. He prods me to stop and evaluate where
I am in this complicated equation of caretaking. It is so damn
difficult for me to see any value in seizing a moment for myself.
At first, I would pursue these sybaritic rituals purely to please
James. I don't want to dismiss him the way I saw my mother re-
ject my father's attentions. I've wanted to let James in all the
way. It is a struggle for me, but I keep beating back the role of
Christian martyr as I hotly pursue Roman indulgence. I do feel
more vital and alive when I take care of myself. And when I
have a slippery, sexy sense of being a woman, it improves all the
people I am.

As I open the door, the scent of lavender fills my nostrils. We
visited the South of France last summer and brought back sacks
crammed full of dried, fragrant flowers. I had intended to make
sachets to give as gifts, à la Martha Stewart. The lavender lan-
guished in my lingerie drawer, until tonight. The pungent fumes
fill my head. James set candles around the tub, and wordless,
wonderful jazz hums in perfect balance in the background. He
has made an exquisite nest into which I can melt. I lie in the hot
water and drift.

When you unwind, where do you go first? If you let it all go,
where does your brain go? I am not proud to say that I begin
with the very mundane. I am floating in lists of laundry, school

clothes, the notes I want to write and the stocks I should have bought or sold. I push to be present and then I begin to lose my firm grip on reality. I shove my brain to a more formless place. Through meditation, I know, I can transform my thoughts. They are mine and can be changed the way James clicks his remote control to whiz past acres of programming. I float, eyes closed with the scent of summer. I conjure the hot sand of Cassis beneath me and smell the South of France. I am there in the midst of New York City winter and no one can budge me from my picnic of white peaches, mirabelle plums, crusty bread, and a divine rosé, chilled to perfection. Sensations fill my mouth, the wine reaches my brain, and just as the doctor ordered, I float.

The music forms a loop of sound that marks time in no way. I luxuriate in unconscious space. James is wonderful because he lets me meander toward relaxation. James never rushes me. Once my spirit has been sufficiently moved, I rise and listen to the counterclockwise whir of water as it winds back to the sea. I step out and notice that mine is a body no longer young. This is not the body I had when floating in the Mediterranean just moments ago. As I muse to destroy the magic the bath created, James sweeps in. He comes behind me with a towel still warm from the drier and wraps it around me. He kisses my neck and bites at my meaty earlobes. His voice is a deep mellifluous hum. The sound is like a cascade of honey in my ear. "Read me the phone book while you make love to me," I once jokingly told him. And in fact there was an occasion when, just at the moment of orgasm, the phone rang and James's voice boomed across the room from the answering machine, filling my ears with tone as his cock emptied into me. As the sounds of his moaning mingled with the controlled business voice on the machine, I savored the aural delight while my cunt tingled with his come.

Now he is behind me and he buzzes in my ear. "Here, my puddin', my sweetie, let me put lotion on you to keep you soft for me." James spins me around. At six feet two with monstrous hands and feet and all the rest that is implied, James is a most gentle giant. He can move me anywhere he wants and he does it with smooth ease. I admonish myself to let the moment unfold. It is in my head that the seduction happens or stops. I can stop the wonderful, sweet sensations as they march across my being. One long glance into laundry land or the kingdom of unfinished projects and I am nervous and unavailable. Now I turn my consciousness toward my pleasure and my partner.

I roll back onto his chest and let my weight go into his taut brown body. He wraps his arms around my belly and I am no longer a middle-aged woman, but young, with creamy thighs and a milky pussy just ready for plucking. "Roll into him, girl, roll and let the time move away," I speak in my head to keep myself present. I do not want to slip away to list land.

"Come into my lair and let me rub you better, little girl," James croons. I start to whine about the children, or whatever I haven't closed or locked or some other diversionary tactics to stop the moment. James picks me up and opens the door to our bedroom. The room is transformed, illuminated by a dozen tiny candles strewn about. "A private party!" James tosses me on the bed and covers me quickly with his form. He is still dressed in businessman clothes. He holds his pleated trousers and Egyptian cotton shirt barely off my creamy body. He bends his head down and fills my mouth with his wide pink tongue. His kisses are so deep, like his fucking. He can penetrate to my core from either direction and he loves the sensation of melting me. I swoon from the delight of the kissing. I purr and groan and leap back to his mouth. He teases me, holding his body and fine clothes inches away as I clutch at him trying to get more and more filled. He brushes his lips butterfly near and the soft baby hairs of his never-shaved mustache tickle my lips. I laugh and James seizes the moment and stands to undress.

I prop myself up on the pillows and stare at him as he begins to remove his clothes. "This is still one of your favorite parts, isn't it, Baby?" He speaks to me in a way that rips the cords of feeling from my gut and lays them at his feet. He forces an answer. He wants to hear me unfold my undying desire for him. "Yes, yes," I sputter and begin to drink in all the pictures I can hold. A visual obsessive, one friend calls me. Someone who loves objects, pictures, bodies, fabric, a huge collection of images catalogued in the museum of my brain. James is center gallery. He doesn't strip as if he were some cheap Chippendale dancer, he takes off his clothes as if he is the most precious package and is justifiably wrapped in tissues, gilded papers, and

ribbons. "Show me what I love best," I mutter. James unbut-
tons his shirt and lets it drop to the floor. "Another one of my
favorite outfits," I tease. James with a naked torso, trousers,
and bare feet. There is something to the heft of his shoulders as
they are displayed. His angular jaw set off by the square
smooth set of shoulders attached to long arms. So hot and bare.
James's back and arms are pure plum smooth. His dark brown
body, now deep purple in the candlelight, is mesmerizing to me.
I watch as he bends his naked chest down to kiss me. I want so
much more. He knows that and this is a part of his game. Tan-
talize me. Roast me. First, in the bath and now with wanting
what he can withhold from me. He rises up. And begins to
undo his belt buckle. "How was your day, Baby, you haven't
told me anything about that white man's racetrack you call the
stock market." I don't want to chatter about my life spinning
straw into gold. He knows that. It is more diversion. Now that
he has my undivided attention he can toy with me. I never mind
because James always finishes what he begins. He preens in my
vision. He makes me turn my head. My attention is drawn to
where he wants me. A corporate lawyer, James can pretend to
be anyone in the world. He is a wise and amazing mimic. He
snaps from street-smart black Will Smith to beyond Oxford in
the blink of a bewildered eye. "Yes, I can see you don't want to
talk to me, do you, Baby? You want me to fix it so that you
can't talk, you can't move or think. You want me to pin you
and all your thoughts to this bed right now. Don't you?"

"Damn you, James, you know I do. So do it!" I am not always the most willing supplicant, but James never gives up. He
stays and plays even in my most tumultuous moments. He
kneels by the side of the bed and takes my foot into his hard,
huge hands. He rubs my feet, crooning with the Johnny Hartman that laps at my ears. He begins in earnest and this time he
won't tease or stop. James rises for a moment and drops his
pants. The change and assorted male pocket accouterments
thud as they hit the floor. I love this sound, the final moment
when the modern industrialized man lets his weapons fall. As
we creep toward the Millennium, the weapons are wallets
crammed with credit cards and minuscule cellular phones to
reach clients on a minute-to-minute basis. He drops all that
with his trousers and is naked and about to be mine.

James slides into bed from the bottom up. He comes in kissing my feet while my hands grapple around his head. I massage his curly follicles and release kittenlike pleasure purrs. "I want you, James. I want to feel you, all of you, inside me, over me. Please." James counters, "Let me take you somewhere first, let me finish the journey you started on your float." I recline on the pillow and begin to spin summer in my head. I travel lost inside my brain. A solitary pilgrim in search of a sexual grail. James holds my leg up to his lips. He crouches at my feet and I open my eyes to regard the pull of his thighs. They are long, longer than my forearms with hands outstretched. They are hard and muscley and they glisten under the flicker of candles. I love this man, I love being lost to his touch and the way he willingly sends me off inside my brain to voyages unknown. I begin to murmur. Truly just moving lips and emitting sounds, utterances that say I am far away in a land of pleasure and you are the only one there with me. "Yes, Baby, yes, I know," James says in answer to my unspoken desires. He always knows. Bound as we are by a force beyond time and space, wrapped by desire, caught by the tail and spinning over my head. James is still touching my legs, his tongue snakes behind my knee and laps up my thigh. I toss my head from side to side and shake dreams into the pillow. I begin to feel my skin being transformed. The surface is alive and seems to change from liquid to solid. I am a lake freezing over. The sensation is delicious, as my flesh hardens my innards melt. James begins to skate across my solid surface. His mouth is in my cunt, all open and fresh for munching. His molten tongue is inside me and his hands, hotter still, traverse my frozen landscape liquefying my core. They explore and find the mountains of my breasts. My nipples are so hard that they threaten to pull my inner flesh into the taut peaks they create. I ache. He knows this and takes the twin peaks between his fingers and tweaks and rolls them. Not in concert but in a deft harmony that tugs at the juices already heavily flowing between my legs.

I need to stay here, in the moment, not to allow my conscious brain to arrive a moment too soon and destroy this passion. I find my concentration flickering into focus and I lose the place where my sensual sensation resides. I feel my orgasm fade as if a cloud blew in to cover the light of the moon. It is up to me to wave the cloud aside and allow the moonlight to bathe me. James knows this and croons to me, "Be here, Baby, bear down on my tongue, on my fingers, as I stuff them into you. Oh, you are so hot, so molten inside. I have to be inside you." I cannot speak, I am in a time beyond speech where to search for the side of my brain where language resides would be to lose my fierce passion. James knows this. He knows that by now I am lost to him and possess neither desire nor volition to resist him. I hover on the brink of coming and he holds me there by a gossamer thread that is elastic and indestructible. I am no longer in the real world. Sound is altered and I exist without a body. I am sensation, an enormous clit that sits up and begs to be devoured, to be taken and ingested so that it can explode. I sense a vibration from deep in my throat, but I do not hear when it emerges. I feel James flip me over onto my side. His hands grip my upper arms and I tense under his grasp. I feel his cock at the entrance to my vagina, he stops and pushes ever so slightly. The tip of his dick peaks into my tunnel. Peaks and stops. I am frantic because I want him. I know this fierce wanting and its conclusion. There is no force that can deny me. I buck back into James and he stuffs himself inside me. "You like that, don't you, Baby. You like that big, fat, black dick far up inside you." James pushes in and wraps one arm around my gut and chest and holds me close. He tugs at my nipples, really clips them with his thumb and forefinger. Tight. I do not know where I am, but I am nearly aloft with sensation and desire. With his other hand, he reaches down to the base of his cock and shoves it further into me. His fingers pull back the furry skin covering my clit and the exposed and excited nerve endings vibrate. I clamp down like a wild dog, my cunt a jaw grabbing his dick, and I release with a spill of emotion. I feel my skin ignite as the lights flash inside my brain. I come and come, a cascade of contractions on James's rigid cock. He arches back and begins to pump with fury. He kneels again above my back and drives his dick deeper and deeper into me. He is behind me and there is nothing between him and his destination. My orgasm opens me wider, permitting his passion to delve even deeper into my cunt and my soul with each thrust. He plants his seed and spirit into me and I love his arch and drive. My hearing returns and the sound is James and his baritone growl as he shakes the come from his bowels. He draws my body to him in a last enormous thrust. I am shocked by the sly runner of a second orgasm that sneaks past me. A sullen base runner who decides to steal home. This click of sensation electrifies my clit and I clamp onto James's tumescent dick. Then I whine and relax back into his curled body. We wait in breathy silence as the music refills the room. Where did all the sound go just moments ago when my ears were filled with cotton wool and the electricity seemed to be speeding across the room? We purr at each other, I cup James's high firm ass with my hand as I descend into the cocoon of dreams.

Someone has blown the candles out, covered me with a downy duvet, and I have fallen deeply asleep as the night unfurled. The boy knocks at my morning door and the coffee wafts its aroma inside my head. "Mommy, today is the ice skating party for the hundredth day of school and . . ." James comes in with coffee, hot, sweet, and creamy. My man takes our son's hand and they kiss me. "Let Mommy wake up slowly, Buddy, she had a long voyage last night."

PART IV

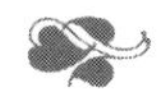

The Environment

The context and the surroundings often play crucial roles in a seduction. In some cases, a sensual environment adds the critical element to an erotic moment. Being in a romantic setting can generate sexual feelings. An isolated and charming bed-and-breakfast, a nightclub alive with intense music and flashing lights, a hot tub overlooking the ocean—all become inseparable from the seduction itself. Particular environments can stimulate your senses and pique your sexual interest.

In "A Conversation About Green Water" by Leslie Cole, the Pacific Ocean is really the main character. "I began surfing this summer and I find the ocean incredibly seductive," Cole admits. "It is thoroughly sensual: the color, the lighting, the sounds, the temperature, the way it moves. And it has mystery because it is so big and can literally overwhelm you. And it's kind of sneaky too." In this surfer story, Cole creates a seduction using the force of the ocean as a metaphor for arousal, unpredictability, and loss of control.

The wild sensuality of the Sicilian countryside conjures the backdrop for the seduction in Lynn Santa Lucia's "A Taste of Sicily." Here we have the perfect combination of elements for the young female lead: a handsome, virile Italian man and the allure of Sicily. "I think the most important element in seduction," reports Santa Lucia, "is a full appreciation of the surroundings and how all the senses are touched in a frozen moment of time with no thought to the past or the future." What makes this seduction memorable is the way the characters are dazzled by the dramatic landscape, the magnificent stone buildings, and the splendid food.

The impact of the environment in Dina Vered's story is a bit different in "Under the Volcano," where she recreates a devastating volcanic disaster. "My protagonist needed an escape from the death and destruction that was having an overwhelming emotional impact on her," says Vered. "It was the only time she'd ever seduced a man, but the seduction was a way to get relief from the intense emotional experience. And the eroticism of Cartagena didn't hurt either." The magic of this hot, sultry, Colombian seaside town helps Vered's character erase the horrific memory of the volcano's eruption. It intensifies her passions and channels them into explosive physical lovemaking.

Whether the surroundings are hot and sultry, powerfully sensual, or dramatically rugged, the physical environment can enlarge and intensify the seduction it encompasses.

A Conversation About Green Water
Leslie Cole

I should have just kissed him the moment he stepped into the ocean. The surf was rising and falling in that sleepy violent way, and every time I closed my eyes I could see a wall of jade green water rising up in front of me.

What does that have to do with it?

Well, the water was inside of me, you know. And I wasn't really a woman anymore, I mean I still looked like a woman, but I was acting like water. And I know he was loving the water rolling over his body, her hands all over him. So it was a perfect setup. He couldn't resist me, with me looking like a woman with the sea water dripping off the ends of my curly hair but tasting like salt and smelling like oysters, and if he had just licked my face or felt the sand all mixed up with my hair he would have been a goner.

Well, why stop there? Why not let him lick that sweet dimple just over your ass?

Because I had a wetsuit on, silly. Everything on me from the neck down was wrapped in black rubber.

Sounds safe, all right.

Well, safe, yeah, but I didn't want to fuck him, I just wanted to kiss him. At least at first, anyway. It was a pure kind of feeling.

Like fucking is not a pure kind of feeling? Like when I've got a hand opening you up and all I can see is wet pink and you're saying fuckmefuckmefuckme and I keep sliding in just about an F's worth and you start screaming "*Please*" and I'm leaving handprints on the inside of your thighs I'm holding you off so hard, like that's not a pure feeling?

Okay, okay, get a grip on yourself, would you? Yeah, so maybe I don't mean pure, I mean simple. This was going to be the kind of kiss that was innocent. Elemental, you know?

So what did happen?

Well, I'd been out on my short board for about an hour, riding the swell up and down. Even before he got into the water I knew I had to touch him, even if it meant running my board up on top of him.

Whoa, girl, that sounds like a hell of a lot more than a kiss to me.

Well, sure, having a goddess ride up onto your backside while you're in the throes of a wave would be a shocker, yes, especially if she's laughing hysterically as she rests her head upon your rubbered ass. But these things happen, I had to consider the possibilities. And besides, he looked like he had just climbed out of bed, his hair was wild and whorled, and his eyes were barely half open, and he was smiling a little like he was still dreaming. He looked solid, substantial, you know, a wrestler body with thick legs and an iron back, and from the way he turned half around to smell the breeze, I could see his muscles moving in one long ripple under his suit. My hands and face were shocked alive from the cold water and my sex ached so bad I had to hold my hand between my legs. But just the sight of him was thawing me out. And the salt in the air was sharp and female and the swell was lifting me up and down, horny but holding back, and I knew I was feeling how it would be to have him inside of me up to the hilt with us rocking in and out like the waves.

You got all that just looking at him?

Looking? I could taste him by then. And then he put his feet into the water and he ran his hand over the curve of his board. That's all I saw at first because I had my back turned to the ocean and a big one swamped me. A surprise, a little water up my nose, nothing serious. Then by the time I came up for air he was already in the water, which was too bad, because I sort of wanted to see him getting in, getting wet, and waking up, because it's sort of like coming. And I wanted to see his face when he came.

So that's why you used to wrestle yourself on top of me and pry my hands away from my face just when you could have anything you wanted. You wanted to see me come.

Didn't you know that?

Well, not exactly. I'd really like to kiss you right now.

You haven't kissed me in seven months. We're buddies now, remember?

Just the same, I don't think I can hear the rest of your story unless I kiss you right now.

Oh. Okay.

Hmm. You taste like apples. So what happened with this guy?

Well, we were both in the water sort of facing out toward the open ocean and sort of toward each other. I must have been turning red, because I figured he could tell what I had been thinking, and I kept trying to point my board away, casually, you know, but the swell or current or something kept swinging me around again.

Did you smile and wave?

Good God, no. I was cramping up the closer he got to me. But then this really steep wave seemed to rise out of nowhere, and I didn't have any time to think. It just rose up under me, gripped my board, and sent me steaming down the inside curl. And for that instant I totally forgot about him and was just back in the water holding on.

Yeah, that top of the roller coaster.

Exactly. Focused abandon. So this wave is so powerful it's taking me right up on shore, practically to the high tide line. And I'm screaming and laughing, and I look over to admire the foam that I'm riding through. It's hissing it's so shook up, and my God, but there he is sharing my wave. He was just a few feet from me. Like a vision, you know.

Yeah, I know.

So I should have just kissed him. And he felt the same way. I reached over and clasped his hand and then just as I was letting go, he gripped me really tight and pulled me toward him. I slipped off my board and slid on my knees over the wet sand right into his lap, right with my thighs wrapped around his waist. It was suddenly so necessary. And then our foreheads touched and our skin was slick from the salt water and his lips grazed my cheek, my ear. I could see his pulse in his neck and the ache between my legs was grinding and there was all this rubber between us. Those suits are so tight and I struggled with his zipper till I finally shoved one hand into the neck of his suit and his skin was hot. And he ran his hands over my breasts and across my ass looking for a way in until finally his hands rested on my bare ankles. So there we were, heads pressed together with our hands on the only exposed skin we could find. Suddenly we were on dry land. I mean, real time, you know? Can you imagine how awkward it can be to pull your hand out of the neck of a strange guy's wetsuit?

So that's where the music stopped? You with your thighs wrapped around his waist and him pulling you in tighter while the backwash sucked out pebbly holes around your knees and your boards banged together in the surf? And you with your hand wedged between his neck and black rubber?

That pretty much sums it up. Yup.

Cruel world, isn't it?

I'll say. And then there was this really long silence and I had to struggle a little to free my hand and I think I mumbled, "Sorry," and he looked at me weird, like I was his big sister or something. Then he pulled his board in and paddled out into the surf without looking back.

Ouch. So what did you do next?

Well, I sat there for a while and just let the waves wash over me. But then I decided the best thing to do would be to pretend that nothing had really happened or that that sort of thing happened all the time. You know? So I pulled in my board, too, and went back out.

Back into cold waters again, huh? Could you open your legs a little? Yeah. Like that. Those long legs make a beautiful line to look at. One big wide U.

Do I look more relaxed this way?

You could say that. I don't think I could have heard the rest of the story otherwise.

So, where was I, anyway? Well, we were both back in the surf and catching waves, but not the same ones. This went on for some time, long enough to play that bizarre little scene over in my head about a thousand times, and then he got out.

You watched him go, of course?

Yes, yes. But even worse than that, I followed him.

Do you mean stalked?

No, I mean lingered after. And that would have been fine,

just playful, you know, some way of working him out of my system, but he turned around and caught me in the act.

Act? What were you up to exactly?

Well . . . he left these perfect footprints in the sand. And he must have been walking really fast or maybe he was leaving in a huff because they were pretty far apart. And since I had only managed to feel his pulse along his throat and look into his eyes for one wave's-worth of a moment, I naturally wanted to walk in his footprints.

Naturally. Say, aren't those my jeans you have on?

You think so? Well, there I was dragging my board behind me on its leash as I leaped from footprint to footprint. I think I had some seaweed in my hair, and I was really starting to enjoy myself, probably flinging my hands up in the air, you know me, and then just mid-leap he turns around and looks at me.

So what did you do?

Well, what would anybody do? I froze in midstep. I must have looked ridiculous. And then I started jumping up and down like I was trying to warm up, but I could tell he didn't buy it. He gave me a good long look and then he headed back toward the parking lot. I ended up loitering around the beach until I was pretty sure he was gone.

You look cold even telling me. Mind if I pull my chair up between your legs? Hey, I can feel your knees shaking a little.

Yeah, warm me up would ya? Okay, okay. Let me finish the story. So I've sort of moped back to my car and had just pulled loose my wristband when somebody comes up behind me and says, "Please don't move." Well, of course I asked why and he says because he wants to get a good look at me if that's okay. So I just sort of nodded my assent and then his hands were in my hair and over my cheekbones and just brushed my lips, and that was such a surprise somehow that I almost turned around to face him, but he stopped me by pulling at the zipper at the back of my wetsuit.

Wait a minute. How'd you know it was this guy?

Well, I just did. He was fresh out of the water, it was dripping off of the ends of his hair, and he smelled a little like a salmon.

Okay. Well that explains it.

Yeah, and then he zipped my wetsuit open just to the top of my back and he kissed my neck and ran his tongue along my

spine up to my scalp. I was getting goose bumps by this time because a slight wind had come up, but it was okay because his
lips were really hot against my skin. And then he pressed into
me and I could feel how hard he was. His prick was making
quite a mountain against me. And by now he had pulled my
wetsuit off my shoulders and down my arms and I was naked
underneath. I felt exposed, pressed against my truck half naked
in a parking lot, but my eyes were closed and all I could see was
that wall of green water. I couldn't stop myself. He was pinching both my nipples and still kissing my neck and the top of my
spine and pressing against me right between my legs. I arched
my back a little, and when I opened my legs wider he slipped
his hand down inside my wetsuit and over my belly and found
my clit with his finger. He just slipped in I was so hot. And then
we started rocking together like that with him hard and sweet
against me. My legs were shaking and I could feel the hot metal
of the truck against my belly and he was breathing hard and I
didn't think I could stand it much longer, when a car drove by
and honked. It startled the hell out of me and I tried to break
away, but just then he pulled me in closer and shoved his finger
deep inside of me. I yelled out and a hot wave passed over and
over and over me. God, what bliss! My legs gave out, and he
caught me and held on to me as long as the wave lasted. Then
I wanted to turn around, but I was afraid to, and there we were
again, in that weird place.

And that was that?

Well. Not completely. After a long moment, I tugged my wetsuit back over my torso and turned around. We both smiled at
each other, embarrassed, you know? Then I reached my hands
up toward his face, and his eyes were the most beautiful color
of green, just like summer water. But then he closed his eyes. He
let me touch him, his face, his prick, his hands, but he wouldn't
look at me.

He was scared.

Hmm. Could be, because when it became clear that I was
aiming to pull his wetsuit off, he stopped my hands. He kept his
eyes closed and then he buried his face into my neck and down
my belly to between my legs. Then he stood up abruptly and
walked away.

And you let him?

Well, I was all confused and jittery. Just half satisfied, you know? I mean, how could he just walk away like that?

I think you should take those jeans off.

Do you now? You show up at my door seven months after you've decided that we're really just friends and now you want me to strip? Are you nuts?

Yes, I am a bit off-kilter. So how 'bout you take your jeans off, and so will I. Besides, I've been a pretty good listener, haven't I? I miss your legs. I really want to see your legs.

Well, use your imagination. But take your shirt off at least . . . hey, you've got sand rings around your belly. Have you been out in the water?

Yeah, just before I came over. Can't you smell it on me?

Um, do you want to hear the rest of my story?

Are you ignoring me?

Shouldn't I be?

Maybe.

Okay. So I pull myself into the cab of the truck. I wanted to get my wetsuit off, but I felt too unsteady to peel it off without falling over. So I leaned over the steering wheel for a minute to savor all the burning hot handprints that he left on my body. I could feel a little sand between my legs from his fingers. Then I noticed that he left me a present.

When did this happen, anyway?

Early this morning. Are you okay? So he left me a row of seashells lined up along the dash. Sand dollars, pink turbans, a perfect miniature abalone. That's all it took. I screeched out of the parking lot in hot pursuit. But it was as if I couldn't see clearly anymore. The gray ribbon of the road looked like still water just at dusk, the green hills were round as huge swells, and the fog was just pushing in from offshore and covering the road. I couldn't see beyond my front bumper, and it was as if the water was pulling me along, water, waves, rivers, swell, surf. I just smelled the salt and felt the truck vibrate up between my thighs.

Did you find him?

Hell no! I didn't even know which direction he had gone in. It was like that feeling where you're taken up by a wave that you're just a little too late for, and over the falls you go, ass in the air, face in the water, turned around, thrashed, and com-

pletely helpless. I was at the mercy of the wave. So I drove on
in this trance, still all suited up, hunched over the steering
wheel, when suddenly I looked up. The hills were brown, the
air was brown, I was hauled in by a stoplight. On a two-lane
road surrounded by commuter traffic the spell was broken. I
thought, "What in the hell am I doing? I don't even know this
guy!" So I turned myself around and headed for home and
that's when it hit me.

What's that?

That he reminded me of you. Everything about you that I've
missed was still in me, and all I could think about was the last
time we made love, the last time you fucked me on that very
beach where we played in the surf and washed in along the sand
on our bellies. Remember how I didn't want to take my suit off
but you kept pressing yourself against me and letting your hair
drip onto my face, my lips, and you kept kissing it off, licking
off the salt until I was so hot I stripped myself and then you
opened my legs to let the surf run over me and you licked me
there, too, in between wave after wave after wave? Remember
how you finally came into me with the surf and then pulled out
and teased me in between until I finally got my thighs around
your waist and forced you to stay? Remember, you shit?

Yes. More than you would believe.

And then I had to pull over. I watched the cars go by as I remembered the last time I saw you and how you told me what a
good friend I was with the emphasis on *friend*. Remember that?
And I remembered what I felt like watching you drive away,
and how you drove so straight down the road without looking
back, and I remembered how I could still feel the kiss you had
left over my eyes, and how your flannel shirt smelled so much
like wet earth and sand, and I remembered how I could see us
both dug in on the beach with the water washing around us and
how all of this slapped at me as I watched you disappear. And
then I remembered that I knew you were a liar.

Oh. And then what?

Nothing. That's the end of the story.

A Taste of Sicily

Lynn Santa Lucia

It's twelve days to Christmas. Visions of chestnuts roasting on an open fire, of sleigh bells glistening, of furtive kisses under the mistletoe are dancing through my head. But I'm home in Miami, alone, facing the prospect of spending the holidays in the hot sun with a beach blanket and a special no one.

Just when I resign myself to the South Florida setting, an overseas phone call from Claudia and Sandro brings tidings of comfort and joy and . . . alas . . . an invitation to share the season's festivities with dear friends, Italian style. Before anyone can change her mind, I'm on a plane to *bell'Italia,* gloating over my good fortune amid fawning flight attendants with Mediterranean accents and names like Mario, Aldo, Ettore, and Luca.

Traveling *sola,* I've never had it so good. The magazines I piled on the empty seat next to me go undisturbed and forgotten, as the boys of Alitalia flight 268 entertain me with their antics—slipping me slices of sweet *panettone* from first class, puffing up one more pillow behind my head—and with stories of their lives in Rome, Piacenza, Verona. I, in turn, talk about the two years I lived in Milan.

"But, *gioia,* why don't you move back to Italy?" one of them asks, after listening to me longing for extended national holidays, buffalo mozzarella, and public displays of uncensored passion.

"Ahh, but what would I do?" I say.

His response, instantaneous: "*Fai principessa.*" Be a princess.

The Italian male's charms and attentions are nothing new to me. I know that the simple fact that I am an unaccompanied young woman impels every Italian male, who feels obliged by hormones and national honor, to shower me with admiration usually reserved for the modern diva. But all the awareness in the world, and all my experience with men from the Med, can't make me immune to their designs.

I lower my head to conceal my blush but keep in my line of vision two sets of eyes, one the color of warm walnut, the other a combustible smoky gray. By now, I've got a permanent pair of companions—the flight attendant foursome taking turns in a madcap in-flight game of Let Us Entertain You—occupying the empty space behind the back of my seat, which is positioned just in front of the aircraft's midsection emergency exit (a detail pointed out by one winking passenger anticipating a need for airborne escape from my oversolicitous friends). First Mario and Luca, then Mario and Ettore, now Luca and Aldo with their lounging limbs strewn out around my head, by my side, atop my armrest.

"So cute, these *lentiggini*," says Luca of the lighter eyes, running a slender finger from the tip of my nose to just below my bottom lashes, then down to my chin, grazing my lips in transit. I can see by his own lips, pitched to one side and turned up at the corner, that he's enjoying this unsolicited game of connect the freckles.

Meanwhile, benevolent, avuncular Aldo, who reminds me of a balding teddy bear, is bouncing my strawberry blond ringlets in the flat palm of his pudgy brown hand. "You are like a child," he says.

"This is true," Luca says. "But"—he's drawing out his favorite English conjunction in a low melodic growl—"you have the look of *una furba.*"

Goose bumps are springing up on my arms. Goose bumps!

"Like a sneaky fox," he repeats, this time in English and *sotto voce,* his mouth to my ear, to make sure I understand, to make sure I catch his meaning.

I feel my cheeks burn. It's a surge of blood that comes less out of embarrassment than from the fire smoldering between my legs. I've lost my knack for repartee and find myself uncharacteristically without words, coming to an unspoken understanding as I hold Luca's suggestive stare, just before he breaks away to business class.

*   *   *

The air underneath the blanket spread across my lap feels hot. Luca's hand, resting on the fleshiest part of my inner thigh, is acting like a branding iron sizzling through my stretch pants. My row companion, the woman who occupied the aisle seat upon takeoff, moved to the back of the plane hours ago to join her friend. From the window seat, Luca has shifted his torso to face me, melting in the middle seat. I catch a sudden whiff of his cologne. Intoxicated by his smell, I kiss him full on the mouth. His tongue presses hard against mine, then slides across it, over and under, over and under in a slow, rhythmic dance that makes my cunt contract. He takes my lower lip between his teeth and I feel my clit twitter out of control. I squirm in my seat, hoping the movement will drive Luca's hand up to my steamy nest. In a flash, his hand is there, his first, middle, and ring fingers—those long and tapered fingers—laid flat on my crotch, sliding up and back on smooth fabric while a nimble thumb hooks itself onto my elastic waistband and tugs down.

I take his face in my hands, pressing on his cheeks so that his lips become round and full between mine. He pushes his fingers down to my crack and into the wet of me. I suck hard on his tongue. He sucks his fingers, then lets me smell and lick them. We are all mouth and face and fingers, lapping, inhaling, nipping, gnawing.

Luca sighs and buries his nose into my neck. "*Che meraviglia,*" he moans. Such a soft mouth, such sweet breath tickling the fuzz on my skin. I let my fingers move down his shirt, slip between two metal snaps, and pop them open to reach the fiery skin of his chest. My hands have a will of their own, circling around and around his hairless nipples until he can stand it no longer and he pushes them down to his crotch. I rub his hard knot, then squeeze. He moans some more and nibbles at my ear and whispers all hot and wonderful in Italian.

In the dim light I see the head of his cock peep out from the top of his pants. A drip of semen glistens and I touch it with the tip of my finger. Tap tap, and then I begin to swirl the sticky liquid around the nub of his rod. Two of his fingers dive into my depths, pull out, and dive in again, pushing me up against the back of my seat. I'm about to cry out. He claps a hand to my mouth just in time, muffling my groan.

A timid tap on my shoulder. I start, stunned out of my

reverie. I am sweating. I look at my watch and see that two hours have gone by and I've missed breakfast. I am being asked to return my seat to its original upright position. We are preparing for landing.

The road to Monreale winds upland five miles southwest of Palermo, Sicily's capital, to nearly 1500 feet above sea level. For twenty nail-gnawing minutes, Luca and I have been careening along the narrow stretch, jitterbugging above beautiful panoramas of the Conca d'Ora valley while skirting oncoming Fiats doing fifty around precipitous bends. My companion is managing his Alfa Spider Veloce like a crazy man at the controls of a clangorous time machine. But the minutes are not going by any faster.

"*Piano, piano,*" I say, imploring him to take it easy.

"*Sì, sì,*" he says, accelerating around the next bend.

I'm overcome with fright, then amusement, then resignation, and finally the kind of pleasant wonderment that a foreigner feels in the presence of an uninhibited and spontaneous Italian: Luca has downshifted into first gear and is pulling off the road. Why? Because the view is "*troppo bella.*" It's true: the panorama is just too beautiful, and beauty has squashed all Luca's need for speed.

Beyond the city, the scenery has rapidly reverted to countryside, tangled brown and green of vineyards and olive groves climbing up the hillsides, splashes of red and yellow wildflowers reaching toward a clear blue sky. We are out of the car, standing on the edge of a precipice. Luca is picking a delicate, long-stemmed flower that's growing alongside the road. Italian, lover of spectacle, he places it behind my ear.

I must be mad. Mad mad mad. My second day in Sicily and I'm on the road with a man, a boy really, eight years my junior, playing the role of lover I've invented out of my own yearning. My hosts believe I'm spending the afternoon with a cousin whose telephone number they saw me retrieve from a folded-up page torn from *Ulisses 2000,* Alitalia's in-flight magazine. I feel guilty about my fib, but giddy about my prospects. I am sixteen again, with the ability to burn for the moment, like extraordinary Roman candles blazing across the sky.

Love and passion and idiosyncrasy . . . Goethe says that in

Rome all the dreams of his youth came to life. Like Goethe, I can be reborn in Italy. I am only thirty years old, but for the last twelve months I have felt lifeless, full of ennui, removed from my body. In the delirious world of Miami—my most recent home—where brilliant colors blind you, heady fragrances stop you in your path, and the oppressive heat weighs like a load of steamy towels draped across your head and shoulders forcing you to your knees, my body shut down in self-preservation. Miami is bold and loud, overwhelming and on display, making me cringe and retract when I am not utterly filled with confidence. Italy, instead, is food for the soul. Italy is sensuous, but gentle. Here, my body feels safe. My body feels whole. Everything good in my nature is nourished here. My heart is full to bursting, and it's so easy and joyful to embrace the one I'm with.

Luca has one arm draped loosely around my waist, as we stand hip to hip looking out over the view. In fact, Luca is staring out over the hillside as I gaze at his unblemished skin that is a beautiful blend of saffron and olive. I wish I could cup the color in my hands and carry it home with me. But surely the tone would lose its bewitching effect without the company of those electric gray irises and that golden hair. He catches me eating him up with my eyes and turns my body in to his torso, up against the hardness between his legs. But I am content not to encourage this moment to culmination. *"Andiamo,"* I say. "Let's go." I won't let him, this imp, have me here.

Within ten minutes we are descending into the medieval town. We are out of the car, stepping along smooth cobblestones on a secret street, cool and mysterious, that leads to a familiar *piazza*. Here the sun is not so evident and everything takes on a fuzzy, ashen hue. It is lunchtime and, without the visitors of high season, the *piazza* is practically deserted. A trio of senior citizens in bowler hats is propped on the edge of a silent fountain, one man sipping from a ceramic espresso cup, the other two striking their walking sticks on the ground to emphasize the points of their argument. A shop owner locks up from the outside, mounts his rusty bike, and pedals off for his midday meal. A jean-clad student straddles his silent moped, taking bites from the square slice of pizza in his hands.

Luca sees me staring at the pizza. "Time to eat," he says, and plants a wet kiss on my lips. I look at him with a raised eyebrow, questioning his meaning. But he has taken my hand and is leading me in long, determined strides across the *piazza* to the only open restaurant in sight.

Pasta is first, *fettuccine* with fragrant *ricci* from the sea, and the dark-haired waiter with a five-o'clock shadow pours an incredible *novello* from Tenuta S.Anna. I am studying the way his thick, black locks—like those of ancient male leaders who wore long flowing tresses as a sign of virility—refuse to stay tucked around his ear, when he catches my eye and winks. I shift my gaze onto Luca, comparing his sun-kissed waves—like a cherub's—and deliver a roguish grin when he tells me how hungry he is.

I, myself, am starving. My hunger has been growing by leaps and bounds ever since we arrived. I feel it not only in my stomach, but in every cell of my body. I shut my eyes, close my mouth over a forkful of pasta, and am aware of the rich red blood coursing through my veins. I blink, watch Luca's graceful fingers twirling his fork into his *fettuccine,* and acknowledge the pleasant tingling across the surface of my skin. I spot our waiter across the room, leaning against the wall, running a hand through his hair as he looks on, and I thrill over the fluttering in my chest. I realize that as my affection for Luca and for my surroundings grows, so does my appetite. It's a craving for every flavor, every texture, every tone . . . every temperament. I want to taste it all. I want to devour everything . . . everybody? . . . in sight.

Between courses, I keep nibbling on the plump green and black olives that have been left on the table. Luca is engaging, as he talks about the extraordinary mosaic scenes adorning almost every square inch of wall in Monreale's twelfth-century cathedral, whose pointed portal faces us from across the *piazza*. The golden mosaics, he explains, depict every Bible story one is likely to know. The scenes are instantly recognizable: Abraham on the point of sacrificing his son, Noah's Ark, the story of Creation. "If you look closely," he says, fixing his eyes on mine and carefully waving a long, thin breadstick in the air, as if it were a wand and he a master hypnotist, "you see that the serpent is in a very strategic position." I gnaw at the olive I'm holding in my clustered fingertips and wait for more. "And Eve, young and beautiful Eve, her breasts droop." I have to think about that one.

"Sicily's favorite dish," sighs the waiter as he sets down a bowl of *caponata*—eggplant, capers, and olives in a sweet and sour tomato sauce. Luca dunks a thick hunk of crusty bread into the bowl big enough for a family of five, and puts the dripping dough, now the colors of the Italian flag, to my lips.

"Open. Take it slowly. *Piano.* Now chew. *Piano,*" Luca directs. I am amazed at his confidence. Every time I think that he's but a boy, he surprises me with behavior that reveals a sexy self-assurance lacking in most American men double his age. And at that thought, he subtly signals the waiter for another bottle of wine while taking my hands in his.

Next comes a wheel of pecorino cheese, plates of sliced green apples and pears, and a glass bowl of dark purple grapes floating in icy water. My head is fuzzy enough, but I find myself accepting a glass of sweet *vin santo* and a plate of *cantucci,* the perfect dipping cookies. We dip and stretch our cookie-laden fingers across the table to exchange bites. We do this over and over again.

"My God, enough! It's all really too much," I say to Luca.

"Yes," the waiter agrees, "but what would you leave out?"

Certainly not his last wink.

The somewhat severe, square-towered exterior of the Santa Maria la Nuova Cathedral—though handsome enough—is no preparation for what's inside: a blaze of glorious, glittering panels portraying God filling his world with water, light, animals, and people. The guidebook says it is the most remarkable and extensive area of Christian medieval mosaic work in the world. And the depictions are just as Luca promised.

Once inside, your eyes scan the animated series that starts with the Creation to the right of the altar and runs around the whole church. Then your eyes are drawn across the wooden ceiling to the all-embracing half-figure of Christ kneeling in benediction: the head and shoulders are almost twenty meters high. Luca digs into his front pockets for some hundred-*lire* coins that will operate the temporary lights for viewing the art. Lighted, the unperturbed Christ broods even more huge and majestic.

I point out to Luca a sign across the central apse indicating admission to the roof: three thousand *lire*. I'd like to go up there, I say. Surely it affords a splendid view of the valley below. In truth, I want nothing more than to get Luca alone, so I can slide my tongue along his neck and press my nipples, hard with anticipation, against him. And with my thoughts running more toward the lustful than to the religious, I want to escape from under the scrutiny of Christ's gaze.

As luck would have it, the roof and the stairs and passageways leading up to it are under construction. A guide informs us that access is not allowed.

"No problem," says Luca, once again taking my hand firmly in his and leading the way. We exit the cathedral, walk around to the south side of the structure, and enter a beautiful cloister enclosed by double rows of columns, many inlaid with richly lustered tiles, others decorated with reliefs.

"Here. Come here," says Luca, his nose up against a column's explosion of color from deep umber to aqua and emerald green. "Look here." In a riot of detail there are flowers, grapes, wise men, snakes, birds, deer. I take Luca by the shoulders and turn him around to face me with his back against a band of armed hunters doing battle with winged beasts. I kiss him. He comes back at me like an explosion. His hands are squeezing my ass, pushing my pelvis toward him. When I twist a leg around one of his for better support, he slips his hands under my shirt and underneath my bra, pinching my nipples erect with wanting him. Our bodies linked, our mouths locked, we slide down the column to the earth floor. We are laughing but ardent in our groping and caressing.

This cloister is the perfect space, exciting and safe. We are in a far corner. Our column and a nearby banyan tree serve to obstruct the view of anyone who should happen to step inside. But our only visitors so far are pigeons cooing from above.

Smells of fresh-cut grass, foliage, and human sweat fill our nostrils, sending us to new heights of excitement. "*Sono arrabatissimo.*" I'm horny, he growls. "*Sono duro tremendo.*" He tells me how incredibly hard he is, as if I didn't know, and plants my hand on his crotch for proof. I hike up my skirt and pull him on top of me. We are writhing away when I notice, above the red-tiled roofs of the cloister, flowered sheets and men's elephantine underwear hanging out to dry. I know if I have to look at the comical sight for one more second, I will burst out in a fit of giggles. So I slide half my body out from under him, turn him over on his back, and roll on top of his thrusting Levi's.

In a knees-to-the-ground straddle, I unbutton Luca's fly and yank his jeans down below his hips. The sexpot is not sporting any underwear. His abdomen is flat and rippled. His penis is straight and long and slender, much like his middle finger. How I want it all! I have to stand up to slide my tights and panties down to my ankles. Then I resume my straddle and finger my clit as he looks on. "*Sei troppo bella. Sei bellissima,*" he groans. "You're so beautiful. I want you." I put my wet, sticky fingers to his lips and drop my mouth to his hard rod. While I run a delicate tongue around his moist head, he gingerly licks at my fingertips. He wraps his lips around my thumb and sucks down to my knuckle. I suck him hard, all the way down the shaft. I can feel him pulsating on my tongue and I imagine thick hot cum coursing through his cock. His thigh muscles tighten, his abdominal muscles turn to steel. He's gripping my wrists when he lets go into my mouth.

My cunt is contracting like never before. I'm rollicking with desire. With his sense of urgency arrested, he begins to tongue me down with amazing care. A slow slide from the tender flesh behind my knee, around to my kneecap, up to my inner thigh, and I'm rolling in ecstasy. Lazy swirls in and around my belly button and I am transfixed. Finally, he's wetting down my pubic hair and gently tugging at it with his teeth. When his full wet lips lock onto mine, I imagine myself a succulent mango for the taking. He sucks every fold, laps at the ridges, and lifts my ass to deliver the meal. A flash breaks the blackness and the breath is sucked out of me. My ears throb, obliterating all sound. I thrust myself against his face, squeezing my thighs around his head, letting my juices gush into his mouth.

Luca releases his suction hold but won't remove his tongue from my dancing clit. He plays with it wildly, wiggling that nimble tongue of his around and around until I move from easy samba to frenetic salsa in no time. I'm incredibly sensitive, tingling and ticklish, so I try to push his head away from my crotch for a moment of rest. Luca stays put, pushing his tongue

deep into my cunt, then along my crack and around the opening of my asshole. This drives me into a new frenzy. He sucks
and laps and swirls in a fury. Then, when he senses my second
climax, he drives his finger up into my behind. Bull's-eye. Blinding flashes of light, the rushing sound of waves in my ears, uncontrollable spasms throughout my body shake my world. I
don't know where I am, or who I'm with. Who am I? Woman
or beast? I cry out in delicious, delightful anguish.

By the time we leave the cloister, dusk has arrived. Luca
wants to pick up a pack of cigarettes before we head back to
the car. But the closest *tabaccheria* is in the opposite direction.
Still shaky, I tell him I'll wait for him on a bench just outside
the cathedral. With a tender kiss, he promises he won't be gone
long.

Once again, I'm ravenous. So when a pastry shop catches my
eye, I'm there in a flash. Entering the establishment, who
should I see at the bar spooning a heap of sugar into his
espresso, but our lunchtime waiter. Not surprisingly, he ac-
knowledges me with a wink. I nod, then turn to the clerk to
make my selection—half a dozen pistachio *biscotti* and two
plump *cannoli* exploding with ricotta cheese filling.

"Can I offer you a coffee?" the off-duty waiter asks, as I wait
to have my pastries wrapped to go. I thank him, but decline, ex-
plaining I can't linger. He brings his cup to his lips and sips,
keeping his eyes on me all the while.

I take my package and proceed to the matronly cashier, seated
near the entrance/exit. As I'm about to pay, I spot a bucket of
roses for sale individually or by the bunch. I decide on a deep red
one whose petals have begun to open up to the size and shape of
a baseball, and I pull its long stem out of the container. "Let me
prepare that for you," the cashier says, taking the flower from
my hand and covering its stem in colored foil.

"Make sure you secure it with a pretty ribbon," says the
waiter from across the room. "Certainly the lovely *signorina*
has someone special in mind."

"Always an opinion. You leave her alone," says the cashier.

"Well, he's right," I say.

The cashier smiles a warm smile and hands me my change,
the parcel, and the flower. *"Arrivederci, signorina."*

I turn from the cash register and take four steps in the direction of the waiter. "This is for you," I say, extending the flower in his direction.

The cashier explodes in a fit of hearty laughter.

With my pretty packet of cookies and *cannoli,* I walk across the *piazza* to join my boy lover. I feel triumphant.

Under the Volcano
Dina Vered

Bogotá

"A volcano just erupted in Colombia," my editor barked into the phone. "One of the worst volcanic disasters in history— more deadly than Mount Vesuvius. You speak Spanish, so I want you to jump on the next plane to Bogotá. We're saving you the cover!"

That night, I landed in Bogotá with my photographer, Max. After flashing around some greenbacks, we found a taxi driver willing to get us to the disaster area fast. He drove us up and down the winding tropical northern Andes. These soaring, misty mountains felt like a tropical Garden of Eden. But we weren't sightseeing, we were rushing at breakneck speed, with a maniac taxi driver. I was frightened by this driver who didn't seem to know how to use his brakes, but Max wasn't—he'd shot too many pictures, covered too many tragedies, hung out at too many hotel bars to be unnerved. While Max snored, I asked the driver in Spanish to slow down. Instead, the driver ignored me and turned up the radio volume.

We listened to the news announcer describe the volcano. "The crater erupted violently inside Nevado del Ruiz. Heat from the volcano's gases melted part of the snowcap. Six-foot waves of mud and volcanic ash tore through the town of Armero and buried it. Many thousands are dead, many thousands missing."

At dawn, we found ourselves in an area studded with towering volcanic mountains topped by snow. Major eruptions were rare here until Nevado del Ruiz, the chain's largest and highest volcano, erupted the night of November 14, 1985. Thirty minutes later, Armero, a thriving town of about 25,000 located just below the volcano, disappeared entirely. When we arrived a day later, signs of the volcano's deadly fury were everywhere. A deluge of mud and water had swept away houses and trees. With all roads and bridges washed out, the taxi driver left us off to hike the few remaining miles to Armero. Max handed him some money and promised to pay him the rest when he picked us up at sunset.

The tidal wave of mud that covered the town of Armero buried thousands of people alive. As Max and I waded through the mud, the silence was devastating. We saw pools of blood on the surface of the mud and then, under a mango tree, I spotted a mattress partially submerged in the mud. On it, I noticed a mother cradling her baby in her arms. My excitement ended when I got closer—both of them were motionless. I felt like someone had kicked me in the stomach, but Max flew into action. Like a machine, he shot picture after picture. Nauseated and in a daze, I wandered off looking for survivors to interview.

Clouds of volcanic ash from the 17,716-foot volcano continued raining down, partially obscuring the sun. I saw more corpses in the mud. Suddenly, the silence was broken by a desperate cry. I looked around and saw a pregnant woman clinging to a tile roof, her body ripped apart. But before I could get to her, she fell into the mud and disappeared. Like her, thousands died awaiting rescue. I kept walking and realized there was no one around, except a few impassive Colombian Army soldiers. Their indifference made me angry.

Then, behind a submerged couch, I noticed two little arms waving weakly from the mud. The mud was too deep for me to enter. I yelled for help. With relief, I saw a tall, bearded man slowly wade through the thick mud. With difficulty, he managed to pull a little boy out. The bearded man carried the boy in his strong arms. When he reached me, he said, "Take care of him," and handed me the naked boy, his clothes torn off. "*Mi madre! Mi madre!*" the boy screamed and pointed to a woman up to her nose in mud. The bearded man rushed back into the mud toward her, but he was too late. The woman's head disappeared. The boy had lost his mother.

I yelled out to the bearded man that there was a girl near him clinging to a tree branch dangling above the mud. He sloughed back in and pulled her down. As he carried her through the thick chocolate-colored morass, he looked exhausted, his beard and brown hair caked in mud. "Take care of her too," he said wearily as he placed the girl on a mound of grass near me. I met his eyes in silent understanding. We'd both seen too many children desperately searching for parents, for parents who would never reappear.

Both the boy and girl were confused. *"Mis padres!"* the girl cried. The burning hot mud had carried her parents away, the girl said. "Where are they? Where?" she sobbed in Spanish, unaware she was now probably an orphan. Five or six American journalists heard her screaming and ran up to us. They shot questions at the children and told me to translate. I ignored them and hugged the children tightly. Then two photographers started taking pictures, treating the boy and girl like cornered animals. The bearded man ran up to the photographers and snapped, "Aren't you ashamed? Trying to make money off this tragedy instead of helping?" His brown eyes were flashing. He looked like an intense Che Guevara. "Can't you act like human beings? These children are in shock." I looked at him gratefully. I realized I'd crossed the line. I was more than a reporter covering a tragedy. I couldn't just cut off my emotions and "do my job." These children were alone. They needed a human being, not a reporter.

Near us, a carefully coiffed blond TV news reporter was standing in front of a pool of muddy corpses. The reporter was looking in a mirror, carefully applying pancake makeup. When he was satisfied with his reflection, he recited his stand-up. It wasn't perfect, so he ordered the cameraman to do another take. And another and another. When the reporter finished, he noticed a grisly scene in the mud behind him: a young girl locked in a death embrace with an older woman. He looked almost gleeful. "Get a close-up of that dead girl's face," he ordered his cameraman. "What a great shot!"

"A great shot?" the bearded man shot back angrily. "Where is your heart? You vulture!" The TV reporter looked embarrassed and ordered his cameraman to pack up the gear. Suddenly, the sounds of a chopper's blades drowned out the bearded man's furious words. The chopper hovered over us and circled lower and lower. I was relieved that the chopper had spotted survivors. Help had finally arrived, I thought, as a man leaned out of the helicopter. But instead of lowering a rope to pull victims from the mud, a long telephoto lens emerged. The idiot was taking pictures! "Do you know why there are no rescue helicopters?" the bearded man asked, turning toward me. "Because American photographers bribed the Colombian government and rented all three of its helicopters!"

I took out my notebook and urged him to tell me more. His English had an accent, but it wasn't Spanish. Even though he wasn't Colombian, he was incredibly well informed. "This tragedy was unnecessary," he said, his words shooting out in a torrent of rage. "We warned the government that danger was imminent, we told them to evacuate the area. But those selfish, corrupt bastards didn't take the threat seriously. All day, ashes from the volcano, thirty miles away, were raining down. People were worried. The local priest came on the radio. 'Note preoccupes,' Don't worry. There is no reason to panic," the priest told them. Then he fled Armero. That night, the mothers, fathers, and children of Armero were at home either sleeping or listening to a soccer match," he said softly, his voice shaking with emotion. "Just after ten, the volcano went off." I looked into the man's sensitive brown eyes. They were glistening with tears.

Just then Max ran up. "I got great pictures!" he said, unaware he was interrupting us. "I gotta rush this film back." I insisted we stay until I got more information. Max shot back that the story was getting old and the corpses already getting bloated.

"We can't leave until I finish getting the real story behind the volcano," I argued. "These deaths were unnecessary and I've got to find out who was responsible."

"We've gotta get back to the taxi by sunset, or someone else will offer the driver more," Max warned me. "Do you want to be stranded here?"

After a few minutes of arguing, I noticed the bearded man was no longer near me. I looked around, searching for him, but he'd disappeared, probably to rescue more people. I didn't know who he was or what he was doing there. But I knew he had a lot more to tell me. He made me realize that there was a shocking story behind this unnecessary tragedy. And even though he'd moved on, I was determined to find out more and expose it in print.

After we returned to Bogotá, Max flew back to New York. I remained behind, checking out the intriguing leads the bearded man had given me. It was true, shockingly true. After I filed my story, I pleaded with my editor for a few more days to write follow-up stories about government corruption and inaction, but he refused. "We've already got enough," he said. "By our next issue, no one will give a damn about dead Colombian peasants. Fly back, the volcano story is finished."

Cartagena

At Bogotá airport, I waited in the check-in line for my Avianca flight home. I was troubled with awful thoughts of returning to my magazine in New York. Numb from seeing too many gruesome scenes, I doubted if anyone in the newsroom would have the empathy for the nightmares I'd seen. I dreaded returning to my dark West Side sublet apartment. It was a lonely, echoing void except for the cockroaches. Then, as I neared the ticket counter, I saw him again across the terminal speaking with a ticket agent. Over her head, a sign was flashing: "Cartagena. Boarding."

"Where's Cartagena?" I asked a Colombian woman standing next to me. "On the Caribbean," she said with a dreamy smile. "It's our most fascinating city, full of charm, with tropical music and exotic beaches." Cartagena. Just what I needed, a balm for my battered mind. Far from the madness of the volcano and the insanity of the newsroom.

I looked over at the passengers waiting in line for the flight to Cartagena. The bearded man had finished and was leaving the ticket counter. He looked stunning, his mahogany skin strikingly set off by a crisp light blue shirt. I grabbed my bags and ran up to the ticket agent and breathlessly asked if any seats were left to Cartagena. When she nodded yes, I pointed to the tall, bearded man heading toward the departure gate. "I want a seat near him," I said firmly.

As I made my way down the aisle, I spotted him sitting in the aisle seat opposite mine. He didn't notice me; he was flipping through papers in his briefcase. As I studied his intelligent-looking chiseled face, I realized I knew almost nothing about this stranger. Who was he? Why was I following him to a place I'd never heard of? I took my seat and began reading *One Hundred Years of Solitude,* by Colombia's most celebrated contemporary novelist, Gabriel García Márquez. After a few pages, I realized how little I knew of Colombia, this land of volcanoes, emeralds, jungles, drug lords, and the mysterious ancient kingdom of El Dorado. Soon after takeoff, I felt his eyes on me. I slowly looked up from the novel. When our eyes met, I feigned surprise. So much depended on what would happen next, I realized. Suddenly, a huge wave of shyness hit me.

"What are you doing here?" he asked in a deep voice. He spoke warmly, as if he were greeting a lost soul mate, not a stranger.

"I'm going to the ocean to cleanse my head from the volcano," I said unsteadily. As I felt his eyes studying me, I felt scared. So much was at stake and I didn't want to blow it. "And you?"

"Exactly the same." He nodded, knowingly. "Only I also have to write a report."

"What kind of report?" I asked, trying to speak calmly.

"About negligence. About ignored warnings to evacuate," he said, his anger building. "About unnecessary deaths." As I saw his intensity return, my muddy memories surfaced. The children. The parents. Forever separated in tombs of mud, water, rocks, and volcanic ash. I sat in silence and realized then that he too was sharing the painful mental pictures.

After that saddening silence, we talked nonstop. Sergio was a Brazilian volcanologist. He'd spent weeks at the volcano installing seismic monitoring stations and drawing up maps showing mudflow paths. "The main goal of volcanologists is warning people to get out of the way in time," he explained. "My team had been inside the crater. We knew it would explode. We drew up emergency plans and warned the Colombian government to evacuate the people. And what happened? Over twenty-two thousand are dead, thousands more missing and injured, and over sixty thousand homeless. Why? Because those bastards ignored our warnings."

Sergio was used to staring death in the face. He traveled from

Mexico to Indonesia to Papua New Guinea studying volcanoes. The world has over five hundred active volcanos, mostly in countries in the deadly Ring of Fire, so Sergio had plenty of work. The Pacific Ocean, he explained, "is ringed by angry volcanoes that have killed before—and will kill again." As he talked, I saw he was addicted, addicted to the adrenaline rush of trying to predict when volcanoes would erupt. I realized that, like me, Sergio loved living on the edge.

After our jet landed in Cartagena, Sergio asked where I was staying. When I told him I had no reservation, he insisted on taking me to a charming hotel he knew. Our taxi drove up a narrow bay to a beachfront hotel. "When they see a blond, blue-eyed American, they'll double the price," he said, motioning me to wait in the taxi. In a few moments, he returned. "All the hotels are full. An international Jaycee convention has taken over the town. It's a sign you should stay with me—my friend left me his house," he said with a great grin. Sergio moved close to me in the taxi's backseat. I hid my excitement and felt his building too.

We drove through the old walled town of Cartagena. This sun-drenched town was a gem, a museum of sixteenth-century Spanish colonial architecture. Sergio visited here every time he came to study Colombia's volcanoes. He pointed out plazas, palaces, and Spanish mansions with graceful facades in pastel shades of tangerine, lime, and lemon. This had been Spain's main Caribbean port, the most well-protected colonial city in South America, founded in 1533. "This is the area where the Spanish stored treasure they stole from the Indians before shipping it back to Spain," Sergio explained. Then he showed me the city's thick walls. "To guard the city from English and French pirates marauding the Caribbean. The Spanish made their African slaves build them." As he spoke those words, he had the same angry look I'd seen in him in the mudfields at Armero.

Our taxi passed through Puerto del Rejol, or Clock Gate, and stopped at an elaborate wrought-iron gate. Behind it was a magnificent whitewashed Caribbean-style mansion with a tiled roof and a bell tower. Sergio put in a key and opened a heavy carved wooden door. His friend's vacation house was magical inside, with old-fashioned vaulted ceilings and Tuscan columns.

The purple bougainvillea peeking out of the wooden balconies gave it timeless elegance. It was hard to believe we'd just seen people buried alive by one of the world's most lethal volcanoes. I asked Sergio about the wooden bars on the windows. "To protect us from pirates," he said, and gently brought my hand to his lips.

"What about the pirate standing next to me?" I asked. He smiled playfully and led me outside to a shady garden. It was bursting with flowers and heavy with the scent of the frangipani. "Nature is generous here," Sergio said, as he placed a delicate white orchid behind my ear. When he pointed to a yellow and black toucan in a tree heavy with mangoes, I told him they were my favorite fruit. Within seconds, he'd climbed up the tree and cut off a ripe mango. As he fed me a soft juicy slice, he looked deeply into my eyes. "I hope you'll always remember Cartagena," he said, caressing my face. As our sticky lips met and then slowly built into an explosive kiss, I knew I would.

As Sergio drew me closer, I felt my body melt into his. There was a special dignity about him that made me abandon all caution. It didn't matter that I knew so little about him, I was pulled to him like a magnet. As our kisses grew more urgent, I kept thinking, "I want this man, I want him inside me." I took a deep breath and tried to slow down and savor the delicious feelings of anticipation. I kissed his ear and then planted a trail of kisses down his neck. Then suddenly, I noticed a large angry scar on the side of his neck. Sensing something, Sergio loosened his embrace. "It was caused by a red-hot rock," he said reluctantly. Then he pulled away from me. Stupidly, I acted like a reporter and probed for more. He tensed up. Then, after a long pause, he continued. "Last year my team was in a crater in Indonesia. Suddenly it exploded with a ferocious force. I jumped behind a boulder and it saved my life. I was the only survivor. The others were buried alive." He turned away and then, in a whisper, added, "My wife was on the team." His scars were still painfully raw. I had to handle this complicated man carefully.

Tactfully, I suggested he show me more of Cartagena. We wandered down little side streets, around the churches, mansions, museums, and crafts shops. We savored the tropical architecture and rich street life. He pointed out some carts selling strange white objects. "*Huevos de ignanas*, iguana eggs, for the adventurous eater," he explained with a mischievous look in his eyes. We stopped at a picturesque square, Plaza de los Coches. But when I marveled at the elegant mansions ringing it, his mood darkened. "Things are rarely as they seem," he answered. I saw his jaw tighten, his intensity return. "This square has a tangled history. Cartagena had the 'official privilege' of being the center of the slave trade for all of Spain's new colonies. You're standing where African slaves were sold, branded, and shipped to Peru, Venezuela, and Ecuador. White Cartagenans had a monopoly on the Spanish slave trade and amassed enormous fortunes."

I noticed that many of the people around us were blacks and mulattos. "Descendants of slaves," Sergio explained. "As you'll discover tonight, they're lively, fun-loving, and spirited, like hot spicy green papaya salad." The play of shadows was beginning to transform both the Old City and our mood. Sergio brought me to an outdoor terrace on the former city wall and we sat at a small candlelit table. As we swapped stories, we could hear the waves of the Caribbean lapping on shore. The maitre 'd greeted Sergio like an old friend and brought us a complimentary bottle of Aguardiente, a strong alcohol that tastes like anisette. Sergio loved the Colombian people. "Because of its corrupt government and bad press, Colombia is South America's forgotten country," he explained. "You'll see that despite its turbulent history, it's also exotic and sensual." By the time we'd finished our plantain and yucca soup and *Langosta caribeña*, a delicious lobster sautéed in coconut milk and flambéd with cognac, the Old City area was vibrating with the sidewalk musicians' hot African rhythms.

"I love this district's charm and lunacy," he said, pointing to a street where a sea of partying revelers were dancing to the *cumbia*, music West African slaves brought to this Caribbean coast. When Sergio got up from the table and led me deep into the crowd of dancers and taught me to gyrate my hips to the hypnotic drum music, I loved his Brazilian charm and lunacy, too. It was pure, crazy fun, a collective celebration of people spontaneously drumming, singing, and dancing. The people were a mix of mulattos, blacks, whites, and Indians. There were sugar cane farmers, teachers, artists, and musicians. As we danced, class and race lines disappeared: the poor forgot their poverty and we forgot the volcano. For hours, the local Ron Tres Esquinas (Three Corners Rum) kept us going nonstop. Our dancing was a catharsis.

Then, the music slowed. Sergio showed me a passionate, erotic dance, a dance Spanish missionaries would have forbade. Our moist bodies, skin to skin, moved in unison to the slow beat. Engulfed by the euphoria of the evening, we let go of our memories of the unleashed fury of the volcano. "Are you enjoying the idea of *'aqui y ahora'*—here and now?" he asked, taking out a white handkerchief and wiping the perspiration from my forehead. When I nodded yes, he planted a kiss on my lips. As we danced, his tongue explored my mouth in rhythm with the music. I shivered with anticipation. I was enchanted by this captivating Caribbean place and this magical man.

But when the embrace of the carnival was over, we shared the same memento—blisters on our feet. At dawn, we fell into bed, worn out. We were friends, exhausted friends. The lover part, I hoped, would come next. Late that morning, I was awakened by tender kisses on my eyelids. Groggy, I slowly opened them and smelled the pungent aroma of strong coffee. As I sat up, Sergio kissed me again and handed me a tray of warm croissants. "Fresh from the bakery down the street," he said. "And now, come see the islands."

Islas del Rosaria

Our catamaran was cruising the Islas del Rosaria, a string of twenty-six pearls in the Caribbean. We anchored off an uninhabited island. I was in my bikini, and grabbed my mask and snorkel, eager for a swim. When Sergio took off his shirt, I saw that the savage red scar on his neck marched all the way down his chest. He noticed my startled look and turned away abruptly. Before I could apologize for my reaction, he dove off the boat into the translucent emerald lagoon. I cursed my insensitivity and jumped in. Immediately, I felt like I had entered an undersea fairyland, teeming with clouds of tropical fish— damsels and yellow butterflies and angelfish. As we snorkeled and played among the magnificent untouched coral canyons, the sea seduced us.

When we surfaced, Sergio swam up to me and held me tightly

in the shallow warm water. We shared urgent kisses. Then I felt his tongue gently work its way down my neck to the top of my bikini. He eased off my bikini top. With closed eyes, I felt his warm tongue play with my nipple, tickling it to arousal. When he untied the bottom of my bikini, I pulled off his trunks. We leaned against a rock, skin to skin. I kissed the scar on his neck and put my hand under the water and massaged his penis. It was soft, but as I stroked it in the warm silkiness of the water, I felt it slowly growing larger and harder. Then I felt his finger gently circling my clitoris—first slowly, then a little faster and faster. With each touch, it grew increasingly more sensitive. Soon, it grew insanely explosive, so explosive that I pushed his hand away. But Sergio stubbornly put it back and continued playing my clitoris like a concert pianist. I closed my eyes, losing myself to him, delirious with the sensations of the building crescendo.

Teetering on the precipice of orgasm, I refocused my mind on stroking his penis. I felt it grow stiffer and stiffer. When it felt like granite, he withdrew it from my hand. I looked up at his face and noticed a wild, wanton look in his eyes. With pent-up urgency, Sergio entered me with slow thrusts while his tongue moved in and out of my mouth in unison with his penis. I quivered with anticipation. Then with a swift, strong stroke, he pushed hard inside me. Then again and again, he shoved his penis in me deeper and deeper and deeper. My body arched, releasing itself from my mind. As Sergio set off my orgasms in rapid staccato succession, I let out a scream that echoed across the lagoon. Just then, I felt him erupt inside me, like a torrent of hot lava, and we exploded together. I looked at him. His wild eyes now had a dreamy gaze, as if he had floated into another world. We held each other like lost souls, sharing deep sharp gulps of the salty sea air.

As we emerged from the water and walked to the shore, I felt a bit shy, my naked body no longer swathed in turquoise water. Sergio took my hand and led me down a powdered sugar beach untouched by footprints. "Welcome to the most seductive island floating in the Caribbean," Sergio said, as he tenderly brushed strands of wet blond hair from my face. The air was fragrant with the perfume of tropical flowers and fruit. We picked *guayaba* (guava), *maracuya* (passion fruit), and mangoes and sucked the fruit from each other's fingers. Exhausted, we lay spent and naked under the nodding coconut palms, a cooling breeze caressing us to a deep sleep. On this bewitching island, I felt as if I'd finally left the drama of the deadly volcano a million miles away. Nothing mattered except sharing this island with Sergio.

The blazing Colombian sun awoke us. Sergio brought me to a small thatched hut, hidden by banana and mango trees. He motioned me to lie on a woven grass mat. He held a bottle of coconut oil to my nose. Its subtle scent, he explained, was from the love-flower, the pink plumeria. Slowly, he rubbed the warm oil on my breasts and then massaged it down my stomach to my inner thighs. "Close your eyes and don't move," he said, as gently, very gently, he spread my legs wide apart. I was aching for him to enter, my desire for this Brazilian fierce, impatient. But Sergio wouldn't let me conduct this symphony. Instead, like a maestro, Sergio made my clitoris respond. First pianissimo, then staccato. Then when he ignited the fire and my body and brain were screaming for more, he abruptly stopped and told me to keep my eyes closed. Then I felt him rubbing something soft and moist in circles around my clitoris. What was it? Then I heard his wet slurping sounds amplified in the tropical stillness. I felt the juices of the mango dripping onto the mat. Then I felt something warm exploring my clitoris. I opened my eyes and watched his head move between my legs. It was his tongue expertly playing me, reigniting the fire in my clitoris. Just as I was about to go off, Sergio turned his body around.

Sergio was on his hands and knees, poised directly above me. "With you," Sergio said, looking deeply into my eyes, "I know the future is today—tomorrow is too late." He bent his head down and planted a sticky mango kiss on my lips. Then, I felt his tongue move slowly in and out of my mouth. I poured coconut oil on my hand and let it slither back and forth over his erect penis. I was aching, aching to feel him thrusting deep inside me. When he gently slid inside my waiting vagina, I shivered with delight. This time neither of us could wait. Our hips heaved in unison, pushed to the limits of uncontrolled passion. He slid his fingers between our pelvises and caressed my clitoris slowly. Then, as if he knew every nerve ending in my clitoris, he stroked it stronger and faster. I was moaning loudly, trying hard to hold off the ultimate, but I couldn't. I burst into a higher plane of fiery sensation. Plunging into the swirling oblivion of orgasm, my strong jerks set off his explosion. As he let out a long, deep sigh, we erupted together.

During our time together, we fell into a delicious routine, addicted to languid days that evaporated one into the next. On our last day sailing around these islands, Sergio handed me a pair of delicate emerald earrings of rare beauty. "So you'll never forget me," he said. As our catamaran sailed back to Cartagena, we both fantasized about throwing our return plane tickets overboard.

PART V

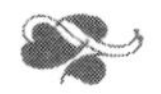

The Dark Side

Seduction has many sides. In an intimate relationship, seduction can convey love and caring. The promise of safety can allow one to enter the sensual world with abandon. But seduction can have a dark side as well. The seducer can be uncaring, self-indulgent, or oblivious to the seduction's impact on his or her partner.

"When I think of seduction, I think of deceit," says Bruce Zimmerman, author of "The Front Runner." "I think of shading yourself, presenting yourself as slightly different from the way you are. An overt seduction is about lust rather than love. It's a bit of a chess match—fun and sexy, but not long-term. It's about enticement and forbidden fruit." In Zimmerman's tale we have a humorous yet disturbing story with the kind of unique twist only an experienced mystery writer could conjure.

Seduction also can be used for more sinister purposes than selfishness; it can be deceptive, hurtful, vengeful. In these instances, seduction is a strategy, a game played with the intent to harm.

Carroll Mavis-Raine creates the ultimate ironic seduction in "Italian Pastry." "Seduction is a multifaceted thing," says Mavis-Raine. "I wanted to write a story about someone who uses seduction to get revenge. Sharon has Tomas completely under her spell. He's helpless as Sharon uses an impeccably planned and strategic seduction to entice him into her lair."

Sinister supernatural forces control the seduction of Analise, a sexually driven rock star who is still a virgin in Staci Layne Wilson's "La Petite Mort." "Analise has no control over the magic spell that has been cast upon her," says Wilson. "She is

swept away. She is lured away from her everyday life by a pro-
found force that is controlling her every move from outside her
awareness. The power is in the hands of the seducer and she
yields completely."

The dark side of the human psyche has a unique capacity to
provoke sexual excitement that has little to do with love, intimacy, or caring—a power that is all its own and that many find
to be extremely sexually provocative and magnetic.

The Front Runner

BRUCE ZIMMERMAN

Martin Kramer drained the last bit of his scotch and held the glass up for the cocktail waitress to see.

"Hey, honey!" he said. "Two more over here."

Bill Spenser shook his head. "Not me, Marty. I've had enough."

"Since when is two enough?"

"Since you're the one on vacation and I'm the one heading back to the office."

Marty smiled, gave his friend a look. Outside the window of the airport cocktail lounge, jumbo jetliners cut through the clear, pale blue Colorado sky. Crisp, end-of-autumn day. Nice now, but snow was around the corner. Marty wondered how blue the sky would be in Tahiti.

The cocktail waitress returned with the two glasses of scotch. She was attractive in a pert, perky, head-cheerleader kind of way, and had a name tag that identified her as "Cindy." Blond, large-breasted, very young.

"Why don't you just give me both of those, Cindy," Marty said, scooting both glasses over to his side of the table. "My friend here's decided to be a Boy Scout."

"Not all of us are on our way to Tahiti," Bill explained.

Cindy groaned with envy. "Tahiti? Any room in that suitcase for me?"

Marty winked. "Cindy, I'd throw stuff *out* to make room for you."

"Better be careful," Cindy said. "I may just take you up on that."

Marty handed Cindy a hundred-dollar bill and watched her as she walked toward the bartender. There were a half-dozen other men at the bar who watched her as well. Men with brief-cases, strong chins neatly shaven. Clones. Earlier it occurred to Marty that this element of the business world was where all those high school football heros ended up once they adjusted to the fact that they would be anonymous for the rest of their lives. A moving, breathing elephant's graveyard for all those who peaked at seventeen.

Up at the bar Cindy dropped a napkin. Her bottom strained at the fabric of her butt-hugging cocktail uniform as she bent to retrieve it. Marty let out a low, appreciative whistle.

"Would you look at that ass . . ." Marty said.

Bill shook his head. "Settle down, Marty. She could be your daughter, for Chrissake."

"I don't have a daughter."

Marty watched Cindy while she waited for the change. Three weeks in Tahiti with her. The thought of it went down as warm and smooth as the single-malt scotch, even though Waitress Cindy wasn't really his type. Other than Karen, his soon-to-be ex-wife, Marty'd never gone for large-breasted blondes. He smiled to himself. Hell, maybe that's why Karen was on her way to becoming his ex-wife.

Suddenly Bill was scooting his chair back and picking up his briefcase.

"Enjoy your scotch," he said. "Enjoy *my* scotch. And do your best to struggle through Tahiti, though I don't know what a hyperactive guy like you is going to do under a goddamn palm tree for three weeks."

"Staying away from signing any merger papers will give me all the excitement I need."

Bill leaned back down and put his face close to Marty. Quiet. Confidential.

"I'm a lawyer, Marty. Judges don't like it when you run away or manipulate business deals so that you don't have to share money with an ex-spouse."

"I'm not running away. I don't know anything about papers. Did that deal go through?"

Marty smiled, but Bill just gave him a look.

"I'm just a tired, overworked businessman," Marty went on, "who needs to get away before making a decision about clos-ing a big deal."

Bill smirked. "Why do I get the feeling you'll decide to go ahead with the merger as soon as your divorce becomes final next week?"

Marty resumed the smile. "Is that the feeling you have?"

"Fifteen thousand miles is a long way to go to save some money," Bill said.

"Four million dollars is a lot of money."

Bill gave Marty one last, lingering, disapproving look, then turned and left the airport lounge. He waved wearily at the door and Marty waved back.

"Thanks for the ride," Marty called after.

Then Marty turned his attention back to his drink. To hell with Bill Spenser. Guy was well intentioned, but he didn't appreciate what was at stake. The divorce with Karen would be official in five days. All he had to do was postpone signing the papers for the merger with Tri-Co until after the divorce and then the money was his, free and clear. If the roles were reversed, Bill'd be doing the same thing.

Marty leaned back in his chair and watched the cocktail waitress some more. Daughter, bullshit. Marty was a long way from being reduced to a father figure to attractive young women. He'd only just turned forty, and he was trim and athletic, with a full head of hair and the kind of looks that still drew interested glances from women on the street. Besides, Cindy was the one who suggested she might want to tag along on the Tahiti trip, wasn't she?

It was time to "run the reel" again. Marty smiled, licking his lips in anticipation. Running the reel was a skill Marty had developed as a young child and as he'd gotten older he'd refined it down to a science. As a kid he would turn out the lights and picture himself in all sorts of heroic escapades, all of it done as if it were a part of a movie. A big-budget feature, starring himself. He even went so far as to imagine the projector running in the background.

Marty sipped his double-scotch and watched Cindy as she leaned forward to say something to the bartender. Of course, the content of the "reel" had changed as he'd grown older. The PG-13 world of cowboys and Indians had turned into the darkest, wildest XXX cinema his brain could conjure up. Low-budget feature, starring himself. Marty closed his eyes, mentally threaded the film . . .

*They rented a car at the airport in Papeete and started
out into the lush Polynesian mountains. Cindy was laughing and hugging Marty. It was an impulse decision to
come with him. She was even wearing the waitress uniform from the airport bar.*

*At the private bungalow they went to their bedroom
and looked out the window at the sparkling blue waters
of the Pacific. Then Cindy turned to Marty, gave him a
lascivious look, and urged him back into a chair at the
foot of the bed.*

*"You've done so much for me," she whispered. "Now
let me do something for you . . ."*

*As Marty sat and watched, Cindy began to slowly un-
dress. Her breasts were large and milky and spilled out
from the confines of her cocktail waitress blouse as soon
as they were loosened.*

"Do you like them?" she asked.

*Marty nodded. Cindy moved closer, put Marty's face
between her breasts, enclosed him. Marty reached up to
press them harder, but Cindy backed off and shook her
finger.*

"Not yet."

*She moved back to the bed, hooked her thumbs onto
each side of her panties, and slowly, teasingly, tugged them
an inch at a time until they were down to her knees. Marty
smiled with appreciation. He was glad to see that she had
a full bush of sandy blond pubic hair. Marty was not like
the new generation of men who liked women shaved or
trimmed so close to the skin that there were no secrets
from thirty feet. Wasn't the whole point to get up very,
very, very close and then discover? Cindy stood before
him, wild, tangled, like an unexplored forest. My, God . . .
a man could be lost in that wilderness forever.*

*Cindy, fully nude, stretched out onto the bed, closed her
eyes, and began to gently touch herself. Almost absentmindedly. Neck, breasts, stomach, lower. She parted her
legs just enough to admit one probing finger. Marty leaned
forward in the chair.*

A knock on the door, but no reaction from Cindy. No

attempt to cover herself or stop the moment. Marty was perplexed, then in the next moment the door cracked open and a lovely Polynesian woman entered the room, carrying a glass of rum. The Tahitian woman handed the frosty glass to Marty, then turned her gaze to Cindy.

"What's going on?" Marty asked.

Cindy smiled, spread her legs a fraction wider. "When in Tahiti . . ." she murmured.

Then, as if it were the most natural thing in the world, the Tahitian woman gave Marty a small, cryptic smile, and knelt before him. She unzipped his pants and took his penis in her mouth, her long, lustrous black hair falling over his lap, obscuring all.

Marty smiled, sipped from the strong, icy drink. Cindy rolled over onto her stomach and lifted her bottom invitingly into the air. As she did, the Tahitian woman increased the tempo and strength of her sucking, reaching down to cup his balls in one hand, the other hand sliding up and down his wet shaft.

Cindy watched from the bed. Her hand was now working quickly between her legs, a quick, controlled clockwise motion with two fingers against her pussy.

"Move her hair," Cindy said, breathless. "I want to see."

Marty gathered up the mane of black hair and swept it aside so that Cindy could have an unobstructed view of the Tahitian woman's activities. The sight was like a sudden surge of hot lava through Cindy. She gasped, made a guttural moan, and pushed herself up onto all fours.

"Fuck me!" she commanded. "Fuck me now! However you want!"

"Here's your change, sir."

Marty jumped, startled at Cindy's voice so near. He blinked once or twice to bring himself back to reality. Damn. His movies were almost getting *too* real.

Cindy put the money down on the table and Marty handed her a five-dollar bill.

"Thanks," Cindy said. "And you enjoy yourself in Tahiti, okay?

"Somehow I feel like I already have," Marty said with a sexy smile.

Cindy shrugged a "whatever" shrug and moved off to the next table. Marty sighed, took a deep breath, and let the last moments of the fantasy linger a bit longer. He loved running the reel, even though his soon-to-be ex would have laughed in his face if she could have seen it.

"How nice of that Tahitian girl to bring you a drink," Karen would have said. "Did she also have the morning newspaper clutched between her teeth?"

Marty smiled. That's *exactly* what Karen would have said. In a funny way Marty was going to miss Karen. If she'd only been more . . . accommodating . . . who knows? Maybe it would've worked out.

Marty looked at his watch. His flight to Papeete didn't leave for another three hours, but Marty was one of those people who loved airports and would find any excuse to come to the terminal early to soak up the atmosphere. Cocktail lounges like this one were especially tantalizing. Sexually charged, transient, anonymous. People on the move, people moving away from the people who would control them. Marty liked the liberty that implied.

He took out his airline ticket and looked it over. Marty was flying Air France, first class. Cost a fortune, but why not? He could afford it. Hell, in three weeks he'd be able to charter his own damn flight. Marty gave some thought to taking advantage of their VIP lounge upstairs reserved for first-class passengers. Quieter, more comfortable, all the free top-shelf booze he could want.

Then she came in.

Marty was halfway out of his chair when the woman entered the bar. He eased himself back down. Jesus . . .

The woman went up to the bar and sat with her back to Marty and ordered a drink. The bartender nodded, took a wineglass down from the overhead rack, and poured out a glass of white wine. The woman crossed her long, slender, well-tanned legs and took a sip while unsnapping her briefcase and taking out a sheaf of papers.

Marty stared at her. Yes, yes, yes . . . this was more like it. Waitress Cindy was fine and well and certainly served a function in his Tahiti daydream, but Marty knew what got his rpm

revved. Marty understood his fantasy life well enough to know
that the voluptuous blond cocktail waitress served primarily as
a way to facilitate bringing the svelte Tahitian woman into the
room. We go to the circus to see the lion-tamer, not the Master
of Ceremonies.

This new woman at the bar was *precisely* Marty's type. She
was medium-height, olive-skinned, with long, dark hair that
spilled in ringlets to a point midway down her back . . . thin
wrists, and an achingly lush body beneath the silky fabric of her
tight-fitting black skirt and cream-colored blouse. It was almost
as if she had been ordered up from central casting.

Marty drummed his fingers on the tabletop and plotted how
he was going to take this woman. That the woman in question
might not want to be taken never occurred to Marty. In business Marty had found that everybody had a price, and the
world of sexual conquest was no different. With women there
was always a button to be pushed somewhere. Always. Some
men were just more adept at finding that button than others.

Marty was about to make his move when a youngish guy
broke out from the pack of television-watching jocks and approached the woman first, holding his beer and packing all the
radiance he could into his phony smile.

"This oughta be good," Marty said to himself. He settled
back in his chair, steepled his fingers beneath his chin, and
watched.

The woman did not blow the guy off immediately. That was
a good sign. Meant she was open to the possibilities. Didn't
have an attitude right off the bat. She returned his smile, set
aside her papers for a moment, took a sip from her glass of
wine, recrossed her legs.

Maybe it was the recrossing of the legs that did it, but suddenly the young guy seemed to falter. He was on thin ice.
Snagged the most luscious fish in all the waters but now she
was working free. When he spoke to her his voice was too loud.
When he listened he was way too attentive. Finally she said
something and pleasantly went back to her papers. Three
strikes and you're out. The guy turned and forlornly blended
back into the pack with his fellow minor-leaguers.

"Okay, Kramer," Marty said to himself, draining the last of
his scotch. "Time to show those kids how it's done."

Marty meandered up to the bar and took the stool next to her. She was working on some spreadsheets and only acknowledged his existence by moving the papers over another couple of inches, out of his way.

"Hello, there," Marty said.

She looked up briefly, smiled. "Hi."

The woman went back to her papers. Her beauty was a little disorienting. Magnificent body. The cream-colored blouse was buttoned to the top, but managed to convey what it would be like to have it unbuttoned all the way to the bottom. A vampy corporate woman. The perfect balance of no-nonsense and come-hither. But all the fabric in the world couldn't hide the tautness of her body. Drop a dime on this woman's stomach and it would bounce twice and rattle to a stop.

"You're a very beautiful woman," Marty said. Lame, but what the hell. At an airport bar you never know how much time you have. Go with the direct approach.

The woman looked up from her papers. "Thanks."

"You probably hear that a lot."

"Yes," she said. "I do."

"The guy who was here before me . . . did he say it?"

"As a matter of fact, he did."

Marty shrugged. "Good. I didn't want to say anything too clever or you'd get the impression that I thought I was better than him."

The woman smiled. "Don't worry. I wasn't getting that impression."

Marty laughed out loud. My God, the woman had spirit, too! Take it, dish it out. She was almost too good to be true.

"My name's Marty Kramer," he said.

"I'm happy for you."

"So let's get right to the point," Marty said. "You want to come to Tahiti with me tonight or not?"

The woman kept examining her spreadsheets. "Don't think my boss in Dallas would understand," she said.

"Not even with a permission slip?"

The woman put aside her papers and took a close look at Marty for the first time. She had the trace of a smile on her lips, and she adjusted herself on the barstool as if trying to bring the bullshit better into focus.

"And what do we do in Tahiti, since it would cost me my job and my wage-earning future?"

Marty shrugged. "Run. Frolic. Then run and frolic some more."

"Something tells me you've got a one-track mind," she said.

"Thanks. You can't believe what I went through to get rid of the other tracks."

This time her grin widened. There was some heat and moisture to it. A funny, humid sort of look in her eyes all of a sudden.

"What's your name?" Marty said.

"Vanessa."

Marty was getting to her. He could tell it. She'd cracked the door just a little bit wider. Marty signaled the bartender to serve up another round for each of them, and she didn't protest.

Vanessa began shuffling about a little with the financial papers spread out before her, but it was aimless shuffling, the way news anchors do while waiting to go to commercial. Marty imagined what it would be like to open her blouse. Suddenly the reel was running before he'd even had a chance to prepare for it. As if it had a mind of its own . . .

Vanessa was all over him, right there on the bar, with all the shocked Dead Elephants watching them from the other side of the room. Vanessa was in a hurry and knew what she wanted and wasn't going to take no for an answer.

Wineglasses shattered on the floor around them as she swept them aside and pushed him flat onto his back and went to work getting his pants down. Marty could feel the financial spreadsheets under his ass, the paper crumpling and crinkling. The bartender absentmindedly toweled off the debris and watched Vanessa with mild interest.

Vanessa was feverish, desperate. Was it the urgency of the imminent plane she had to catch? Or was the thought of ravishing Marty so exciting, she couldn't control herself?

"Help me!" Vanessa cried out to the bartender.

The bartender matter-of-factly put down his towel and climbed onto the bartop and went to work removing

Vanessa's skirt while she yanked Marty's pants down to mid-thigh.

Hungry, like a ravenous animal, she gathered his hardening cock into her mouth, using only her lips, her hands bracing herself on the bartop.

The bartender took off Vanessa's skirt and pulled down her panties and took a moment to stare at her exposed bottom before slowly unzipping his own pants. She spread her knees further, almost to the point where they were slipping off either side of the bartop. Her mouth bobbed furiously up and down on Marty's rock-hard cock. She let it slip out of her mouth and it slapped against his belly. She bent down again and licked his balls—big, greedy, full-tongued licks, like an animal at a salt lick.

Behind her the bartender had his pants down and he methodically placed one hand on each ass cheek and opened her up a little more. Vanessa's eyes fluttered half-shut . . . a mild brown-out, then they opened wide as the bartender entered her.

From the other side of the bar the half-dozen former high school football quarterbacks walked over. They were nude from the waist down, all of them in a high state of excitement. They lined up behind the bartender, each waiting his turn. Two of them stood on either side of Vanessa and started fondling her breasts while the bartender took her from behind and her lips slid up and down Marty's saliva-slickened shaft. She stared at Marty.

"When I get you hard enough," she gasped, "this is what I want you to do . . ."

The bartender set their drinks before them.

"—expensive?" Vanessa said.

Marty took a moment to adjust himself. Cleared his throat and erased the image of an overheated Vanessa half-naked on the bartop.

"I'm sorry," Marty said. "What did you just say?"

Vanessa sighed. "I said, isn't going to Tahiti a little expensive?"

"Oh," Marty said. "Don't worry. It'd be my treat."

Vanessa shook her head. "My whole *life* is going to have to be somebody's treat unless I get to Dallas."

"Why's that?"

Vanessa sipped her wine. "Have you ever been to the dog races?"

"You mean out at Mile High Stadium?" Marty said.

Vanessa nodded.

"Sure," Marty said. "Lots of times. I'm a member of the Turf Club."

"Well, I went just once, last night. A girlfriend told me they were fun, and easy to bet on. So easy I lost practically all my money."

"No kidding?"

"Six hundred fifty dollars, right down the tubes."

"All the more reason to dry your tears in Tahiti," Marty said.

But Vanessa wasn't really listening. She was holding her wineglass with both hands, looking out the window and smiling a bemused smile.

"Know how I lost my last race?" she said.

"How?"

Marty didn't give a damn how she lost her money. He was busy trying to keep the reel from running on its own again. He'd had enough of fantasy. He wanted to take this woman somewhere and see what she was like in real life.

"I bet all my money on a dog named 'Rocket Dancer' in the last race," Vanessa said. " 'Rocket Dancer.' A name like that, how could he lose, right? So right out of the blocks he's way, way ahead. None of the other dogs were even close. You know how they have that electric rabbit that goes around the track to make the dogs run?"

Marty nodded. "Rusty the Rabbit."

"Right. Well, guess what? My stupid dog went so fast it caught up with Rusty the Rabbit."

"It did?"

Vanessa nodded, shook her head at the memory. " 'Rocket Dancer' took a bite of that rabbit and got an electric shock that almost took its head off. The dumb dog just went staggering around in circles, a goofy look on its face. Came in last place."

Vanessa sighed, took a sip from her wine. "Anyhow, there went 'Rocket Dancer,' and there went my money."

"This story's getting sadder and sadder," Marty said. "Maybe some Polynesian skies would cheer you up."

Vanessa gathered up her papers and put them in her briefcase and shook her head.

"So that's a definite no on Tahiti?" Marty persisted.

"Afraid so."

Marty nodded, rubbed his chin. "How much time do you have before your plane to Dallas?"

Vanessa looked at her watch. "About an hour. Why?"

"How about this?" Marty said. "I've got a key to the VIP lounge at Air France upstairs. No palm trees, but they speak French and the champagne's free."

Vanessa stared at Marty, trying to assess him. Size him up. Then there was a roar from the group of jocks at the other end of the bar, all of them thrusting fists and looking at the television and talking football. Vanessa glanced at them, then picked up her briefcase.

"I can trust you, right?"

"To do what?"

"To not be an axe-wielding psycho?"

Marty held up his right hand, Scout's Honor style. "You can definitely trust that I'm not an axe-wielding psycho."

"Then let's go," she said.

The Air France VIP lounge was snooty and just-so and, much to Marty's delight, completely empty. There were only three flights a day out of Denver, two to Paris, one to Tahiti, and none of the flights were even close to boarding. At this hour even the hostess area was empty, and Marty used his electronic pass to get in.

Vanessa took a moment to survey the room. To take it all in. "Nice," she said.

"Can I get you some champagne?"

"No."

Marty already had the bottle of champagne in his hand, but Vanessa's abrupt answer stopped him from getting a couple of glasses.

"How about some wine, then?"

Vanessa shook her head. "No."

"Cheese? Bread? A little fruit?"

"No."

Marty put down the bottle and turned to face her, folding his arms across his chest.

"What *would* you like, then?"

Vanessa hesitated, fidgeted, moved away to the far side of the lounge. "I don't know. Maybe just rest a little . . ."

Marty moved closer. He came up behind her and put his hands on her shoulders. She tensed briefly beneath the touch, then relaxed.

"Your flight leaves in forty-five minutes," Marty said soothingly. "Why don't we use our imagination and make the most of the time?"

Marty decided to take the plunge. He let his hands slide from Vanessa's shoulders to her sides, then let them slowly insinuate themselves around to the front where they gently cupped her breasts. They were fuller than Marty expected. Firm. The nipples hardened beneath his fingers.

"I don't think this is a good idea," Vanessa said.

"Why not?"

Marty kept his right hand on Vanessa's breast, and let the other hand slide down to her hips. She may not have thought it was a good idea, Marty noted, but the woman was not making any effort to break it off.

"Somebody could come in," she said.

"Nobody's coming in."

Marty's breath was coming quicker. So was hers.

"I mean it," she said. "You had a key. Other people could have a key."

Marty turned Vanessa around to face him, looked down into her anxious but willing eyes. "Anybody coming in here is probably French," he said with a smile. "They understand about this sort of thing."

Vanessa looked at the door, chewed her lower lip, then came to a decision. She took Marty by the hand and led him to the most remote corner of the lounge, behind a high-backed couch. If somebody buzzed themselves into the room, they would have a reasonable amount of time to get themselves back together.

"Okay," Vanessa said once they were tucked away. "Now!"

Marty undid the buttons on her blouse while she stood before him, arms back so that her breasts strained against the fabric of her bra, one eye on the entrance to the lounge.

Marty parted her blouse and took a moment to look at her.

"Let me do the bra," she said. "Sit on the couch and close your eyes."

"Close my eyes?"

"Please."

Marty eased down onto the couch and closed his eyes. He could hear Vanessa shrugging out of her bra. Then he could smell the freshness of her skin, very close.

"Open your mouth," she said throatily. "Just a little bit."

Marty opened his mouth. In the next instant he felt the firm, hard tip of her nipple tracing his lips, running along the edge of his tongue like the tip of an eraser on a brand-new pencil, just aching to be used for the first time.

"Suck it," she said.

Marty did. Then she moved and the nipple was gone, only to be replaced by the other nipple. Marty greedily licked it, sucked it, played with it with his tongue. Now and then he could feel her finger as her hand cupped her own breast to better maneuver it in his mouth. Then the nipple was suddenly gone again.

"Keep your eyes closed," she said.

Marty nodded, but cheated a little, opening his eye an unde-tectable amount to watch Vanessa. She was lifting her skirt and pulling down her panties, still nervous about the entrance door. Then she inched closer to him, the sweet pubic triangle getting nearer and nearer to his mouth. He felt both her hands grasp him behind the head.

"Why are you doing this?" he said.

"Don't you like it?" she breathed.

"Yes."

"Then let me do it how I want." She paused. "Put out your tongue."

Marty extended his tongue and suddenly his mouth was filled with the explosive taste of her juices. Her hands were off the back of his head and were parting her vagina, pulling back the lips of her pussy. Marty angled his head and licked deep be-tween her legs, almost to the point of her anus, and he could hear her groan above him.

Incredible, Marty thought to himself. Absolutely incredible. How ironic that when he ran the reel his fantasy was all visual with no real, true sensation. And now that he was up in the Air

France VIP lounge with the woman of his dreams, he was denied the visual completely. It was nothing but taste and smell and texture and the sound of Vanessa's approval. He liked this method better.

Then she eased back. "Keep your eyes closed," she said.

Marty nodded, but he cheated again, glimpsing her in a gauzy half-vision as she reached to steady herself against the couch. Her gorgeous breasts hung loose. Vanessa's own eyes were closed, and she was kneading one of her breasts with one hand and sliding her other hand between her legs. She put two fingers, three fingers, deep, deep inside her. They came out slick and shiny, and Vanessa moved toward him again.

"Open your mouth," she insisted. "Wide."

Marty clenched his eyes shut and opened his mouth, ready to devour the fragrant, wet, sticky fingers. Already he was thinking about what he was going to do to her when it was his turn. He was about to explode. It was delicious to contemplate exploding inside of Vanessa. He was going to put her back on that plane to Dallas disheveled, dazed, fucked utterly senseless.

"Wider," she whimpered.

Marty opened up his mouth as wide as it would go and suddenly he felt something strange jammed between his teeth. He immediately opened his eyes to find himself masticating on a yellow manila folder.

Marty yanked the folder from his mouth and spit out the musty taste of impersonal stationery.

"What the hell . . . ?"

Vanessa had already moved away from him, a good twenty feet on the other side of the room, near the door. She was pulling herself back together. Panties up, bra fastened, blouse buttoned.

"Hope it was good for you, too, Marty," she said with a smile.

Marty got up off his knees and held the papers aloft. "What is this?"

"Contracts for you to sign," Vanessa said. "Your ex-wife will be expecting you in court next week. Sorry if I messed up your vacation in Tahiti."

Marty's face collapsed. He dropped the manila envelope as if it had turned into a hot coal, burning in his hand.

"You. . . ! You *tricked* me!" Marty shouted.

Vanessa shrugged, buttoned the last of her buttons. "What are you talking about? You came to me. I was just sitting at the bar, minding my own business."

Marty stood for a moment, looking down at the floor, trying to assimilate it all. Puzzle it out. Make the nightmare go away.

"Look at the bright side," Vanessa said. "Usually I charge five hundred dollars a pop. You just got a freebie. It's not every ex-wife who'd give her ex-husband a treat like that."

Vanessa went to the door, opened it, paused to look back with a smile.

"By the way, my name's not Vanessa. Just in case you were thinking about getting even."

"What is your name?" Marty heard himself ask.

The woman shook her head, put two fingers to her lips. "Trade secret. But you can call me Rusty."

Marty blinked, looked down at the manila envelope resting on the couch. The weight of it seemed to sink into the fabric of the cushion. The weight of four million dollars lost.

"Rusty," he mumbled. "Like the rabbit."

"That's right," the woman said. "*Precisely* like the rabbit."

Then she turned and left. Marty stood in the empty room and watched her go. The woman was so much his type it was scary. Almost as if she had been sent over from central casting.

Italian Pastry

CARROLL MAVIS-RAINE

Tomas Marcolini saw the shapely blonde at Carrie Andrews's funeral. *Who was she?* In the six months he'd dated Carrie, he'd surely met every one of her large extended family. He remembered meeting one wrinkled face after another at that family reunion she'd dragged him to last summer. Except . . . hadn't she mentioned an older sister who was always off on some archeological dig in Egypt or Syria or some weird place? Who knew? Their romance had gone sour long before the egghead sister had shown up, and he'd had to break it off.

It was really too bad about Carrie. She was a cute kid. *Had* been, anyway. Tomas still remembered the day he'd met her. It was in Norway during the Winter Olympics. He'd just won his second gold medal in the Men's Downhill. Still jubilant with victory, he'd gone over to see the women do their thing in the Giant Slalom. Carrie, an eighteen-year-old nobody from Colorado, blew away the competition and became America's newest media darling.

He'd taken one good look at her long golden-brown hair, her clear green eyes, and pretty freckled face and decided that America's media darling needed to meet Italy's media darling. He'd made his way through the crowd, which immediately parted for him as soon as they recognized him. Wearing his warmest smile, he introduced himself to Carrie, although an introduction was *definitely* not necessary. After all, one would have to be living on an ice floe in Antarctica not to have heard of the great downhill racer Tomas Marcolini.

Seducing America's newest celebrity had been remarkably easy. All it took was a couple of bottles of good French wine, an elegant dinner in one of Oslo's best restaurants, and his undivided attention. He had it down pat—the constant eye contact that told her she was the only woman in the room, maybe the *world* as far as he was concerned. He'd kept his voice low and intimate, and of course, his Italian accent hadn't hurt, either. American women swooned over it.

After dinner Carrie had returned with him to his hotel room, where he'd taken her virginity. Her innocence astonished him. Sure, she was only eighteen, but most girls, especially American ones, had experimented with sex earlier than that. But because Carrie had been so caught up in ski racing since the tender age of twelve, he supposed she hadn't had the time or the opportunity for romance.

Tomas was glad about that. Teaching Carrie about love had been intoxicating—so much so that he'd stayed with her much longer than he did with most women, even following her to Colorado for the summer and moving into her house in Vail. That's where he'd met all her weird relatives.

It was inevitable, though, that he'd become bored with Carrie's "apple-pie" wholesomeness (although he had to admit she'd turned into quite the little wildcat in bed and wasn't averse to learning a few tricks—even flirted with S&M). Still, Tomas was used to variety when it came to women; it was amazing, really, that he'd stayed with Carrie almost seven months. And in that time, he'd remained faithful, screwing only two other women, a barmaid and a stripper—just a couple of one-night stands.

As summer ebbed into fall, Tomas's thoughts turned to Europe . . . to Celeste in Paris, who could do amazing things with her tongue and dark sweet chocolate. To Shawna in London, a six-foot black model who craved back-door sex. Oh, and of course, Gina in Rome, who often invited another nymphet to join in on their bedroom games. Not to mention all the thousands of young nubile girls he'd yet to meet.

Unfortunately, the breakup was uglier than he'd expected. Poor Carrie was crushed. It seemed that she'd thought he was in love with her. He'd tried to be gentle; he'd told her how sweet she was, how she'd someday make a wonderful wife for some lucky man. But not him. He couldn't see himself *ever* being husband material. He was too much of a wild spirit. Surely she could see that. But she hadn't.

Yes, it was a damn shame about Carrie. What a waste! Her deterioration hadn't been sudden. She'd gone back to ski racing the following winter after the breakup, but it was obvious that something had gone out of her. Experts said it was her drive, her will to win that was missing.

And then she'd had that horrible accident at Garmisch. Lost her concentration for a split second and careened down the mountain, smashing her leg in three places and her arm in two. That had been the beginning of her drug problem. The painkillers got her hooked. Nothing to do with *him*. Oh, sure, Tomas had got her to try a little coke once or twice, but she hadn't had a drug problem when he broke up with her. No fucking way.

No one was going to blame *him* for her death. He'd heard the rumors. That before she'd gotten mixed up with him, she'd been a bright, effervescent young woman, destined for greatness. Now, at nineteen, she was dead from an overdose of phenobarbital and alcohol.

But it wasn't *his* fault! Why was everyone here giving him such dirty looks?

Tomas returned his attention to the shapely blonde sitting with Carrie's grief-stricken parents, wondering again who she was. Could it possibly be the sister? If so, she wasn't anything like he'd imagined. Somehow, he'd thought she'd be an old hag with skin the texture of a sun-ripened raisin.

The funeral ended and the immediate family stood up and began to make their way down the aisle toward the doors. The buxom blonde moved gracefully, almost felinely in a clinging black dress, exuding a sexuality that triggered an immediate reaction in Tomas. Sheer, unadulterated lust. A dark veil hid her face from view, but he could see that her hair was honey-colored, short, and silky. And her breasts were gorgeous—firm and full beneath her rayon bodice. *Who was she?*

As she reached the last pew, he felt her gaze, but of course, couldn't see her eyes. She hesitated for a split second and then passed by. Tomas released a deep, explosive breath, feeling his heart pounding like a piston. His prick had gone as hard as a block of cement . . . just because she'd looked at him. Christ! He'd never felt such an overwhelming sense of arousal. He had to find out who she was.

He didn't see her again until he joined the mourners at the

cemetery. After Carrie's coffin was lowered into the earth, each of her family members, including the woman in black, tossed a clump of soil into the grave. Tomas stared at her, unable to disguise his fascination. Her legs were gorgeous—long and slim. Could she be a model? She certainly had the body for it now that tits were back in style.

As the mourners left the grave and headed back toward the long line of limousines nearby, Tomas stood still, staring down at Carrie's coffin and wondering how he could possibly approach the blond woman in black.

But incredibly, it was she who approached *him*. Her fragrance wafted toward him, a heady Oriental scent. Sultry and sensuous. She stood only a few inches away, much closer than was socially acceptable.

"I know you," she said in a husky Demi Moore–type voice. "You're Tomas Marcolini. Carrie told me a lot about you."

"Really?" He felt vaguely uncomfortable. What had Carrie told her.

"Oh, yes." Slowly, the woman lifted the veil and drew it back over her hat.

He inhaled sharply, unprepared for her incredible beauty. Her eyes were smoky-blue and widely spaced, fringed with dark lashes. A perfect nose, a full, sensuous mouth, creamy porcelain skin. And a tiny mole just to the left of her lower lip. But it was much more than that. It was her earthy sexuality, so powerful that he almost reeled from it.

At her approach, his cock had again stirred and now was so hard, it felt like a hot brick had been placed in his pants. All because of her proximity. If she touched him . . . Christ . . . what would that do?

She extended her gloved hand. "I'm Sharon, Carrie's sister."

"I'm sorry about Carrie," he said, taking her hand. Even through her glove, he felt her warmth. His senses swam. Jesus Christ! What was happening to him? He looked into her eyes, and all he wanted to do was fuck her right there next to Carrie's grave . . . right then.

She smiled, gazing deeply into his very soul, and somehow, he knew she was reading his mind. "Are you as good as my little sister said you were?" Her voice was so low, he wasn't sure he'd heard her correctly.

But before he could respond, she turned and walked away. His eyes locked upon her swaying hips. "Wait!" he called out.

She turned and looked him up and down, a slight smile of amusement on her lips. "Yes?"

He swallowed hard, for once in his life feeling out of his depth. Impossible! Tomas Marcolini out of his depth with a woman? It couldn't be happening. "Can we . . . you know . . . get together for a drink? Talk about Carrie?" Jesus, he was *stammering*.

"I'm leaving for Central America tomorrow."

He stared at her, his mouth slack with dismay. "For good? Please don't say for good."

She smiled, her eyes penetrating. "For a few months. I have a study to complete." At his look of total bafflement, she went on, "I'm an anthropologist. I spend a lot of time in South America."

"Do you ever get to Rome?" he asked eagerly.

She lifted one shoulder in a slight shrug. "You never know."

His fingers trembled as he drew his business card out of his wallet. "Here is my address. If you do, call me."

The Mona Lisa smile remained on her lips. *Did she find him amusing?* She took the card and tucked it into her purse. "Perhaps I will. Then again, maybe I won't."

Two months passed, and Tomas didn't hear from her. Still, she was in his mind constantly. At night, his dreams were of her . . . erotic dreams beyond all imagining. The things she did to him . . . God . . . he'd wake in the middle of the night, his cock granite-hard and pulsing. He tried making love to other women, and for the first time in his life, he found himself impotent. It was as if Sharon had put some kind of curse on him. His cock wanted only her. What was she? Some kind of witch?

Masturbating was his only relief. But even with that, the only way he could maintain an erection was to think of Sharon. Sleazy magazines, adult videos . . . none of them would do the trick. Only Sharon.

And then, one afternoon three months after he'd met her, she turned up at his manager's office while they were in the middle of a meeting. Walked right in. She wore slim faded jeans, cowboy boots, and a flesh-colored crocheted vest that did nothing to hide her round, luscious breasts. Both Tomas and his manager stopped talking in mid-sentence to stare at her. She gave them a cool smile and asked to speak to Tomas alone. He wasted no time in getting his manager out of the office, then turned back to Sharon, catching his breath as he noticed the tiny brown nubs of her nipples through the openings in the crocheted vest. Her short blond hair was slightly mussed by the wind. She gazed at him with her deep indigo eyes for a long moment without speaking.

"About that drink," she said. "I'm staying at a friend's villa outside the city. Here're are the directions. It's rather remote, so leave early. Be there at nine o'clock tonight." With that, she turned and left the office, leaving behind that alluring Eastern scent he'd noticed that day at the cemetery.

The hours couldn't pass quickly enough for Tomas. He raced back to his apartment and, after showering, dressed in casual pressed slacks and one of his favorite printed shirts. He brushed his dark brown hair and stared into the mirror, knowing he looked great, as usual, but somehow, he still felt insecure. No other woman had ever made him feel insecure. What *was* it about Sharon?

At nine o'clock sharp, he knocked on the elaborate front door of the villa. She opened it and stepped back. He stifled a gasp as he caught his first sight of her. She was dressed in a short silk dress with a plunging satin neckline that revealed her ample breasts. Silky black hose encased her long legs, made even longer by the four-inch strappy heels she wore. Her hair was pleasantly mussed, as if she'd just dragged herself out of bed after hours of long, lazy lovemaking. But her makeup was flawless, her lips red and pouty.

He stepped inside, his hands clammy with nerves. "I'm afraid I'm a bit underdressed."

"No matter," she said, taking his hand and leading him into a huge drawing room.

He tried to ignore the tingle her touch sent racing through him and, instead, gazed around the room. It was decorated in a Middle-Eastern motif—big fluffy pillows, silken scarves, and woven tapestries. Tapered candles burned in different places and spicy incense permeated the air. On a low table in front of a large L-shaped white leather sofa, a bottle of red wine chilled in an ice bucket. Two crystal goblets were half-filled.

"I knew you'd be on time," she said, her eyes resting on the glasses. "Please, sit down."

"You are very sure of yourself, are you not?" he said, trying to sound offhand, but it came out awkwardly. Contrived.

Her eyes sparkled as she met his gaze. Was she laughing at him, he wondered?

"There are some things everyone *should* be sure of," she said, settling down next to him on the sofa and reaching for her wineglass.

Her heat hit him like a blast from a furnace, yet she hadn't touched him yet. As before, his cock had hardened the moment he saw her. Now it lay rigid against his stomach. Could she see it? But how could she not? It bulged against his trousers, plainly outlined against the gabardine fabric. Yet she appeared not to notice as she drained her glass.

She placed it down on the table and turned to face him. Her gaze was direct. "I have two rules," she said huskily. "Do you want to hear them?"

His heartbeat picked up. He knew exactly what she meant. "Yes," he said.

"Okay. Number One. You can look, but you can't touch. Not until I give you permission."

He swallowed hard and managed to answer. "And Number Two?"

Her eyes hardened. "You can't come until I allow you to. If you do . . . you're out of here."

He tried not to show his consternation. Still, he wasn't too worried. He was the kind of guy who could keep it up for hours if he wanted to. Looking at Sharon, he decided he wanted to.

"That will not be a problem," he said.

She nodded. Her hands went to her crossed leg and slowly slid up her nylons, her eyes watching him. He felt his breathing go shallow as his eyes followed the movement of her hands. They reached her thighs and moved upward, pushing the silk fabric of her dress higher. Finally, they slid up and under the skirt to the juncture of her thigh and belly. Slowly, still watching him, she uncrossed her leg. Her fingers moved between her parted legs, touching herself. Her mouth parted, and her tongue snaked out to lick her lips. A dazed expression had lodged in her eyes as she became lost in her own caress.

His cock bucked against his zipper. He could feel the engorged blood coursing through it, demanding release. It was agony. Sharon's eyes had darkened as she continued to stroke herself. She turned slightly so he could get a better view, and for just a moment, she withdrew her hand so Tomas could clearly see she wore no panties, only a garter belt to hold up her nylons. She smiled lazily as he gazed hungrily at her revealed pussy, and then, slowly, she slid two fingers in and began to fuck herself right in front of him.

Tomas groaned and pressed a hand against his erection.

"Uh-uh . . ." she said softly, shaking her head. "No touching, remember."

"But . . ." he gasped. "No touching you, you said."

She shook her head again, still sliding her fingers in and out of her cunt. In the silence, he could hear the sucking, moist sound of her wetness. It was making him crazy.

"No touching, I said. . . ." Her voice was soft, almost as if she were hypnotized. "Not even yourself." She pulled her fingers away from her pussy and leaned toward him, rubbing her juices over his lips. "You have my permission to lick my fingers."

He reached for her hand, but she shook her head. "Just your tongue. No other touching."

Avidly, he licked her pussy juices, and again, felt like he was going to explode. What was she doing to him? After he'd licked her fingers clean, she stood up and left the room.

Quickly, Tomas unzipped his pants and slid his hand inside, closing on his rigid penis. He knew he was playing with fire, but he had to touch his cock. Nothing on earth could stop him. One . . . two strokes, and already, he was close to coming. He heard her footsteps coming down the hallway and quickly withdrew his hand and zipped up. He felt the hot color flood his face. Oh, man. She was driving him mad.

She stepped into the room. He gasped at the sight of her. She stood before him, completely nude except for her black nylons, garter belt, and high heels. Her breasts were large and supple; her nipples dark brown and hard. He saw immediately by the tawny color of her pubic hair that she was a natural blonde. She looked so good, Tomas almost creamed in his pants right then.

"I had to get my toy," she said, smiling sweetly. In her hand, she held a huge dildo, veined and lifelike. She smiled at him and, slowly, began to lick it, her tongue swirling around it as if it were a Popsicle. Her eyes held his as she performed fellatio on the lifeless object, oh, so expertly. And it was almost as if she were doing it to him. He moaned as she flicked the tip with her tongue and then withdrew it from her mouth.

She switched on a button and the thing began to buzz. Smiling, she settled down on two large pillows on the floor, parted her legs, and began to fuck herself with the vibrator. Her other hand alternated between her breasts and her clitoris, and all the time, she gazed at him, right into his amazed eyes, a tiny smile on her lips.

Oh, God! His cock was a live thing inside his pants, straining to get out, straining to plunge inside her like that dildo was doing this very moment. As her strokes intensified, she began to grunt in a soft sexy way, and Tomas felt his senses swim with each sound. He arched his pelvis and felt his cock rub against his zipper. He couldn't touch, but he could get a bit of friction that way. As she rose higher toward her peak, Tomas did the same. He began to moan in time with her grunts, his heart pounding against his chest wall.

"Please, *cara mia* . . ." he gasped. "Let me touch . . . let me touch . . ."

"No . . ." she mumbled, between grunts. "No . . . permission . . . ahhh . . ." She grimaced and shuddered as she came, grinding the dildo inside her frantically.

Tomas thrust upward, rubbing himself against the fabric of his pants and, suddenly, he was so close to coming, he knew it would only be a matter of seconds. Even in the middle of her orgasm, she realized what was happening to him.

"Don't do it," she gasped. "Not if you want to stay!"

He forced himself to stop grinding his pelvis. And he stopped himself right at the brink. His cock remained like a hot rod in his pants, just millimeters away from erupting.

"Oh, Christ . . ." he murmured. "I cannot believe this . . . you are killing me . . ."

"Think about something else," she said, rising gracefully to her feet.

Tomas couldn't believe it. She wasn't even out of breath from her orgasm.

She grabbed the wine bottle from the bucket. "More wine?" she whispered, smiling catlike.

He nodded, and she filled his glass. He gulped it frantically, trying to get his mind off his swollen prick.

She sipped her wine daintily, her eyes amused as she watched him. After draining her glass, she stood up. "Why don't you bring your wine upstairs to my bedroom? This time, I might let you touch."

His heart skipped a beat, and almost immediately, he felt his cock grow even harder. He'd never met a woman like Sharon before. She was a witch. A delicious, spellbinding witch. And if he didn't fuck her tonight, he'd surely die.

Meekly, he stood up and followed her up the wide, curving marble stairs, his eyes fixed on her full curveous buttocks, her long smooth back, and tapered waist. What a woman. All woman. He was practically drooling.

Inside her spacious white-furnished bedroom, she placed the wine bucket and her glass onto the bureau and turned to him. His eyes swept her body; she looked so incredible, clad only in that black garter belt, nylons, and heels. What gorgeous breasts, full and firm. And that tawny thatch of hair that guarded her honey-pot. Oh, how he wanted to sink his tongue into that crevice, make her cry out as she had when she'd fucked herself with the dildo.

She lifted the two refilled glasses of wine from her bureau. "Drink up, and let's get started."

Tomas took the wineglass and drained it in one swallow.

She smiled. "Strip off your clothes. All of them. And lie down on the bed." Her tone brooked no argument. In her hands, she held two long silken scarves. Immediately, he did as ordered. He loved silk scarves. Gina used silk scarves in her sex-play. But compared to Sharon, Gina was about as sexy as flannel. He stretched out on the bed, his cock at full-mast. This time, he knew there would be skin-to-skin contact. If not, he'd surely lose his mind.

She tied his hands to the bedposts in a tight but not uncomfortable knot. Still, he knew he wouldn't be able to release himself without considerable work. She'd done this before, and she knew how to do it right. For a moment, she stared down at him, her blue eyes cloudy with lust.

His cock had been granitelike before he'd stripped down. Now, it reared hungrily, like an impatient animal, ready for the kill. Sharon gazed at it, and licked her lips sensuously.

"Please . . ." he growled out. "Do not make me wait any longer."

He was full, pulsating. It was as if he hadn't climaxed in years.

She smiled and moved toward him in her feline way. She straddled him, her knees pressing on each side of his waist, but not touching him. Her eyes gazed into his. He arched his head enough so he could see her inviting pussy, just inches from his navel. "Oh, Christ . . ." he mumbled. "What are you waiting for, woman?"

She grinned and slowly sank down, pressing her wet cunt against his stomach. He felt his cock rub against her buttocks and thrust toward her. Immediately, she moved away from him. He growled out in frustration, and she only smiled. Again, she lowered herself, rubbing her pussy against his stomach. He bucked against his ties, wanting nothing more than to be able to use his hands to grab her sexy buttocks and slam her down onto his rigid rod. As if reading his mind, she scrambled over him and positioned herself at his right side, making sure that none of her skin touched his.

"Oh, *cara* . . ." he moaned. "Quit teasing me . . ."

She laughed. A soft, sexy sound that made him even hornier.

"Do you want me to suck you off, Tomas? Is that it?"

"Yes . . . damn it. *Yes!*"

"Okay . . . but remember Rule Number Two. You can't come until I say so."

He nodded frantically. "Just . . . *do* it!"

She began at his chest, kissing and licking. He moaned and thrashed on the bed, wishing his hands weren't tied. He wanted to touch her, feel those breasts, slide his fingers inside her wet pussy. She inched her way down, swirling her tongue along his quivering stomach muscles, dipping it into his navel. God, her tongue was hot. Finally, her hand grasped his shaft and it jerked spasmodically at her touch. Her mouth closed over its head and slowly, oh, so very slowly, his hot tool slid down her throat. Oh, God . . . he thought he was dying. It had never felt like this . . . too fucking wonderful for words. Her tongue was magic as she sucked him, licking the length of him, her fingers stroking his scrotum, her mouth sliding up and down, tongue stroking in circular motions, and finally, reaching his very tip, where it flicked teasingly until he was near screaming. And then, just as he was about to explode in her mouth, she drew away.

"No!" he grunted. "Please . . . don't stop."

She laughed and strolled toward the door. His eyes feasted on her perfect body. Christ! He wanted her like he'd never wanted anyone. And she hadn't even let him touch her pussy yet! Not once.

"I'll be back. I like my Italian pastry with chocolate on it."

She was only gone for a few minutes, but it seemed like hours to Tomas . . . and his cock. It reared at the ceiling, pulsating and engorged. He closed his eyes, grimacing. How much longer would the torture go on before she allowed him the satisfying release? He heard her footfall and opened his eyes. She stood at the side of the bed, smiling down at him with those gorgeous indigo eyes. In one slim hand, she held a jar of thick chocolate sauce. She dipped an index finger into the viscous goo, and slowly, her eyes fastened to his as she slid her finger into her mouth, sucking rhythmically. He almost creamed right there and then, and she knew it. She gave a delighted laugh and tilted the jar over his cock. The thick, dark chocolate covered the head of his cock and slithered languidly down its length, and the feel of its soft velvet warmth made him, incredibly enough, even hornier.

"Oh, yeah . . ." he groaned. "Lick it off, baby. Lick it all off."

"All in good time," she whispered. "There's just one more little extra I need to get out of the bathroom."

What, he wondered? What more could she possibly need? Tomas closed his eyes, groaning. "Just hurry," he gasped. "I cannot take much more of this." He heard her walk into the adjoining bathroom.

She seemed to be in there a long time. He felt the chocolate pooling stickily at the shaft of his cock. If she didn't hurry up, there wouldn't be any left on his flagpole to lick off.

"Hey!" he called. "What is taking you so long, *cara mia*? I am going crazy in here!"

"I'm coming!" she replied.

"That is what I have been trying to do for the last fucking hour," he muttered.

She stepped into the room.

"It is about time," he said, and opened my eyes. "What the fuck?"

She was completely dressed, wearing a pair of jeans and a sexy white silk blouse. In one hand, she held a suitcase, and in the other, a rectangular glass box. She smiled at Tomas apologetically.

"I'm sorry, Tomas, but I just remembered I have a flight to Belmopan to catch. But I'll leave you something to keep you company."

She placed the glass box on the bed next to his thigh, and carefully opened the cover.

"What is that?" His eyes fastened upon the box.

"Oh, this?" She gave a soft laugh. "Surely you've seen these before. It's an ant farm. Almost every young boy has one. But these ants . . ." She laughed again. "Oh, *these* ants are special. Because, Tomas, you deserve nothing but the best. Nothing but the most unusual. Have you ever heard of the species *solenopis*? Oh, probably not. You're probably more familiar with its nickname. The fire-ant?" Her smile disappeared and her smokey-blue eyes grew icy. "Known for its particularly vicious bite."

"Jesus Christ!" he blurted out as realization set in. "You cannot be serious!"

She turned the box on its side, the open end of it facing his groin. "How can you know when I'm serious," she said, taking a step back from the bed. "You hardly know me at all. Just as you didn't know my sister. Because you didn't take the time to know her. You just fucked her and threw her out with the garbage."

She was at the door, suitcase in hand.

"*You cannot leave me like this,*" Tomas screamed.

She paused, her brow furrowed. "I can't?" She appeared to think about it for a moment. Then she shook her head. "I don't see why not." Then she stepped through the bedroom door and closed it behind her.

"*Sharon! I am serious! You cannot do this!*" He heard her footsteps as she descended the marble stairs. "Okay, okay! I am sorry for what I did to your sister! But it was not *my* fault she killed herself. Besides, we do not even know if it *was* a suicide!"

He waited for a response. Nothing. His eyes darted to the

open ant farm. A long line of the tiny black bodies was already trailing across the rumpled sheet toward his groin.

"*Sharon!* This is not funny!"

From downstairs, he heard the villa door close with a thud. The first of the ants began to climb onto Tomas's stomach, heading straight for his chocolate-covered cock that now lay listlessly against his leg. A blossom of pain exploded in needle-like pricks over his stomach and thighs as the swirling ants began to bite.

Just before he opened his mouth to scream, he thought he heard Sharon's laugh from outside the villa. But maybe that was his imagination.

La Petite Mort

Staci Layne Wilson

He was there in the audience again. "Analise," he called to her, without saying a word.

The blinding lights, the fog of cigarette and pot smoke, and the shadows cast by the massive sea of humanity usually blended together in a collision of visual haze when she was onstage. But even way out there, several rows back, Analise could see his pale face, dark, piercing eyes, and long, shining silver hair quite clearly. This was the third night in a row he'd come to see her show, but this was the first time he'd ever spoken to her. But how could he? She could hardly hear herself sing, let alone hear the sweet, beckoning whisper she imagined.

Imagined. That was all it was. As for him coming to see her three nights in a row, that was nothing unusual. She had quite a following. Analise, the young, sexy rock singer, attracted many "groupies"—male and female alike. But this man was older. It wasn't just the lines in his face and the silvery hair that hung in loose waves to his shoulders; it was something in his eyes. Something wise and knowing. Something hungry.

Analise tossed her head in time to the driving beat of the music, trying to shake the image loose. She closed her eyes and made her guitar scream louder. She could feel the aggressively sexual beat in every nerve ending. It came right up through the floor, shooting through her high-heeled leather boots, up her bare thighs, pulsing in her clitoris, tickling her belly and breasts, and finally bursting out her mouth. She sang the next verse, roaring like a lioness and pushing her hips in time against her candy-apple-red Fender Strat. Her henna hair flew in the wind created by the many fans placed around the stage, and it felt good.

It felt so good. This is what Analise had dreamed of ever since she had been a young girl. Yes, she had lusted after the jean-clad, thin-hipped seventies rockers whose music she and her girlfriends loved. The difference was, her girlfriends wanted to be *with* those icons—Analise wanted to *be* them.

Robert Plant. Steven Tyler. Mick Jagger. All of them so aggressively, unabashedly sexual. Their music had been called "cock rock" and Analise loved it. Sure, there were a few female rockers out there, but when Analise hit the stage at the age of seventeen it was as if musical history had been rewritten. Even though she was in her mid-twenties now, to her fans Analise was just discovering the rapture of sexual salvation. Even in these times of fear and repression, Analise's randy ways were a shining ideal to many.

Analise tossed her long, silky hair again and made the song come to an abrupt climax. She walked over to the mic stand and smiled, her light hazel eyes dancing over the crowd. There were so many beautiful young men out there. She took deep breaths and her breasts heaved, barely contained in their leather harness. "Who wants to fuck me?" she shouted, her challenge echoing out. The crowd's cheers and whistles reached an almost deafening level. Security guards had to beat back several of the people in the front row who attempted to rush the stage.

Analise beamed at them. "You really do love me, don't you? Okay then, let's rock and roll!" She launched into another burning number, just she and her electric guitar up there before a crowd of over 50,000. And they all wanted her.

Little did they know she was a virgin.

Analise opened the chocolate-tinted window of her limousine just a crack and craned her neck. Once she was able to get a better look, she decided that he was not what she wanted. The skinny young Latino on the street corner, unaware of the rock star's scrutiny, took a deep, final drag of his cigarette and flicked it away. The embers illuminated his pockmarked face for just a split second before they died out.

It was late at night, and there wasn't much out there but the least desirable of prostitutes. The dregs, those not yet picked up. Analise really didn't like to pick up hustlers, if she didn't have to. She preferred to find regular men, just working guys, or students out looking for a good time. Normally she went to clubs, and sometimes she even hand-picked a man from her audience and brought him back to the hotel room. Colin, her manager, told her time and again it was more discreet to hire an escort if she *had* to do this sort of thing at all, but Analise had never found them very exciting.

"Hold it here, Earl," she said to the limo driver. "I want to take a look at that one. The blond over there."

A handsome, well-built man, about twenty or so, was hurrying across the street. He had a briefcase in his hand and was dressed in jeans and a long-sleeved dress shirt. He had a gray wool blazer draped over his arm. He wasn't a hustler, so what was he doing out at this hour? Analise wondered. He intrigued her, and she liked that. "Get him for me, Earl."

The driver, an aged Englishman, the picture of British reserve, pulled into a parking place along the curb and exited the long, sleek car. Wearing his white gloves and bowler hat, he looked decidedly comical running in his short, hasty steps across the nearly deserted city street. "I say!" he called after the blond man, who slowed, then stopped.

Analise couldn't hear the conversation, but she watched as Earl approached the tall, broad-shouldered man. The chauffeur said a few words, then indicated the parked limo. The blond looked over, squinting, his brows knit. The limo's windows were tinted, and there was no way he could see who was inside. He looked dubious as Earl continued to talk, then he turned and slowly followed the dignified, older gentleman to the car. People always trusted Earl, and they always got in the car once they saw Analise sitting there.

She pushed the button that rolled the back window down as they drew close. Oh, he was quite something. And most definitely not a hustler. His eyes were curious and intelligent, not dead and unfocused. His mouth was full and sweet, not slack and disinterested. He carried himself with youthful pride mingled with a touch of uncertainty, not as though he bore the weight of the world.

The blond caught himself just slightly when he saw her. "It's really you," he blurted. His cheeks flushed.

"In the flesh, baby," Analise replied in her husky voice, made even raspier by the night's performance.

"Wow, I can't believe this," the blond gushed. "I wanted to get tickets for tonight's performance or tomorrow's, but no dice. So, I just worked late tonight and tried to ignore the sound coming from the stadium."

"You could hear the concert from here?"

"Barely. If I had my window open." He indicated an office building across the way. "But, not quite. Which is even worse than not hearing it at all, y'know?"

"How would you like a ticket for tomorrow night? I think maybe I could arrange something." Analise smiled, sticking the tip of her tongue between her teeth ever so slightly.

The handsome man smiled, his eyes lighting up even more. Could it be true? *The* Analise flirting with him? "So, what brings you here? I mean, are you lost? Can I—"

"Yes, you can," Analise purred, and opened the limo door. She'd showered backstage and changed from her concert outfit into a long, clinging satin gown of ice blue. It covered everything, but concealed nothing. The blond instantly noticed that she wore no underwear. Analise followed his eyes with pride.

He slipped into the seat beside her and murmured, "I must say, you do live up to your reputation."

Earl started the car and pulled smoothly out into the street. He raised the partition between the front and back, then put some smoky jazz on the stereo.

"My reputation? And what's that?" she asked softly, leaning back and letting her knees fall open. The silky fabric fell between them, just covering her sex.

The blond cleared his throat and looked slightly discomfited. They usually did. Analise found that most men, especially the younger ones, only thought they liked the idea of a sexually aggressive woman. Once they got started with her little game, they often hesitated. But she could always talk them into it.

"Go on," she said. "What do you mean?"

"Well, you are a very sexy woman. You see what you want, and you take it."

"Does that make you feel uncomfortable? That I want you? That I have you in my possession?"

He thought for a moment, then he leaned close to her and

brought his mouth up to hers, their lips just a fraction from touching. "No," he whispered and reached up to touch her hair before kissing her.

Analise drew back and smiled seductively. "Ah, ah, ah. It doesn't work like that, honey. I call the shots. Now I want you to get over there." Her voice was firm as she pointed to the blue velvet-covered seat across from them.

He furrowed his brow briefly, but did as he was told without question.

"Now," she said matter-of-factly, "I want you to touch yourself."

"Huh?"

"Come on, right there. Between your legs. I can see the bulge, baby. Mmmm, you are so hot."

The blond did as he was told, stroking tentatively at first, then rubbing harder with his short fingernails against the denim material, as he looked directly into her hazel eyes. His manhood grew, straining against the confinement.

Analise sucked in her breath and suddenly there was nothing in her world but that busy hand and that burgeoning cock. Her nipples hardened, tingling, and the pulse beat in her clit urgently. Oh, if only that hand could be on her, rubbing, stroking, touching, teasing. She shifted, letting the silky material of her dress caress her ever so slightly. She shivered and sighed, "Let me see it, baby." She didn't know his name, and didn't want to.

He moaned as he unzipped his pants and let himself free. She noticed with a thrill that he hadn't been wearing any underwear either. He lifted his hips up off the seat and began to take his pants down.

"No, no," Analise breathed, her heart fluttering in her throat. "That's enough. I just want to see it." Her lids half-closed, she took in the beauty of the man's stiff penis. She knew it was clichéd, but she thought it was like a missile, so straight and so hard, ready for its mission. It jerked in the air, as if straining to come to her. She felt the pleasant, moist heat begin between her legs. She wanted it so bad.

But she couldn't. Something always held her back. Maybe she was afraid that the act itself would pale in comparison to the capture, the anticipation, the longing for the unknown. What would it feel like? Taste like? Those questions excited her beyond belief. And that was enough for now. "Touch it again, honey."

"I want you to touch it, Analise. I want to be inside you." There was a desperate longing in his voice, a nearly sorrowful yearning.

Analise felt the desire in his voice almost as a physical caress. She felt a chill creep up her thighs, across her engorged labia, into her tingling breasts and her pulsing throat. "Oh, yeah, baby. Talk to me."

"Just talk?" he whispered huskily, leaning toward her, his shirt still on, his gorgeous penis sticking through the opening in his jeans. "I can do more than that."

Analise allowed the spell to break for just a moment. Yes, the panic button was within reach. She never actually feared rape, but she did think about it, and she made sure that Earl kept a loaded pistol in the glove box up front. Her eyes wandered back to the flushed, excited blond.

"I'm sure you can, sweetie," she sighed. "But this is the way I like it. I want you to perform for me. I want to watch you. I want to see you come."

"Mmmm . . ." he moaned, leaning back on the cushion. He took his engorged cock in his hand and stroked the length of it. He began to play along. "It's so hard for you. It's throbbing, just like the beat of your music, Analise." His hips began to rock and his muscles tensed. "You know what? I've done this before, listening to you sing on my stereo. You make me so hot . . ."

This practically sent Analise into the stratosphere. She loved it when they loved her. But still, she did not touch herself. She just watched him and enjoyed the sensations that coursed through her slim, taut body. "Do it, baby," she said. "Do it for me."

His hand moved faster, the head of his penis almost becoming a blur. She could hear the friction of flesh on flesh and felt the heat rise in the small space they shared. Her breath stopped as she watched. She knew the time was near. His testicles drew up into his body, his back arched, and his face contorted. He was so beautiful. And then—then the climax. She watched the pearly liquid shoot from him with such force it hit the ceiling of the rented limo. Analise opened her mouth and cried out with him as he came.

They panted together in the afterglow, each in their own separate seats, not touching, not looking at one another. Analise squeezed her thighs together and her swollen lips tingled against the pressure. "Oh, honey. You were great." She sat up and ran her fingers through her hair. Their eyes met.

"What now?" the blond asked, fully expecting to be taken back to her hotel room for the main course.

Analise smiled softly. "Now, my dear, we stop the car. I let you off and you go home. Be sure and write your name down for Earl, and I'll make sure there are two tickets waiting for you at will-call tomorrow. You do have a girlfriend, don't you?"

He nodded. "Well, I don't know what to say . . . Thanks."

Good. He wasn't going to argue with her on this. She was dying to get back to her hotel room, and she wanted to be there as soon as possible. She was about to burst.

She would miss this suite. As hotels went, this was one of the finest she'd stayed at in some time. She'd been there three nights so far, and had another one to go. After that, it was off to California. Then on to one quick show in Las Vegas, and finally she would start the European leg of her tour. London, Paris, Amsterdam, Rome. Aside from her villa in the Hollywood Hills, she felt most at home in Europe.

But right now she wanted to be in bed. She passed the grand piano and walked up the elegant spiral staircase to the master suite. The four-poster bed's pastel pink spread was awash in the moonlight shining down from the skylight above. It was like a beacon. Analise pulled the covers back and slipped in, still dressed in her gown and fancy high-heels.

She nestled her head deep into the soft, satin-clad feather pillows. She let her hands travel down her soft, satin-clad breasts. She closed her eyes and circled each nipple with the tips of her forefingers, then felt down her ribcage with her palms, over her taut belly, and finally to the mound between her legs. The muscles in her thighs and butt flexed and hardened as she rose to meet her hand. The throbbing began and she sighed wistfully as she touched herself.

She pictured the blond stranger now, the hardness of him . . . his willingness . . . his eagerness. He'd wanted her so badly. He'd wanted to be inside her. Analise's knees came up and the hem of her dress slid over her thighs and settled onto her belly. She put her fingers inside, feeling what he would have felt, had she let him. Such warm, velvety softness.

She sighed and opened her eyes dreamily. She stopped her stroking, suddenly. What was that? She opened her eyes fully and looked up at the skylight. A face? No, it was impossible. No one could get up there. But still. She thought she'd caught a glimpse of a pale, predatory face, long hair silvered by the moonlight. Him.

She sat up, looking intently. There was nothing up there, just the starlit night beyond the window's clear glass. She laughed self-consciously at herself. Why was she so shaken up over that man? So he'd come to a few concerts. That didn't mean she'd have to start obsessing over him, imagining things. Like when she thought she'd heard him speak her name earlier. His cognac voice had made her name sound like a prayer. "Analise." An incantation, a mantra. "Analise . . ."

Analise swung her legs over the side of the bed and she stretched. She was tired, and no longer in the mood. "Damn," she whispered. The blond had been so good, she'd been sure that the image of him would last her for days. Now she could hardly remember the encounter at all.

Analise spent most of the next day in her hotel room. She'd been in Albuquerque many times before, and had seen all it had to offer. Although she loved performing—lived for it, really—Analise did find the rock and roll lifestyle unbelievably dull at times. She didn't do drugs, she wasn't into watching TV, she had few real friends, and she seldom spent any time with men outside her limo. That meant a lot of time to fill between shows. One could only read and sleep for so long.

She began to get restless by late afternoon. She didn't have to do a sound-check that day, so she had time to kill. She'd tried sitting at the piano and composing something, but all she could play was "Stairway to Heaven." She took a bubble bath and let her hands slide over her oiled body in the hot water, but she couldn't get into it. She ordered room service and nibbled at some fettucine. Finally, she decided to pick out her stage clothes for the evening's performance.

Analise was lucky. She'd been blessed with a tall, slender, full-bosomed body that was easy to clothe. She looked as smashing in jeans and a T-shirt as she did in a black rubber minidress. She stood before the mirrored wall-length closet and let her terry-cloth robe drop. At twenty-seven, she looked amazing and she knew it. Analise was not conceited, but she knew she was beautiful and had a knockout body, though she really couldn't take credit for it, since she was born that way. In fact, she often thought of herself as the Jessica Rabbit cartoon: a tall, statuesque redhead with her sultry singing voice and her "I'm just drawn that way" philosophy.

Sometimes she wondered, since she had so much time to think, if perhaps the perfection of her face and body was somehow a tangible symbol of her virginity. Maybe if she had sex, it would all fade. She smiled at herself in the mirror. That's ridiculous, she chided herself silently. But even without makeup, her full lips were rosy, and her long lashes framed startling hazel, gold-flecked eyes that stood out like jewels against her café-au-lait skin. "You may be lucky in looks, but not love," she said aloud to her reflection. "So don't get cocky."

She slid the mirrored door open and looked at what she had. Most of her stage clothes were with her costumer, and she only had about ten outfits with her at any given time. Analise wasn't sure how she felt today. Like a pagan goddess? Like an elegant torch singer? Like a medieval temptress? Like a bad little girl? A flaming rock star?

Finally she decided on a skintight, white minidress, black over-the-knee stockings topped with satin bows, and a pair of wicked combat boots. Now all she had to do was occupy herself for another two hours.

"Colin, have you happened to notice an older man in the audience over the past three nights?" Analise was sitting in the back of another rented limo, riding to the stadium with her manager, Colin, and her bass-player, Sherman. Her drummer, Hadrian, and the backup singers had already gone on ahead.

"No. Why, Luv? Is he bothering you?" Colin was a big, burly Brit, always looking for a fight. And he loved to protect his Analise. Right from the start, when he'd discovered her at the age of seventeen, singing in a cheesy talent contest at the Northridge Mall in Southern California, he'd been very protective of her. He often expressed this desire to safeguard her with his fists. It was as if she was his own daughter, though he'd never married or had any children—"None that speak English, anyway," he liked to joke.

"No, nothing like that. I was just wondering. It's so strange to see anyone over twenty at my shows. I guess he just kind of stood out."

"Hey, I'm over twenty," Colin shot back.

"Me, too—and so are you," Sherman said.

"Don't remind me," Analise muttered.

"Oh, go on now," Colin guffawed at her false fret. "You'll be forever young."

"Yeah, whatever," she said. "If you see that guy out there tonight, could you get someone to bring him backstage after the show? He's been sitting in the first loge seat, in the center, just to the right of the mixing board."

Colin giggled. "He tickles your fancy, does he? Tired of the jailbait, are we?"

Analise grinned back and arched her thin, chestnut eyebrows, but inside she wasn't smiling at all. She couldn't make sense of her feelings for the strange man, but she thought maybe if she could meet him, speak to him, she would see that he was nothing special and forget about him.

Analise was fanning her face in the dressing room. The air-conditioning couldn't begin to penetrate the inner heat she felt after a performance, but sometimes a strong breeze could. She'd put on a really hot show, and she could hear the audience screaming for more, stomping their feet and demanding an encore. They wanted her, and she couldn't wait to get back out there and give herself to them once again.

As she'd half-hoped, half-dreaded, *he* had been there again. He sat in his loge seat, just watching her quietly with those onyx-like eyes of his. Unlike most concert goers, this man did not mouth the words to her songs or nod his head in time to the music. He didn't even stand up or shake his fist in the air. He just sat there, perched very tall and straight, watching her. Although he was several rows back, the man's luminous white face was like a beacon, drawing her eye several times throughout the night. Analise was a professional though, and she never let on that she was distracted. The only indication that she'd seen him at all was to point him out to Colin after the last song, as she headed for her dressing room.

While she was out playing her encore, he would be brought in, and finally, she would know him.

Analise took a deep breath and stood. She headed for the door and went through it, just as the guys' dressing room door across the hall was opening. She gave Sherman and Hadrian the thumbs-up and said, "Let's do it!"

Analise rushed through her two encore songs, and consequently made several mistakes when she noticed that he was no longer in the audience. He must be backstage, waiting for her.

She waited until the guys went into their dressing room before going into hers. She opened the door to find—

No one. Her dressing room was completely empty, which was unusual after a show. Usually Colin could be found in there, one or more of her backup singers, wanna-bes from the record company, a couple of groupies who'd wheedled their way backstage, and so on. But tonight it was quiet, and very still. It was almost as if the room was in a state of suspended animation.

Analise walked inside and sat down in front of her makeup mirror. There, lying on the table, was a single red rose. Held beneath the swell of the ruby bud was a tiny card, decorated with a border of assorted flowers. In the center was the handwritten message:

> My little voyeur—
> I am watching you.

Analise picked the card up and looked at it closely. She did not recognize the handwriting, which was so bold and deep, it was practically etched into the paper. Whose writing could it be? The blond? He was here tonight, watching her. But then, so was *he*. And this lettering just seemed to be like him. Strong, hard, compelling. Analise wasn't sure how she knew, but she did—and the knowledge made her heart pound.

Just then, the door swung open. She sucked her breath in as she turned. It was Colin and one of the roadies.

"Sorry, Luv. We tried to find that gentleman for you, but he must have left before the encore."

"That's okay, Colin," Analise sighed. Suddenly, she was very tired.

As the storm tossed the little chartered plane about in the night sky, Analise couldn't help but think of Buddy Holly, Patsy Cline, Duane Allman, Stevie Ray Vaughan, and all the rest. For some reason, she mused, Thor, the Norse god of thunder, must not like musical performers. Or was it Zeus, the Greek ruler of the heavens? She sighed, wondering if such absurd thoughts had passed through the minds of those other doomed performers.

But doom was not to be Analise's immediate fate, after all. With a shimmy and a shudder, the plane landed safely on the runway of the Los Angeles International Airport. She would be home soon.

She would only be in California for a few days, but she would be *home*. Analise longed to see her beautiful Spanish-style house again, to be inside its old, cool walls, to touch her bare feet to the icy tile-and-stone floors. She loved being in her home best of all when it was stormy like this. The rooms were so open and airy that some might consider it too drafty, but Analise loved to hear the gusts of wind whistling through the vents and to listen to the windows shake as the rain beat against them. It was almost as if the house were being seduced by the storm. *Can I come in?* the wind would whisper, as Analise lay in bed, the covers pulled up to her chin.

"Your car is here," Colin said, breaking Analise's reverie. "Are you sure you want to drive? It's awfully dark and wet out there. I can get Earl. . . ."

"No thanks, Col," she said. "If you could just get my bags delivered to me tomorrow, I would be eternally grateful." She hugged her manager and waved to the rest of her entourage. "See you guys at the Forum, day after tomorrow. Take it easy!" she called over her shoulder as she headed for her classic Silver Ghost, which had been driven right up to the plane for her.

A young woman got out of the car and held the driver's door open for Analise. Analise slid onto the cool leather seat and put the car in gear.

The steady rhythm of the windshield wipers was practically hypnotic, and before Analise knew it, she was home. She opened the huge wrought-iron gate with the remote control she kept in the glove box and drove in. As always, she kept an eye on the rearview mirror, making certain that no one followed her in. As she drove up the winding, tree-lined driveway, Analise noticed that some new flowers had been planted. Their colors were merely a blur in the driving midnight rain, but Analise was sure they would be beautiful. It reminded her of the rose she'd been given the night before, and the giver of that gift. Would he follow her to California? Would she search the Forum's audience for his face, and would she find it?

Suddenly, the rain stopped. It was as if a switch had been thrown, and the full moon shone from above, casting its cloudy cloak aside. Analise cracked the window and breathed in deeply, the wet flowers' fresh aroma filling her.

Coming around the final turn, her beautiful Spanish villa loomed into view, its whitewashed exterior and red-tiled roof shimmering beneath the full moon. Her heart swelled. It was good to be home. Analise used her remote control again, this time to open the garage. She pulled the grand automobile inside, and the large door shut silently behind her. She got out of the car and went into the house through the side door that connected the dwelling to the garage.

Analise flicked the switch on the wall. There was a spark, and then nothing. The electricity had gone out. She peered through the kitchen, across the dining room and into the den. The house appeared to be lit. Yes, there was a full moon, but this light held a warm, an amber glow. Candles.

There had to be hundreds of them. But who . . . ? Analise walked deeper into the house, following the trail of light. Her eyes were drawn to the staircase. It was *him*.

He stood there at the midway point, a resplendent, regal figure. His alabaster face was warmed by the soft glow of the candlelight, but the shadows cut eerie, dancing figures across his gaunt cheeks. His eyes were like burning coals, and his magnificent hair hung in silver waves to his proud, straight shoulders. He wore a white linen suit that fit like it was custom-made. He wore no shoes on his feet, and in his arms was a huge bouquet of blood-red roses. Slowly, he descended the stairs.

Analise was rooted to the spot, speechless. She let him come to her.

He stopped just in front of her and selected one rose from the bunch cradled in the crook of his right arm. He held it up with his left hand and stroked her cheek with it, staring into her eyes. Analise was spellbound. The rose slithered across her jawline, down her throat, and teased at her décolletage. Analise unbuttoned her white poet's shirt and opened it for him. The silky petals kissed her rosy nipples and they swelled with excitement. Analise caught her breath. She wanted to ask him who he was, how he had found her, what he was doing . . .

He put his finger to her lips, stopping all those unasked questions. She fell into his inky eyes and followed him without hesitation when he turned and walked into the den. Flames were blazing in the fireplace, and the storm, raging anew, could be seen outside beyond the glass wall.

Fire and rain.

He dropped the roses to the stone floor and took her hand in his. His flesh was cool and smooth, and his fingers were long and conical. Artist's hands. He bent at the knees and brought her down with him onto the white fur rug that lay before the crackling blaze. He pushed the shirt from her shoulders and it fell in a feathery heap behind her.

Analise eased herself onto her back and unzipped her tight blue jeans. She wanted to undress for him. She wanted him to watch her.

She slipped the shoes from her feet, and she was naked. The shadows cast from the dancing flames licked at her body and Analise shivered with pleasure at the sensation of their warmth. She looked up with dreamy eyes and saw him, still on his knees and fully clothed, watching her.

She started down at her angular hipbones, stroked her thighs, then let both hands travel back up and over the curve of her waist and the swell of her breasts. Her fingernails grazed over her skin, moving back and forth. Analise moved back down, stroking at the downy hair between her legs, and slid one finger down into the folds of soft flesh. She was already slick with desire. She closed her eyes and felt . . .

. . . a caress on her quivering thigh. He had disrobed, and his slender, rock-hard body reminded her of the ancient white marble statue of a majestic Greek foot soldier she had seen in the Louvre years before. His fingertips caressed the length of one leg, then the other. He leaned over her, his silver hair framing his angular face. She lifted up, her lips straining for a kiss.

He kept just out of reach and looked at her with such hunger, such desire, Analise cried out in frustration. She had to have him inside her. She reached between their bodies and found what she sought: She closed her hand firmly around the silky smoothness of his erection. It was like an iron fist in a velvet glove, a delightful contrast of softness and hardness. She thrust her hips upward, dying for their most intimate parts to meld as one. The muscles inside her contracted, begging to hold him in their feathery grip. She had waited so long for this moment.

But he withheld it from her, teasing her unmercifully. She moaned again, pressing her hot, heaving chest against the cool pebbles of his nipples. Analise put her arms around him and felt the hard planes of his ribcage and spine as she tried to pull him down onto her.

He brought his face close to hers and whispered in her ear, "Are you mine now, my little voyeur?" He had a heavy French accent, but Analise had no trouble understanding his words.

"Yes, forever yours," she gasped, each nerve ending tingling.

Before she knew it, he was inside her. There was a brief moment of blinding, ripping pain, then an exquisite agony. "Oh, yes," she moaned, grasping his hips with both hands and driving him deeper inside her. She twined her legs around his and began to move in the rhythm she knew so well. It was like playing her red guitar, lost in the melody. The thunder roared outside, competing with her climactic wail.

He, too, was in the throes of passionate release. He arched his spine and threw his head back, his mouth open. Analise saw the two sharp fangs glinting in the firelight just before he swooped back down and bit into her neck.

He kissed her neck harder. The pain was exquisite. Analise felt a warmth and knew he had penetrated her skin. And then the waves came. She moaned with ecstasy, and saw supernovas shooting beneath her tightly closed lids. She felt as though she were being hurtled through space. She was hot and sweating in one instant, then ice-cold and shivering the next. She tried to open her eyes, but could not. She tried to move her arms, but could not. She tried to remember where she was, but could not.

And then it all vanished. She was left feeling very weak, and her once-racing heart was suddenly dying. Dying! Now she knew where she was. Now she could open her eyes. And she saw the blood. Her blood, shiny black in the candlelight, dripping down the chin of her undead lover. His eyes were like a cat's, reflecting back the light, showing her nothing.

But suddenly, she knew. She knew everything: His name was Avenant, and he'd been born in Nice, France, centuries before. He had come to her one night as she lay sleeping in her bed, when she was a just-flowering young girl. He'd promised her he would be back when she was ready for him. Avenant told Analise to save herself for him, and when the time came, they would be together forever.

The vampire smiled, his long white fangs a beautiful and awesome sight. His eyes, now soft and moist, were full of love. One amber-hued tear, sparkling in the candlelight, slid down his cheek. "You remember," he whispered.

He raised his slender hand slowly to his lips and punctured his wrist with his own fangs. Analise felt the pulse-beats in the hollow of her throat and between her legs again. Weak, but there. Wanting. Needing. The blood, a ruby-black rivulet, splashed on her heaving breasts. It was hot and it stung, as if filled with a preternatural electricity. As lightning shot through the night sky, he brought the weeping wrist to her mouth.

Biographies

Wickham Boyle has been a writer since childhood. She has kept journals and edited her school yearbook. For her Finance final at Yale she wrote a parody called "Alice in Numberland." Ms. Boyle has worn many hats, including experimental theater producer and Wall Street stockbroker. Currently she is the director of Wizard, a consulting company that solves all sorts of problems. Wicki has a husband and two cool children. She always rides a bike in New York City for transportation and writes erotica, theater reviews, and finance for fools. She is working on a book called *Between My Legs*.

Edward Buskirk lives in rural upstate Michigan. His erotic fiction, ranging from comic to crime-thriller, has been published under various pseudonyms in numerous adult-oriented magazines. Readers of Lonnie Barbach's previous anthology, *The Erotic Edge*, may recognize James and Brenda, the married couple in "The Other Woman," from Buskirk's short story "Other Men," which was later adapted to film as *The Voyeur* by director Deborah Shames. Buskirk is currently working on a novel featuring these same characters.

Dave Clarke ponders life from the home in the foothills he shares with his inspirational wife and two amazing daughters. He's written on everything from polo to prep schools, the romance of luxury train travel, to California's most romantic coastal inns. His work appears in national and regional magazines coast to coast. An erotic thriller, *au Bleu*, will soon be followed by a tale of political suspense, *Aid and Comfort*.

Leslie Cole is a writer and teacher who lives in the hills above Occidental, California. "A Conversation About Green Water" is her first outright erotica, although most of her work is sensual in nature. The author derives great inspiration from the natural world, and is currently completing a book of short stories.

Tee A. Corinne is a writer and artist who lives in the Pacific Northwest. She is the author of *The Sparkling Lavender Dust of Lust* (a novel), *Lovers, Courting Pleasure,* and the small-press best-seller, *Dreams of the Woman Who Loved Sex.* Her short stories and poetry have been anthologized in *Pleasures, Erotic Interludes, Intricate Passions, Riding Desire, The Poetry of Sex,* and *The Body of Love.* Her *Cunt Coloring Book,* first published in 1975, is still in print. *What Difference Does Poetry Make?* is her most recent poetry collection.

Kate Fox is a slight variation of the author's real name, Kate Foss, adopted as a pseudonym because she finds it just "a little catchier." Kate grew up in the San Francisco Bay Area and received a degree in English from the University of the Pacific in Stockton, California, in 1996. She moved to New York six months later to begin her career in publishing, and is now the publisher/managing editor of *Akkadian,* a quarterly writer's magazine.

Hannah Katz is a pseudonym for a woman living with her husband in Northern California. This is her first piece of erotic fiction. She loves writing, traveling, hiking, and science fiction, and recently has decided to spend more time with her computer.

Nancy Sasha Long is a writer, performer, social worker . . . Loves to write about food, conflict, men, and erotica. Has an insatiable curiosity about people, romance, film, literature, and foreign lands. Has traveled, lived back East, held numerous day jobs, including dancer, teacher, assembly-line slave, and taxicab driver. Made her way through grad school, marriage, divorce, birth of twin girls. Recently coproduced "Writers on the Edge" (a Bay Area group of writers who perform and write their own life stories).

Carroll Mavis-Raine is the pseudonym for a writer living in Manassas, Virginia. Her erotic fiction has appeared in *Genesis*, in America, and *Erotic Stories* and *For Women* in England. Her story "Phantom Grey" appeared in Lonnie Barbach's previous collection, *The Erotic Edge*. She is married to a sexy Italian who is definitely *not* the inspiration for Tomas Marcolini in "Italian Pastry."

Phoenix McFarland is an American writer who lives in a charming seaside village in British Columbia. Her erotica has appeared in *All Acts of Love and Pleasure*. She is the author of *The Complete Book of Magical Names*. She's won awards for her short fiction. Before becoming a writer, she was a nude artist's model, a gun-slinging Old West stuntwoman, a TV newsroom secretary, a drill rig geologist, a Hazmat worker, and a ground crew member of a hot air balloon; she has also mapped Africa from space.

Ethan Monk is the pen name of a California attorney with a former Entertainment Law practice. In the early nineties Monk did stand-up comedy and had his own one-man show: "Monsters in My Closet." Currently the president of a large nonprofit arts organization, this is his first venture into erotic writing, and he hopes it will bring him "interesting and inviting mail from readers throughout the world." Monk is currently working on a humorous look at the aging of the baby-boomer generation.

Doraine Poretz is a poet and playwright who teaches an ongoing poetry and prose writing/reading series entitled "Writing Down the Music of Your Life." She also instructs monthly writing seminars in poetry and the Tarot and facilitates readings at the Bodhi Tree Bookstore in West Hollywood on sacred poetry in world literature. Four books of her poetry have been published by Bombshelter Press, Los Angeles, and her poems have most recently appeared in *Grand Passion: The Poets of Los Angeles and Beyond*. She is currently working on a revision of her play about the diarist and erotic writer, Anaïs Nin.

Lisa Prosimo, originally from New York, now lives and works in both Southern and Northern California. Her stories have appeared in *Sauce Box*, a journal of literary erotica. One will be featured in the upcoming *Herotica 6*.

Lynn Santa Lucia is a professional magazine writer and editor who recently relocated to New York City from Miami. Originally from Buffalo, New York, she has lived in Italy and Spain, and has found inspiration for much of her creative writing through her travels. This is the first time she has tried her hand at an erotica story. She is currently working on a collection of "travel erotica" pieces set in Mediterranean locales.

Renate Stendhal is a German writer and translator who now lives in Berkeley, California, after having lived for twenty years in Paris, France. She has published *Gertrude Stein in Words and Pictures* (Algonquin Books, 1994) and co-authored (with Kim Chernin) *Sex and Other Sacred Games* (Times Books, 1989) and *Cecilia Bartoli: The Passion of Song* (HarperCollins, 1997). She is currently working on a Parisian memoir.

Joseph S. Teller is married and has lived in San Francisco for the last twenty years. He has a degree in music education from the University of Colorado and traveled with a band for two years and freelanced as a musician in Los Angeles before moving north and settling down. Joseph started writing a few years ago and has published an erotic vampire novel and a mainstream short story. He is currently working on a book about voodoo.

Dina Vered is the pseudonym of a screenwriter and award-winning international journalist. Her articles appear regularly in major newspapers and magazines.

Saskia Walker lives in the seaside town of Brighton, in England. Saskia is interested in exploring and expressing the sensual, through literary and visual imagery. She began writing in earnest a year and a half ago and has had several stories published in a variety of genres and publications. Another erotica story, entitled "In Pursuit of Knowledge," appears in an anthology called *Sugar and Spice* (Black Lace, Virgin, 1997). Saskia has also published art reviews, photography, and Gothic fantasy. Saskia dedicates her story to BK-S, who made it all happen.

Staci Layne Wilson lives in the Southern California beach community of Rancho Palos Verdes with her husband, three cats, and three horses. Staci had her first article published in a national magazine at the age of twelve and has been writing ever since. She's had hundreds of nonfiction magazine articles published, but her true love lies in fiction writing. "La Petite Mort" is her first erotic story and her third fiction piece to be published.

Bruce Zimmerman is a novelist and screenwriter. His published books are *Blood Under the Bridge*, *Thicker than Water*, *Full-Bodied Red*, and *Crimson Green*, the first of which was nominated for an Edgar Award as Best First Mystery. He is currently selling his soul to the Devil in Hollywood, and lives in Santa Monica with his wife and two sons.